SECRET SINS

LORA LEIGH

St. Martin's Paperbacks

This is a work of fiction. All of the characters, organizations, and events portrayed in this novel are either products of the author's imagination or are used fictitiously.

SECRET SINS

Copyright © 2012 by Lora Leigh.

All rights reserved.

For information address St. Martin's Press, 175 Fifth Avenue, New York, NY 10010.

ISBN 978-1-250-23054-6

St. Martin's Paperbacks edition / December 2012

St. Martin's Paperbacks are published by St. Martin's Press, 175 Fifth Avenue, New York, NY 10010.

P1

SECRET SINS

PROLOGUE

She couldn't stand it.

She couldn't stand being around him. Watching him, wanting to rub against the hard corded strength of his body, desperate to taste a kiss from the controlled line of his sensual lips.

He looked like a pirate. Like a desperado pretending to be a sheriff, and he made her want to run even as he made her want to cling to him.

She couldn't stand it.

No, that wasn't true, Anna Corbin thought, looking over at the too-handsome sheriff. She loved being around Archer Tobias and had since she was a young girl. The problem was he didn't seem to see her. But she was eighteen now and she could make him see her, if her grandfather and parents would stop shipping her off, like they were proposing to do once again.

"You'll love France," her mother was saying, her smile bittersweet and filled with longing, though she refused to look up at Anna. "It's beautiful there."

"Jacques said you can start as soon as you graduate college. Beginning two years early will allow you to begin in an excellent position before you turn twenty-one," her grandfather, John Corbin, informed her. "His company is really going places, Anna. You'll be there to watch it grow into a major accounting firm."

Yippee. Wasn't that sure to be boring?

Looking up, Anna's eyes met Archer's before he quickly turned his gaze back to his meal.

Lifting her glass she sipped her wine, before setting the glass back by her plate. She silently ran her fingers up and down the slender stem.

"Jacques is really looking forward to having you come in as his assistant," her father said quietly, watching her intently.

"Of course he is." Her head snapped up as the words escaped her mouth. "It will be so much easier to cop a feel if I'm right under his thumb."

Silence filled the room as everyone but Archer stared back at her in shock. For his part, Archer simply stared back at her, the ice that suddenly filled his gaze sending a chill up her spine.

"What are you saying, Anna?" Her father, Robert Corbin, frowned, his expression dark and forbidding as he turned and glared at Gran'pop.

"Anna." Her Gran'pop's voice was chiding as he stared back at her with disappointment. "Jacques explained that." Turning to his son he breathed out heavily. "Jacques fell against her while he was here last summer and unfortunately brushed her back end. It was an accident."

She could feel her teeth automatically clenching at her grandfather's explanation. When her eyes lifted, she saw that Archer was not looking at her, but was instead staring at his plate, fingers gripping his fork, eyes glaring at his food, his expression hard. Her heart thumped. Was Archer angry at hearing that another man had touched her? Anna shook her head. Even if he was, Archer saw her more as a little sister, so if he was angry it was probably the anger of a big brother. Her shoulders slumped a bit. How sexy.

"It wasn't an accident," she said stubbornly.

"You can't come back here." That was Gran'pop, cutting right to the chase.

Anna looked defiant. "I'm not going to France."

John Corbin shrugged. "Then I'll find you a job in England."

"Let me be clearer, Gran'pop." It was now or never. "I'm not leaving the States. I'm not working on the West, East, or Southern coasts."

"You are not coming back here." His silverware clattered against his plate.

"Then I will stay in Sweetrock."

"Over my dead body." His aged, wrinkled face showed his age and his command.

"I hope not, Gran'pop." She shook her head as she lifted the napkin from her lap and laid it politely next to her plate. "I believe I'm finished. If you'll excuse me."

"No, I will not," Gran'pop declared as she moved her chair back and started to rise. "We have company for dinner, Anna. You will not embarrass this family."

Archer was staring back at her now, anger sparking in his gaze as her brow lifted.

"This is probably one of the least explosive arguments Archer's witnessed over the years," she assured her grandfather. "Sorry, Gran'pop, but I'm not sitting here and pretending to like how very easily my parents and grandparents are planning my life for me. Especially when every one of you is very well aware you're breaking my heart."

"You will not do this, Anna," her grandfather ordered then.

"Do what, Gran'pop? Have a life? Have something

to do with cousins you've kept me from all my life? Cousins who are so obviously not the monsters you've made them out to be?" Her voice rose, anger, hurt, that odd hunger to know the cousins reviled for so long both confusing and drawing her.

"That's all—this is over!" he yelled, his fist hitting the table hard enough so that the dishes vibrated with a discordant sound. "Those fucking Callahans."

"Those fucking Callahans?" she sneered. "One of whom is your *only* grandson. Let's lay it out on the table, shall we? For years you've been trying to keep me away from my own family. Away from Logan, Rafer, and Crowe and for years I had no choice. You've kept me so isolated, I feel like an orphan myself! But I'm eighteen now and I can make my own decisions. You can't keep me away any longer."

"The hell I can't," he snarled, all but shaking with fury as all eyes turned to him. "I'll be damned if I'll allow it, Anna. You will return to college and you will do so immediately, or I promise you, I swear to you by all that's holy I'll make damned sure Crowe Callahan pays for it." Anna felt herself pale. She could see the determination, the certain conviction in her grandfather's expression and she knew he meant it.

"The day will come that you can't hurt him any longer," she said. "When that day happens, Mr. Callahan"—she wouldn't call him Gran'pop again—"I promise you, I'll be back."

Moving from the table she strode quickly from the dining room and then from the house as the first tear fell.

France and the pervert. England and God only knew what kind of deviant. Anywhere but where she wanted to be. In Corbin County with her family.

And Archer.

* * *

Archer glared at John Corbin, then at his son, Robert, and daughter-in-law, Lisa.

Anna's place in Corbin County and on the family ranch had been a heated topic since the year she had been shipped off to boarding school at age nine. As he heard it over the years, each vacation, holiday, or family visit Anna had screamed, raged, begged, and pleaded to come home.

She had bargained for homeschooling or tutors, and swore she'd obey every request, want, need, or command that her parents could come up with. When that had failed, she had become a terror on two legs with pretty emerald eyes.

Each time a school had threatened to send her home, John Corbin had paid them for whatever trouble she had caused and then paid them more for whatever trouble she might cause in the future.

She had for nine years been involved in a war that neither Anna nor her parents had escaped unscathed. And now, it seemed, she was upping the stakes. She was eighteen, they couldn't force her into the college of their choice, and it seemed she wasn't going to allow them to force her into the job of their choice.

"She doesn't understand," John muttered. "Sorry 'bout that, Archer."

"Why the fuck do you keep doing this to her, John? Or for that matter, to Crewe?" Archer couldn't hold back his own anger any longer. "She's your granddaughter and you do everything you can to disown her without actually doing so. And who is this bastard you keep defending who dared touch her?"

"This is none of your business, Archer," he began.

"You brought me into this family, John. You made it my business, especially when I learn she's in danger of being molested by someone you keep trying to throw her at."

"That's not it—" John grated harshly.

"Archer, stay out of this." Robert spoke from the other end of the table, his voice firm. "This is family business."

It was always family business when they didn't want to explain their unjust actions toward Anna. He was getting damned sick of it.

"Understood, Robert." Following Anna's example he lifted his napkin, wiped his lips, then folded it and laid it next to his plate with icy precision. "Thank you and your family for dinner, John, but it's time I go."

John grimaced. "Thanks for coming by, Archer. It's always nice to see you."

Fuck, as though he hadn't just witnessed Anna having her heart torn out and one of his best friends trashed by the Corbins' determined refusal to allow Anna to know a cousin she obviously ached to know.

It might not make sense, but Anna didn't have to make sense to him when it was clear her family was making demands that were so blatantly unfair.

Shaking his head as he swept his gaze between the three of them, Archer left the table and strode from the room. Things had always been damned strange in the Corbin household, but now, they were approaching Twilight Zone level.

Stepping onto the wide wraparound porch and closing the door behind him, he let a smile touch his lips at the sight of the curves leaning indolently against the SUV.

Well-worn jeans, and a light gray stretchy top that clung to her breasts, waist, and hips to end at the band of those low-slung jeans.

His gaze lifted to her breasts again.

A perfect handful, he thought, his palms suddenly tingling at the thought of those firm, rounded curves fitting his palms.

He gave himself a mental shake.

Had he lost his fucking mind?

Long black hair, waves upon waves of it, tumbled from her head, over her shoulders and one breast, and down her back almost to her curvy, tempting hips.

With her arms folded beneath those breasts, her head tilted to the side, and those lush, enticing curls flowing around her, she was the image of a tempting, sensual little angel.

One he was dying to touch.

God have mercy on his self-control.

She was a woman now.

Archer felt his breath pause in his chest, felt his entire body go hot, then cold.

Son of a bitch, she was a woman now.

Stepping across the porch he felt the blood suddenly rushing through his body and heading south just as fast as possible.

All for one tiny, tempestuous, trouble-making package.

God help him.

"They're going to try to make me go back, Archer." She lifted her head and the sight of her emerald eyes, sparkling with jewel-like brightness beneath her tears, was nearly more than he could bear.

"They're trying to do what they think is best for you, Anna." He sighed as he moved beside her and leaned back against the vehicle, crossing his arms over his chest.

He didn't believe they were, but hell, what was he supposed to say to her at this point?

"Can't you talk to them, Arch?" Straightening from

the car she moved to face him, standing way too damned close as she laid her hand on his forearm and stared up at him beseechingly.

"I tried," he said softly, dipping his head down toward her before he could consider the need to touch those pouting lips. He straightened quickly, a grimace pulling at his expression. "Your daddy told me to stay out of it."

She laid her head against his arm, and he wanted nothing more than to return to a time when he could have hugged her and not worried about her feeling the hard-on he was fighting.

"I don't want to leave," she said, the pain in her voice so filled with aching loneliness that Archer wanted nothing more than to fix it for her.

"Go to college," he told her and, unable to help himself, his arms opening for her.

Pulling her against his chest he laid his head against hers. "Do what you have to do first, then do what you want to do."

"I don't want to go to France."

"Good." He pretended to breathe a sigh of relief. "Protecting you from all those depraved Frenchmen would be hard to do from here, you know."

A little laugh escaped her.

"Will you miss me?"

"More than sunshine." He grinned. He'd been telling her that for a lot of years now.

"They don't have sunshine where I'm going," she said, sadly.

"California?" He pretended disbelief. "Darlin', I have it on the highest authority the sun shines there every day."

Her head lifted and the pain in her eyes, in her face, broke his heart. "My sunshine is here, Archer."

Cupping her cheek his gaze flicked to her lips.

Awareness suddenly exploded between them. Like a live wire sparking around them, through them, it blazed like wildfire.

His gaze jerked back to hers.

She was too innocent to hide it, too damned young to know what it could do to both of them.

"Are you finally going to kiss me, Archer Tobias?" she whispered, her breathing sharp and heavy, her fingers curled against his shirt as though terrified something, or someone, would jerk her away from him.

"Your granddaddy's standing in the living room window," he said. "And I know your daddy's not far behind. It would look real bad if one of them killed the sheriff his first year in office. Especially considering how hard they campaigned for him."

But he wanted to kiss her. God help him, he wanted to kiss her.

"Will you call me sometime?" she asked, those emerald eyes so sad, so brokenhearted that, for a moment, he hated her family for forcing her away.

"I'll call sometime," he promised, easing her away from him.

"Will you kiss me sometime? I've been waiting a long time, Archer."

"One of these days," he promised softly, opening the door to the vehicle and getting in as she watched him with tear-filled eyes. "One of these days."

She was too innocent, too unaware of the evil that existed.

"I had a sister once," he said, his voice soft.

"I remember." She nodded. "I heard she had died, but no one ever told me what happened and I didn't want to bring up bad memories by asking."

"Dad didn't know about her until after he married

Mom and I was already born. She came to the house a lot, though, after she found Dad. She was always full of laughter, always demanding what was due her."

"What happened?"

"A serial killer in Washington state." He frowned as he stared through the windshield. "She was only four years older than me. I'd just shipped out to the Marines. The Washington state police contacted Dad weeks after it happened. Her mother hadn't called him. He called me that night and I managed to get leave."

Reaching through the open window she touched his shoulder softly. "I'm so sorry, Archer."

Covering her hand with his he stared back at her, wishing he could make this easier for her.

"You know, maybe that's why your family doesn't want you in Corbin County, Anna," he suggested. "We still don't believe the Slasher was actually caught. Until he is, no woman is safe here. Especially no woman with ties to the Callahans. If it were me, and you were my daughter, I'd keep you the hell away from here, too."

"You'd just move, too," she said regretfully. "You wouldn't just send your child away, Archer."

She had him there.

"They love you. I know that for a fact, sweetheart."

"Not enough," she said, stepping back from the vehicle. "They obviously just don't love me enough."

Starting the Tahoe, Archer slid it into gear before pulling slowly away from her. He'd told her the truth. He didn't blame the Corbins in the least for wanting her to be protected. It was how she was being protected that he found fault with.

If she were his daughter, he would have gotten her the hell out of Corbin County, too. But Anna had been right as well. He wouldn't have just sent his daughter away; he would have made damned certain he was with her. Because as bad as the Slasher was, there were worse, far worse, monsters in the world. The brutality inflicted on his sister attested to that fact. Archer didn't know if he could face losing Anna in such a manner.

At least Anna was safe a little while longer.

She was eighteen, as beautiful as a sunrise, and he had no doubt the day would come when she would return to Corbin County with all intents of staying.

And when she returned, there would be no sending her away again. He only prayed she didn't become a target.

CHAPTER 1

Six years later

She had only been home for less than a day and the first thing she had done was seek out Archer Tobias. The man she was determined to seduce. But now, as she stood there, staring at him, she started to lose her breath.

Anna could feel her body weakening, a sensual, overwhelming surge of sensations flooding her, whipping through her, tearing across her flesh like an erotic tidal wave.

Dark gold eyes watched her through lowered lashes, his face set in an expression that, even in her limited experience, she knew was filled with hunger.

His lips parted as she licked hers to relieve their dryness, his gaze dropping to them, then lifting to her eyes once again.

She had only wanted to dance.

The music was pulsing through her blood, filling her with energy as the beat wrapped around her, and invisible notes seemed to be dragging her onto the gazebo patio used as a dance floor.

The evening air was turning cooler, but as she began to move—as Archer watched, his gaze caressing her body—heat flooded her. Perspiration dewed across her skin and a fever burned beneath her flesh as she turned to him once again. Her hips swayed, long black hair trailed down her back as she slowly, slowly shed the long-sleeved, Victorian-style velvet shrug she'd worn over a white silk camisole.

The feel of the velvet rasping over her bare arms sent a shiver racing over her, electric pleasure sizzling through her.

Did he see her reaction?

His eyes seemed to flare with some dark emotion or hunger as the muscles of his arms bunched, his fingers clenching where they gripped the support post of the awning he stood beneath.

Dropping the shrug to the top of the bistro table near her, Anna tipped her head back, feeling her hair brush past her hips. Heat surged through her. Her nipples ached, hardened, her breasts swelled in painful need.

Between her thighs the swollen bud of her clitoris throbbed with the need for his touch.

The feel of his fingers—his lips . . .

Oh God, the feel of his lips doing all the things she had ever fantasized of.

She needed his touch.

She needed him like air, like water—

Forcing her eyes open, Anna met his gaze again. Letting her hands caress her hips, her sides, stopping just beneath her breasts before stroking down once again, Anna teased him.

Her hands reaching her thighs, she stopped, stroked back to her hips, then lifted her arms over her head and swayed, moving for him, her hips shifting and swaying—

She lost her breath.

Releasing the hold he had on the post, Archer moved slowly down the steps, striding toward her with slow, purposeful strides as the music slowly changed.

The hard, driving beat slid slowly into an erotic pulse of sensual chords. Couples filled the floor as he reached her, his arms surrounding her a second before he suddenly jerked her against his hard body.

"Archer—" Breathing in roughly, her hands gripped his shoulders, holding tight as she felt the hard length of his erection pressing into her lower stomach.

Sensual heat swept through her. Pounding, fiery sensations burned through her, weakening her knees and her womb before they struck at her clit with such pleasure that her breath caught and new heat flushed through her face.

"You're teasing a very hungry man, sweetheart," he growled as he began to move, stroking against her, his arms holding her as she stared up at him, caught, held by the dark hunger in his gaze.

"Or you're teasing a very hungry woman," she suggested breathlessly. "And I'm tired of waiting for you, Sheriff."

His hands tightened at her hips as his dark gold eyes flared with open lust.

"You could be asking for more than you can handle, Anna," he warned her.

"I've wanted you for so long that I feel as though I've lived my entire life with this hunger, Archer. I don't think I've lived a day without burning for you." Such an admission could end up breaking her heart.

And she didn't care. A broken heart could be a small price to pay for the chance, for just one night in the arms of the man who had held that heart forever.

How many times had her friend, Amelia, warned

her that Archer would destroy her heart? That he was the type of man no woman could ever forget? The type of man who might never belong to one woman, forever.

She'd suggested that perhaps Archer wasn't capable of loving anyone but the law.

Once, though, he had loved a sister. Anna had heard the regret and loss in his voice as he had talked about her that last night she had seen him.

Smoothing her hands over his shoulders to the hard, bunched muscles of his biceps, Anna told herself she didn't care. She wasn't going to let herself be afraid of the pain that could come later, when the pleasure was awaiting her now.

Her lashes drifted closed as his head lowered, but he wasn't moving to kiss her as she hoped.

At least, not on her lips.

Instead, his lips brushed over her closed eyelids, moved to her neck, their rough velvet stroking against nerve endings so violently sensitive she couldn't hold back the breathy moan that tore past her lips.

"I need you," she said breathlessly.

Thank God she had slipped out of the house, that her family hadn't known where she was going. She prayed no one called her gran'pop. Or, Lord forbid, her parents.

"What do you need, Anna?" His fingers pushed beneath the hem of her top to find bare skin, his fingertips rubbing and caressing in the small of her back, beneath the veil of her hair.

"I need you," she answered, eyes closing, her body moving instinctively against his as she felt her juices spill between her thighs, dampening the lips of her pussy and the silk of her panties. "Touching me." Forcing her eyes open she stared up at him. "Kissing me. I need your kiss, Archer. You've never kissed me, and you did promise."

"I've kissed every inch of your body in my dreams," he growled, sounding almost angry. "You torment my sleep."

"So, pay me back for it," she suggested, her womb clenching so hard it was like a punch to her lower stomach, shortening her breath and weakening her knees.

"You've been teasing me since you were seventeen," he accused her roughly.

"I've been teasing you since I was thirteen," she countered. "You just refused to notice."

A sense of satisfaction rose inside her at the shock that filled his eyes at her statement.

"I'm glad I didn't notice," he breathed out roughly. "Thirteen?"

"I had some very naughty dreams." She let her nails scrape down the fabric that covered his upper arms. "Dreams of us—"

"Uh, damn, Anna . . ."

"Of you holding me when it was dark," she whispered, remembering those long, tear-filled nights when she'd faced the dark with no one to turn to. "Dreams of your laughter, and the way you teased me over my hair, or scowled at the older boys who flirted with me."

"Damn perverts is what they were," he muttered as his head lowered once again, his cheek resting against the side of her head as they moved to the music, easing further into the shadows at the far end of the patio-style outdoor dance floor.

His fingertips moved farther up her back, beneath the stretchy material of her camisole top as he slowly eased her into position to allow his knee to slide between hers.

"Then my dreams started getting really naughty," she breathed as his thigh pressed into the soft silk of her skirt, rubbing the material between her clit and the hard muscles of his upper leg.

"Please tell me you were at least eighteen." He sighed.

Despite the hungry need pounding inside her, Anna had to grin in amusement at the resignation in his voice.

"The night of my eighteenth birthday—remember?— you were there."

Archer nodded slowly, the hammered gold of his eyes darkening further as he stared down at her.

"I dreamed you followed me to my bedroom and gave me a very special birthday kiss." Trembling, heat flushing her body further at the memory of that dream and how often it had repeated itself.

His fingers flexed at her hips, pulling her closer as he moved them deeper into the shadows and into one of the small, private grottos, surrounded by fragrant blooms and tall evergreens kept expertly manicured.

"What kind of birthday kiss, Anna?" he questioned, his voice hoarse, rough.

"Do you remember the dress I wore?" she asked, tilting her head back as his lips moved along the shell of her ear.

She ached for his kiss. He had never kissed her. She had never felt his lips on hers, and she needed it.

"I remember," he growled.

The dress had been white, long and flowing, the soft chiffon a caress against her flesh and falling around her like a waterfall of material.

"You lifted me to my dresser and pressed me back to the mirror. You pushed my gown above my thighs as you spread them, and you kissed me there."

She couldn't stop the flush that surged beneath her skin at the declaration.

His breathing was rough and ragged as his fingers flexed at her hips, then slid around to her rear. Clenching the rounded curves and lifting her, he ordered, "Spread your thighs, baby, grip my hips."

His cock ground against the mound of her pussy, nothing but the silk of her panties and Archer's pants between him and the slick dampness spilling from her sex.

Anna's mind froze. For one long moment she couldn't think or process the sensations racing through her.

"I think I can make that dream come true soon," he groaned as she felt her rear settling on the top of a table and his fingers speared into her hair and pulled her head back.

The sharp, heated sensation that tugged at the roots of her hair shouldn't have been pleasure, and it shouldn't have been arousing. But it was.

Then his hand moved, sliding around to her cheek, her jaw, his fingers cupping it as his thumb glided over her lips. The rasp of his flesh against the sensitive curves had them parting as she drew in precious air.

Eyes narrowed, he watched her, the gold of his gaze mesmerizing her as the pad of his thumb stroked, caressed, building the heat inside her to an inferno.

Finally, he parted her lips, the broad digit pressing against them as she flicked her tongue over the pad of his thumb.

Archer froze, a hoarse growl leaving his lips as she licked, then sucked it inside and loved the feel, the taste, of him. Rubbing her tongue over the pad, she suckled at it. She felt the hard, aching clench of her womb and the heated wetness as her juices flowed from her pussy.

"Damn you, Anna, you're going to cause us both to get arrested if I end up fucking you here," he groaned, pulling his thumb free of her lips.

"What's wrong, Sheriff?" she asked. "Afraid you can't stop with a kiss?"

"One kiss would never be enough."

Staring up at him breathlessly, lips parted, Anna waited with adrenaline-laced anticipation as his head lowered and his lips touched hers.

As her lashes feathered closed, sensation began erupting inside her. His lips rubbed against hers, stroked and smoothed until a whimper of longing spilled from her lips.

"Please, Archer, kiss me. Just once." Trembling, adrenaline and pure hunger crashing through her system as her nails bit into his shoulders, Anna didn't think she would survive if he didn't kiss her.

His teeth caught her lower lip, gripping it for a second before releasing it, and then he gave her the kiss she had always dreamed of.

It wasn't hard and rough. His lips settled on hers with a firm heat and an erotic caress. His tongue licked at the plump curves of her lips, parting them, catching the lower lip between his lips and licking over it before taking advantage of the fact that her mouth had parted for him.

Slanting his lips over hers, his tongue slid over her lips, licked against them, and possessed her with tenderness.

Oh, yes.

Pure erotic need shot through her senses.

Her lips parted further beneath his, her arms wrapping around his neck as her knees tightened at his hips and he ground his cock between her thighs. The rasp of material, his and hers, over the swollen bud of her clit sent waves of furious need whipping through the oversensitive bundle of nerves and striking to the heart of her womb with burning heat.

Pushing her fingers into his hair, Anna fisted them in the thick strands, desperate to hold him to her. He nipped at her lips, licked the little wound, then came back to take hard, heated tastes of her.

One hand slid from her rear, then his fingers stroked beneath the fabric of her skirt to find the curves of her rear left bare by the thong she wore beneath the frothy material.

Her knees tightened further against his hips, shudders working over her body as he stroked lower, curving between her thighs to find the hot, silken juices gathering at the entrance of her pussy, saturating the silk of her panties.

His fingers eased slowly, so damned slowly beneath the elastic of the thong—

His head jerked up as he found the tightly clenched entrance at the same moment that slick dampness spilled from her again. Anna trembled against him, tiny, whimpering little cries escaping her lips as she felt the violence of the pleasure threatening to erupt into flames inside her.

"Come home with me, Anna." His gaze locked on hers, his body demanding, the need inside her insisting.

Come home with him?

No one had ever said those words to her before.

Come home—

She'd never had a home, but the need to leave with him was suddenly as fierce, as strong, as the need to have him. As strong as the need to belong—

"Sheriff, we have a situation." The voice that came through the radio at his hip was like a shock of ice against the heat raging through Anna's body.

Archer stilled, stiffening against her, his lips drawing back from hers as she bit back a cry of denial.

Forcing her eyes open, staring up at him as he slowly eased her to her feet, Anna wanted to grab the radio and throw it away. Throw it so far that they could never be destroyed by it again.

"Sheriff, you there?" John Caine, Archer's deputy, repeated, his voice low but no less demanding.

Pulling the radio from the case at his hip Archer brought it to his lips. Lips swollen by their kisses, sensual, sexy.

"I'm here," Archer answered, the hammered gold of his eyes slumberous with the need for sex but quickly clearing, as though that hunger had never been there. "What's your location?"

"I'll meet you on the western edge of town, out near the Hopkins' place. I'm on Hopkins Creek Pass, at the clearing," John answered. "Give me your ETA."

"ETA is thirty minutes unless you need me faster."

His gaze didn't leave hers. He didn't blink, and Anna felt her throat tighten with the need to scream, to rage, to deny the fact that he had to leave.

It had taken so long to get her nerve up. So long to tease him, to tempt him to her.

"Thirty minutes." Caine sounded as though the time wasn't the problem.

Disconnecting the radio, Archer lowered it to his hip and pushed it into the case again.

"You have to leave," she said, her hands sliding down his hard chest to the clenched muscles of his stomach as she licked her lips, suddenly uncertain.

He nodded slowly.

Nothing else?

She waited, staring up at him, knowing, praying she was wrong; praying it wasn't over.

Surely he would ask to call her? To see her? Perhaps have her wait for him—in his bed?

"I better go," he said softly.

Her throat tightened and she felt the rejection coming. She was intimately acquainted with being left behind, but this time it had been the last thing she had imagined happening.

"Archer—"

"Shhh." A finger against her lips reinforced the command. "Think about this, Anna. Think about it, and be sure, be very sure, this is what you want."

Before she could assure him that it was, he had moved away from her and disappeared along the shadowed path outside the small grotto. The protest forming on her lips was left unsaid, and the tears that filled her eyes, as always, were left unseen.

She couldn't believe this.

Staring into the dark, with music, muted voices, and laughter surrounding her, Anna realized she should have expected it. After all, she couldn't remember a time that she hadn't been rejected, in some way.

Blinking back her tears and drawing in a deep breath, she too left the grotto. Unfortunately, she couldn't leave the memory of what had happened in it behind her.

Pulling into the clearing next to Deputy Caine's four-wheel-drive Tahoe, Archer turned the engine off and simply sat in the vehicle, staring at where Caine sat on his haunches next to a pale form.

Son of a bitch.

Son of a bitch.

Pushing open the door he stepped from the interior, the chill of the late summer air rushing at him as he closed the door and watched the other man straighten before moving toward him.

"Did you call anyone else?" he asked the deputy as the other man neared him.

"No, sir." Caine breathed in heavily.

"Who called it in?"

Caine shook his head. "I was driving by when I thought I saw lights out here. I turned in to investigate and saw the same thing you just saw when I pulled in."

The glow of headlights off a silken, pale body.

A lifeless body.

Pushing his fingers through his hair, he steeled himself for the inevitable. Striding the remaining distance, he hunched down and stared into the expression of pain and horror that twisted her features.

"Fuck," he muttered as the girl's identity registered. "Ah, hell."

What the hell was going on here?

Katy Winslow, one of the waitresses from the Tavern. Her father had reported her missing the night before when she hadn't returned home from work.

"The wounds are consistent with the Slasher's." John sighed heavily. "And it looks like she's been raped."

Yes, she had been raped.

Heavy, dark bruises marred the skin of her inner and outer thighs, as well as her small breasts. Her eyes were open, staring out in unseeing horror and pain. A knife had cut into her body in far too many places to count them all in the dark. The most telling cut, though, was the puncture wound to her side and the one across her throat. The Slasher's trademark wounds.

Blood marred her body.

She hadn't even been cleaned before she had been deposited in this clearing.

"Rafer Callahan's place, the old Ramsey Ranch, is just over the rise." Caine nodded in the general direction.

"Callahans didn't do this, John." Archer wiped his

hand wearily over his face before rising to his feet. "Call Nash in. See if he can justify that high-ass salary he demanded."

Callum Nash, Corbin County's new crime scene investigator, had been hired specifically for crimes such as the Slasher's.

"Sheriff, Katy Winslow isn't on the list of past Callahan girlfriends," John stated quietly, turning to face him. "Hell, Crowe's the only one not involved with someone right now. He would have told us if he had signed up with someone new, and he makes a point not to talk to any of the women in town."

"Yeah, I know." Archer was well aware of that fact, just as he was aware that Crowe deliberately ensured there was no way the Slasher could target another woman because of him.

"Has she been seen flirting with the other two? Talking to them?" Archer asked.

John was a regular at the Tavern and Bar. It was there that most of the gossip and rumormongering began or eventually filtered through.

"As far as I know, Katy doesn't talk to many men at all. She's been dating the bartender there since she was in high school." Confusion filled the deputy's voice. "Why kill her if she's not associating with the Callahans?"

"Fuck if I know." Archer sighed. "Call in Nash and Chayna. Let's see what we can find, and start praying that bastard hasn't found a reason totally unrelated to the Callahans to start killing again."

Turning, Archer stomped back to his Tahoe, rage festering in his gut at the thought of the Slasher striking again.

The Slasher's attention had seemed to focus on Rafer and Logan's fiancées, who were now under the protection of Ivan Resnova. There had been some incidents, but he hadn't managed to seriously hurt either woman. But why had he targeted Katy Winslow? It didn't make sense. Sliding into the driver's seat, Archer slammed the door before grabbing his cell phone from the passenger seat and dialing Crowe.

"Sheriff?" Callahan answered on the first ring.

"Crowe, how well do you know Katy Winslow?"

A dead silence came over the line for several seconds.

"I only know who she is, and where she works." Crowe's voice was hollow, emotionless. "I've never spoken to her. Not to say hello, excuse me, or good-bye." He paused before breathing out wearily. "She's dead, isn't she?"

"It looks like one of the Slasher's kills," Archer confirmed his suspicion, his teeth clenching. "When I catch him, Crowe, and I will, I'm not promising I'll save him for prison."

Katy was a good kid. She and her boyfriend had been saving up for an apartment together. She was always smiling, always filled with laughter.

And now, she was dead.

"You'll have to beat me to him," Crowe informed him, his voice so icy cold it would have sent a chill up a lesser man's spine. "Are you at the site now?"

Archer gave him the location before disconnecting the call, knowing Callum would have a fit over the interference, but also knowing the Callahans well enough to know that by not telling them he would have been risking the threat of them attempting to investigate or draw the Slasher out on their own.

Leaning back in his seat and closing his eyes, he deliberately brought Anna's face to mind. He let himself remember the touch of her, the taste of her, the warmth that surrounded him as he touched her.

She was his weak spot.

For far too many years Anna Corbin had been the woman he ached for the most, and the one he knew he couldn't have.

At twenty-four, she was sweet as candy, as temperamental as a volcano, and just as hot. And she was his.

He'd been claiming her since the evening he'd realized, to his soul, to the base of his hardening dick, that she was a woman.

Six years.

For six years he'd done everything he could, fought every battle, cursed himself, fought his desires, and ached for her.

She'd haunted his fantasies, invaded his dreams, and tonight, of all nights, had filled his senses with a pleasure he knew he wouldn't be able to hold himself back from.

He'd told her to be certain what she wanted, because he knew once he got her in his bed, escaping it might not be easy for her if that was what she eventually decided she wanted. He was too hungry for her.

Fuck that, he was too damned horny for her.

The lust that raged through him where Anna was concerned was one that no other woman could assuage. If another could, then he would have ensured it was taken care of before now.

Before he touched her.

Before he tasted her.

Before he allowed himself to become addicted to the feel of her close to his chest, in his arms, and somehow awakening hungers he'd never known he had.

Archer could feel the fact that Anna was home to stay tightening in every bone and muscle of his body. She was a woman now, and he recognized that steely confidence he had seen in her eyes. She was a woman who knew what she wanted. He'd take her into his bed, but he would not let her into his heart—at least no more than she had managed already. Damn it, a man had to draw the line somewhere if he wanted to preserve his own sanity. In the meantime, he was going to ignore the voice in his head telling him that it was already too late.

CHAPTER 2

Two weeks later

"I'm not going back to college."

Anna tried to ignore the four sets of shocked gazes that stared back at her as she stepped into the kitchen and walked to the coffeepot.

She'd made her declaration, and now she was going to make her stand.

"I didn't hear you right," her father replied coolly. "I could have sworn I just heard you say you were throwing away thousands of dollars already paid, on tuition alone, to one of the finest colleges in the state of California."

"Not to mention one of the most secluded, out-of-the-way colleges on the face of the planet," she retorted. "One I first begged you not to send me to, and have since demanded to be able to leave for another."

"And that doesn't count the apartment, furnishing it, clothing and food allowances—"

"Oh yeah, and that's so much money in that dried-up little corner of the world," she snorted. "Especially considering your so-called apartment is one owned by the school itself."

She would have given her father's argument much more respect if it weren't for the fact that the college she was attending, as exclusive and high-priced as it was, was little more than a home for wayward children who gave little respect to the fact that their parents only wanted a future for them.

It was all but a prison.

And why was she there?

She hadn't figured that one out yet.

She was three years through a four-year program, and she still couldn't make sense of her family's choice for that college.

What she had done, though, was cram those four years into three, and had the degree she had been sent there to attain in business management and consulting.

"Not to mention the fact that Jacques Dermonde's offer of a position at his company in France is dependent on the completion of those courses," he continued.

"And it also doesn't take into account the fact that I hated France when we visited it, and no consideration is given to the fact that I've said countless times that I refuse to work there. Especially for a man who forced his daughter into marriage with a man twice her age, and considers women no more than children who have to be controlled and fondled as he pleases."

And what had ever made her parents believe she would allow herself to be controlled by anyone, besides themselves? And only then because of her love for them.

Pouring a mug of coffee she turned back to her family and felt her stomach clench in dread and trepidation.

This wasn't the reaction she had expected.

There was no warmth, amusement, or even resignation in their gazes. For a moment, before she could turn her head away, Anna was even certain she'd seen rising fear building in her mother's eyes.

"Lisa." Her gran'mama, Genoa Corbin, addressed Anna's mother as she rose slowly to her feet, reaching for the cane that sat by her chair. "You and I should let John and her father handle this."

Lisa rose to her feet and Anna noticed her mother's hands shaking.

"Yes, run away, Momma. This is, of course, the Middle Ages rather than the twenty-first century and I'm certain none of your business," Anna retorted painfully.

"Have some respect for your mother, Anna," her grandfather snapped, slapping her emotions with the brutal chastisement. "I raised you better than that."

"Did you, Grandfather?" Straightening her shoulders and lifting her chin in determination, she faced him squarely. She hadn't called him Gran'pop for several years now, for a reason. "You raised me to stand up for myself until I was nine, then you shipped me off and never did more than let me know which exotic location we'd be vacationing in during my breaks, despite my pleas that I be allowed to come home, just for a little while."

"And here you are! Just look how you've repaid me for that," he accused her, his tone forbidding and bleak.

"Anna," her father snapped. "Stop acting like a spoiled brat. You will return to school today."

"No, Father, I won't. I've had the dean's letters to the ranch collected before they ever left the school for the past three years. You've only been sent what I wanted you to see. I graduated before showing up here last week. I won't be going back. If you and Grandfather won't let me work with you here on the ranch, then I'll find a job in town."

"No one will hire you," her father promised her.

It wasn't just anger that made her father's voice hoarse, vibrating with a rough, dark emotion. It was indeed fear, just as it had been in her mother's eyes.

"They already have," she stated quietly, clasping her hands in front of her. "I've been hired as assistant to Mikhail Resnova at the Sweetrock offices of Brute Force."

She could have cut the tension in the room with a butter knife as pure terror seemed to flash in her father's eyes.

Brute Force was her cousins' business. Rafer, Logan, and Crowe Callahan were equal partners along with Ivan and Mikhail Resnova in the security venture.

"What are you scared of, Dad?" Forcing the question past her lips was one of the hardest things she had ever done. And she wouldn't have asked if it weren't for the fact that she knew he was frightened of something.

"Of your determination to ruin your life and your future," he stated, his voice still hoarse. "I can't believe you pulled this, Anna."

But there was more. She knew there was more. She could see it in his eyes. Just as she could see the fear and desperation in his expression.

Anna shook her head. "Working on the family ranch, or for my cousins in town, is not the destruction of my life or my future," she informed them. "And neither will any other dream I have. Dreams I deserve, Dad. I don't deserve to be locked up in a college for wayward children, nor have I deserved to be separated from my family since I was nine years old."

She'd hated that. She still couldn't forget it. Nothing could ever hurt her as much as being taken from her family had broken her heart.

She'd been jerked from the home and the family she

loved, and placed in private schools. She had called home when her fear of the dark had overwhelmed her, and they had refused to come get her.

She had cried, she had begged, she had demanded, and still they had refused.

"I'm tired of begging," she told them when neither man spoke. "I'm not going back, and I refuse to beg further. I haven't been a part of this family since I was nine years old, and I refuse to give you the courtesy of having any say in my future any longer. I'm staying in Corbin County, whether you like it or not."

"No, you will not." It was her grandfather who rose to his feet. "Fine, you've graduated without telling us, but that doesn't mean you'll work for anyone in this County or in the state of Colorado without my permission. You can take the job in France or you can leave with nothing but the clothes on your back and see how easy it is to feed yourself with nothing more than that. And don't expect that no-account cousin of yours to do anything but laugh in your face. Because, by God, he hates us all."

And if it had been only anger in his gaze, something other than that flash of terror that filled his eyes, then she could have hated him. She could have allowed the years of desertions, the dark, lonely nights and even more desolate days to feed the anger growing inside her.

She had no friends but one. She hadn't had family to depend upon. She'd just been alone in one private school after another, with each move, each year until she swore she couldn't bear another.

If she had seen disinterest or just anger in her family's eyes, in their faces, then she could have hated them as she wanted to.

That wasn't what she saw, but it wasn't enough to hold back her own anger.

"Disowning another grandchild, are you, Grand-father?" She gave a facsimile of a mocking laugh, but nothing could cover the pain spilling from her. "Why doesn't that surprise me?"

"If that's what I have to do," he snarled.

"Dad!" Her father's tone was a shocked warning as he spoke to his own father.

"She's been pushing for this for years," her grand-father snapped. "She's been begging for it. Always fighting over the fact that we preferred to meet her for a nice vacation rather than having her come here. Al-ways running her mouth about her lack of family. Her lack of consideration in everything we gave her—"

"What did you give me?" she cried out painfully. "An education? Clothes? That's all you gave me."

"And just exactly what did you think we owed you?" he growled back.

"You owed me a family," Anna yelled with over-whelming fury, so filled with pain and anger she was shaking now. "You owed me the same love and devo-tion you gave me before I turned nine. That was ex-actly what you owed me. That, or to tell me what the hell I did to make you hate me so much."

The tears fell then. They filled her eyes, blurred her vision, and ran until she wondered if she would ever be able to stop them.

"Why?" she sobbed desperately. "Why do you hate me?"

"God, Anna, we don't hate you." Her father came out of his chair in a burst of anger so ferocious even Anna stepped back. "Why can't you just accept that we're doing our best to protect you?"

She shuddered, shaking with her sobs as she faced him.

"Because I don't need to be protected from living. I

need a life, Dad," she cried, the pain building, burning inside her until she was terrified it would consume her. "Is that so hard to understand?"

"Then get out there and get you a life." Her grandfather waved his arm to the door. "But don't expect it to be easy. I promise you, no one in Corbin County will dare help you. Especially Crowe Callahan."

"Like no one helped him, Rafer, and Logan?" she sneered back at him. "I always thought he must have done something so vile, so unforgivable, to have been denied your love. But that's not the truth, is it, John Corbin? What they say in town, that you punish him because you can't punish his mother for leaving and allowing herself to die in that car accident all those years ago, is true."

His face spasmed with pain. An agony unlike any she had ever seen filled his face.

"And if she had done as I asked, then she would be alive now," he stated, his voice hoarse as another sob shook her body. "I won't make that same mistake with you, Anna. You can start packing for France, or you can be cut out of our lives just as easy as David Callahan's little brat was."

Pain filled his voice and struck at her heart, but it was too late to back down. She had made her stand, just as her grandfather had now done.

"Is this how you feel as well, Dad?" she asked bitterly. "Would you cut me out of your life so easily?"

His jaw tightened as he refused to speak.

As far as Anna was concerned, that was answer enough.

"I'll get my things and leave."

"No you won't." The fury in her grandfather's voice made her pause. "You haven't bought a damned thing you call your own. Everything you have someone else has bought for you. You can leave this house the same way you came into it, with nothing. You should be thankful I let you have the clothes on your back," he reminded her. "That's all you leave with and you can count yourself lucky that I'm allowing you that much."

Her chest tightened, her heart constricting until she was certain she would die from the agony tearing through her.

This was her grandfather.

She'd loved him all her life.

He'd spoiled her when she was a child, swore he would protect and love her, then he had sent her away, swearing it was for her own good.

He'd lied to her, cheated her out of a childhood, and now, he was attempting to cheat her out of the rest of her life.

"Daddy?" she asked. "Are you going to let him do this?"

Not even her purse? Or the car they had bought her for her sixteenth birthday?

The one she had so rarely gotten to drive?

None of her clothes, or her shoes?

Nothing of the mementos bought for her through the years that she treasured so much, not even a picture of her parents?

"And don't fool yourself into thinking I'm not well aware of what you were up to with that damned sheriff in town when you slipped off to the social weekend before last, either," her grandfather informed her then, his tone brutal. "The reason you want to be back here so bad has nothing to do with your family and everything to do with whoring around with that son of a bitch. Stay the hell away from him."

Shaking in fury, outrage, and the shattering of her heart, Anna didn't bother to fight back her tears.

"Go to hell!" she cried out. "I'll whore with who-ever the hell I please. It would be a far sight better than trying to be perfect enough to be a part of this family. It's pretty damned evident that no matter how anyone tries to love you, or hold onto you, the only thing you know how to do is turn on them."

"I turn on enemies," he told her with a cold smile as he finally rose from his seat. "Now make up your mind, little girl. Take your ass to France or get out."

"Ah, least you're allowing me a choice," she sneered. "It's more than you allowed Crowe, isn't it?"

"At least I'm prepared to give you a choice," he snarled back at her from the table, his arms crossing over his chest imperiously. "I don't recall giving him one."

The callous disregard in his tone was at odds with the look in his eyes, the turmoil and pain she could have sworn glowed within them.

She turned to her father again.

He was at the table, his palms flat against the top of it as he stared down at the circular glass top rather than at her or his father.

He wouldn't look at her, refused to acknowledge her.

"Why, Daddy?" she asked. "Why are you letting him do this?"

Slowly, his head lifted. His gray eyes looked tor-tured, his face drawn and years older than it had been minutes before.

"It's the only way I know how to protect you." He turned and left the room.

"Make your choice, Anna," her grandfather de-manded.

She didn't see anger in his gaze, though; rather, she saw a resigned misery, as though he had known this day would come, and still, he hadn't been prepared for it.

Tears were soaking her face, she realized, running from her cheeks and dripping onto the silk cami she wore with her jeans and sneakers.

"I've made my choice." She could barely force the words past her lips as she turned and walked from the kitchen.

Surely her father would stop her.

Her mother?

She had to force herself to walk across the wide, dark wood floor of the foyer to the front door.

With no luggage, no money, and no ID, she left the only place she had ever called home and stepped into the cool morning air as daylight filtered over the mountains.

A sob tore from her chest then.

Then another.

Moving down the steps, taking one step at a time, her heart broke into fragments. The knowledge that no one was going to stop her, that no one cared enough to stop her, destroyed her.

And, she realized, she didn't feel any more alone now than she ever had.

But that didn't mean she had to obey his whim.

Sniffing back the tears, though nothing could hold back the pain, she paused, trying to think, to plan.

Her purse, ID, and what little cash she had, along with the key to her safe deposit box, were in her room.

She had some jewelry she could sell, though only as a last resort.

With what she had, perhaps there was enough to get an apartment and pay the down payment and rent until she began working.

Making the decision quickly, she turned around the side of the house and ran to the heavy wood trellis that ran up to her bedroom window.

She didn't have to obey anyone implicitly any longer. And she would be damned if she would just walk away with nothing that belonged to her.

Climbing swiftly up the trellis she slid the window open, thankful she'd forgotten to lock it the night before when she'd had it open, and slipped into the room.

Quietly, quickly, she rushed to the closet and found the stylish leather backpack she kept there.

It wasn't big enough to carry much, but the essentials should fit. A couple of handfuls of silken lingerie, two sets of the vintage silk nightgowns and robes she so loved. Several changes of clothes suitable for the job she'd been hired to do, and a pair of flat-heeled business-type shoes. Several pairs of socks and stockings, the small box of jewelry.

There was a little room left if she really stuffed it so she threw in some jeans and T-shirts.

When she finished, the buckles were bulging and she was still leaving behind so much.

As she packed, holding back the tears was impossible.

It was killing her. Inside her chest she could feel her heart breaking, feel the hope she'd had when she'd first faced her father and grandfather drain away. The tears were impossible to hold back now.

She was stealing her own clothes, her own jewelry. She was being forced to walk out of the house that hadn't been a home since she was nine years old.

And she couldn't imagine anything that could hurt more.

As she pushed the window open again, the sound of her mother's voice in the hall outside her door made her pause.

"How could you let him do this?" her mother cried out, her voice rough, almost unrecognizable.

She'd never seen or heard her mother cry, though. "You know what this could cause, Genoa. You have to do something. Please—"

Her mother's voice broke as she began sobbing, the sound of her pain causing Anna to cover her lips to hide the sound of her own agony.

"Lisa, you know he had no choice. Neither of them did," her grandmother protested.

"No, there's always a choice," Lisa Corbin cried out desperately. "This was the wrong one. Oh God, it was the wrong choice."

Seconds later, her parents' bedroom door slammed, cutting off the sound of her mother's tears. But it didn't stop Anna's. Leaning against the window frame, her face buried against the sheer curtains, she couldn't hold them back. The silent sobs shook her body, and the pain causing them ripped at her heart until she wondered if she were going to be able to leave. Or if she would beg, plead with her grandfather to change his mind and to let her do as he wanted. But leaving again would be like cutting her heart from her chest.

Hell, she'd prefer to cut her heart from her chest.

She had never had a home, she had no family. So she would make her own home, her own family, or, she swore, she would die trying.

Archer Tobias stared at the map on the wall in his study for long minutes before inserting the yellow, round-headed push pin he held into its proper position.

The pin represented the Slasher's latest victim, Katy Winslow.

His grandfather had started this map fifty years ago, during his election campaign when he ran for sheriff of Corbin County.

Each pin represented a suspicious death, murder, or suicide in the County.

Katy's pin was bunched in with more than a dozen others.

"A favorite killing ground," he remembered his father saying as he stared at the map.

The red push pins represented a Callahan who had died, and each blue push pin represented the death of someone connected to the Callahans. The white-headed pins represented deaths that couldn't be connected, but those bodies had been found on or near Callahan property.

For instance, Logan, Rafer, and Crowe's parents and Crowe's infant sister's pins were all there. They had gone over a cliff during a winter snowstorm while on the way back from Denver. The boys had only been eleven and thirteen at the time. They had been with Rafe's mother's uncle, Clyde Ramsey, while the parents had made the trip.

There were other colored pins on the map of Corbin County as well.

Green pins represented areas where marijuana had been found growing, pale blue marked burglaries, purple marked assaults.

Brown represented suicides. Black represented murders of those not connected to the Callahans.

The deaths of those connected to the Callahans threatened to outnumber them.

Bad luck, being a Callahan. Or knowing one.

Other than the Slasher, Corbin County wasn't a place that drew much crime.

His eyes returned to Katy's pin.

Why Katy? he wondered again.

Shaking his head, Archer turned and left the study,

locking the patio doors as securely as he had the inner
doors that led to the rest of the house, then setting the
security system Crowe had helped him install in the
spring.

Moving to the SUV he drove, the trip to the sheriff's
office was made in less than five minutes. His home
only sat two blocks from his office, one of the older
buildings behind the main street courthouse.

Pulling into his designated parking slot, he restrained a sigh at the sight of the County attorney,
Wayne Sorenson, as the other man walked down the
back courthouse steps and turned to head to the sheriff's office.

The text the attorney had sent earlier that morning
had sounded dire.

Must see you at nine. Imperative.

Shaking his head, Archer reached for the Stetson
he'd laid on the passenger seat before exiting the
vehicle. Settling the hat on his head, he adjusted
it automatically while hitting the door lock to the
SUV.

The warmth of the morning sun beat down on Sweetrock like a lover's caress, stroking across the town
with the promise of more heat to come. There were
clouds building over the mountains above that promised rain in the valley though and a possible blizzard
higher up.

The season might be summer, but the mountains
paid little heed to the calendar.

It was the middle of August, but already the chill of
an early winter was invading the temperatures at night,
and the old-timers swore there was a hint of snow in
the air.

They hadn't had snow in Corbin County before October in nearly twenty-five years. The last time it had snowed that early, JR and Eileen Callahan had died on that mountain road.

He made a mental note to warn the Callahans to stay off fucking mountain roads this week.

Waving at the two old men sharing a bench across the street, Archer strode quickly to the white stone sheriff's office and connecting jail.

Unlike many counties, Corbin County didn't have a separate detention center. The six cells that had been built housed any overnight, and some monthly, prisoners. If more secure accomodations were needed, then there was the detention center in Montrose that they transferred the prisoners to.

Judge Pascal was firm, but he didn't sentence a lot of jail time unless the crime really warranted it. Violent criminals he sent to Montrose, anyway, because Archer wasn't comfortable keeping them in the lower security cells.

Stepping into the outer office he nodded to his model-turned-secretary.

"Mornin', Madge," he greeted her.

"Mornin', Sheriff," she drawled, a sure indication she wasn't happy. "Attorney Sorenson is awaiting your arrival in your office." She rolled her eyes in disgust. "He didn't seem to want to sit out here and entertain me until you arrived."

In other words, the other man had entered the office without informing Madge he would be doing so.

Archer's lips quirked. That was Wayne; he didn't stand on ceremony for any man—or woman.

Striding to the closed door, Archer pulled it open and stepped inside the overly scented room.

He didn't know what scent Wayne was wearing,

and though it was only slightly stronger than the scent he used to wear, still the stuff reeked.

"Archer, good to see you." Rising to his feet from the chair that sat facing Archer's desk, Wayne extended his hand as he smiled at him.

"Counselor." Archer nodded as he drew his hand back. "How can I help you?"

Moving behind the desk, Archer removed his hat and laid it on the side of the desk before taking his seat and watching Wayne expectantly.

"Well, Archer, I had a call from the governor and Sweetrock's mayor first thing this morning. Governor Ferguson was in Boulder and couldn't find time, I guess, to actually travel to Sweetrock and grace us with his presence." He snorted rudely.

Archer let a mocking smile pull at his own lips. Governor Ferguson was damned busy, he knew. Just as he had been damned busy from the moment he'd been voted in as governor. Chief among the jobs he'd set for himself was finding and identifying his only child's killer, the Sweetrock Slasher. County attorney Sorenson had managed to make it onto the list of suspects. Not that Archer had informed him of that fact.

"I assume he wasn't calling to invite us to dinner, then?" Archer wasn't going to tell him either.

Wayne's snort was heavy with sarcasm. "Nope, I reckon he wasn't." He chuckled then. "Though from what I hear about that man's personal chef, I wouldn't have minded."

Archer let a chuckle rasp his throat, but it was a cursory one, intended only to observe the rules of courtesy.

"No, it wasn't for dinner," Wayne repeated as he sighed heavily. "It was more of a threat." His gray eyes met Archer's brown ones.

"A threat?" That didn't sound like Carson Ferguson. "What kind of threat?"

"He's threatening to send us 'help' if we don't step up our efforts to identify and apprehend the 'Slasher.' "

Archer grimaced at the news, though he'd known it was coming, still he maintained an air of surprise.

"Fuck, we don't need this," Archer murmured as he rose quickly from his chair and stomped to the door of his office. Jerking it open he found Madge. "I'm going to need coffee." He sighed. "And fix it strong."

"Try decaf," she advised as she rose from her chair and moved around her desk. "It's healthier for you."

"Slip that crap in on me, Madge, and I swear I'll fire you for real," he growled.

"Instead of for fake?" Madge only chuckled. "I'll have it in there in a sec, boss," she promised.

Archer paced back to his desk and took his seat once again.

Wayne watched him with quiet sympathy. "It's been damned hard on the Callahans." He sighed. "And those girls." Shaking his head, Wayne cleared the emotion in his throat. "Cami, Rafer's fiancée, and my Amelia used to be damned good friends until I learned Amelia was getting mixed up with them." He pushed his fingers through his brown-and-gray hair with a grimace. "Terrified the hell out of me. I may have even made her hate me, the way I jerked her home and forced her to disassociate with the Flannigan girl she was such good friends with."

Wayne looked away for a moment, obviously torn about how he had handled the matter. Wayne's sympathy and attempts to help the Callahans were one reason why Archer found it hard to believe he was a suspect.

"Ah, hell, it beat having her raped and murdered,"

he bit out angrily on a hard breath. "But that's neither here nor there. How are we going to handle this? We have to figure out who that bastard is and where he is or we're going to have company. Something that hasn't been accomplished in twelve years."

Archer pursed his lips thoughtfully as he leaned forward in his chair, his arms bracing on the desk. "Well, Wayne, I'm not sure at the moment. I do know I don't want 'help' invading my County."

The FBI was, of course, already there and had been for a while now. Not that they were finding anything more than Archer had.

"My God, that's the last thing we need," Wayne agreed, his gray eyes darkening with anger. "It would become a three-ring circus. But if we don't have any leads at all, then how will we stop it?"

"We're just going to have to figure out a way to draw the Slasher out," Archer stated. "I'm working on a few ideas. Give me a few days and we'll go over them and see what works."

Wayne nodded, though he didn't appear in the least relieved. "Let's hope those ideas are at least working ideas," Wayne grunted sarcastically as he rose to his feet. "Is that the best you can do, Sheriff?"

"Considering the girl we found the other night had no known connection to any of the Callahans, I seem to just be at a dead end," he growled in frustration.

"No connection at all?" Wayne murmured, surprised. "But they've always been the Callahans' past lovers."

"Not this one." Archer shook his head firmly as he lifted one hand to rub at his cheek thoughtfully. "Like many of the other women in Corbin County, she was polite to them, but that was it. She and her boyfriend had just rented an apartment in town and she was scheduled to start business courses in the fall. But she was definitely in no way connected to the Callahans."

Wayne breathed out roughly before shoving a hand in a pocket of the summer-weight gray slacks he wore. "Let's just get this done without any damned outsiders coming in," Wayne ordered broodingly. "I really don't relish that kind of hassle."

Not that Archer did, either.

Archer watched as the County attorney left the office, the door slamming behind him. Almost immediately it reopened and Madge entered with an irritated look. "You know, he saw me coming with that coffee. He could have left the door open."

The tray holding a thermal pot and a ceramic cup proclaiming FAVORITE SHERIFF thunked down on his desk as Madge straightened and propped her hands on her hips. "I don't like your friends, Sheriff."

"I never said he was my friend, Madge," he pointed out with a grin.

She smiled back at him then, causing Archer to pause, his hand reaching for the cup. That smile was enough to make a grown man shudder in fear. The pure glee in her light blue eyes was enough to make him turn, tuck his tail, and run.

Hell, he pitied the man that ever married her.

"What is it, Madge?" he asked as she continued to stare down at him with that damned Mona Lisa curve to her lips.

"Well, you had a call while you were in your meeting," she informed him.

"Did I?"

"Uh-huh." She nodded. "Miss Lonhorne called. She told me to tell you that you're going to be hearing from her lawyer. It seems she found another of her expensive purses, a Choo, I believe, clawed up, and used as a litter box. She's none too happy. Perhaps you should contact that lawyer of yours now."

Snickering, she turned and left the office as Archer sat back in his chair in disgust.

Dammit, he'd told Marisa not to bring that crap to the house. His cat, a chocolate-brown Maine Coon cat with the temperament of a rabid lion, hated her. Archer had warned her Oscar would shred anything she owned that the cat found lying around, but she'd refused to listen.

She'd demanded he get rid of the cat instead, so she could move in.

When Archer had refused, she'd arrived with her luggage anyway, and decided she was going to fight Oscar for her place in his life. She'd then thrown the cat's pillow out of the bedroom, locked the door on him at night, and thought she would get away with it.

Chuckling, he made a note to call his lawyer and let her deal with Marisa, if she ever actually decided to sue. Until then, he needed to talk to the coroner and wanted to head back up the mountains to where Katy Winslow's body had been found.

There had to be something, somewhere, that would give him a lead on the Slasher and the partner he had to be working with. The FBI hadn't changed their profile, but they agreed the man killing the young women had changed after the death of the assailant who had attacked Rafer Callahan's fiancée, Cami Flannigan.

The FBI had yet to take over the case, though, because the minute they had tried to do so in the past, the killings had simply stopped. Of course, it had also coincided with the Callahans' departure from the County.

It had been Archer who had gone to the agency when the first victim in twelve years had turned up the summer before. The FBI was here, not that he knew who it was or where that person was, but he'd bargained for just that. An undercover agent rather than having the case taken over by the agency might give them a greater chance of finding the bastard.

Opening the door and peeping in, Madge stared at him with a frown. "You have a call on line two from Lisa Corbin. She says it's urgent."

A frown furrowed his brows as well as he picked up the phone and pressed the button to line two as Madge stepped back and closed the door.

"Lisa, is everything okay?" He didn't know her well, despite the years he'd spent vacationing with her family. What he did know was that she was Anna's mother, and despite the distance he'd always seen between them, he'd always sensed the love she felt for her daughter.

"No, it isn't. You said if I or Anna ever needed anything, you'd be there for us," she reminded him.

Archer tensed, dread suddenly striking his chest as he felt the flesh down his spine begin to crawl in warning.

"What do you need?"

As he listened, disbelief, fury, and some dark, unknown emotion began exploding within him.

"I'm going for her now, Lisa," he promised as he rose from his chair and jerked his hat from the side of his desk. "Don't worry, I'll watch out for her."

Lisa hung the phone up slowly before wrapping her arms across her stomach and releasing the sobs she'd been fighting to hold back.

Again.

"Not again," she sobbed painfully as she felt her husband's arms wrap around her, felt his tears against her cheek as they held each other. "Oh God, Robert, please, please don't let me lose my baby again."

CHAPTER 3

Anna was silent as Sweetrock came into view from the curve in the road that wound around the mountain. It wasn't one of the more dangerous roads. The four-lane had heavy steel guardrails stretching along it, ensuring there were no winter accidents.

The road itself wasn't as elevated as most. Where they couldn't cut through the mountain, excavation had centered on cutting *out* the mountain instead.

The view wasn't as incredible as many of the scenic routes were, but neither were they as dangerous as the one now named in honor of the Callahans who had died on it.

Callahan's Peak, the sharp curve that had taken Crowe Callahan's grandparents, and then his parents, uncles, and their wives, was a treacherous stretch of road when even the lightest of snows fell.

She wasn't on that road, but the decisions she faced felt nearly as dangerous as that cliff had become. And she felt as though her situation was just as precarious.

What was she going to do now?

No doubt she wouldn't be able to afford the exclusive,

boutique-only underwear and gowns she preferred for a long time, she thought in rueful amusement.

She would be lucky, if she could make the money she had stretch to afford dinner on a daily basis until she began getting paid.

"Are you sure you don't want to stay with me?" Archer asked again as the Tahoe passed over the small stone bridge that spanned Corbin Creek and marked the last mile to the city limits.

He'd made the offer when he first picked her up.

She'd turned him down then, too.

"That's okay, Archer." Shaking her head, she stared straight ahead, loath for him to see the confusion and indecision she knew would show in her eyes.

Or the tears.

She was still battling those hated tears.

"Why?"

The question made her pause.

Turning to him, Anna called up the only defense she had against the emotions and fears weakening her.

Anger.

"You didn't want me there two weeks ago, so why would you want me there now?" she asked him, the hurt from that night still lying inside her, brought fully to the surface by the rejection of her family.

"I didn't say I didn't want you there, Anna." The golden brown of his gaze, the mix of colors reminiscent of an eagle's, touched her as he glanced at her with predatory intent. "I said I wanted you to be certain, damned certain, of coming to my bed, before you made that decision."

Her lips pursed bitterly. "You pushed it pretty far before making the offer. You could have at least let me orgasm to be certain, one way or the other, before rejecting me."

She hadn't stopped aching for him.

If the hurt building inside her weren't so brutal, so filled with anger, then she would still be aching for him.

Hell, she *was* still aching for him. Aching to be held, to be touched—God, she was dying to live for a change rather than keep herself in some kind of abyss to prove her love for her family.

Archer didn't say a word. Flipping on the turn signal, he took the turn that led into town rather than turning into the hotel parking lot as they passed it.

"I didn't say I was certain I was ready to go to bed with you," she reminded him pointedly.

"I have a guest room." The shrug of his muscular shoulders indicated he didn't care either way, but the heat in his gaze told another story. "You can stay there until you're sure."

"I heard you have a cat that loves to shred leather purses, too," she retorted, sitting back in the seat and letting go of the seat belt latch she'd been prepared to unbuckle when the hotel came into sight.

"Hmm, only when he gets thrown out of his bed." A grimace pulled at his lips as he glanced at her, his gaze filled with mirth. "Come on, don't tell me you already heard about the cat?"

"And Marisa." And how jealous she had been.

She'd wanted to scratch the other woman's eyes right out of her face, and might have, if she'd known who she was. All Anna had heard was her name, as her grandfather's maids laughed over the rumors of the other woman's attempt to move in with Archer.

"Marisa's not there, Anna. She left. And Oscar's a big ole lap baby," he told her as he glanced back at her with a grin. "He just wanted to keep his pillow at the foot of my bed. Marisa threw him out instead. She put

his pillow in the guest room, and when he sat outside
my bedroom crying she took him to the guest room
and locked him in with her extra purses and her luggage."

"While she occupied your bed," she filled in, her
jaw clenching as spikes of jealousy raged through her
again. "I'm sure Oscar appreciated your loyalty."

Archer chuckled.

"Actually, I was called out that night." Rubbing
at the side of his face, his fingers rasping over the
closely cropped beard growing there, he glanced at
her with devilish amusement. "She didn't spend the
first night in my bed the whole month she was there.
Oscar would start squalling every time the bedroom
door closed."

She was in love with Oscar, that was simply all there
was to it.

The remainder of the drive to his house was made
in silence, and an uncomfortable one at that. Anna
could feel a tension rising between them now that hadn't
been there in all the years he had vacationed with her
family in the exotic locales they had chosen.

Bermuda when she was sixteen. That was the first
year he had flown in with her grandfather.

He had been twenty-six. He'd just been discharged
from the Marines for medical reasons. She remembered the cast he'd worn from his ankle to above his
knee, and the jeans, cut short on that one leg, revealing
the bronzed, hair-spattered flesh that seemed to fasci-
nate her.

The next year, he'd sported a scar from his thigh to
his ankle, thanks to the surgery and the metal pins
that had fused the shattered femur in his thigh, and the
tibia below his knee. The shattered bones, courtesy of
an IED, had taken the military career he had been

working on, but, as her father had explained to him the summer he turned twenty-seven, it didn't have to destroy a very promising career in law enforcement.

Seven years later, he was on his second term in the sheriff's office, and it didn't appear he would have much competition for a third term.

Unmarried and unattached, he was considered the most sought-after bachelor in Corbin County and the counties surrounding it.

How often had she listened to her father and grandfather chuckle in amusement over the number of women chasing after Archer? Marisa was merely one in a long line of women who thought they could break Corbin County's favorite stud, her grandfather had drawled in amusement, unaware that Anna had been on the balcony above them, her heart breaking at each amused observation made.

She'd loved him since she was a young girl. As a teenager, he'd been the man she measured every boy against and, as her interest in the opposite sex began maturing, it had been Archer she'd dreamed of kissing, touching, loving, and nothing over the years had changed that. And now, here she was, uncertain in the face of the needs she couldn't seem to make sense of, the building pain of the desertion of her family, and the certainty that what was left of her heart would be lying in tatters, just as it had been left that morning.

"You're too quiet," Archer observed as he pulled into the sheltered parking pad next to the house he'd inherited from his parents.

"What do you want me to say?" Shaking her head at the bitterness she couldn't seem to fight, she pushed open the vehicle's door and jumped out.

"For starters? 'I'm sorry, Archer, yes, I'll let you practice all those manners your momma beat into your brain before her death and sit nice and still while you open my door and help me from the vehicle,'" he quoted with an edge of mocking censure.

Anna looked from the door to the seat as he rounded the front of the vehicle.

Drawing in a deep breath, she knew there was no way in hell to fight not just what she felt for him, but also the physical need for him.

It was mixed up with her need for this county, the need for her family, and the need to just belong.

"I'm sorry, Archer." She sighed as he glared down at her. "Unlike you, my momma didn't teach me all the finer points of responsible manners."

"No, but I know damned good and well all those fancy girls' schools you attended taught you that, and more," he grunted as he gripped her arm and moved to lead her up the steps from the front curb to the porch.

"I'm not a child." Pulling her arm free of his hold she stared up at him archly. "I know how to walk on my own."

His touch did something to her that she had no idea how to combat. She wanted to throw herself in his arms, beg him to touch her, to take her, to drive her crazy with his kiss.

"Hell, woman, you're going to drive me to drink." He sighed as she moved up the steps, strode quickly across the small front yard, then up several more steps to the front porch.

"Do you really think I will?" Cocking her head to the side she watched as he stepped on the porch and unlocked the door.

"Well, let's hope not," he stated. "But if you do, it's my fault alone, and none of yours."

Stepping into the house, Anna looked around at the heavy dark wood of the furniture and matching dark

curtains that kept the room to a bare glimmer of light
that managed to spill into it.

As Archer stepped into the house and closed the
door, Anna watched in complete wonderment as a
huge, dark brown shadow stalked slowly from the <u>hall</u>.
Body crouching in predatory mode, belly low to the
ground, golden brown eyes, nearly identical to those of
his owner, peered around the side of the couch.

Anna deliberately ignored him as she hoisted the
strap of the backpack higher on her shoulder and followed Archer through the foyer to the sunlit kitchen at
the far end of the large entryway.

"Oscar, be a good kitty," Archer chastised the cat
behind her as they entered the bright, roomy kitchen.
A wide archway led to the living room, another to the
dining room beside it, and then what appeared to be a
study from the other side of the room.

"You can put your things down," he told her as he
moved to the coffeepot. "I'll show you up to the guest
room in a minute."

After the inevitable interrogation, she guessed.

"I'm not in the mood for twenty questions, Archer,"
she informed him. "This hasn't been one of my better
days, and I'd like to just lie around and feel sorry for
myself for a while. I have a feeling you don't consider
your guest room pity-party central, though. Right?"

His gaze was like a heated caress against her flesh.
A caress she had no choice but to pretend to be unaware of.

"What happened, Anna?"

The question hung between them as she dropped the
backpack and purse at her feet.

She'd known he was going to ask. Archer should
have been a prosecutor rather than a sheriff.

"What makes you think anything happened?"

Wrapping her arms across her breasts, she turned and paced to the wide sliding glass doors that looked out to the private balcony beyond.

"Now, what would make me think anything happened?" he asked mockingly. "Could it have been the fact that you were walking down that damned mountain road like a little waif?"

Like a little waif—

"A waif is defined as a person, especially a child, who has no home or friends," she murmured mockingly. "I actually had cause to have to define the word last year."

She could hear the tears in her own voice, feel them tightening her throat.

"Anna, tell me what happened." The gentleness in the demand almost broke the hold on her tears.

Lifting her eyes to his reflection as he moved to her, Anna watched as his hands, so large and broad, settled against her shoulders, his thumbs stroking gently beneath her nape.

"Do you know your mother called me?" he asked when she didn't answer.

"What did she say?" Jerking her gaze to the reflection of his eyes, Anna felt her heartbeat becoming sluggish and heavy as her chest tightened painfully.

The sound of her mother's tears earlier had cut at wound in her soul that still bled.

"She said your grandfather had thrown you out and you were walking alone toward Sweetrock." The sound of his voice left her wondering if perhaps her mother hadn't had much more than that to say.

Tightening her lips as they threatened to begin trembling once again, she said, "I refused to take the job in France that Jacques Dermond extended. That damned pervert." By now she was barely holding back the tears as they filled her eyes. "I wanted to come home. I worked myself almost into exhaustion to cram eight years of classes into six, so I could come back home. So I could get to know my parents and grandparents." She swallowed tightly, inhaling with jerky breaths. "I was supposed to be in college four years, Archer. Just four." Outrage colored her voice. "Do you know John Corbin changed my major when I refused to go to France that summer?"

"I heard," he sighed. "I'm sorry, Anna."

"What did I do that was so wrong, Archer? That was so bad?" There was no holding back the pain that filled her. Her voice echoed with the consufion inside her. "What was so horrible about wanting to know family? The Slasher hasn't struck out at family, only lovers."

"Nothing that I could ever imagine." He sighed heavily, his arms lowering to wrap around her stomach and pull her back against him. "I honestly believe they wanted nothing more than to keep you safe, sweetheart. They've gone about it the wrong way perhaps, but it was done out of love."

A bitter laugh escaped her.

Turning from his reflection she faced him, a certain knowledge rising inside her.

"He never regretted losing his only grandson. Why would he regret losing one worthless granddaughter?"

"John Corbin has more regrets, I believe, than he admits to," he stated as she pulled away from him.

The loss of his warmth, the loss of that feeling of not being so alone in the world, caused the battle with her tears to only become harder.

"It doesn't matter." Drawing in a deep breath, Anna forced herself to shrug it away. "None of it really matters now, Archer. And things are really no different now than they ever were, other than the fact that I now know they never really wanted me with them."

All the years of vacations in exotic locales, and pushing her off on business associates when they couldn't accompany her. The times she had cried and begged to come home, and the excuses they had given, all well-practiced and regretfully voiced.

If she had looked like a waif earlier, then it was because that was what she had always been, and that wasn't how she wanted Archer to see her.

"This isn't going to work—"

"You're not leaving," Archer spoke over her, his expression, his tone, suddenly more arrogant than before.

"Excuse me?" Crossing her arms over her breasts, she fought to push back the need for his touch and the arousal that look sent spearing through her traitorous body.

"You heard me, Anna." Neither his expression nor his tone eased. "You're not leaving. You can stay right here, where I'll know you're safe."

Safe?

"From what?" Incredulity filled her. "Or do you think I need to be saved from my own poor choices just as my family does?"

He snorted at that. "I think leaving that house is the best decision you could have made." His gaze became smoldering then, dark and intently sexual. "That doesn't mean I'm going to let you spend the last penny you probably have on a hotel room, or that I'm going to let you forget what happened the night you nearly came on my fingers. I think I'm ready to collect on that promise now."

She couldn't breathe.

Anna felt her body heating instantly. Her breasts swelled, her nipples tightening and beginning to ache with the overwhelming need to be touched.

Her stomach clenched, her womb flexing as a surge of electric sensation raced through her clit.

"I don't remember extending a rain check, Archer." She stared back at the smoldering sensuality in his expression as though she had never seen it.

The truth was, that look of lust and hunger had her creaming her panties so furiously that it was all she could do to keep from throwing herself in his arms. To keep from begging him to finish what he started in that little grotto.

"Oh, baby, the rain check was there," he countered. "In every drop of your response raining on my fingers—"

Her lips curled mockingly. "Every drop of my response?" She sniffed delicately, though her body ached in response to his words. "Does that line actually get you anywhere?"

Delight flickered in his gaze.

Oh, hell, what had she managed to ignite in his evil little brain?

He advanced on her, one predatory step at a time, as she fought to stand her ground—and failed miserably.

Anna felt her back flat against the refrigerator, his front pressing against hers, the hard wedge of his cock imprinting through their clothes to the aching depths of her womb.

Oh God, she needed to come.

"Actually, I was trying to be a good boy," he murmured as he caught her wrists and stretched them over her head, securing them against the cool metal of the appliance with one hand.

The other pressed beneath her shirt, easing up until his palm cupped her breasts.

"You know how to be a good boy?" Anna widened her eyes in surprise. "Why, Archer, I'm certain I never recognized that quality in you."

"I'm going to push my cock so deep inside that slick little pussy, Anna, that you'll wonder how you ever breathed without the feel of me fucking you."

Yep, there went her breath.

"But first." His head lowered, his lips caressing the lobe of her ear as he spoke. "I'm going to spread those pretty thighs and eat you until you're screaming with pleasure. Until you're coming on my tongue and begging for my dick."

"My, how confident we have become." It was all she could do to push the words past her lips. "Were you going to do that before or after I put your balls up in your throat?"

She'd managed to slide her knee between his legs, lifting it until it rested against his balls.

He didn't release her.

He grinned.

A slow, anticipatory grin that should have warned her.

Before she realized what he was doing he shifted, lifted her, edged his hips to the side and, before she could do more than take a breath, had her thighs at his hips and his erection grinding the seam of her jeans into her clitoris.

Oh, hell, it felt good.

The heat of him seemed to surround her.

The heat of his cock speared through the clothes separating them, causing her clit to swell further, to ache in need as her juices flowed from her vagina.

"Now, where are my balls going to be?" His voice caressed her senses, the hoarse, hungry timbre of it stroking against her senses.

"Shouldn't you know?" She couldn't stop the grin that tugged at her lips. "They are your balls, after all."

His chuckle was one of amused surprise.

"So they are," he murmured, his thumb stroking against the tight hardness of her nipple and sending waves of electric sensation surging to the sensitive bud of her clit. "I'd say before the day is over they'll be pressed against the entrance of that snug little pussy as it tightens and milks my cock with your release."

The tender bundle of nerves clenched and ached with painful pleasure. The need throbbing through it was a hunger she had no idea how to process.

The explicit earthiness of his words sent heat flashing through her, weakening any objections she might have pretended to have and leaving her weak against him.

"You're all talk," she said, panting as his fingers flicked open the buttons to her top. "You've been promising to teach me not to tease full-grown men since I was eighteen. I have yet to figure out why."

Her thighs tightened at his hips, her hips rubbing against him, grinding against the thickness of his erection as it pressed tight and hard between her thighs.

"Oh, baby, I absolutely intend to show you exactly why pretty little girls such as yourself should never play games with full-grown men."

The fingers of one hand tangled in her hair, tugging her head back as a gasp parted her lips. His lips covered hers, the wicked, heated stroke of his tongue licking against hers, pulling her into a surplus of pure sensory overload.

Her fingers fluttered against the breadth of his hard chest as he released her hands. She ached to touch him, to find some way to delve beneath his shirt to the heated skin beneath.

She had to touch him. She had to feel his flesh against hers, to stroke and caress his hard body. This was her fantasy. The need for it tormented her dreams with almost nightly consistency. She couldn't escape it. She didn't want to escape it.

She pushed past the material between the top two buttons to find the coarse hair-covered flesh beneath.

Heat met her touch.

The feel of his heart beating, thundering beneath her fingers, easily matching the beat of her own as his fingers found the latch of her bra between her breasts and flicked it loose.

Releasing her lips with a groan he pulled back, his head lifting, staring down at her as she felt the buttons of her light summer blouse being released.

The experience and sheer confidence in his touch wasn't lost on her. Just as her own inexperience wasn't lost on her.

Would he be surprised to learn she was a virgin?

Would he be pleased to learn she was a virgin?

"Release my shirt, Anna," he growled as he pushed the shoulders of her blouse and the slim straps of her bra over her shoulders. The tug of the material pulled her arms down until he could pull it free of her and send the clothing fluttering to the floor. "Come on, baby, show me what you want."

What she wanted?

All of him.

Lips parted, fighting to draw in breath as he brought her hands to the buttons of his shirt.

She fumbled with the first.

As certain as she had been that she could slip each rounded disc through its hole, she found herself fumbling.

An aching moan left her throat as his head began lowering, his hands cupping her breasts, lifting them.

"How fucking pretty," he rasped, the wild, predatory color of his gaze lifting to hers, gleaming with hunger through the heavy veil of thick lashes. "I've dreamed of tasting your nipples, Anna. Of sucking on them until that soft, soft pink turns a pretty raspberry."

"Archer—"

How was she supposed to unbutton his shirt when he—

"Oh God, Archer."

His tongue licked over the hard tip of her nipple.

Flaming sensation washed through her body as pleasure surged like a rogue wave through her senses.

As she tried to catch her breath, to right her senses, his lips were surrounding it, his mouth covering the tight nipple and sending shafts of fiery pleasure surging straight to her clit.

Moving her hips, grinding her clit on the hard shaft pressing into it, nothing mattered but finding relief now. The pleasure was torturous. It tore through her, blazing a path of such indescribable sensation through her body that she forgot about getting his shirt off.

Head thrown back against the fridge, little moans of pleasure rising unbidden from her lips, Anna slid her fingers beneath the collar of his shirt as she flexed her nails against his flesh. Eyes closed, surrounded with lush, fiery sensation, pleasure clenched her womb with desperate contractions.

She needed.

Oh God, she needed so much more.

The feel of his mouth drawing on the violently

sensitive nipple was excruciating pleasure. The rasp of his tongue as he tasted it, the rake of his teeth against it as he teased and tormented it, was like lashing whips of sizzling pleasure-pain.

Each suckling motion, each incredibly heated draw of his mouth had the need, the lashing flares of desperation rising, striking at her clit, tightening her womb with increased force.

"Fuck, baby," the harsh growl came as his lips lifted from the needy flesh and his fingers slid to the rounded curves of her rear. "Come on, we're not doing this here."

As he moved to turn, her knees still gripping his hips, the radio at his hip began issuing rising static before the dispatcher came over the connection.

As she listened, Anna's lips parted; the code, despite having given no information a layman could have deciphered, wasn't hard for her to understand.

After hanging around Archer and his father for years, she had picked up enough to be able to follow the code.

Deputy Caine had found a victim's vehicle, and the only one she knew of missing was the one belonging to Katy Winslow.

Drawing back, Archer pulled the radio slowly from the holster at his hip, his gaze still locked on hers.

"Sheriff Tobias en route," he answered. "Inform Deputy Caine to remain on location."

"Ten-four, Sheriff Tobias, will appraise Deputy Caine of status," the dispatcher said as Archer moved back, allowing her legs to slide from his hips and hold her own weight.

The loss of his touch, of the warmth and pleasure she'd experienced in his arms, was a sensation she could only describe as painful.

"Don't you leave," he warned, the dark rasp on his

tone, the dominant command in it sending a shiver racing up her spine.

"I'll think about it." Shrugging in apparent unconcern, she stared back at him as though she were going to do whatever the hell she wanted to do.

The sad fact was, she wanted to stay. She wanted to stay so much it was a hunger inside her. A hunger that burned inside her with a flame she knew she wouldn't be able to deny.

"Yeah, you do that," he growled as he snagged his hat from where he'd tossed it to the kitchen table and jammed it on his head. "And when you're done thinking about it, I'll be back." He paused before turning away. "And you damned well better be here."

Drawing in a deep breath she watched as he turned and stalked from the kitchen before moving quickly through the wide foyer and out the front door.

He slammed the door closed, but took the time to stop and lock the deadbolt.

Anna's lips quirked before her fingers lifted to the swollen curves, a sensation of weakness flooding her womb and vagina at the memory of how they'd become swollen.

It was only then she realized she was still naked from the waist up. Her shirt and bra on the floor—

At least, they had been on the floor.

Looking around, her lips tightened to hold back her grin as she propped her hands on her hips and pretended to glare at the monster cat on the other side of the room.

He was lying on her shirt, the lace-trimmed strap of her bra hooked around his neck.

"Go ahead and keep it," she murmured to the cat as though unconcerned. "Your owner can just buy me a new one."

Hefting her bags to her shoulder she turned, found the staircase and headed up it quickly.

Of course, she was staying. At least, for now.

Just to see what happened.

Just to see if there was any chance of stealing Sheriff Archer Tobias' heart.

CHAPTER 4

It was Katy Winslow's car.

The little twelve-year-old sedan had been sent over Callahan's Peak, the sheer drop the Callahan grand-parents and parents had gone over.

There was a message here, Archer could feel it as he drove the SUV down the rough track that led to the rocky valley below.

Katy's car was a burned-out wreck. At the base of the cliff it still smoldered sullenly, giving a gloomy cast to the late afternoon sun.

Pulling his vehicle alongside Deputy Caine's, Ar-cher leveled a low, considering look at the other man.

John Caine had arrived in Corbin County just be-fore the Callahans had returned. Just before the mur-dering duo dubbed the Slasher had struck for the first time in twelve years.

The deputy had found that first body and each one after that. He'd been the one to find each piece of evi-dence and uncover each clue. He was on Archer's short list of suspects.

As Archer watched him, the deputy tipped his hat back on his head and stared back at him.

Stepping from the Tahoe, Archer moved across the distance to the little sedan and stared at the burned-out remains. Propping his hands on his hips he blew out a hard breath.

"Why?" he murmured as the acrid scent of the vehicle burning surrounded his senses.

"Why crash it here?" the deputy asked. "It's connected to the Callahans obviously, just as her murder was," he answered the question building in Archer's mind.

It was the obvious answer.

"This is out of character," Archer stated.

"Or the vehicle held prints or other evidence the Slasher doesn't want found. What better way, in an amateur's mind, to hide that evidence than to burn it."

Not exactly what Archer expected from him.

Crossing his arms over his chest and rubbing at his jaw thoughtfully, he slid a look to his deputy once again. "Did you contact Callum?"

"He's twenty minutes away." The deputy nodded.

Archer glanced at him again, seeing the practiced expression of emotionlessness. He hated that fucking look on any man's face. It made him instantly suspicious, instantly curious as to what he was hiding.

"What did she do to deserve his attention?" Archer murmured thoughtfully as he continued to stare at the smoldering car. "She wasn't sleeping with a Callahan. She hadn't slept with one in the past and she wasn't helping them in any way. Like many of the women in town, she kept a very careful distance."

"Then she saw something she wasn't supposed to see?" the deputy asked. "That's the only thing that makes sense, isn't it?"

"It's the only thing that makes sense now," Archer breathed out roughly. "But what? Or who?"

The deputy shook his head slowly as he crossed his

arms over his chest before lifting a hand to rub at the side of his face. "The Callahans and their properties, are the objective, though," he murmured then.

"The objective in what?" It was a question neither Archer nor his father had been able to answer. "What makes it so damned important that one or more has cut a swath of blood through this County?"

The deputy gave a hard, sarcastic grunt.

"That one, Sheriff, is buried, and even I, the master of gossip, rumor, and shady deals, have yet to uncover it."

"Master of gossip, rumor, and shady deals, huh?" Archer murmured as he glanced at the deputy once again.

Caine grinned with cool mockery. "We all have our talents, Sheriff, we all have our talents."

Archer wondered if those talents could have led to murder.

Maybe someone else had those answers, though.

As the deputy walked away, Archer made a call.

"Hello?" John Corbin answered on the first ring.

"I want answers, John." Archer stared around the canyon, the bleak stone walls, the hint of a pine struggling to anchor to a soft ledge above.

"Archer . . ."

"I said, I fucking want answers," he snapped. "You'll be at my place before dawn, or I'll be there. You hearing me?"

Silence filled the line for long moments.

"I hear you."

The line disconnected.

Anna awoke to the most incredible sensation.

It wasn't sensual, hot, or filled with lust or sexual hunger. It wasn't sensual or sexual at all.

It was like the softest silk—no, softer than silk. It was the softest touch rubbing against her shoulder, slow and easy, caressing down her arm. It was warm, comforting. It was a sensation of living warmth, accepting and vibrating—

A frown tugged at her brow, drawing her further from sleep.

It was vibrating against her shoulder.

No, it was purring.

Forcing her lashes to open she turned her head to stare into the slitted golden eyes that peered at her as Oscar rubbed the side of his face against the curve of her shoulder.

A peek at the clock on the living room wall assured her it was well after two in the morning. Archer had been gone all day and now most of the night.

A plaintive meow rumbled from the cat's throat as he rubbed against her shoulder again.

"What do you want?" she mumbled. "Can't believe you're harassing me after stealing my bra and shirt. Those were damned expensive, you know."

A rumble between a purr and a meow sounded again as Oscar stared back at her with such arrogant command that she couldn't help but think of Archer.

"What do you want, anyway?" She really didn't want to get out of bed. "Don't you know I have to show up for work in like five hours? I need my beauty sleep."

The feline growling purr sounded again. This time, instead of rubbing against her shoulder, Oscar pushed at it with his big head.

"Bossy." Sitting up, she was prepared to push herself from the couch to get whatever the demanding fur ball wanted only to watch in surprise as he moved farther onto the couch and settled into the corner where her head had been resting.

His eyes closed, shoulders shifting as he perfected his position and settled into sleep as though he hadn't awakened her to do so. As though he wasn't even concerned with her presence after forcing her awake so he could take his favorite position.

"You ass," she accused him, surprised by the animal's audacity. "I was sleeping myself, you know."

And he obviously didn't care. He didn't even twitch at the anger in her voice.

Shaking her head at the animal, Anna glanced at the front door, then at the clock again.

"Did he finally wake you?"

She swung around, nearly falling from the couch in surprise as Archer moved into the living room from the opposite doorway, obviously having come from upstairs and the shower.

Damp, darker than its normal sandy blond, his hair lay around his face, obviously having just been dried with little care as to style. The ends curled haphazardly as the heavy strands framed his darkly tanned face and made his golden brown eyes appear more like hammered gold than normal.

Broad, bare, his hard, darkly tanned chest, with a thin covering of male curls just lighter than the hair on his head, tempted her fingers. Tempted them with the need to touch him, to experience the feel of them against her sensitive fingertips.

"How long have you been back?" She frowned at him, surprised that he had managed to come into the house without waking her.

Surprised at how he had entered the living room.

Hell, she had been sleeping not ten feet from the damned door and he'd slipped right up on her.

It was all she could do to keep her gaze above his hard abs because she could see the muscles beneath the bronzed flesh tempting, drawing her gaze.

"A couple of hours." He shrugged as though uncertain.

She bet he knew almost to the second exactly what time he had walked through the front door.

"You should have woken me." She watched his face, seeing the heaviness in his gaze, in the somber expression on his face.

"You were sleeping too well." His lips quirked with an almost gentle smile and his eyes seemed to warm as he watched her. "Besides, I knew Oscar would run you out of his corner eventually."

Glancing at the monster cat who took up at least a cushion of the couch by himself, she sniffed at his presence.

"Damned fur ball," she muttered. "The least he could have done was wake me when you arrived."

"He likes you." Leaning against the door frame, his lips kicked up at one corner. "Anyone else would have had at least a scratch by now. Oscar doesn't really tolerate strangers in his home well."

Anna pushed her hair back from her face, staring at him, at a complete loss for words.

Sweet heaven have mercy on her, he was aroused. Powerfully, unapologetically aroused.

Beneath the cotton pants he wore his cock raged, hard and heavy, pressing against the material with insistent demand. Lifting her gaze slowly, Anna encountered the lust-driven dark gold of his gaze.

It became hard to breathe.

Anna could feel her heart racing, beating between her breasts like fists rapping, hard and heavy. Lips parting, she fought to drag in oxygen, to make herself breathe through the adrenaline pounding through her.

Suddenly, she could feel parts of her body that she was only aware of whenever he was around.

Her lips—

God, she needed him to kiss her, she needed to kiss him.

Her nipples—

Between her thighs—

Need, deep in her womb.

Her knees were weak and she wasn't even standing.

Suddenly the room was filled with such tension, with such an overwhelming air of hunger, that Anna could barely breathe for it. That hunger pounded through her, burned through her, and tore aside any veil of disinterest or screen of objection. There was only the wild, burning hunger, and her need for Archer.

Lifting her gaze, Anna wondered if it was normal to feel such constriction in her lungs; if she could actually live without air. Because she couldn't seem to catch her breath.

Especially when he moved toward her with that predatory look in his gaze.

"You can sleep in the guest room or you can sleep with me," he stated as he stopped in front of her, the heavy proof of his arousal now at eye level.

Lifting her gaze again, Anna swallowed tightly. The fierce hunger swirling in his eyes warned her that the need was building just as high inside him as it had been in her.

"If I choose your bed?" she asked.

"Then it's without promises, Anna," he warned her, his gaze darkening. "Don't make that mistake, for both our sakes. I won't tell you I love you, and there's no wedding ring waiting when it's over."

"Have I ever asked for a wedding ring, Archer?"

Yet she couldn't deny that dream was there. It was a fantasy she'd had since she was a teenager. The white dress, the veil—and Archer.

"It's in your eyes." His jaw tensed, fire blazing in the golden brown gaze watching her. "It's been there since the night you turned eighteen."

"Are you sure the desire you saw was for a ring, or something a little less—" She let her lashes lower to half-mast. "—acceptable, perhaps?"

Before common sense, embarrassment, or any other sterling qualities her mother had no doubt tried to teach her could kick in, Anna reached for what she had hungered for most. Before inexperience, uncertainty, or fear could overcome six years of fantasy and hunger, she reached out for what she'd always seen as hers alone.

Archer.

Still staring into those wild eyes, Anna reached out with both hands, her nails rasping down his hips as she leaned forward. Her lips pressed against the hard-packed muscles of his flexing abs, her tongue peeking out to take him.

Archer's jaw tightened, his fists clenching at his side as she tasted his flesh.

Licking over the indent of his navel she was forced to hold back a moan, one of pure, desperate desire. Slightly salty, heated, clean, and intently male. His flesh was warm beneath her tongue, the hard muscles flexing with innate power.

"Fuck! Anna!" One hand moved, strong fingers threading through the hair at the side of her head.

Clenching, his fingers tightened as his expression became darker, more brooding with sensual, sexual heat that burned through her senses.

She'd had years to prepare for this night. Years to ensure he never forgot her touch once she had the chance to touch him.

Years to make damned sure he never forgot being with her.

Fingers bending and hooking in the elastic band of the pants, she slowly eased the material over the thick, heavy length of his cock. Thickly erect, blood throbbing through heavy veins, the impressive stalk of male flesh caused her to swallow tightly as she fought back her trepidation.

Fear thundered just beneath the adrenaline rushing through her system. A fear she refused to pay heed to. Fear of failure. Fear of being unable to measure up to past lovers, no matter the research she'd put into the subject of giving a man a blow job he would never forget.

Watching him from beneath the veil of her lashes, Anna flicked her tongue around the shallow indent of his navel again, teasing it with tasting licks as she pushed the material of his pants to his ankles. Standing still and silent before her, he just watched her, his body as stiff as his cock, his expression sensually brooding.

Stepping from the light cotton at his feet, Archer continued to watch her, as though certain she would stop. Certain that the intimate caress would not be forthcoming.

Oh, he definitely had a surprise coming if that was what he thought.

Easing back, watching his gaze darken, his jaw tighten, Anna let a small smile tug at her lips.

"I was waiting for you when I fell asleep," she said softly, her nails rasping down the outside of his thighs.

"Were you?" The heavy rasp of his voice sent a shudder of hunger clenching her womb and nipping at the sensitive bud of her clit. "Why is that?"

"Because a girl can only wait so long to live a fantasy, Sheriff," she said, her hands sliding to the insides of his thighs where she made a U with the fingers and thumb of one hand and tucked them beneath the taut sac that held his testicles.

A sharp, indrawn breath assured her Archer's attention was fully centered on her now.

Lowering her head, pursing her lips, she blew a soft breath against the surprisingly curl-free male flesh, luxuriating in his response. His hand tightened in her hair, the other gripping her shoulder with a firm hold.

"Anna, be sure about this," he growled.

Oh, she was sure.

Leaning forward, her head bending, she tasted the male flesh, first with her tongue. Licking over the tight sac, probing at the base of his cock, then parting her lips and drawing it inside.

She was going to orgasm from excitement alone.

Both of his hands were in her hair now, his legs shifting, spreading further as she sucked one side of his ball sac into her mouth and laved it with her tongue before moving to the other.

She'd never done this, but he loved it. She could feel him loving it. The iron-hard thickness her fingers had no hope of circling, the rush of blood beneath the silky flesh, the tautness of the sac she caressed, all proved he was loving it.

And if she had any doubts—

"Fuck! Damn you, Anna." His back arched as the rasping curse tore past his lips.

His fingers tightened in her hair, then kneaded her scalp as his thighs parted further, giving her tongue, her lips, room to play.

And how she did enjoy playing there.

Lavishing attention on first one side of his testicles, then the other, she lived the first fantasy. Shuddering, a groan rumbled from him. With his cock throbbing in both hands now, she stroked it with firm caresses before another drawing of his flesh into her mouth and suckling at the sphere contained there.

Feeling the heavy throb of blood through the thick veins, Anna licked, laved, tasted the hard, heated flesh before releasing it with reluctance.

"Anna." The rasp of his voice was a sensual stroke of eroticism against her senses.

"My fantasy," she whispered.

Pressing her hand into his chest she eased him back a step and came slowly to her feet.

"Waiting until I lose control is the wrong time to change your mind," he warned her, his expression, his voice, dark and filled with hunger.

"Change my mind?" Anna lifted her hand to the tiny silk tie that held the white robe over her breasts and pulled it free, slowly. "Archer, the last thing I intend to do is change my mind."

Archer had to clench his teeth to hold back a demand that she hurry. That she wrap her lips around his dick and give him the blow job she was promising.

"Ah, hell, Anna." The words felt ripped from his throat as he fought to hold back the pleasure and the unfamiliar demands rising inside him. "Ah, baby, that sweet, sweet mouth."

She was destroying him with it.

Keeping his teeth clenched tight, he held the demand

back. His arms were stiff at his side. His gaze narrowed, he stared down at her, fighting to deny what he saw in her gaze.

Feminine hunger was tempered by love. Confidence was tempered by inexperience. Need was fueled by all the above—the sight of it was enough to terrify him.

He wasn't terrified enough to pull away from her, though. He didn't dare. His cock would probably send agony streaking through his body at the slightest attempt.

As he watched, she rose slowly to her feet and dropped the robe she wore.

That gown was a fucking wet dream.

No—

A wet dream dressed in breast-hugging silk and spandex—in a gown so fucking romantic, so damned bridal, despite the color, it had his chest tightening with some emotion he could make no sense of.

From the soft lace that cupped her breasts and lovingly conformed to the gentle curves of her slender waist, to the silk that flowed to the floor in sweeping abundance, it was a bride's gown pretending to be a wicked temptress.

A seductress going to her knees.

"Anna, you don't have to . . ." The offer cut off in a hoarse groan as her fingers gripped the thick flesh, stroking it in slow, even strokes as she brought the heavily flared crest to her parted lips.

Sweet heaven have mercy on him, she was actually going to do it.

Perfect, sweet lips parted.

Free of makeup, pretty green eyes staring up at him with slumberous passion through sooty lashes. Her heated, damp tongue peeked out, lashed at the crown, then began tonguing it with pure wicked pleasure as her eyes closed and her attention became completely devoted to pleasuring his dick.

Tonguing the satiny head, sweet lips taking heated kisses, and silken hands stroking the thick shaft, she destroyed any doubt that might have flashed through his mind.

Parting her lips further and sucking the head inside, she then set out to destroy his control, which she did far quicker than he could have ever expected.

With lips, tongue, and heated suckling of the too-sensitive crest, she swept his misgivings to the side and convinced him—even as he knew better—that no virgin could ever embrace the sweet, wicked moves she used on his throbbing cock.

Tucking beneath the head of the fierce erection, her tongue licked, stroked, tasted, then swirled in intimate abandon around the flared edge. Sucking him back inside the heated depths of her mouth, the vibration of her moans had his thighs tightening, his hands clenching in her hair.

Kneading his fingers against her scalp, Archer bit back a hoarse groan, fighting to contain the wild impulse to push her to the floor, hike her gown above her hips, and fuck her until they were both screaming in orgasm.

Pleasure exploded through his senses, tore across his nerve endings, and laid waste to any preconceived notions of the pleasure she could give him.

Staring down at her as he watched her lips redden, watched his cock fuck past them in shallow thrusts, Archer knew the thin threads of his control were unraveling by the second.

There was no way to hold back the response or the pleasure erupting inside him.

She pulled back, surprising him by releasing the

head of his cock, her tongue flattening, her head tilting to the side as her tongue tasted the broad length of his flesh.

Pulsing, tightening, his cock throbbed in painful pleasure.

"So fucking good. That sweet, hot mouth is so fucking good."

Heat unfurled inside him. It blazed across his nerve endings, shot through his senses and—fuck!

His knees were weak.

Catching his breath, watching as her head moved lower, that sensual little tongue dancing over his cock like an erotic flame, she all but destroyed him. Pleasure burned over his flesh, sank into his pores, and pulsed through his blood like a fever raging out of control.

"Ah, baby, that's fucking good." Threading his fingers through her hair, letting her lips, her sweet tongue, and mouth have their way, Archer luxuriated in the pleasure. "That tongue's a fucking wet dream come true."

Even his fantasies about her hadn't been this damned good.

Moving those sweet lips over the head of his cock once again, sensation shot through his system. Pure, fiery, pleasure like nothing he'd known before whipped through him.

Flattening her tongue, she licked and laved that ultrasensitive spot beneath the crest. Flicking against it, nudging at it, stroking it with hungry heat until he was certain he was going to go mad with the need to fuck her.

He was losing the ability to withstand the sensations building in his balls and whipping through his cock. Every muscle in his body was tightened to a point that he felt locked in place, unable to stop the agonizing pleasure. He was unable to stop it and unable to give in to it.

To give in to it meant to take far more from her than he knew her innocence was ready for. Confidence and preparation were two different things. She might be hiding her innocence well, but he could see it in her eyes. In her actions.

She wanted, and she hungered—and her need for him was possibly as great as his need for her. But that need couldn't possibly prepare her for what he wanted from her.

What he needed from her, what he wanted from her, went far beyond what she could possibly be prepared for.

CHAPTER 5

Archer knew he was reaching the point of no return.

At the first pulsing flex of his cock and the pre-come that spilled onto Anna's lips, he knew he was nearing the edge of his control and threatening to fly over it.

A ragged groan tore from him as his fingers tightened in her hair and forced her head back from the tortured shaft. Staring down at her as she lifted those thick, sooty lashes, he stared into the pretty green eyes and acknowledged the fact that he was in way the hell over his head. Where this woman was concerned, he was drowning in her, and he had no idea why.

Or how to stop it.

All he knew was that he had to have her, and he had to have her soon.

Throwing her to the floor and fucking her into mind-less orgasm was his favorite option. It was the option his body was demanding.

She was pure fucking pleasure, and she was destroying him with the nearing ecstasy rushing through his body.

She wasn't just pure pleasure.

She wasn't just the most incredible sensations he'd ever known with a woman.

She was pure romance, and she was destroying him with it.

She was the ultimate wet dream wrapped in sweeping silk and lush pleasure.

And Archer couldn't help himself.

She was, and always had been, his weakness. Admitting to that fact hadn't been easy. It still wasn't easy.

Pulling her to her feet, Archer bent to her, one arm going around the back of her knees, the other behind her shoulders as he swung her into his arms.

The feel of silken arms wrapping around his neck made his groin tighten painfully, his cock throbbing in pure lust.

"What the hell are you doing to me?"

He didn't expect an answer. Hell, he didn't want an answer. There was a part of him that was terrified to know.

"What can I do to you?" she asked, the breathy sound of her voice slicing at that last, thin-as-air thread of control he possessed as he mounted the stairs.

"You can destroy me," he retorted, his jaw so tight it felt ready to splinter as he carried her, cradling her in his arms, feeling too strong—or did she feel too fragile?

She was fragile.

Of body, of heart, and he knew it.

God help him, he knew it, and still he had no choice but to take what she was offering. What he had fantasized about for far too long.

Carrying her into his bedroom, careful to kick the door closed in case Oscar should decide to have one of those jealous tantrums of his, he carried his precious, too-delicate burden to the bed he'd dreamed of having her in.

Lowering her to her feet beside it, the first thing he did was slide the tiny straps that held her gown over her breasts over her shoulders. As they slid down her arms, the embroidered lace fell from her breasts as the weight of yards of silk dragged it along her body until the gown pooled at her feet.

Oxygen, needed, life-giving, was sucked silently from his body. The sight of her naked body—perfectly rounded breasts tipped by cotton candy-pink nipples, her gently rounded stomach, slender, curvy hips, and rounded thighs were like an oasis in a sensually dry desert.

Between those perfect thighs—

He dragged in air desperately.

Between those prettily rounded thighs the curls had been removed, leaving silken, bare flesh that shimmered with a layer of sweet, feminine juices.

The sight of the dew-rich flesh again had him willfully controlling his body's response. The urgent need to fuck her, to pound inside her and claim her immediately, nearly overrode the contradictory need to worship her body, to kiss each inch and bind her to him so elementally that no part of her would ever be free of him.

Just as he sensed the fact that he would never be free of her, either.

"My God," he said, his hands lifting, cupping the swollen mounds of her breasts as a whimper of need parted her lips. "Sweet, beautiful Anna."

She was trembling. Archer could feel the fine shudders shaking her body as his thumbs found the hardened little buds topping her breasts.

"Perfect breasts," he whispered. "So pretty, Anna. So damned pretty and sweet that all I want to do is devour them."

Her hands lifted, covered his.

The sight of her hand on his, so small and pale against his much darker, much larger hand, was almost humbling.

What the hell was he doing even considering this? She was so damn small against him, so delicate that, for a moment, he was terrified of breaking her.

"What are you waiting on, then?" she asked, the edges of her lips turning up in a siren's smile.

A second later they parted in a surprised gasp at the feel of his fingers and thumbs gripping each distended point and applying just enough pressure to ensure her complete attention.

He wanted every nerve ending, each sense, her entire being completely focused on him.

On him, and all the pleasure he intended to ensure she received.

Staring up at him, Anna felt her heart racing impossibly fast.

It pounded against her chest, each pulse of blood shuddering through her body as his gaze darkened further and dropped to her breasts.

The calloused flesh of his palms massaged the undersides of her breasts, adding to the erotic sensations racing through her.

"I've dreamed of this," she said, hoping the weakness in her knees didn't become worse.

She could barely stand as it was.

"Sweet Anna." The odd tone of his voice had her holding back anything else she would have said.

He sounded almost—regretful.

"The things I want to do to you should be considered illegal," he said, his voice low, dark. "Hell, it probably *is* illegal in several states."

"I wouldn't protest."

She wanted his touch, needed his touch, as she needed nothing else in her life.

"Wouldn't you?"

Her lashes lowered, threatening to close as his head moved down, his lips brushing against hers, teasing them as she fought to hold his gaze, to watch the shifting colors of his predatory eyes.

"Well, I might not be into pain, if that's your fetish," she quipped with a spurt of amusement. "But, at your hands, I might be willing to try."

His lips quirked.

She loved that little half smile, the way his eyes gleamed with hidden laughter and his expression seemed to soften marginally.

"I promise not to hurt you," he murmured as his lips moved along her jaw. "At least, no more than necessary."

Her soft laughter was cut off, the slow relaxation of her body stilled, and tension took over as his lips moved beneath her jaw.

Sensation rushed through her nerve endings as Anna drew in a harsh breath. Caressing, gently nipping, his lips and teeth seemed to be making a delicate meal of her flesh, throwing her into a maelstrom of need with each touch.

"Archer, it's so good," she moaned, unable to hold back the moan that filled her words. "Better than I dreamed."

And she'd had a damned good imagination when it came to dreaming of this with him.

"It can get better, I promise."

His kisses moved down her neck, brushed across each breast. Before she had a chance to catch her breath or vocalize what she was aching for, those diabolically experienced lips found the tip of her breast.

"Oh, yes," she moaned as his lips played with her nipple, his tongue licking at it erotically as she watched, barely able to breathe for the excitement and pleasure shuddering through her. "I want more," she all but demanded as her fingers slid into his hair and clenched in the strands. "Suck it, Archer. Please."

The tender bud was aching, throbbing to feel his lips and mouth surrounding it. The need to have the heated interior of his mouth drawing on the peak, sucking at it hungrily, had her begging for it.

"This is going to tear both our lives apart," he warned her, but his head was lowering, his lips hovering over her nipple as he spoke.

"My life has already been torn apart, remember?" And at this moment, she didn't even care. All she cared about was having his mouth surround her nipple, close on it, suck it, give her more of the pleasure tearing through her.

Arching against him, her breath caught as the hard tip pressed against his lips and felt the damp, moist interior of his hot mouth.

"Fuck!" The exclamation came a second before he gave her exactly what she was begging for.

His lips surrounded her nipple. Wet heat pierced it and less than a second later he was suckling it like a man starved for the taste of a woman.

Cupping the gently rounded flesh and pressing it closer to his lips, his teeth rasped it. Enclosing it once again with his lips, he drew on her nipple, his cheeks hollowing as male hunger filled the groan that rumbled in his chest.

Sensation flared at the firm contact. A sizzle of

electric pleasure that only built the hunger already burning inside her. Her breathing became harsh, heavy. Her hands tightened in his hair, her knee bending, lifting to his thigh to press herself closer to him.

Suddenly the firm suckling stopped, and a second later his lips covered hers again. Fully. Without warning, he possessed her lips.

If he had any indication of her innocence, he gave no concessions to it. His lips parted hers with practiced ease, his tongue flicking against them, licking with sensual hunger as Anna gasped at the pleasure that tore across her nerve endings and began burning in the pit of her stomach.

She felt eighteen again, desperate for that first kiss, seeing Archer's face in her mind as the college boy she was kissing handled her with such rough inexperience that she'd wanted to kick him.

She'd known he would never kiss like an inexperienced boy. He kissed like a grown male in his prime and hungry for a woman. His tongue swept against hers, tasted her as she tasted him.

He'd been drinking coffee. The dark essence of the drink infused his kiss and wrapped around her senses as he kissed her with dominant demand.

Lowering her to the mattress, his hard body coming over hers, her thighs parting further for the breadth of his hips, he settled against her, and she moaned in burning need.

This was what she needed. She felt as though she had waited for it all her life. Waited for this kiss, this man, this touch. She needed it like the air she breathed. Needed it to the point that her entire body was beginning to ache for it.

Anna found herself gasping for air as his lips moved

to her jaw, his rough kisses moving over it as one hand slid up her thigh.

The rasp of his calloused palm sent shivers of incredible sensation moving through her. Heat blazed across her clit and through her vagina to tighten her womb with clenching spasms. As his palm eased up the curve of her hip, then slid to her stomach, she held her breath, head tipping back as his lips moved to her neck.

Stinging kisses were spread across the arched column as Archer's hand stroked up her stomach before cupping the rounded curve of one swollen, touch-hungry breast again.

Sensation lashed at her senses as Anna arched, desperate to press her flesh further into his hand, to feel him as close, as deep as possible. Raking his thumb over her nipple, his flesh rasping against the tip, dragged a cry from her. The need to be closer to him, to feel more, to experience more, was making her crazy.

Heat radiated from her body, perspiration dampening her flesh as her breathing became more harsh, the moans harder to hold back as his kisses moved lower, his tongue licking against her collarbone. His lips licked the swollen curves of her breasts and the hard, distended tips of her nipples.

Anna forced her lashes to remain raised, watching as the dark blond head lifted from her neck, his golden brown gaze, heavy-lidded and filled with lust, staring down at her. Watching her with so much heat that her pussy wept in need.

His lips were as swollen as hers felt, his expression as dazed as she knew hers must be.

"Don't stop." It was a plea, a demand.

Aching, her hips lifted against his, stroking the swollen bud of her clit against the length of his cock.

She could feel her orgasm moving closer, building to that point where she knew the pleasure would catapult her into sensations she had only heard others talk about until now.

This would be nothing like the weak releases she'd found when she'd orgasmed in the past.

"Do you know what you're doing to me, Anna?" he groaned, his expression filled with torment as his eyes flicked to the hard tips of her breasts. "What this could do to both of us?"

"What could it do to us?" she demanded, frustration tearing through her now. "Will the world end, Archer? What catastrophe could rip through Sweetrock if we have sex?"

If he made love to her?

If he risked opening just a small, very small, undefended part of his heart and gave her a chance to slip inside?

"God, you amaze me." For the briefest moment, amusement glittered in his gaze before his eyes dropped to her breasts once again. "But catastrophe could definitely happen," he breathed roughly. "God help us both, Anna, I'll be damned but I think it would be worth it."

"Then stop talking and start sexing," she suggested breathlessly as his head lowered, turning just enough to allow the rasp of his cheek to brush against the soft mound of a breast.

"Stop teasing me, Archer." Her pussy was on fire, her breasts swollen and aching.

If he didn't take her soon, if he didn't fuck her soon, she was going to go insane from the need.

Archer felt as though he had fought this attraction to her for his entire life. Definitely for the past six years. He'd been fighting since the day she turned eighteen and he'd recognized the beautiful woman she was turning into.

Beautiful, graceful.

She was headstrong and determined, for sure. They had always been two of her most challenging qualities. It wasn't a childish stubbornness, though. It was that of a woman who knew what she wanted and what she was determined to have.

And what she wanted was in direct opposition to what her family wanted from her, and for her.

Easing into a kneeling position his knee slid between hers, parting her legs, opening her to him as he gripped the hard shaft of his dick and prepared to lean into her. Below, a heavy sheen of juices coated her swollen pussy lips, drew him, made him hungry to taste her, to fuck her.

He paused, because for a moment he couldn't decide which he needed worse. The taste of her against his tongue, or the feel of his cock burrowing inside her.

As he paused, Anna moved.

Sitting up, her fingers curling around the width of his cock, she leaned over him, covering the engorged head for the second time that night. Her hot little mouth engulfed him with pleasure.

Archer stilled, his body tightening as the heat of her mouth sucked him in and worked the head of his cock like a favorite treat. A delicate hand settled at his hip and gripped it firmly. A harsh groan tore from his lips as she sucked him deep, the back of her throat suddenly caressing the violently sensitive crown as she moaned with her own pleasure.

Innocence filled the touch, but also hunger and an awareness of what she was doing. Her short, neat little nails bit into the flesh of his hip as her tongue rubbed against the underside, stroking nerve endings so close to the skin that every muscle in his body tightened in response. The other hand stroked from the base of his dick to her suckling lips and back again. She was making him crazy with pleasure and he loved it.

She was a virgin. Archer had known for years that she didn't have other lovers. John Corbin had told him several times how closely he had his granddaughter watched, and how proud he was that promiscuity wasn't a path she had chosen.

Why did he have her watched? That question had often plagued him.

That question flitted through his mind before her suckling mouth wiped it away.

He couldn't keep himself from looking down, just as he had earlier. Watching as she took him with an intimacy other women with a hell of a lot more experience didn't enjoy nearly as well as Anna was enjoying him now.

Pulling back, her lips swollen and red, her slender fingers pumped the hard, wide shaft, and he nearly lost that last hold on his ability to hold back his release.

The engorged crest was flushed dark and throbbing in lust as moisture sheened it. The narrow slit at the tip beaded with a creamy drop of pre-come.

Archer watched. His heart nearly stopped as her soft pink tongue emerged to swipe over the bead of lust. She tasted him with an intimate hunger that burned through his senses and sent chaotic shudders of pleasure racing up his spine.

A snarl snapped past his lips as pleasure overcame his reserve. The fingers of one hand buried in her hair. They tightened in the strands as her tongue caressed the violently sensitive flesh of his cock head once again and he growled with the heightened sensation.

"Ah, hell. Yes, Anna. Suck it like that, baby. Suck my dick just like that."

How often had he fantasized about this? With his fingers fisted around his shaft, stroking it as he brought just this sight to his imagination. Eyes closed, he'd imagined her lush little mouth moving over the engorged flesh. He'd pictured her lips stretching over the broad tip, her tongue lashing at the ultrasensitive spot just beneath the hooded crest.

"Fuck, that's good." He couldn't stop watching her lips move on the head of his cock. "Ah, yes, baby. That's so damn good."

She was doing far more than he'd ever imagined, and giving him far more pleasure.

Moving up and down on the engorged head, sucking and stroking with lips, tongue, and her suckling mouth, she took him like a woman starved for the taste of a man.

The innocence in her expression as she glanced up at him was at odds with her confidence and the pure hunger blazing in the dark green depths of her eyes.

Her innocence didn't stop her now, though, any more than it had earlier. His stomach tightened as she slid one hand between his thighs to cup his balls, her fingers rolling them gently, firmly.

Destroying him with pleasure.

There was no going back.

There was no saving her innocence, his conscience, or the consequences he could sense would rise from this night to bite him on the ass.

Brushing her hand aside he gripped the base of his dick. He pulled free of the exquisite heat of her mouth, then angled it to her lips once again. Rubbing the wide crest against the swollen curves of her lips, his teeth clenched as a moan slipped past them. Her gaze darkened further, and as he watched pure emotion fill them, Archer swore he could feel something inside his soul reaching out to her.

Emotion threatened to ambush him, threatened to break free despite his determination to hold it back. Lust. This was lust. It was about hunger. It was about physical need and pleasure.

A pleasure she was sharing with him.

The sound of her pleasure in him caused his balls to tighten in spiraling lust. His need for her was moving through him. Slamming into his senses, tempting him to take over, to take her.

It was all he could do to hold back the powerful dominance that was so much a part of him.

And he had no idea why he was holding it back.

He was already a dead man. He might as well enjoy every second of the lovely, sensual creature sitting before him, her tongue peeking out to lash at the head of his cock.

Yeah, he was a fucking dead man and this was his last meal. A lovely, delicate, sensual little feast, and he intended to enjoy every second of pleasure he found in her.

Anna glanced up at him, the battle to keep her lashes raised nearly overwhelming her.

She wanted to see his dark face, the savage contours and tense hunger in his expression. The chaotic emotions and pure dominance that filled his eyes excited her and intensified her own arousal.

She couldn't believe all the years of fantasizing about him had finally come to an end. All the years of reading about the act were at an end. She had watched it in videos, listened to every story her friends told of giving a man pleasure, and amassed the knowledge that she prayed would mark this man with her touch.

He didn't love her, but she wanted to make certain he remembered her. That he remembered her touch and the heat burning between them. That he never forgot that she had waited for him—

Parting her lips to take the wide crest between them once again, Anna sucked the engorged head into her mouth and let her tongue rub against the ultrasensitive area just beneath the throbbing head.

The taste of male heat and lust filled her senses as a harsh growl sounded above her. Archer's fingers tightened in her hair as the fingers of his other hand tightened around the base of his cock.

Anna tightened her lips and mouth around the pulsing flesh, sucking him deeper, more firmly.

She could barely take more than the thick head, but the overwhelming sense of femininity that filled her only stoked the flaming hunger higher.

Lifting her gaze to his once again, Anna couldn't help but whimper at the savage intensity of his expression. His fingers tightened in her hair once again as he moved her head back, slowly, before pulling her mouth back onto the thickly flared crest.

He filled her mouth, fucking it slow and easy, as the rasp of his breath and her muted moans filled the room.

Anna could feel her juices easing from her aching vagina as her clit throbbed in painful need.

Electric fingers of sensation raced over her nerve endings, sensitizing every inch of her flesh. The fingers of one hand tightened at his hip while the other weighed and caressed his testicles.

Her mouth followed the guiding motions of his hands and thrusting cock as he fucked past her lips. The muscles of his thighs bunched as his testicles drew closer to the base of his cock, and the crown filling her mouth throbbed.

She couldn't hold back a muted cry as the subtle taste of his release teased her tongue and his cock throbbed again.

She sucked at the thick head hungrily, wanting more. Her tongue rubbed and stroked as the need for the taste of him overwhelmed her.

She needed more of him.

She ached for more of him.

Archer was dying.

The need for release was torturing his balls, drawing them tight beneath his dick as his thighs clenched to iron hardness. Holding back the release throbbing in the tight sac was torture.

Groaning, torn between the hunger to take her as he'd always dreamed of taking her and the knowledge of her innocence, he was caught in a battle between the two impulses that he had no idea how to ease.

"Fuck, enough, Anna," he groaned, pulling his dick back from the temptation of her mouth and the come threatening to spill from his balls.

Spill, hell—if he let it go, he'd explode in her mouth with a force that could have him shouting with the pleasure.

"Archer, please," the plea for more, for exactly what he wasn't yet ready to give her, almost broke the control he was exerting over his lust. "Don't stop."

CHAPTER 6

"Stop? Not in this lifetime." Archer groaned as he pushed her back to the bed, coming over her and taking her lips with his own in a kiss that burned through his senses like a laser through butter.

With one hand still buried in the thick silkiness of her hair, Archer pulled her head back, his tongue sinking past her lips to find hers in a dance of sexual heat.

She arched into his hold, her slender, fragile body seeking his as the heavy width of his erection pressed demandingly against the silken flesh of her thigh.

Kisses weren't enough.

The need raging through him now was impossible to resist. As sweet and soft as her lips were, the swollen globes of her breasts with their hard-peaked nipples drew his hunger. They were yet another fantasy. A tempting sin he'd often found himself imagining, pressed close together, his dick tunneling between them.

Hell, he could fuck those pretty tits as he taught her to lower her head, to part her lips, and take the thick crest as it emerged from them. He could feel the silk of them, play with her tight nipples and watch her face as he spilled his release into her hungry mouth.

But not tonight. There was no time, no chance, for every fantasy he'd ever had where her body and his dick were concerned.

But there was the chance to taste her breasts, to devour the hard tips of her tight, candy-pink nipples.

Easing down her body he caught one of the little buds between his teeth to nibble at it. Rasping it with the edge of his teeth, he couldn't help but watch the sensual, feminine hunger in her face. Watched her lashes flutter closed as her body stretched beneath him, arching to him as though to push her nipple deeper into his mouth.

Instead, he released the tight little tip, his head lifting to stare down at her demandingly.

"Watch me!" he growled as her lashes lifted. "Watch how much I love pleasuring this sweet, perfect little body of yours."

Anna forced her lashes to stay open, her whimpering cry shocking her with the husky, pleading sound of it.

A surge of clenching, overwhelming sensations flooded her pussy. They struck at her swollen clit and sent spasms racing through her aching vagina as his head lowered, his gaze still locked with hers as his tongue curled around the hard tip of one nipple.

With his free hand Archer flattened his palm against her thigh, the calloused rasp of his touch smoothing up her sensitive flesh. Electric pinpoints of fierce pleasure raced through her nerve endings and fired exquisite flares of sensation through her body.

Arching, her hips rolling, desperate to have his stroking fingers against the swollen folds of her pussy, Anna tightened her fingernails against his hard shoulders. Kneading the powerful muscles as his palm stroked and caressed her thigh, edging closer to the heated center of her sex, Anna couldn't hold back her whimpering moan of rising need.

Moving from one nipple to its mate, Archer groaned as he covered the hard tip. Anna gave a matching cry as his fingers met the slick, heated juices beginning to dampen her inner thighs. Her legs parted further, her vision blurring as pleasure crashed and clashed through her senses.

Hard flares of sensation raced from her nipples to her clit, striking into her vagina and sending her juices rushing past clenched muscles to further dampen the folds.

"Oh God, Archer," she moaned, her hands moving from his shoulders to his hair, her fingers clenching in the strands as he released her nipple and began spreading heated kisses lower.

Moving down her body, his gaze held hers as his lips kissed, his tongue licked her sensitive flesh. Anna felt intoxicated by the rising pleasure and the desperate sensations building inside her.

With her fingers buried in his hair, his gaze holding hers, she could only watch, her breathing restricted, as his kisses began moving across her stomach to her abdomen, and moving inexorably to the aching flesh between her thighs.

She could barely breathe. Held mesmerized by his gaze, by the incredible pleasure building inside her, she could only watch as he placed stinging, roughened kisses on her thighs.

"Archer, please." Arching to him as he paused just above the throbbing bud of her clit, his gaze still holding hers, Anna tried to lift herself to the heat of his lips.

"Please what, Anna?" he tempted her, brushing his

chin against the sensitive mound. "Tell me what you want. Tell me how you want it."

What she wanted?

How she wanted it?

Moaning, she shook her head. How the hell was she supposed to do that? She'd never been touched like this before. Reading about it, or watching it, didn't give her a clue what she wanted or how she wanted it.

"Archer—"

"What do you want, sweetheart?" he tempted her further. "Tell me, and I'll give it to you."

Tightening her fingers in his hair as she licked her dry lips, Anna fought to push past the need to cry out at the rising desperation building in her body, in her senses.

"Please, please, Archer." Finally forcing words past her swollen lips, she arched to him again, needing his lips there, his tongue, his kiss.

"Tell me what you want, Anna." His voice was more demanding, rougher than ever, as the brush of his breath against the sensitive flesh drove a shaft of searing sensation racing through her pussy and throbbing through her clit.

"God. Archer, please. Like my nipples. Take my clit like you did my nipples." She couldn't bear the need any longer.

Hunger trumped shyness and sent her racing headlong toward the flames threatening to consume her. "I want your tongue, Archer. Your lips." Her breathing hitched on a moan. "Now, Archer. Please, God, put your lips on my clit."

The words were no more past her lips than his tongue found her. Swiping through the saturated slit, rasping the sensitive flesh hungrily as Anna felt such ecstatic sensations tearing through her that she would have screamed if she'd had the breath to do so.

She didn't have the breath.

Parting her legs further, her knees lifting and spreading as her heels dug into the mattress, she fought to get closer to him. Anna lifted to his questing tongue. As Archer licked with hungry demand around her throbbing clit, it felt as though a thousand suns exploded through her taut muscles and over sensitive flesh.

A wail tore from her lips, only to be caught halfway as his lips suddenly clamped on the exploding nubbin. His thumb pressed into the clenching entrance of her vagina, barely penetrating, stroking as his lips, tongue, and the suckling heat of his mouth sent her hurtling through ecstasy.

She couldn't cry out.

Anna lost her breath to the incredible sensations tearing through her unprepared senses. Even her own fingers, her knowledge of her own body, had never produced such rapture. She was locked in it, her body shuddering, jerking against him as his suckling mouth, his rasping tongue, and knowing fingers delivered such sensual chaos that Anna could only ride the fury of the sensations as they tore through her.

Rapid bursts of ecstasy were still firing inside her as he moved. Ignoring her desperate cry of denial, Archer came to his knees between her thighs, his knees pressing her legs further apart as he gripped the base of his cock and covered her shuddering body.

The wide, pulsing cock head pressed against the clenched entrance, stretching her slowly as his kisses began to devour her lips.

She could taste herself on his kiss, but rather than pulling her free of her arousal, it only built it.

Flames of pleasure-pain began tearing through her as the blunt, engorged head of his cock pushed inside her, stretching the tender entrance. The impalement of previously untouched muscles burned her flesh as he worked the blunt head slowly inside.

The iron-hard crest raked across previously hidden nerve endings, striking at her senses with so many alternating sensations that she could barely process them.

"Oh God, Archer!" Crying out his name, Anna watched through pleasure-blurred eyes as his head lifted, his fierce eagle gaze locking onto hers as his hips moved again.

Pulling back, pressing deeper, Archer worked the thick, hard flesh against the clenched, untried muscles of her pussy. He possessed her with a single-minded intent that stole all semblance of control.

As he pulled back again, Anna felt the throbbing crest poised at the entrance of her vagina as his thighs tightened and the muscles of his hips bunched. A second later he was surging inside her with a fierce, hard thrust that sent the thick shaft pushing past the veil of innocence she had been saving for him.

Anna could only hold on for the ride.

Her fingers tightened on his shoulders, ragged cries falling from her lips as he began to move with powerful thrusts, pushing deeper inside her with each inward movement. Anna arched her hips toward him, desperate to take all of him.

Every sensation, every harsh groan, every stroke of his thick erection shafting inside her sent ecstatic explosions converging on her senses as ecstasy built higher inside her.

Driving into the clenched depths of her pussy, past previously untouched flesh and bared nerve endings, Archer drove his erection in to the hilt. Pleasure ruptured with blazing force inside her, each explosion ripping through her senses and marking her soul.

He was possessing her.

Dominating her every response.

He was taking more than her virginity, more than the sensitive depths of her responsive body. With each fierce, plunging thrust, she swore he was stealing her heart.

Building, rapturous pleasure, violent in its intensity, began exploding through her. As though there were too many sensations, too much heat——

Anna exploded again, crying out his name, her head tilting to the side as stinging kisses were delivered to the sensitive flesh of her neck.

The additional pleasure-pain amplified the explosions, the pleasure, until Anna could only cry out again with the force of them. She gave herself wholly to the force of the orgasm as it possessed every molecule of her body, every ounce of her emotions.

She was only dimly aware of Archer's ragged groan as the force of her own climax began to ease. Her vagina still clenching, rippling around his erection, her breath caught as he forcefully pulled free of the clenched grip she had on his cock.

A ragged male growl echoed through her senses as the heated, damp spurts of his release spilled against the swollen, sensitive flesh of her clit.

His lips were parted against the side of her neck, the burning bite of a fierce, possessive kiss against her flesh mixing with the echoing waves of her completion.

Exhausted, physically sated, she lay beneath him, unable to move, barely able to breathe. Lying against her, his hold still tight and possessive despite his completion, Anna luxuriated in the warmth of his flesh, the beat of his heart.

She could lie in his arms, just like this, forever.

She didn't have to move, she decided. There was no reason to even consider leaving the bed and his hold, until she simply had no other choice.

Archer was moving, though. Easing from her, she expected him to collapse beside her, but instead he was moving away. The feel of him leaving the bed sent regret and aching hurt racing through her.

Keeping her eyes closed, she told herself she wasn't going to call him back. She wouldn't beg, rage, or cry as she had heard of other women doing when their lovers eased away from them and found another bed to sleep in.

He'd given her a pleasure she couldn't have expected—

The sound of the bedroom door closing behind him wasn't what she heard, though.

A frown flitted between her brows as she heard water running in the bathroom. Seconds later her eyes opened quickly at the feel of his hands parting her thighs.

Archer moved between her legs, his expression pensive as he took the cloth he carried and tenderly cleaned the wetness from the tender flesh between her thighs.

"What are you doing?" She was shocked at the action.

She had never heard the girls who bragged of their sexual conquests saying anything about this.

"You'll sleep better," he promised, as his lips quirked at the side in a slight smile.

She would sleep better?

Watching as he finished cleaning the proof of their release from her, Anna admitted that Archer wasn't a man she would ever figure out easily.

But she wanted to.

She wanted to know him, to know his touch, his pleasure, his agonies, and even his regrets.

She wanted to know why he wanted her, and why he hadn't let her know before now that he desired her.

And she would ask him about it, she promised herself, just as soon as she had slept and recovered from the pleasure that had sapped the last of her strength.

Moving from the bed and returning to the bathroom, Archer ran more water, then, as Anna felt drowsiness stealing over her, returned to the bedroom and the bed.

Even more shocking, he eased her back into his arms as he settled in beside her, her head coming to rest against his chest.

"We'll talk in the morning," he stated, his voice quiet and intent.

"Okay," she agreed, though she wasn't certain what the discussion was going to be about.

No doubt he wanted to discuss the whole lack of emotion, lack of relationship rules. She almost smiled at the thought of it. Too late for that on her end.

For now, all Anna wanted to do was lie against him, to sleep, and to luxuriate in the completion that filled her.

She might never actually recover from it, though.

She knew she would never recover from the man and the intensity of the pleasure he'd given her.

Anna knew there would never be another touch that could ever compare to that of the man who held her now.

A man she feared she could never possess as he now possessed her.

Body.

Heart.

Soul.

She just might well belong to Archer Tobias.

CHAPTER 7

A man was stepping into a minefield when a woman had the power to make him forget something as important as the meeting he had scheduled several hours before dawn that morning.

Archer was just beginning to drift off to sleep, Anna held securely against his chest, when the silent vibrating alarm in his watch went off. It wasn't a response to alert him to the time, but a trigger set off by the alarm system in the house.

Gently detaching himself from the fragrant warmth of the woman resting against his chest, Archer quickly slid from the bed, found the pants he had kicked off earlier, and pulled them over his legs hastily.

As he moved from the bed he collected the weapon he kept tucked just beneath the head of the mattress.

He doubted the weapon was needed, but it was better to be safe than sorry. Archer had never considered John Corbin an enemy, but, now that Anna was here, in his bed, anything was possible.

With the Glock tucked against the side of his leg, he moved to the door of the study that he'd left ajar by several inches before going to bed and angled his head to look inside the room.

He could see John Corbin standing in front of the large map of Corbin County that Archer's grandfather had commissioned. Using yellow tacks, Archer had marked the position of each body the Slasher had left for the authorities to find.

John was frowning at the map, his heavily lined expression reflecting his grief over the situation he'd found himself in, and his inability to find a way to resolve it.

Archer narrowed his eyes at the older man, waiting to see if he moved.

It had been John who had come to him ten years before, when Archer's father had first begun showing the signs of Alzheimer's.

Randal Tobias had been quietly investigating the Slasher's kills, attempting to pinpoint some common individual the girls had associated with, besides the Callahan cousins, who might have had such murderous tendencies, or such an overriding hatred for the three young men.

With Randal's illness, John had been desperate. His granddaughter, Anna, had been a teenager, barely fourteen, but already begging to return to Corbin County when her parents moved back to the ranch for the spring to help John with the ranch during calving.

The older man had claimed he kept his granddaughter from the county because of the Slasher, and because of Anna's curiosity where her Callahan cousin, Crowe, was concerned. It seemed no matter the excuses they made or how often they tried to tell her it was too dangerous for her in Corbin County, she refused to believe it.

The Slasher only struck at the Callahans' lovers,

she argued once she'd understood the significance of the targets the killer chose. She wasn't a lover, she was simply a cousin.

Every occasion the young girl had been home it seemed the opportunity arose that she'd run into Crowe or one of the other cousins. She'd always spoken to them, always attempted to draw them into conversation, and always ended up in tears when they refused to talk to her.

How the new job working as Mikhail Resnova's personal assistant was going to work out for her, Archer had no idea, because Mikhail's and Crowe's offices were side by side.

Not that Archer could blame the cousins, especially in those days. It seemed every move they made while home on leave was watched suspiciously. As though Rafer, Logan, or Crowe would fall upon some hapless female and murder her in front of the whole town.

When John didn't move from his position, Archer pushed the door open slowly and stepped inside.

John's silver head turned in his direction, his fingers burrowing through the thick coarseness of his hair as Archer came to a surprised stop and stared at the other two men in the room.

"You said you wanted answers tonight," John stated. "They aren't mine alone to give."

Of course not, Archer thought sarcastically. He should have guessed that.

The "Barons" were called such because they owned the largest ranches in the area, had the most employees of any businesses in the County, and because their family, along with the Callahans, had first founded the County more than a hundred years before, their claim on the land extending even before the first recorded non-native settlement.

Along with John Corbin was Marshal Roberts, Rafer Callahan's paternal grandfather, and Saul Rafferty, Logan's grandfather.

Each man was around seventy-one or seventy-two, and each moved like a man two decades younger, despite the heavily lined weariness in their expressions.

"Now why didn't I guess that if one of you was involved in something, then all of you would be?" Archer snorted as he moved to the front of the heavy walnut desk that had once been his grandfather's and rested against it, his arms crossed over his chest as he watched each man demandingly.

Breathing out roughly, John paced across the room before turning and moving back to the chairs that sat in front of the desk.

Grabbing a matching chair from along the wall, he placed it to the side of Saul Rafferty before taking his seat and staring up at Archer imperiously. "You'll want to sit down for this."

He would want to sit down for it.

Great.

Whatever might be stalking the cousins, there was little doubt that it originally stemmed from these three men.

Archer's father had first made the prediction, his expression tight with anger, as he'd pushed a red pin into place on the map.

Moving behind the desk Archer took his seat, leaned back, and waited.

"Forty years ago, there was an unfortunate event that the three of us happened to come upon. None of us were involved in it, but having arrived when we did, it gave someone we still have yet to identify the opportunity to frame us for it," John began heavily. "Because of that one situation, and our inability to foresee that by not telling anyone what had happened, whoever had set it up would be able to destroy our lives.

"Because of that event, Archer, we were forced to disown our daughters when they married men who interfered in whatever plans this person had. Then we were forced to turn our backs on our grandsons and disown them as well. Because of whatever godforsaken plans the bastard has, nearly a dozen women have been murdered because of their connections to our grandsons. And now"—John's voice roughened—"because of a situation we could not control, and could not prove had not happened, I've had to disown my granddaughter because this person finds it, for whatever reason, inconvenient for her to be in Corbin County. If you don't convince her to leave, if you don't get her out of Colorado, then she could die for her stubbornness in staying, and for aligning herself with her cousin in that job she's accepted at the head offices of Brute Force. You have to get her to leave, Archer. You're my last hope to save her."

He didn't pretend to hide his shock.

Sitting back in his chair, he stared at the three "Barons," wondering if his father had ever suspected any of this.

No, he couldn't have, Archer thought. If his father had suspected it, he would have surely told Archer, or left him that information before Alzheimer's had taken his mind and a massive heart attack had taken his life.

"Well, fuck me," Archer breathed out roughly as he stared at the three men, not even pretending he wasn't speechless.

Hell, his father had always surmised the Barons had more to do with all of this than any of them could ever imagine, and how right he had been.

"What happened?" He let his gaze touch on each man.

John answered for them all. "Once you figure out the identity of the Slasher and his partner, then we'll tell you everything. We'll tell you about a conspiracy of blood and death that possibly stretches back far longer than any of us want to consider. But until both killers are taken into custody, revealing the secrets we've kept for so long will do none of us any good. Least of all my granddaughter."

Archer stared back at him silently.

He remembered the first time he'd met the older man. Archer had been no more than seven, motherless after Mera Tobias' death, and lost. His father hadn't quite known what to do with him, so Randal had taken his son to the Corbin Ranch and left him with his friends, John and Genoa Corbin, for the summer.

Archer had grown fond of the fatherly John, and he'd begun looking forward to those visits. As he entered his teens he'd taken summer jobs at the Corbin Ranch until he joined the Marines.

He'd gotten to know John well enough that he could read the determination in the older man's gaze. That glitter of stubbornness ate at Archer. For ten years, even before he'd left the Marines, Archer had been investigating the rapes and murders of the original six women, and any possible connections they could have had to the Callahan cousins and whoever had been attempting to frame the boys for those murders.

To learn that the killings might have begun long before he'd imagined made fury churn in his gut. It was bad enough he couldn't even come up with one suspect, let alone a list from which to identify the Slasher and his partner, but to have what could be vital information held back from him only pissed him off further.

"You have knowledge of a series of murders that could predate twelve years before, and you're refusing to reveal that information to an officer of the law?" he asked the three men, careful to keep his tone quiet and controlled.

"To tell you now, without proof, will only hurt us," Saul Rafferty spoke up, his voice a dark rasp that still held the deep baritone of command. "You will still have no suspect, and without proof of what happened, no way to identify even a possible suspect. But if knowledge of it became known, then the three of us could be blamed for it, and for so much more. Forty years, Archer. We've had to stand aside, disown the daughters we love more than life, and then to disown their children, or see their blood spilled and our hands appear to be stained by their blood. I'd rather die than see those boys suffer further."

"And now I've lost Anna as well," John grated out, his voice filled with bitterness. "If we tell you what we suspect, and what we know of the past that's being held against us, it then endangers not just our grandsons, but our entire families. If we wait until you identify the Slasher, or at the very least his partner, then you can pin far more on him than the murders the Slasher thus far claims."

"That's not enough," Archer informed the three men as his jaw tightened with anger. "You could have information that would help me identify the bastard and you're withholding it."

"No, there's nothing that could help you," Marshal Roberts promised as he spoke up, decades of grief

lining his face and filling his voice. "Nothing we know
could help you. If it could have, I swear to you on my
own life, you'd have the entire story, no matter the
danger to us personally. My grandson means everything to me, and to my wife. Just as the others meant
everything to John and Saul. We'll only endanger
them further if it's ever learned we told you even this
much."

Hell, this was going to come back and bite him on
the ass, and Archer knew it. But he could also sense
that the three men weren't going to give him whatever
it was they were holding back.

At least not yet.

"Does any of it tie into the murders that have been
used to attempt to frame Crowe, Logan, and Rafer?"
he asked them.

"I suspect they're tied together by the killer, the
Slasher himself." John sighed.

And he was supposed to accept their word for that,
of course.

Archer didn't think so. What he would do instead
was look into any major events that had occurred in
the time frame he had just been given.

"And this is why the three of you came together to
this meeting?" he asked mockingly. "Why can't I believe that, John?"

"We came together because it's not a story that
belongs to just one of us, or to just one of our family
members. It involves all of us," Saul reaffirmed. "Besides, Anna's as close to my family and Marshal's as
our grandchildren are to John. Seeing her hurt because
of this would break us all." For a second, moisture
sheened his eyes. "Archer, we've lost too much already.
None of us can bear to lose more."

"And that's why you have to convince Anna to leave

until this has finished," John demanded, his tone harsh now. "You know she's not safe in Corbin County, Archer."

"Anna's safe as long as she stays here," Archer informed them all, surprised at the ferocity of his statement. "I won't force her to leave. I won't ask her to leave."

John lifted his head, his expression tightening as he stared at Archer coldly from intense blue eyes. "You're sleeping with her, aren't you? The rumors of you two being seen all but naked and fucking in one of the park's grottos were true."

"Watch what you say, Corbin." Archer stared back at him, doing nothing to hide the fury rising inside him. "I don't know what the fuck you said to her before you forced her out of your house with nothing but the clothes on her back, but I know you destroyed her."

"And who the fuck do you think was standing there with Robert and Lisa when she called you?" the other man grated. "Do you think I'd leave my granddaughter helpless and alone for even a second? I knew when she shimmied up that trellis into her bedroom and collected that backpack and her purse. She'd have her car, too, if she hadn't been so pissed she forgot I always leave the side door to the garage unlocked."

"Then the fact that she's sleeping with me should comfort you rather than upset you, shouldn't it?" Archer snapped. "Because having her in my bed wasn't a decision I made lightly. I will protect her, John, with my life if need be."

"But will it be a decision that involves a ring?" John growled. "I won't let you treat her like you have your other women, Archer, never doubt that. My granddaughter isn't a fucking mark on your bedpost."

* * *

It was a lack of warmth, a feeling that something wasn't quite right, that woke Anna.

At first she felt disoriented, uncertain why she was naked and why the blankets were tangled across the bed, not quite covering her enough to keep her warm.

In a second, the memory of Archer's touch, his kiss, and the incredible pleasure he'd given her flashed into her mind. A flush stole across her face before racing through her body with remembered warmth. And renewed arousal.

He'd been beside her when she went sleep. She couldn't imagine he would lie next to her, let her think he was going to sleep with her, only to change his mind so quickly and leave his own bed to find another.

Oscar was there at the bottom of the bed.

His own pillow, her ass, she thought with a smile as she felt the furry warmth at her feet.

Archer couldn't have gone very far, and leaving the house itself wasn't something she believed he would do without waking her or leaving a note next to her first.

Rising from the bed she found her gown and robe, which he must have lain across the back of the chair. Barefoot, she left the bedroom and silently began moving through the house.

Anna had made a point earlier to pay attention to which floorboards squeaked and which weren't quite flush with those around them as she had made herself familiar with the house.

Avoiding those particular pitfalls, she made her way downstairs and continued through the house until a sound made her pause several feet from the study. Her head tilted to the side to identify the sound of voices coming through the narrow slit between the door and its frame. It hadn't been closed fully, leaving an inch or so view into the room.

Archer was meeting with someone? At this time in the morning?

Moving closer she paused near the narrow opening to hear if she could recognize the voices and make certain it wasn't intruders. What she heard lit a flame of anger so deep and so hot inside her it was all she could do to remain hidden.

"Then the fact that she's sleeping with me should comfort you rather than upset you, shouldn't it?" Archer snapped. "Because having her in my bed wasn't a decision I made lightly. I will protect her, John, with my life if need be."

"But will it be a decision that involves a ring?" John growled. "I won't let you treat her like you have your other women, Archer, never doubt that. My granddaughter isn't a fucking mark on your bedpost."

"My relationship with Anna is our business, not yours," Archer stated coolly. "Remember that, John. You're the one who threw her out rather than being honest with her. I won't lie to her, and I'll be damned if I let you endanger her further."

"You'll get her killed," her grandfather accused him fiercely, his voice echoing with a vein of deep, tortured fear.

"I'll protect her with my life," Archer retorted. "And with the truth. Until the three of you decide to come clean with that little commodity, then you have no say in how I protect her. I'll take care of her and I'll take care of my own end of things. Until then, you do your part and see if you can't find a few more truths to give me to help figure this crap out."

"Fuck my part. And don't think for a second you won't get her killed if you tell her what we've just divulged. I've protected her from the so-called truth for a reason. She's a damned good girl, but she trusts people, Archer. Too much. She'd need someone to talk to and she'd tell someone. She tells her friend Amelia everything. I can't tell you the times Wayne Sorenson has snickered over Anna sneaking out of the house to catch sight of you at those damned socials over the years. Or how often his daughter has told him about the arguments Anna has with me. Because Anna can't keep her mouth shut. And that's beside the fact that she doesn't know how to stay the hell away from those boys. They'll get her killed." Her grandfather was raging, albeit without the raised voice she was normally used to.

Her fists clenched as humiliation tore through her.

Her grandfather didn't trust her with whatever this "truth" was, because she told Amelia about their arguments? Or because she'd slipped from school a few weekends, hoping to see Archer or find a moment to talk to the cousin who had been so unfairly ostracized?

She had been told all her life to stay the hell away from the Callahans. Crowe was her cousin and she wanted to get to know him, especially now that she had been disowned as well.

But to be thrown out of her family, to be forced from her home and never told why, because they based whether or not she could be trusted on those few instances?

It was beginning to feel as though there was a hell of a lot more going on than her family's arrogance and determination to have their way. She'd always known something dark existed in her family, but she'd never revealed that suspicion. Not to anyone. Even Amelia.

Still, her family didn't trust her.

It hurt.

Oh God, it hurt so bad.

That knowledge was digging razor-sharp talons into her chest and ripping her apart.

She was twenty-four years old, not a baby. She was a grown woman, and regardless of what her grandfather believed, there were a hell of a lot of Corbin family secrets she did know. Knew, and had never told another soul.

"The Callahans aren't a threat, John," Archer argued. "But they could damned sure help. And don't try to tell me how to do my job or how to protect Anna. I won't stand for it."

Anna's eyes narrowed at his tone. He sounded awfully possessive for a man who had already made the whole no-emotion-no-relationship rule. And it was beginning to sound as though the feeling she had of a conspiracy revolving around her was true.

"Whoever's behind this knows you're sleeping with her." Her grandfather's harshly voiced declaration had Anna flushing with mortification, even though she knew there wasn't a chance anyone could know about it. Hell, it had only happened little more than an hour before. "It's one of the reasons I agreed to meet you, Archer. Not just to explain what we could, but to try to get you to see how much he knows and how dangerous he is. That bastard has been blackmailing us since before those boys were born. And no more than hours before you called, he contacted me. He knew she was here, and he knew she would be sleeping in your bed."

Who the hell was this "he"? There had been no time for anyone to have known anything.

"He told you he knew Anna was here?" Archer asked carefully. "If you don't know who he is, John, then how does he communicate?"

Anna could feel the confusion building inside her now.

"He calls. I can tell his voice is disguised, and tracing the call to find the number has been impossible over the years. He's furious that she's here, and still in Corbin County. When she came home two weeks ago he contacted me by letter. Said she would die if she didn't leave. He's threatening to make certain she pays for it if I don't get her out of your house and get her out of Colorado."

"If he's becoming angry, then he'll make mistakes," Archer decided.

"He knows the two of you were in that grotto two weeks ago. That's how I found out about it. God, Archer, please listen to sense. She can't know about this, and she can't stay here."

"If he doesn't like her living arrangements, then he can take it up with me," Archer drawled, his tone dangerously low. "Because Anna will be with me, and I promise you, to get to her, he will have to go through me. You're not going to keep her safe by lying to her, or hiding this from her. She has to at least know her life is in danger. She can make the decision after that."

A flood of weakness—fear- or anger-induced, Anna couldn't differentiate—raced through her body. She could feel her knees trembling, her lips shaking as she lifted her fingers to them to hold back the rage that wanted to consume her.

The fact that Archer was demanding she be told the truth did nothing to ease the unbelievable knowledge that her family had kept such things from her.

What the hell was going on? What had her grandfather and his friends managed to get her mixed up in? And why, why hadn't her parents ever told her this?

All the years of being alone, of being so lost and feeling so abandoned, all because they refused to trust her with the truth?

"You're using her as bait," her grandfather charged, giving voice to the suspicion rising inside Anna.

"For God's sake, John, she's a target no matter where she's staying. If he was going to strike out at her, he would have already. Trust me to know what the hell I'm doing here. And trust Anna. She's not a child, nor is she unable to keep this to herself."

Confusion filled her, but it didn't obliterate her anger at her family. There was some awful conspiracy shadowing her family and threatening her? And they couldn't tell her?

As for Archer, she had no doubt he was using her, especially if he had somehow suspected whatever was going on. His desire to use her in whatever this situation was hadn't made his dick hard, though. He wanted her for other reasons and she knew it.

She had been a virgin, but she wasn't stupid. She was a woman, and a woman knew when a man wanted her simply because he couldn't keep his damned hands off her.

She might not have a chance at his heart, but in Archer's arms, she had a chance at something almost as important. The chance to learn why she'd been pushed away by her family so long ago.

CHAPTER 8

It was all she could do to stand in place, to listen, to make herself absorb what she was hearing. Remaining silent through it was one of the most painful, heart-rending things she believed she had ever done in her life.

She wanted to rush in, ask questions, and demand explanations.

She wanted to rage and cry and scream—

Oh God, she wanted to scream at her grandfather, to slice at his heart as hers had been sliced over the years because of the forced isolation from her family and from coming home.

She wanted to cry. But if she cried, if she let the first tear fall, then the objectivity she was forcing herself to use would be lost. She would be a child again, crying into the night and begging Mommy and Daddy to please, please let her come home.

So much of it didn't make sense. And so much of it was destroying her even as it gave her a glimpse into all the questions that had raged in her mind for so many years.

"There's no way to keep the Callahans out of this,

or Anna away from Crowe, John," Saul Rafferty stated, his tone weary, surprising Anna with his presence. She hadn't known he was there. "Whoever's behind this, his only focus is destroying us and our grandsons. If she stays hidden, if she stays in the shadows and we continue to do as he orders, then he'll never reveal himself."

"And I've tried to convince you that girl could give a clam a run for tight lips if she knew the truth of this." Marshal Roberts sighed. "I understand your need to protect her better than anyone does, but Archer's right. We haven't protected her. All you've done is let that little girl grow up without family and without friends because some madman found another way to punish you. Let Archer fix this, before it's too late for any of us."

"She's too damned stubborn for her own good," her grandfather grumbled. "If she had just gone to France she would have been protected."

"And you would have lost even more time with her than you're losing now," Archer growled. "That's beside the fact you should have known she would never agree to it."

"She's far too much like Kim was before she died." The grief in her grandfather's voice made Anna's chest tighten.

The family had never recovered from her aunt's death. It still shadowed them, just like whatever danger was shadowing them, and her as well.

"Was he right about your relationship with Anna?" Her grandfather ignored Archer's previous statement. "Are you sleeping with my granddaughter?"

Her fists clenched at her side as she laid her forehead silently against the wall and closed her eyes.

This was none of his business.

He would have seen her living a solitary, cold life rather than trusting her. He had no right to know if she was sleeping with anyone or who she might be sleeping with now.

"My relationship, whatever it may or may not be or develop into, is none of your business, John. But let the Slasher believe whatever he wants if it means taking them out of their comfort level and making them angry enough to make a mistake." Archer's tone remained respectful, despite the fact that he had just told her grandfather it was none of his business if he were sleeping with Anna.

Had he brought her to his home and to his bed to catch a killer? Was she wrong? Had the thought of catching the Slasher, or whoever was threatening the Corbin family, actually made his dick hard?

"She has a heart, Archer," her grandfather gritted out. "A tender one. And one I'd prefer not to see broken. She's not had a lover, and I know she hasn't taken one because she thinks she's already in love. Once she gives the man she loves that gift, she will never stop loving him. No matter how he hurts her, she'll always love him. And if you don't realize that, then you're a bigger fool where she's concerned than I ever thought you were."

Thanks, Grandfather. That was exactly what she wanted her new lover to hear.

"What the hell do you mean by that?" Archer growled.

"I mean you've been too blind to see that Anna's been in love with you since she was a teenager. And she's refused to settle for anyone else. She's always considered any other man second best."

Anna cringed. She hadn't thought anyone had realized

just how deep her affection for Archer had actually grown.

"Anna's too smart for that, John," Archer argued, though his voice had changed, thickened. "Love like that is a fairy tale for little girls playing dress-up with their mother's clothes. Anna's not a little girl anymore."

Her heart broke. Right then and right there, standing outside Archer's study, wearing one of the sexy gowns she'd always imagined seducing him in, she felt her heart break in half.

Because her grandfather was right; she loved Archer Tobias. She loved him with all her heart, and nothing would change that.

She couldn't deal with this anymore.

In a single conversation she had learned her grandfather was somehow tied to the Slasher through a conspiracy that now involved her, and that Archer was possibly using her to draw the Slasher out into the open.

She was turning to leave when her grandfather said, "I've lost not just my baby girl, but also her son—the grandson I have found so much pride in, Archer. Genoa and I would have given our lives to know Crowe. Now that bastard has forced us to push Anna out of not just our lives, but also her parents'. My son hates me, and rightfully blames me for all of it. My daughter-in-law and my wife haven't stopped crying since she left. God help us. If we lose Anna, it will finish the destruction of the Corbin family."

They were forced to disown her because of all this? Her heart was racing, adrenaline coursing through her veins as she tried to make sense of what was going on.

"The Callahan brothers and their wives were murdered, weren't they?" Archer's question nearly stopped

her heart. "By the same man, or men, calling themselves the Slasher?"

God, she wished she could see her grandfather's
face, and though she expected him to answer Archer,
it was Marshal who spoke up instead.

"I was the one who advised the three girls to change
the terms of their trusts to their children once they
acquired them. We prayed it would ensure their safety.
No one knew they had gone to do so that day, together.
But it was the only time the couples had gone out together in years. They had known that to do so was too
dangerous. The confusing part was the couples had all
left separately and at different times in their own vehicles. Yet only one vehicle had been used to travel
back in, while the two others were left abandoned in a
mall parking lot. We don't know if it was the Slasher
who killed them, just as we don't know if it's the Slasher
who's been destroying us all these years, Archer. We
suspect there's a plot to acquire the Callahan land. We
just don't know why, or how someone could ever imagine killing our daughters or destroying their sons could
help acquire it. Or why they would want it so damned
bad."

Archer stared at the three men, careful to keep his
expression blank.

So Crowe, Logan, and Rafer's parents had indeed
been murdered.

"I know you suspected it, Archer," Saul stated.
"Your father knew. He was sheriff at the time. But
there was nothing he could do. There was no evidence,
and no way to prove murder. All we had was that bastard and a note he sent to each one of us. *If you had
listened*— And that was all it said."

"Listened?" he questioned them softly. "To what?"

"To his demands that we find a way to force the girls to leave their husbands and deny their sons," John said, shaking his head, confusion flashing in his gaze. "God, Archer. They loved those men. Loved them like you couldn't believe. We even tried telling them the truth. Tried explaining it and urged them to change their trusts and their wills. And still, we couldn't save them."

John swallowed painfully, turned away, and blinked at the moisture filling his eyes.

He would prove it now, Archer assured himself. The minute he identified the bastards, he'd make damned sure he proved their connection to not just the young women who had died at the Slasher's hands, but also the deaths of the Callahans.

"It's time we go." It was Marshal who glanced toward the curtain-covered windows warily. "Dawn's coming, and we don't want to be seen here. We have to leave before it begins getting light."

"Do you need a ride? Help getting to your vehicles?" Archer rose to his feet, suddenly concerned about the three men. Hell, they were in their early seventies—not exactly the best age to be tromping through the woods at night by themselves.

"If we can't make it, then we deserve to drop where we stand," Saul muttered as he picked up the cane he had set by his chair and rose to his feet.

"Didn't remember you carrying a cane before, Saul," Archer drawled.

The old man gave a bitter half grin before gripping it with both hands and pulling free a long knife from one end. "I only need it when I want to, Sheriff. Only when I want to."

Shaking his head, Archer watched as the three men

slipped from the study through the back door and made their way into the darkness.

Closing and locking the door after them, he stiffened, feeling the presence that stepped into the room as he silently cursed with a virulence he hadn't used in years.

Turning, he faced Anna, and in that second knew she had heard far too much.

"You could have told me you were just fucking me to draw a killer out," she drawled. "I might even have gone along with it."

"I think you know better than that, Anna."

He could see the pain and the confusion in her eyes. Chaotic, soul-deep, the emotions tearing her apart now were clearly reflected in the deep, emerald green of her eyes, and he'd be damned if he could blame her for any of them.

Uppermost in her gaze, and filling her expression, was bitter betrayal. The emotion darkened her eyes, but it also caused her face to pale and revealed the ultra-light scattering of freckles across the top of her nose.

Hell, and why had he just noticed those? There wasn't a chance in hell she was going to let him brush his lips across them as he suddenly wanted to.

Her gaze dropped down, eyes narrowing at the evidence of the hard-on pressing against his cotton pants.

A grin tilted the corner of his lips. "I think you just might have made me hard again, sweetheart."

Her lips tightened in anger, but that flame of arousal he glimpsed in her eyes hadn't been doused. Hell, it might even be a shade brighter now.

"Don't think you're good enough to make me forget a single word of what I heard tonight," she warned him. "And don't think for a moment you're not going to fill me in on every word I might have missed."

"Just exactly what did you hear?"

She was smart, and despite John's assertions, Anna knew how to keep her mouth shut, especially when it came to the only friend she had in Corbin County.

"I believe it might have been the part where my grandfather was asking you about the ring and the commitment. And I didn't miss the part where you assured him I wasn't into fairy tales, either."

Ouch.

Now that part he would have preferred she hadn't heard. Because Anna did have fairy tales she still lived by, but there wasn't a chance she'd believe his explanation, either.

Anna was smart enough to know love rarely, if ever, happened at first sight. It came with knowledge, it came with understanding.

And that wasn't a discussion that was going to walk hand in hand with explanations of the danger she was currently involved in.

He breathed out wearily and glanced at the clock before meeting her gaze once again.

"You didn't miss much," he growled as he rubbed at his lower jaw in irritation. "The reason they placed you in private schools, and kept moving you, was because, according to your grandfather and his friends, they've been blackmailed for decades, Anna. That's why they disowned your aunt, Crowe, and now you. If you didn't leave Corbin County, then he was to disown you and ensure you had no option but to leave the county to survive."

Graceful, charmingly innocent, she lifted one hand to rub at her forehead, her brow creasing thoughtfully.

"My parents moved with me for several years," she

said softly as she turned from him, the white gown and robe sweeping softly at the floor as she moved. "Until I was nine."

He remembered that. Her father had traveled often between the ranch and wherever she'd been enrolled in school.

"I don't know why they stopped." He knew the unvoiced question before she turned and stared back at him, her gaze tortured. "Those are questions you can ask later. But I think you know it's not a question you can ask right now, Anna. You have to maintain the illusion that you are indeed disowned. Not just being protected. As your grandfather said, even your only friend, your best friend, can't know the truth. The chance that she would confide, in anyone, would be too great."

Delicate nostrils flared as a jerky breath shook her body and she gave a tight nod. A shudder worked down her spine.

God, if she started crying it was going to destroy him.

Instead, she wrapped her arms across her breasts before pacing to the map on the wall and staring at it unseeingly.

"Why?" she asked. "Why all this conspiracy just to claim property that could have been sold? Hell, it *was* sold. Crowe's grandparents sold it in three parts to the remaining Barons. Remember?"

"The property was tied up in their daughters' trusts after JR and Eileen Callahan's deaths. JR and Eileen had the property placed in trust for their sons in the event of their deaths. According to papers filed several days before their bodies were found, they had sold the property to Corbin, Rafferty, and Roberts on the condition that the property went into their daughters' trust funds. Everyone knew JR and Eileen had a soft spot for the other three Barons' daughters. They wouldn't have sold to your grandfather, Rafferty, or Roberts, though, after they refused to help Eileen while JR was in the hospital. Especially considering her youngest child's death occurred at the time she was begging the others for help." He frowned at that knowledge.

Unless they hadn't actually sold that property, he thought.

Forty years.

That would have been about the right time if JR and Eileen had been murdered. Then, to frame the remaining Barons, that property had somehow been placed in trust for their daughters?

Still, none of it added up.

"Archer, it doesn't make sense," she pointed out what he already knew. "Why make it so damned difficult if the point was to get the land?"

Giving his head a hard shake, he focused his attention back on Anna.

"Unless the point was to frame your grandfather and the others for JR and Eileen's deaths," he murmured.

What the hell was he doing? He'd told himself he wasn't going to discuss this with her, yet he was.

Archer tightened his lips, determined to hold back any other observations he might have.

Hell, she wasn't a trained law enforcement agent or a deputy. She was a tender twenty-four-year-old ex-virgin with more dreams than experience, and more stubbornness than any woman had a right to possess.

And that stubbornness went hand in hand with her soft heart, her generosity, and her open nature.

Yet, who else deserved the information? Who else could he discuss it with besides Anna and the Callahans? Crowe, Logan, and Rafer would have to have the information. And, no doubt, Ivan Resnova as well. Resnova would have the resources to get answers they couldn't.

That added four others who could possibly reveal the secrets the Barons had kept for so long.

Fuck.

"If they were framed for JR and Eileen Callahan's deaths, then once the trusts were acquired, he'd have to have something in place to ensure he had the property," Anna pointed out logically. "Their daughters were teenagers then. He couldn't marry all of them when they came of age, which is what he would have had to do if gaining the property was the point."

Archer nodded. "Dead end," he murmured.

"Why demand I be taken out of the County and placed in a different school every year?" The years of loneliness filled her voice. "How could I have played in this scheme, Archer? What makes me so important?"

"That's a question only one person can answer." He sighed. "Hell, there are a lot of questions only the person who began all this can answer."

"And the Barons believe that person is the Slasher," she stated, rather than asking for affirmation.

"That's what they believe." He nodded. "So far, there have been three different men committing these murders. Thomas Jones killed twelve women twelve years ago. Lowry Berry killed three women this past spring and tried to kill Cami Flannigan. Now, someone else, so far unidentified, has killed at least two women, and possibly a third. Yet there are too many similarities to rule out the same man being involved in each death."

"The FBI profilers have always said there were two or more men involved." Her frown deepened.

Archer grimaced. Hell, he couldn't keep his mouth

shut here, and this endless round of questions was going to get them nowhere.

"I didn't take you to my bed to catch a killer." It was
time to change the subject.

Rather than arguing the statement, she stared back
at him silently, the bitter betrayal in her expression
never wavering.

"Then why did you?" she asked him. "You've had
every chance to take me since I turned sixteen."

"And I was an adult," he snapped. "Do you really
think I would have touched you at that age?"

"That wasn't what I said, Archer," she retorted, her
own tone heated now. "I said you had every chance.
Since I was sixteen, every time I saw you, I flirted so
blatantly it's a wonder the words 'Fuck me' weren't
stamped on my forehead."

His jaw tightened. "Should I apologize for waiting
until you were old enough to understand what the hell
I might want from you?" he growled.

Her nostrils flared, eyes narrowed. Well, hell, wasn't
she just pissed off now?

"What you should do is forget the whole thing," she
snapped. "While I move into your very comfortable
guest room."

Oh, he wanted to fuck her. He wanted to fuck her
with a hunger that belied the fact that he had already
had her once that night.

As she turned to stalk from the room, determination began to burn through him.

Before he could stop himself, he was pulling her
around and jerking her to him. "Damn you, Anna, I
don't think I'll ever have enough of you. I could fuck
you until the end of time and I'd still want you." And
he didn't look in the least happy about it.

There was nothing so sexy, so sensual, as the lust

burning in his gaze, tightening his face. Nothing that could have held her in place easier than the pure erotic heat that surrounded her.

Before she had a chance to argue, even if she had wanted to, his lips covered hers, possessed them, and stole any fight still hiding inside her.

She couldn't fight this pleasure. She couldn't fight his touch. She loved it far too much. She loved him far too much. Her fingers gripped his shoulders, her nails digging into him as she strained against him, desperate to get closer now. Her lips parted, accepting his tongue, stroking it, tasting him and becoming drunk off the need spilling from his kiss. Moaning, aching for him, Anna pressed closer to the hard wedge of his cock as it centered between her thighs. Rolling her hips, riding it, aching for more, she dared him with every move to take her. With the hard wedge of his cock centered on her sensitive pussy, Anna couldn't help but move against him. Whimpering with pleasure and rising need she rode the iron-hard erection her body craved, torturing them both with her hunger.

As she felt her back meet the wall, Anna moaned at the sexual promise inherent in the move. Her fists uncurled, her nails biting into his shoulders as she arched against him. She couldn't get close enough. No matter how she tried, her gown and the cotton pants he wore kept their flesh from touching, kept his cock from demanding entrance inside the aching depths of her sex.

"Oh hell, no, you little wildcat," he growled as she tried to push the elastic band of his pants over his hips. "I'll be damned if I'll let you have it that easy."

Archer pulled back, placed her on her feet, then shocked her again. Just when she thought he was going to release her, he gripped her gown and robe in both hands and, before she could fight him, had both

over her head and tossed to the floor, leaving her naked before him. His head lowered, lips parting, and
as Anna gasped, his teeth gripped a tight, hard little
nipple.

Worrying it first with his teeth, Anna felt the electric jolts of sensation shooting from the tender tip to
her swollen clit and the clenched depths of her pussy.
Her hands buried in his hair, pulling at the thick strands
as she strained to force him to suck the needy tip.

Anna cried out in desperate pleasure at the lashing
sensations surging through her sex with each hungry
draw of his mouth. She was only dimly aware of him
removing his pants as his tongue licked at the tortured
tip before moving to its mate. Pleasure, desperate and
burning in its intensity, rocked her senses.

What was he doing to her?

She should never, not in a million years, allow him
to touch her now. As furious, as hurt as she was, she
should be anywhere but here.

But, oh God, it was so good.

The pleasure bordered on pain. It rode an edge of
sharp sensation so incredible that Anna couldn't resist,
no matter how hard she tried.

And she did try.

Pride was most often her downfall. Yet with each
touch of Archer's knowing, experienced hands, her
pride melted, bit by bit, for the pleasure her body was
beginning to crave. His touch was addictive. His kiss
was like a drug.

Lifting his head from her breasts, his expression
was tight and hard with lust. Archer stared down at her
with narrow-eyed hunger and dominant sexuality.

"Did you think I would let you go so easily?" he
growled.

Her lips parted as she fought to drag in air, to breathe

rather than gasping with each hard pulse of pleasure racing through her body.

"I won't let you go," he snarled when she refused to answer him.

He wouldn't let her go? But he didn't love her. He didn't need her.

Archer believed love was a fairy tale, something only children believed in. As much as it hurt, as deep as the pain went, she couldn't fight the pleasure. But she sure as hell could build her defenses against him, once he wasn't throwing her senses into chaos.

And her senses *were* in chaos.

As Archer's lips roved over her neck to her lips, stealing yet more kisses, her pleasure was spinning out of control. The hard length of his cock pulsed and throbbed against her stomach while her pussy wept in need.

"Please, Archer," she cried out, the melting ache in the depths of her vagina demanding the hard thrusts of his cock.

"Please what, baby?" His head lifted, the fierce demand in his gaze bordering on command. "Please fuck you? Please give you all the pleasure we've both ached for?"

Damn him and his arrogance.

His dominance.

"Damn you, Archer, fuck me," she made her own demand. "Fuck me like you mean it."

"Oh, baby, every stroke, every cry I pull from your pretty lips, trust me, I mean it."

His lips covered hers again. Briefly. One hard, stinging sip of her lips before he pulled away and quickly pulled her around to bend her over the wide desk beside them.

Before Anna could process the fact that he was

coming in from behind her, his hard hands were gripping her hips as he came over her.

Surrender echoed in her pleading cry. Sensual surrender rushed through her as the thick crest of his cock parted her intimate lips and she felt her pussy beginning to suck him in. Her juices flooded from her inner flesh, making it slicker as he began to stretch the inner muscles and work his way inside her.

"Archer." Arching to him, losing her breath, nothing mattered but the feel of his hips pressing, rolling, penetrating her vagina with fiery thrusts.

Rubbing, stroking, the thick, hot crest rasped the tender tissue, burned as it stretched her and sent flaming pleasure tearing through her. His lips brushed against her ear, nipped, then sent her senses spinning further as he began to speak. "Damn, baby, I love how sweet and wet that tight little pussy is around my dick."

His voice, tight and filled with lust as he pressed his dick slowly inside her. Moving in, then out, thrusting in to his balls before pulling back and fucking inside once again.

Wide and steel-hard, his erection rasped over nerve endings so sensitive she cried out at each stroke, poised at the edge of release and on the point of screaming to be pushed over. The need to orgasm burned through her, her hunger for it clawing at her senses.

"Do you like it, sugar-girl?" he groaned at her ear. He thrust harder inside her, his cock shuttling to the hilt with each stroke. Each impalement sent a rush of radiant heat and pleasure-pain radiating through her. She felt ready to fall into a maelstrom of erotic sensation so brilliant that nothing else mattered.

Reaching back, Anna grabbed his thigh, desperate

for some part of him to hold onto. For some part of
Archer to hold onto.

"Do you want more, sugar-girl?" he demanded, his
voice hoarse, his own pleasure building. "Do you want
to come for me, Anna? Do you want to send that sweet
pussy clenching and raining over my dick?"

"Yes," she cried out, unable to deny him anything
now. "Oh God, Archer, let me come. Let me come all
over your cock."

"Do you love it, Anna? Do you love coming for me?"

"Yes," she cried out. "I love it, Archer. Oh God, I
love how you fuck me, how you make me come—"

Groaning, his thrusts became harder, faster. Drill-
ing inside her, the thick width raking and caressing
delicate nerve endings drove her insane with the building sensations. With his hands tight on her hips, holding
her in place, he shafted inside her with such powerful
inward strokes she became lost in the dizzying rush to
release. She couldn't hold back. She was lost in him.
She felt so much a part of him at this moment that she
wondered if she could ever live without his touch, his
possession.

Each thrust pushed her higher, burned brighter inside her.

Anna whimpered his name, begged, pleaded for
release. When it exploded, it tore through her senses
and, for a moment, destroyed any idea she'd ever had
of pleasure.

Behind her, Archer fucked her through each explosive pulse of release. He pounded inside her, taking
her fiercely until, at the last second, he pulled free of
her, spilling his release to the rounded curves of her
rear.

Archer was branding her with his touch. He was

stealing parts of her that she had no idea how to protect. He was tearing through any walls she could have built against him and anchoring himself so deep inside her that she feared he was going to end up owning her soul.

CHAPTER 9

Two days later

Anna was going to make him crazy.

Sitting at his desk, Archer tried to keep his attention on the reports he was supposed to be working on, but he was damned if he could do it. All he could think about was Anna, her pain-filled eyes and the sense of betrayal he'd glimpsed there.

Hell, it wasn't as if he'd run over a damned pet or something. Yet she'd had that same look in her eyes.

Trying to shake the memory wasn't easy. And fixing it was going to be even harder. She'd been betrayed by everyone around her, and now she was expecting Archer to betray her as well.

He forced his attention back to the report on the abandoned vehicle he'd found on Main Street that morning. The car was registered to Elizabeth Haley of Sweetrock, but Archer hadn't been able to locate an address for her. The address listed was one that hadn't been used in years. The house on the property was falling in and the name on the mailbox was dried and faded, though still legible.

That name wasn't Haley.

He'd checked with Talia Beckett in the clerk's office and, though they had the same information he had, she couldn't remember an Elizabeth Haley, either. And Talia, it seemed, had known everyone in the County by name and by face until this one.

As he frowned down at the information, the sound of his secretary's voice pulled him from the report.

His secretary, Madge, wasn't pleased.

"Just try to hurry, Mr. Sorenson. I've been trying to get those reports out of him for days."

"Stop fussing, Madge. He can take ten minutes for me."

Archer grinned at the querulous tone of the County attorney's voice before the office door opened and Wayne Sorenson entered quickly.

Tall, reed-thin with a slight stoop at his shoulders in a subconscious attempt to appear shorter, Wayne Sorenson had that studious, lawyerly look portrayed in movies for decades.

With serious brown eyes and a face lined from years of squinting over law books and worrying about clients or cases, the other man had just celebrated his sixty-fifth birthday and was still going strong.

Hell, Archer hoped he had half the energy at that age as the County attorney had.

"Damned bulldog," Wayne muttered as he closed the door and frowned over at Archer. "Where the hell did you find her? She's a menace to society, Archer, and a pain in my ass whenever I have to deal with her."

Archer snorted. "At least she's not making you do reports."

Pushing the files to the side while motioning Wayne to have a seat, Archer pushed the intercom button.

"Yes, hon, what can I get for you?" Madge answered with her best Southern-charm voice.

Archer lifted his brows in surprise as he glanced at Wayne, before letting a grin curl at the side of his lips.

"Madge, could you get some coffee? A pot, please, and two cups. And if you don't mind, a few pieces of that banana-nut bread you brought in?"

It was a hell of a way to have to get some of that bread himself. She'd turned him down until he finished his reports. Hopefully, she wouldn't deny him in front of Sorenson. She should know that was just a breach of good manners.

"Are those reports finished yet?" Madge asked sweetly, causing Wayne to chuckle in triumph.

"Not yet," Archer growled. "And if I don't get my coffee *and* bread, then you'll be lucky to get them before the week is out, let alone my shift." He disconnected with a swift click of the line before she could bring up an argument that would just piss him off.

"Lord have mercy, that woman needs a husband and a passel of kids to chill her out and keep her out of trouble," the older man grumbled.

"Hell, then I'd just have to lock one of 'em up for killing her." Archer grinned, glancing outside the smoked-glass window as Madge rose from her chair, glared through the window, then turned and headed for the break room.

"Damn woman," Wayne muttered before giving Archer an appraising look. "Loan her to me for a few months. Maybe I could get caught up on my paperwork."

Archer really didn't want to have to arrest Madge for killing the county attorney. That would just be a hell of a mess.

"Sorry about that, Wayne." Archer shook his head, grinning back at the other man smugly. "As irritating as she can be, I think I'll keep her."

Wayne nodded, though Archer could see the instant calculation filling the other man's eyes. If he thought he could bribe Madge away, then he had a surprise coming. There wasn't a chance in hell Madge would leave the sheriff's office, and Archer knew it.

"If you ever change your mind, let me know," the other man bargained instead. "I at least want first choice at hiring her."

"That I can do," Archer promised, grinning at the thought. "You'd return her in a day flat, though."

Leaning back in his chair he watched as the slender, doe-eyed young woman opened the office door and stepped inside with a large coffee tray.

Madge had spent five years in Atlanta, Georgia, working for an upscale designer, modeling the clothes they made.

She had instead elected to stay in Sweetrock to look after her parents while her brothers and sisters ran around the globe and had fun rather than continuing in the career she had chosen.

Her father had begun developing Alzheimer's the year before, and her mother had only recently had a stroke.

If Madge was bitter about the choice, she never showed it. No matter where Archer saw her, or how bad her day might have been in dealing with him, she still seemed to keep her cool.

Setting the tray on the corner of his desk, she gave the obviously uncompleted stack of files a hard look before turning her attention back to him.

Archer narrowed his gaze on her. "Two hundred

years ago you would have been burned at the stake as a witch," he informed her.

"Not hardly, sugar," she drawled. "Especially if the judge's files were in the same shape yours are."

He had to give her that one. No doubt Madge would have survived when many others went up in flames.

Waiting until she poured the coffee and sliced the bread into small, thin slices, Archer took the opportunity to watch Wayne from the corner of his eye.

The other man couldn't take his eyes off Madge's legs, encased in silk hosiery and black heels.

Setting Archer's cup and saucer in front of him, Madge then turned and placed Wayne's at the end of the desk.

"Hold my calls until we're finished, Madge," he told her as she finished.

"I'll take care of it," she promised as she turned and walked gracefully from the room before closing the door behind her.

Archer enjoyed the slice of bread, small though it was, and sipped at his coffee as he gave the other man a chance to do the same.

"Why do I think I was privileged to a slice of that heavenly bread because it was the only way to get your own?" Wayne asked ruefully as he finished it, then brushed any possible crumbs from his gray slacks.

Archer chuckled. "She's a slave driver."

"She reminds me of Amelia before I forced her home and took something very important from her." Wayne sighed. "She's not been the same since," he lamented again.

Archer had to admit Amelia had changed over the past few years.

"Where is Amelia?" he asked the other man. "Anna

was worried about her. She hasn't answered her calls since Anna returned to Corbin County."

Wayne sighed, shaking his head. "I talked to her last night, but getting her to answer the phone isn't always easy. I keep telling her she's going to have to pull out of this slump, but—" He shrugged helplessly as he lifted his gaze to the window behind Archer. "Hell, she stopped confiding in me a long time ago."

"When you talk to her again, would you let her know Anna's worried?"

Wayne nodded. "I'll make sure she calls, Archer. Anna's one of the few friends Amelia has left. I'd hate to see anything happen to destroy that friendship."

Archer rather doubted it was that imperative, but he didn't tell Wayne. Sometimes, Archer had the feeling that the other man manipulated his daughter far more than anyone suspected. Wayne just wasn't the type to beat her as far as he knew.

"So, then." Archer leaned back in his chair, putting his arms on the padded rests at the side. "What can I do to help you?"

Wayne's eyes crinkled at the corners in amusement. "Straight to the point. I liked that about you, Sheriff."

Archer glanced at the files. "Reports. Or someone might have to arrest Madge for shooting me."

Wayne glanced back at the smoked glass before giving a light laugh in response. That amusement dissipated quickly though, leaving Wayne's expression to tighten in displeasure instead.

"I just left another meeting with the chief of the state police and our esteemed governor. I believe there may well be chew marks on my ass, Archer. They ripped me up one side and back down the other."

Archer grimaced in frustration. "Go ahead," he snorted in frustration. "Kick me while I'm already down."

There was no smugness in Wayne's expression or in his gaze now. There was only disgust and a glimmer of impatience.

"Ms. O'Brien's foster father, our governor, isn't in the least happy that it's taking so long to find his foster daughter's attacker," Wayne bit out furiously. "They stopped by my office to give us a few ultimatums. Ones our mayor seems to agree with completely."

Archer wasn't in the least concerned with the mayor, but he cared about as much for official ultimatums as Wayne did. Besides, this seemed a little fast since the last ultimatum Wayne had been given.

Hell, this day wasn't turning out to be one of his better ones.

"Such as?" He was beginning to think Wayne was going to make him beg for the information.

The other man's nostrils flared, his dirt-brown eyes glaring in remembered ire. "They reminded me that if another victim is found, or another comes up missing, then the state police will be given the investigation immediately, while the FBI will handle local questioning and continued profiling. We have six weeks to find and arrest the Slasher, or the investigation will be taken from us immediately. And you know what that means, Archer."

Nothing could foul this situation up worse now.

"Hell," Archer cursed. "We don't need this."

"I believe I may have expressed the same sentiment myself," Wayne assured him before finishing his coffee and setting the cup back on the tray. "How would you like to handle this, then? There has to be some way figure out who the hell the Slasher is, Archer, and whether or not he does indeed have a partner." Wayne had never believed it was a team, but rather a series of copycats.

Wayne's lips tightened when Archer sighed wearily. Hell, the man didn't have the patience of a two-year-old.

"How, then, are we going to proceed?" The same question repackaged.

Lifting his brow mockingly Archer said, "Well, Wayne, if you have an idea how to proceed that I haven't yet used, then let's hear it."

He was getting damned tired of the demand for results and the lack of cooperation in the case.

Wayne sighed heavily. "There was no offense intended, Archer," he promised. "The thought of Sweetrock under siege by the FBI and state police makes my skin crawl, though. They haven't lived through this, nor have they seen what we've seen."

And wasn't that the damned truth.

"Agreed." Archer rubbed at the back of his neck as he leaned forward and stared at the files he'd shoved to the side of his desk.

Lifting his gaze once again to Wayne's, he breathed out roughly. "Let me think about this—"

"And let you contact the Callahans and see how they want to proceed?" Wayne's jaw tensed, a muscle jumping at the side of his face as his brown eyes grew cool and filled with disdain. "Is this your investigation or the Callahans'?"

Archer forced a hard, cold smile to his lips. "Why don't I give it to the Callahans and we'll see if a difference can be seen."

The whole damned County would see a difference then.

"What about Anna?" Wayne's demeanor shifted to one of concern. "The whole County is buzzing. The maids were on the phone within seconds of her leaving to spread the word that Corbin had thrown her out." He shook his head with a grimace. "That son of a bitch sure as hell knows how to destroy a kid, doesn't he?"

"She's dealing with it, just not easily." Archer shrugged with a heavy sigh.

Damn, he was glad he had learned how to lie in the military.

"Poor kid." Wayne rose to his feet with a heavy sigh. "I'd better return to my own paperwork." He nodded to Archer's files. "I'd like to meet with you and the deputies you have working the case tomorrow, though. We have to figure this Slasher thing out, Archer. And we don't have a lot of time to do it in."

"Set it up with Madge," Archer told him. "And I'll see you then." Unless he could get out of it.

Archer had no intentions of sharing any more information with anyone that he didn't have to.

Archer had learned by watching his father, and listening to him discuss the case, to trust only the few proven to be trustworthy. It wasn't that he didn't trust the county attorney. Hell, Wayne had as many hours on this as anyone did, but still, the less said about some things, the better. Especially with a man Archer's father had identified as a suspect years before.

Rising to his feet, he walked across the office to the set of wide, old-fashioned windows that looked out on the back lawn where the sheriff's department and courthouse employees took their lunch.

Propping his hands on his hips he stared out at one of the shaded benches that sat next to an ornate cement fountain.

He had no doubt about the direction he was following

in the investigation. He'd already begun a more extensive search into his deputy John Caine's background, but he was coming up with several dead ends. For a period of five years the man hadn't existed. Not surprisingly, that period coincided with the summer the Slasher had first struck, twelve years before.

Striding back to his desk and taking his seat, Archer pulled his cell phone from the side of the desk and made a call. He hadn't wanted to make this call, but he was out of options.

"Hello," Ryan Calvert answered. The child Eileen Callahan had sold to save her husband and her ranch was a man now. A man with a cause, and that cause was centered in Corbin County.

"Are you ready?" Archer asked.

"As I've ever been." His voice was slow and easy. "We meeting at your place?"

"The study," Archer agreed.

"Give me three," Ryan replied. "And I'll be bringing a friend. The boys have been working on this for several years now, so don't worry. Once you meet him, you'll understand why I trust him."

Ryan knew Archer's secrecy issues well, just as Archer knew Ryan's. He'd meet the other man, but that was all he was promising.

"If I'm not in the study, I'll know you're there," Archer promised. "It might take a minute to get there."

"Let's rock and roll, then," Ryan said.

"As long as we're the rock." Archer sighed, hoping—praying—he had this figured out. "As long as we're the rock."

The newly renovated building that now housed the main offices of Brute Force Security no doubt had the classiest interior of any office in the County.

Anna felt a sense of pride that morning as she stepped inside the tastefully furnished reception area with the sleek, curved receptionist's post that drew the eye rather than the security guard's matching post in a far corner of the room.

The computerized wonderland that each sleek electronic top held, hidden behind the raised front panel that greeted guests, was a technological marvel as far as Anna was concerned. And it was completely unlike anything she'd seen in some of the more high-tech offices in New York and California.

The fact that her cousins—well, only Crowe was actually her cousin, but she liked to claim all three of them—were part owners of the business was the source of that pride.

They'd been disowned, fought a legal battle for more than a decade for what was rightfully theirs, and they were now using that inheritance to create something, rather than simply living from it.

Not that any of them would accept it if they knew that was what she felt.

Moving along the plushly carpeted hall of the upper-floor offices, Anna carried the electronic pad used to transfer documents and record signatures between offices. Until the new interoffice network and encrypted e-mail system was online and tested, Crowe and his partner, Ivan Resnova, had ordered that the electronic pads be used instead.

Anna loved them.

Stopping at the heavy, dark oak door to the large meeting room, she wiped first one hand, then the other, down the side of her skirt before knocking firmly.

"Enter," Crowe called out, his dark, brooding voice bringing to mind the boogie man naughty children were frightened of.

She almost grinned at the image before opening the door and stepping inside.

And there was Archer. As well as the two Callahan cousins she'd believed had left earlier, the Resnovas and Archer.

Anna almost paused before closing the door. She tried to ignore Archer as she stepped to the long, oval, dark walnut table where Crowe, Ivan Resnova, and Mikhail Resnova, as well as four of the security agents employed by Brute Force, sat.

"The employment agreements you requested, Mr. Callahan," she stated, placing the electronic pad on the table beside him.

"Thank you, Ms. Corbin." He accepted the pad but didn't glance at it. "Would you have a seat now?"

"Excuse me?" The soft command made her pause.

"The chair beside Archer." He indicated the empty chair.

Anna narrowed her gaze at the top of Crowe's head. He didn't even bother to look up at her.

"Why?"

She was pretty certain it was Archer snickering, but she didn't give him the benefit of so much as a glance.

Crowe did turn his head and glance up at her then.

Slowly, he pushed his chair back and moved to rise.

"Don't make a mistake I'll help you regret, Crowe," Archer warned him, his tone suddenly dark.

Crowe slid his gaze to Archer as he planted his hands on the table before his eyes zoomed back to her. Like the wolf it was rumored he lived with, even more predatory, more intent than Archer's, his eyes sliced into her.

"Because, *cousin,* I thought you might like to have an opinion where your protection's concerned in the coming weeks. I have a feeling Archer's wrong about your ability to handle the truth. Perhaps I should have just put bodyguards on you and left you in the dark where they were concerned. I have no doubt they're good enough that you would never know they were there."

Her protection?

She glanced at Archer, inhaling sharply rather than blasting him with a scathing retort, before she turned back to Crowe.

"You can shove your protection, *cousin*." She didn't have to hold back with Crowe. "I've lived for twenty-four years without your help, and I can live without it just fine for the rest of my life, thank you very much."

But she knew that look on his face. She could protest until hell froze over and he would still do whatever the hell he pleased.

"Anna, please sit down." Archer's request was a careful, thinly cloaked warning in an order that pretended to be a request.

She might hate men.

Anna sat down slowly, watching as Crowe took his seat once again.

"You may remember seeing Thaddock, Stryker, and Brolen around town," he introduced three of the men she had seen. "The fourth is new to Brute Force, but he comes from an exceptional family with excellent references." He nodded to a handsome younger man. "This is Rory Malone, from Texas. He'll be the one ensuring the other three aren't glimpsed. He has no security background, but he's from a well-respected security family."

Anna stared at him thoughtfully for a moment before smiling. "You're Sabella Malone's brother-in-law. You came to Edgemoore Girls' School with her when she gave her class on basic auto mechanics."

It hadn't been nearly as informational as Anna had hoped at the time. How to change a tire, who to call in case of a roadside emergency. How to check the oil and refill the wiper fluid. Anna had known that much by following her grandfather around on the farm before being shipped off to school.

His head tipped to the side.

The youthfulness that had once filled his face was no longer there.

"I remember you, Miss Corbin." He nodded. "It's been a while."

It had been well over ten years.

"How's Sabella doing?" she asked.

Rory's sister-in-law had been struggling with a failing business, but she had still taken time out to come to the exclusive school.

"Are you finished with the pleasantries now?" Crowe asked mockingly. "Or would the two of you like us to return?"

"Not really." Anna smiled back at him tightly. "I don't get to town much, *cousin*. Remember? And polite conversation is just so hard to come by."

The other three security agents were the ones snickering now. At least until Crowe and Archer sent a warning look their way.

"As I was attempting to point out, I'm not in the mood to see another of those helpless, obviously tortured bodies of a young woman who dared to have contact with me, Rafer, or Logan. Especially not the only cousin who had the good grace and generous heart to reach out to us every damned time she saw us," Crowe snapped. "So you can pretend they're not there and accept it."

Anna stared at him silently for long moments before replying. "Thanks for speaking back all those times." She leaned back in her chair and crossed her arms over her breasts defensively.

"And thank you for not attracting the Slasher's eye and getting yourself killed," he grunted. "Now, if we have the pleasantries out of the way, can we continue this meeting?"

"Crowe, the two of you will never stop sniping long enough to get anything out of the way." Ivan laughed from his position at the side of the table, across from Anna. "Shall I handle this for you, my friend?" he asked, his Russian accent filled with amusement.

He was a handsome man. Not as handsome as Archer, definitely dangerous, and not one to suffer fools easily, she had found.

"Why do you think I need protection?" She turned to Archer. "I know you're behind this, so why don't you explain it? He's not handling it very well." Her nose wrinkled with charming disgust.

At least she wasn't completely refusing to cooperate, Archer thought, amused. It would have been uncomfortable if she had made him appear a liar after he'd said she was entirely reasonable.

"I'm handling this fine," Crowe growled.

"Sure you are," she agreed mockingly, her expression filled with blatant disbelief. "But I think Archer can handle it better."

Crowe's lips thinned.

A second later they twitched as his brown and gold gaze flickered with amusement. "You can tell we're related."

Anna's eyes rolled at the comment. "Really? The way you ignore me, I would have thought differently."

Crowe grunted at the comment. "Because of information that has recently come to light, it's the decision of the owners of Brute Force to ensure your protection.

You will have two agents shadowing you at all times. *Shadowing you*," he emphasized. "You won't tell anyone they're watching you, and they will ensure no one notices them watching you."

If she didn't know better, by his posture, the tone of his voice, and his gaze, she would almost swear he might give a damn if she lived or died, Anna thought.

She knew better, but she let him keep talking.

From the look on Archer's face, as well as the Callahans', she knew arguing would do her no damned good at all. Besides, she didn't have a death wish. She might not like having bodyguards, but it beat being forced to leave Corbin County again just to stay alive.

As he talked, and the others clarified or threw in their own ideas, Anna remained silent and just watched.

She mostly watched Archer and Crowe.

She knew why she was fascinated with Archer, especially now that he'd shown her the pleasure he could give her.

Crowe was just a cousin who had ignored her every time she'd attempted to speak to him. Crowe, Rafer, and Logan. They'd all but disowned her from the moment she'd been born.

Until it appeared she needed them?

She couldn't understand the change in attitude, and she wasn't certain she wanted to understand it.

Crowe's change in demeanor didn't just extend to her, though. It had begun, as she understood it, just after the Slasher had attacked him, his cousin Logan, and Logan's lover, Skye, at Crowe's cabin.

Crowe had been rendered unconscious for several hours before a huge she-wolf burst through a window and chased the assailant off. That wolf had saved not just Crowe's life, but also Logan's, Skye's, and that of Skye's unborn child.

The story behind the animal? Anna wasn't certain. She knew the rumors of it were spreading like wildfire.

Everyone who knew Crowe had commented on the change from hard, bitter, and icy to one of a more thoughtful, if often confrontational, demeanor.

He'd always been slightly mocking, but never too prone to call individuals on their switch between hating Callahans and supporting Callahans as he was known to do now.

After more than twenty years of deliberate cruelties that had been dealt to them, it seemed everyone loved them now that he and his cousins had secured their inheritances.

Especially after helping to establish two new businesses with the potential to be long-running, and rumors of turning the previous Callahan and Ramsey ranches into a resort. The respect was pouring from the fine citizens of Corbin County with such sickening sweetness it was pathetic.

"Is this all agreeable to you, *cousin?*" He emphasized the relationship once again.

"The next time you call me cousin, *cousin*, I suggest you do so without the tone." Leaning forward, she confronted him irately, knowing that even though she wasn't being forced from the County again, her life wasn't yet her own. "I've never treated you with anything but respect, and damn you, Crowe Callahan, you won't treat me any differently."

Tension filled the room for long seconds as his gaze locked with hers, and Anna felt pure determination burning inside her. She'd be damned if she would let him treat her as though she had.

His jaw clenched and his gaze flared with momentary anger before his lips tilted just slightly. A second later a glimmer of amusement sparked in the oddly colored depths of his eyes before he inclined his head in agreement.

"Very well, cousin *Anna,*" he emphasized her name instead. "Are you willing to work within the parameters we've set up?"

"Do I have a choice?" she muttered, sitting back in her chair once again as she breathed out wearily. "Who knew wanting to come home could turn into such a life-or-death decision?"

"It could be worse," Crowe pointed out, bitter pain flashing in his eyes now. "You could be facing the death of every past lover you've had."

She slid a look in Archer's direction.

Hell, she didn't have past lovers, thank God. What she did have was one far-too-stubborn lover who seemed to think he was now responsible for her life as well as her pleasure.

Which would have been okay if love were actually involved on his end, rather than just lust.

Her gaze then turned to Rafer and Logan, both of whom now lived daily with the knowledge that if they made one mistake, blinked too long, or dared to drop their guard for a second, then the women they loved would die.

In Logan's case, his unborn child would die as well.

"I don't know how any of you have borne that pain," she finally said compassionately. "Or how you've borne what this County and your families have done to you and your cousins over the years. It was wrong, Crowe. But there are so many who were not a part of those years who are willing to stand behind you. Who are willing to help you. Don't turn your back on them because of what others did in the past."

His lips pursed for a moment, the roughly handsome

features frighteningly savage for one long moment. "Lectures weren't on my agenda today, nor was anyone's pity. If you don't mind? Now." He turned to the bodyguards. "Thaddock, Stryker, and Owen Brolen are invisible. As for Rory, he's known Archer for several years and he's in town to visit for a while. He's renting the Brocks' garage apartment next to Archer. His morning jog will coincide with your walk to work. He'll get off work next door about the same time you do, and he'll walk you home if Archer isn't available to see you home."

He would never stop resenting her, she feared. And a part of her couldn't blame him. She would have argued it, but at the moment she had a far more imperative battle to fight.

"Why? Why is someone so determined to keep me out of Corbin County? To keep me from associating with the three of you?"

"That's what we're hoping to find out, quickly," Archer assured her, his dark voice sending an unbidden thrill of sensation racing up her spine. "We'll figure it out, Anna, I promise."

Archer always kept his promises. She just hoped the price they paid for the truth was one they could all live with.

CHAPTER 10

"Very well, then." Crowe gave a slow nod of his head as he rose from his seat. "Thaddock and his team will head out and, within hours, at least one will be in place at all times to ensure you're protected. Rory will leave as he came in, unobtrusively."

"In the trunk of Thaddock's car." Rory snickered. "Mine was left in Montrose."

"He'll return this evening and move into the apartment," Crowe finished as he picked up his files. "I'm sure you'll probably have more questions. Archer can answer them. We went over the plan extensively with him before calling you in."

Oh, had they?

Wasn't it rather nice of him to discuss it with her?

She felt as though her life was being taken over again. Controlled again.

Nodding, she waited until they all filed out, then watched as Archer rose from his chair and moved to the door. The click of the lock was loud, causing her head to jerk around as she watched him, her eyes narrowing.

He looked hot as hell.

He was dressed in his customary uniform of jeans and the dun-colored sheriff's shirt, his badge clipped to his belt next to his holstered weapon. Scuffed, well-worn boots covered his feet. His expression was frankly sensual.

"You didn't discuss any of this with me first," she pointed out. "I hate that, Archer."

Surprise had his brows lifting as he stared down at her.

"I assumed you would know I wouldn't leave you unprotected, Anna. Just because you're living with me doesn't ensure you won't be in danger. For some reason, a madman decided you were never to stay long in this County after you turned nine. I want to know why, but I also want to make damned certain you're not hurt in the bargain."

"And you couldn't discuss it with me?" The knot of anger that had been growing inside her began to tear.

Coming to her feet, Anna confronted him, feeling her hands shaking with anger even as her body burned with arousal for him.

She couldn't shake the need for him, even in anger. She couldn't shake years of fantasies and an aching hunger for his touch, no matter how she tried. Even now, in the face of the knowledge that he was making decisions for her, that he wasn't discussing them with her, she couldn't shake that need.

"You're getting angry over nothing." His arms went over his chest as he glared down at her. "You should have known, at some point, a decision like this would have to be made."

"Just as I assumed, at some point, you would discuss it with me first." Placing a hand on her hip she tapped her index finger slowly to hold on to her patience. "I don't like being controlled, Archer, especially by you."

It seemed that no matter how hard she tried, the madder she became with Archer, the more it hurt and the more she ached for him.

"Anna, I wasn't trying to control you—"

"That's exactly what you're doing." Pushing her fingers through her hair, she turned and stalked to the other side of the room before turning back to him. "You had me called in here like a child, and the decisions were made as though my opinion didn't matter. And it should matter. My opinion matters, Archer."

It should have mattered, she told herself. It was her life. Just as it should have mattered to her family. Once she was old enough to hear the truth, she should have been told.

They should have let her come home.

"Controlling you was the last damned thing on my mind," he growled. "When I told Crowe and his cousins about the meeting with the 'Barons,' the subject of your safety became uppermost. It's not as though we were discussing it for weeks, dammit. It was done right here in this fucking room, the decision made thirty minutes before you were called in."

Anna clenched her teeth. Seeing the logic in it didn't help.

Of course she could see how it could have happened, but it shouldn't have happened.

"The minute my name came up in the same sentence with protection, you should have had them send for me," she cried out. "Don't do this to me, Archer. Don't treat me like my family has all my life. Don't take the choice out of my hands, because I won't have it." Before she could stop herself she was striding to him, her hand jerked from her hip, her index finger pressing firmly into his chest with furious demand.

"Not from my family, not from Crowe, and I damned sure won't have it from my lover."

"Exactly, your fucking lover." He jerked her to him.

One hand held her hip, the other wrapping around her back as she found her body suddenly flush with his, her hands pressing against his chest in surprise. "I'm your damned lover, Anna. You are my lover, and don't think for one minute I won't do exactly what it takes to protect you. You want to work? Work. You want to live in Corbin County, Aspen, or Tim-fucking-buktu, then that's your decision if I can't talk you out of it. You want to buy a new car? New shoes? A fucking horse to ride to work? I don't give a damn. But by God, when it comes to making damned sure you're warm and safe, then don't think for one fucking minute I won't do exactly what I have to do to keep you warm and safe."

Shock reverberated through her.

He glared down at her as though what he felt for her might, just might, be more than just lust.

"Next time, discuss it with me first," she demanded furiously, though she could hear the weakness in that demand. And she could feel the hunger for him beginning to race through her bloodstream at the feel of his erection pressing against her lower stomach. "I don't care where or when the discussion comes up. My protection, where I live, when I live, is all my business and I won't be left out of the conversation."

And she really needed that demand to sound more like a demand.

"If you're there." His head lowered, his lips inches from hers. "If whether or not you agree with the decision makes a difference in the decision being made. And as long as it has nothing to do with whether you live or die."

Her nostrils flared. Her lips parted to flay him alive for his arrogance when he suddenly covered them.

Before she could snap her teeth down on his tongue as it pushed past her parted lips, his hand was at her jaw, preventing it. His kiss demanded, moved over her lips and, far too quickly, there was no chance in hell of daring to actually bite his tongue for its demanding invasion.

A moan tore from her despite her attempts to hold it back.

Pleasure began to invade her, the anger-based adrenaline suddenly turning to hunger, to flames of need striking at her clit, her vagina, and racing to her nipples. All the flesh in between began to heat as well, each cell in her body suddenly aching for his touch.

She was hungry for him. It had only been hours since he'd had her, since the hard length of his cock had filled her, possessed her, and she wanted it so desperately now that arguing with him was a thing of the past.

She had no idea what the argument was even about any longer.

A shiver raced up her spine as heat sparked, hot and tempting, spearing straight to her womb as her pussy began to ache, to clench in hungry need.

She'd told herself she wouldn't do this, wouldn't allow it. That she would not let him control any part of her. But he controlled this. The need, the desperation for his touch. He controlled it with such need she was moaning for more.

"I've been dying to fuck you since seeing you in this skirt this morning. If you hadn't run out so fast, I would have had you before you left the house," he breathed out roughly, his hands sliding from her hips to her thighs, bunching the material in his hands, pulling it up far enough that his hands could cup the curves of her ass left bare by the silk of her thong panties.

Slick and hot, her juice gushed from her vagina, the feel of it sliding over the sensitive inner flesh dragging a low moan from her.

Archer's lips covered hers, his tongue licking over the seam of her lips. Pleasure washed over her, through her, as his lips sipped at hers, his tongue licked and stroked, penetrating her lips with a slow, sensual glide.

She could be pissed later, Anna decided. Right now she wanted him, ached for him.

She wanted to fill the loneliness with his touch, the hurt and betrayal that lived inside her with pleasure.

Parting her lips, Anna's tongue peeked out as his licked over the lower curve. Her hands, at first pressed against his shirt, then moved to the buttons holding the material together.

Clumsy, fumbling, Anna struggled with the too-tiny discs until, finally, the last one came free, revealing the hard contours of his chest and the light mat of dark blond curls that tempted her fingers.

Pushing back, Anna stared up at him, and Archer had no idea what was causing his chest to tighten. His body hardened with such feeling that making sense of it was impossible.

"Archer," she whispered, her hands tightening on the material of his shirt, trying to still the trembling he'd glimpsed.

There was a need in her eyes, a hunger he couldn't decipher.

Her lips trembled before she stilled them as well, but she couldn't erase the unconscious plea in her gaze that she had no idea she was showing him.

"Whatever you want, Anna," he told her, his lips

brushing against hers, watching her pupils flare, watching the lust, seeing some deeper, darker emotion he couldn't allow himself to acknowledge in the dark sea-green of her eyes.

Clenching his fingers in the curve of her ass, feeling the muscles beneath his hold, left him fighting the need to take her as fast, as hard as possible.

But it wouldn't be enough, Archer knew. It wouldn't be enough for him, because he could sense what she was silently aching for, feel it in the tightening of his chest though he was unaware of exactly what it was.

"Tell me, Anna," he said. "Tell me what you want, baby. Don't you know I'd give you anything you asked for? If I have it, it's yours."

If he could give it to her without asking, then he would. If he could read the desire raging in her eyes, then he would do whatever he had to, to ensure she had it.

She licked her lips, the sight of her little pink tongue tasting her lips tightening his balls. Her breathing accelerated, her breasts rising and falling beneath the light, silky material of the white sleeveless blouse.

Her gaze turned somber then, a flash of uncertainty sparking deep in the pretty green orbs.

Archer lowered his lips to her ear again, caressing the curve of the delicate shell.

She arched against him, her head tilting to the side to give him greater access to the flesh beneath her ear as he began kissing the soft curve.

"Please, Archer. Take me now. I don't want to wait." She shook her head and he could see the uncertainty, the hesitancy raging inside her.

She could ask him to take her, but whatever need was eating her alive, she wasn't yet comfortable asking for.

"Don't you trust me, Anna?" he whispered, kissing the corner of her lips.

Her lips trembled.

There were no tears in her eyes, but the need was only growing, burning hotter inside her.

"I trust you with my life."

But did she trust him with her dreams?

Lifting his hand, his fingers touched her cheek, his thumb brushing against her lips. "Sweet Anna."

A part of him knew what she wanted. Knew and ached to give it to her.

Burying his face against the curve of her neck, a grimace tightened his expression as he fought to hold back, to at least take her easy.

The knowledge of what she wanted, the knowledge that he couldn't give it to her here, ate at him. What he could give her was the pleasure, though.

There was a hunger in Archer's kiss that Anna hadn't felt before, a need she hadn't known could exist, except in her.

When his lips covered hers, gently—oh God, so gently—his lips moved over hers, rubbing against them, stroking, warming them as sensation mixed with emotion to flare in heated pulses rushing through her.

Wrapping her arms around his neck, Anna's lips parted further as she eagerly accepted the deeper intensity that filled the kiss.

This was what she had needed.

This was what she had ached for.

As Archer's lips devoured hers, his tongue pushing and teasing hers, the hard curve of his knee tucked high between her thighs. The heated warmth against the sensitive flesh of her silk-covered pussy pulled a moan from her lips. It was so good. It was the most incredible kiss she had experienced. Even in her deepest fantasies she hadn't known a kiss that fired her blood, her heart and soul, as well as her pleasure at once.

The slow arch and lift of her hips rubbed the aching bud of her clit against his knee, blindly following the sensations suddenly tearing through her.

Burying her fingers in his hair, Anna licked at his lips as he had hers. Moving into his kiss, a muted cry of pleasure was lost beneath the harsh male groan that rumbled in his chest. The combined sounds of pleasure moved through her senses, multiplying the intensity of her pleasure.

Tightening her thighs on his knee, Anna's fingers slid from his nape, along his neck, then to his chest. Lowering her other hand, instinct and need guiding her actions, Anna was pushing at the material of his shirt, needing to feel his flesh against her own.

As the soft cotton slid over his powerful shoulders, catching on his hard biceps, Archer suddenly moved back from her, jerking the shirt off and letting it fall forgotten to the floor.

Lifting her to the conference table Archer stared down at her, his breathing accelerating at the sight of the short skirt pushed above the silk of her panties as he lifted her knees and moved between them. Gripping her legs he parted them before his hands slid to her hips, drawing them to the edge of the table.

Lying out before him, her long, dark hair spread out above her, her pretty green eyes watching him with slumberous heat, she was the most beautiful thing he'd ever seen in his life.

Moving one hand between their bodies, Archer quickly loosened his belt, flipped open the metal button of his jeans, and eased the zipper over the furious erection pressing against it demandingly.

"Oh, yes!" Need passed her lips as she spread her thighs, her knees lifting to grip his lean flanks.

Quickly rolling the condom he'd pulled from his back pocket onto his cock, Archer bent to her.

"I love fucking you, Anna. Being inside you, feeling the heated grip of your pussy caressing me." He gripped the thick stalk of his cock and he eased the engorged head through the swollen, juice-laden folds of her pussy.

"Oh God, Archer, I love it." A moan parted her lips as the thick crest pressed into the now oversensitive entrance. "It's so good."

"Watch," the hoarsely voiced order had her gaze following his.

Reclined back as she was, her thighs spread wide, Anna could see the hard flesh of his cock parting the intimate lips. The swollen curves hugging the wide crest, her juices clinging to it as he began pressing inside.

The slow, controlled stretch of her delicate inner muscles had pleasure rising rapidly as the fiery pleasure-pain began streaking across her nerve endings.

"Archer." The intensity of the pleasure began to overtake her. "It's so good, Archer."

Moving against her with slow, shallow thrusts, he parted the inner tissue, stretching it in burning increments as sensation began slicing through her senses.

Angling her hips to him, her fingers gripping his arms, Anna watched as, with a final hard thrust, he buried to the hilt inside her.

The heavy pulse of his cock had her knees tightening on his hips as the imperative need to orgasm began racing through her.

Lifting her gaze to his, Anna felt her chest tighten, almost felt the tears that would have filled her eyes.

The look on his face—

Her breath hitched, a whimpering moan filling the air around them as he began to move again, his hips thrusting, dragging his cock nearly free before pushing inside her. He worked the heavy flesh to the hilt, pulled back, then thrust hard and heavy inside her again.

The stroke and caress of the heavily veined shaft and the thick, blunt head had pleasure building violently inside her.

Each sensation rose in intensity as overexcited nerve endings began to burn, to flare. Thrusting harder, faster, his gaze locked on hers, Archer's expression was so tender, so—what?

What was it?

What emotion was whipping between them?

The intensity of it, like the ecstatic pleasure, only strengthened, increased.

"Archer, please." The need, the overwhelming sensations, were pulsing, expanding inside her.

Groaning, perspiration running in rivulets down his chest, along the side of his face, his golden brown eyes seemed more brilliant, more predatory—

"Anna. Sweetheart—" His groan was hoarse, his body tightening as he lifted one hand from her hips to cup her cheek. "Sweet Anna—"

Archer's teeth clenched as Anna cried out, her pussy tightening around his cock as it shuttled back and forth, harder, faster.

Flames erupted inside her.

Electric, pulsing ecstasy exploded like fireworks inside the clenched, pleasure-tortured depths of her vagina.

"Fuck! Baby!" His hand tightened at her cheek, some

battle raging in his expression as she felt his release suddenly tear through his corded body.

"Ah, fuck!" His face tightened, his gaze turning savage. "Anna. Ah, God. Mine!" His hips slammed forward as she felt his cock flex, pulse.

The muscles of her pussy rippled and tightened around him.

"Mine! Damn you, you're mine!"

His lips covered hers.

Possessive, demanding. The kiss marked her soul and stilled the words being torn from his lips.

Caught together in the cataclysm swirling through them, Anna swore she felt a part of herself merge with him. Felt a part of him merge with her.

And for one precious moment out of time, Anna knew what it meant to belong.

Crowe glanced from his office to the hallway, his jaw clenching tighter at the knowledge of what must be going on inside the conference room. It had been all the sheriff could do to keep his hands off Anna while they had been in there during the meeting.

Archer had sat with his fingers curled into fists as he sat back from the table, or flexing his fingers as he obviously kept himself from touching her. The air of tension and sexual connection between them was so damned thick it was all a person could do to stand to be in the room with them.

"Surveillance of the house hasn't been showing much," Rory reported as he watched the monitors they'd connected to the wi-fi cameras positioned outside Archer's house. "You'll be able to tap into these cameras from the ranch, or your cabin as well, but I don't think anyone would hit the house."

"Why?" he asked, still watching the hall.

"Everyone who knows Archer knows he's paranoid about security," Rory answered. "Hell, I had no idea who he was the first two days I was here doing recon and I knew he was paranoid about security. If they dared strike the house, it would be disguised as you, Logan, or Rafer, just as they were when they took Marietta Tyme."

"Are we sure the Slasher will even come after her?"

Were they making a mistake focusing on Anna rather than elsewhere?

"If he's the one that's kept her out of the County since she was nine, then having her back here and working for you and your cousins would enrage him. For whatever reason, he's put a lot of time and effort into keeping her away. He wouldn't let the fact that she was back slip by him."

"What does Jordan think?" he asked, referring to Rory's uncle, a former Navy SEAL.

The rumor that Jordan Malone was also commander of a silent, shadowy mercenary group hadn't been lost on Crowe when he'd heard it ten years before. Jordan was the type to be involved in something that covert, but he was also a man with the knowledge and presence to make it work.

"He agrees. If it's the Slasher, then he won't wait long before he grabs her."

Crowe wiped his hand over his face and glared at the hallway now.

Damn, why was he so fucking pissed off over the fact that Archer was obviously fucking his cousin behind those doors? Just as he couldn't figure out why his protective instincts had gone crazy over the years every time he'd seen Anna Corbin in town. There was something about her that just pissed him off every time he saw her.

"We were always afraid he would focus on her," Crowe growled.

"Maybe Ivan's right," Rory pointed out. "Having her show her faith in you would give more credence to your innocence than anything else could. And it's always been more than obvious she's believed in the three of you."

"Maybe," he murmured, shaking his head at the thought before checking his watch again.

Hell, they'd been in there a half hour. Would they come out already?

He had to leave soon. He had things to do. After Archer had appraised them of the information the Barons had given them the night before, Crowe had known the confrontation with his grandfather was coming.

Thirty-four years of hell because they had wanted to "protect" their grandchildren?

He didn't think so.

Whatever event they had been framed for was the key to this, and he wanted to know what the hell it was.

The door to the conference room opened and Anna and Archer stepped out.

Anna tucked her hair behind one ear, looking up at Archer with somber intensity, a shadow of uncertainty, and all the love a woman could hold in her heart, and Crowe froze inside.

It was always like that. Every time he saw her she did something, said something, that reminded him of his too-delicate mother.

He'd only been twelve when she'd been killed on that mountain, but he remembered her so clearly sometimes that it felt like only yesterday. The sound of her voice, the way she would hold his infant sister and sing so sweetly to her. The same way she would cuddle him when he'd been a child, and tell him how much she loved him.

He'd adored his mother.

She had been the center of his young universe, and losing her, his father, and the baby sister he'd cherished had killed something inside him.

Anna nodded as Archer said something. The sheriff let his hand trail gently down her arm in an intimate caress that assured Crowe the other man was definitely in over his head where Anna was concerned.

He'd have been pissed as hell if anything else were the case.

And he had no idea why.

CHAPTER 11

Watching this bullshit was going to drive him to drink.

Anna should have left Corbin County by now. She should have missed her family, her money, her car, all the little comforts the Corbin money bought her, and done what it took to be back in their good graces.

Instead, she was fucking that sheriff like some cat in heat, and hadn't even bothered to contact her family. And he knew she hadn't bothered to do so. He had enough spies in the Corbin household that he would know if she were in contact with them.

She hadn't called. They hadn't called.

And she hadn't left town.

Watching as she left the new offices of Brute Force, he did nothing to restrain the erection rising beneath his slacks.

He'd warned John Corbin to get her out of town, out of the County, or suffer the consequences. And still she was there.

Those consequences would be visited upon her soon.

As he watched, the newcomer to town stepped from the bar and with a quick grin fell into step with her.

Rory Malone.

The black-haired bastard was from Texas. He'd come in several mornings before and applied at the bar for the position of bartender that was being advertised.

He'd rented the garage apartment the Brocks had advertised near the sheriff's house, and in the past few days had seemed to become quite cozy with Anna. He walked her to work each morning as he went in himself, and walked her home as he was getting off from work.

Archer could have a rival for her affections if he wasn't careful, he thought with amusement. And perhaps, if he was lucky, he could manage to convince his partner to strike out at her for that reason alone.

The thought of his partner left a grim anger sparking at his senses.

The bastard.

The rules he had once found so quaint were now becoming a pain in the ass. Not enough of a pain to get rid of him, of course. Good partners were damned hard to come by in his line of employment.

He couldn't chance her presence in Corbin County much longer, or in the sheriff's bed. The sheriff was much too close to the Callahans, and his knowledge of them was possibly dangerously deep.

The only way she could be allowed to live was if she lived out of the County.

This was what he got for allowing the treacherous weakness he felt for her mother to rule his good sense.

"Please, please don't hurt her," her mother sobbed as she cradled her child to her breasts and knelt next to the body of her dead husband. "Please. Oh God, Wayne, please don't hurt her. She's just a baby. She's just a baby."

"A Callahan baby," he raged, the fury of her betrayal making him sick to his stomach. "She could have been mine, Kimberly. She could have been our child."

How he had loved her. She had been the world to him. And now she sat before him, sobbing for her dead husband and the child they'd had together.

One of the children they'd had together. If her son, that trashy Callahan bastard, had been with them, he would have put a bullet in his head as well.

"Please, Wayne," she continued to sob as the baby whimpered from the cold, her little limbs turning blue from where he'd jerked the blanket from Kimberly as David Callahan's body had collapsed onto the ice and snow. "Please, I'm begging you."

Her head had bowed.

How defeated she looked with her long red hair cascading over her baby's fragile body, her shoulders slumped and all the fight seeping from her body. He wished he hadn't revealed himself. He could have let her live.

Fisting the blanket in his hand for long moments, he finally tossed the thick covering to her.

Her head jerked up, tears still pouring from her incredible green eyes.

God, how he loved her.

"I'll save the girl," he told her. "Your brother's child died this morning in the hospital in California. If he'll return home and take Sarah as that child, then I'll let her live. If he doesn't, she'll die, Kimberly."

He had to harden his voice. He had to harden his soul.

She wrapped the covering snugly around the baby, kissed her forehead.

"Mommy loves you, Sarah Ann," she whispered, the sobs tearing from her soul. "Always remember how Mommy loves you."

The baby whimpered weakly.

Slowly, her arms trembling, she extended the baby out to him.

She was delicate, light.

For a moment he was tempted to toss her over the cliff out of pure hatred.

But the look in Kimberly's eyes stopped him.

She trusted him.

Shock trembled through him. He had just killed her husband, and she knew she was going to die in this blizzard as well, and still she trusted him.

Opening his coat, he tucked the girl against him and rebuttoned it.

As she moved to lie next to her husband, he snarled in fury.

"Move away from him. I won't let you die beside him. I won't let you cuddle to him in death, Kimberly."

She was sobbing. Weak. Cold. The bodies of her brothers and sisters-in-law were scattered around her. Dead.

With each step she took away from her husband she cried harder until she had only the strength to cry, and collapsed in the ice and snow several feet from him.

She stared back at him, her tears falling so fast they were like streams down her face as he leveled the gun at her head.

"I love you," he whispered. "I always loved you, Kimberly. You were to be mine. We could have ruled Corbin County together."

He wasn't even aware the moment he pulled the trigger.

It was a perfect shot straight into her heart.

He didn't put a bullet in her face. He couldn't risk damaging her perfect face.

She crumpled to the ground and, damn her to hell, if she had had a breath left in her he would have killed the brat in front of her for her final betrayal.

As she fell to the ground, her arm reached out, her fingers burying in her husband's all-but-frozen hair.

A howl of rage brought a cry from the baby. A whimpering little sound of distress that struck at his heart. At a heart he swore he could not still possess the day he'd realized how she had betrayed him.

But she was so like his own daughter. So small and fragile. And he did love his own child. His flesh and blood. Amelia wasn't Kimberly's daughter, but she was still his own.

Together they wouldn't find a treasure others could only dream about. Together they wouldn't create their own family. And now, he would never see her smile or know her laughter again.

It wasn't the daughter's fault, it was the son's.

That little bastard. If she hadn't become pregnant with him, then David Callahan could have never convinced her to marry him, Wayne was certain of it.

As he stared at her fallen body, the first teardrop fell.

He'd murdered the Callahans' parents, and even then he'd felt no sorrow. He'd felt none until his precious Kimberly had fallen, her hand reaching out to touch her beloved husband.

Beloved.

She loved him.

The baby girl whimpered at his chest again and his tears only fell faster.

"Kimmy—" he sobbed, and rushed to her.

Holding her daughter to his heart, he lifted her to

*him, cradled her head to him, her daughter cushioned
between them, and he sobbed.*

"Ah, Kimmy. Kimmy, why did you have to take him?
Why? Ah, Kimmy, why?"

*He shed his tears in her silken hair, so like sunlight
and warmth. He sobbed his soul out to her, sobbed his
heart out to her. And there, beneath a blizzard that
later hid the fiery explosion that all but obliterated
the bodies in it, he'd killed the only woman who held
his heart.*

Obliterated his Kimmy.

A tear slid down his cheek. The first tear in twenty-
four years.

Their anniversary was coming soon, just as Anna's
true birthday was coming. That blizzard had rolled
in during September. Anna celebrated her birthday
September tenth. Her true birthday was August twenty-
ninth.

This August, she would die, no more than weeks
away.

He would take her and laugh at her, though inside,
he knew he would shed again each tear he had shed the
night he had taken her mother's life.

He would rape her and watch her cry.

He would slice into her body with his cock and then
with his blade, and his soul would weep.

And he would send her to Heaven to her mother's
arms.

A soft knock at the office door had him turning, a
smile pulling at his lips as his daughter entered.

His flesh and blood.

As fragile as Anna, as delicate, and just as corrupted
by the Callahans.

His Amelia would never forget the night Crowe

Callahan had held her, just as he couldn't sever that invisible bond of brother and sister between Anna and Crowe.

"I found the information you were searching for."

He blinked back at her in shock. "Excuse me?"

She entered the room, all smooth, delicate grace.

She looked as he'd always imagined his daughter with Kimberly would look. His hair, his Kimmy's eyes. Her smooth, creamy complexion with just that hint of freckles over her nose.

She moved across the office, balanced on five-inch heels that made her appear all legs, and laid the file she'd brought in with her on the desk.

"I'm not sure what all of it means." She sighed. "The private investigator I hired in California was rushing out on another job and I was late for my plane." She shook her head.

She was tired.

He'd had her on the road for weeks, since the day before Anna had returned to Corbin County. But she'd tracked down the information he'd sent her after.

"You found him, then?" he queried.

Sitting down in the leather chair in front of his desk she nodded tiredly. "Marcus Duclock is currently residing in San Quentin on a life sentence for the rape and murder of a prostitute. He's been there for over ten years."

"Well, then, we know he had nothing to do with Katy Winslow's murder." He sighed, knowing full well that the bastard hadn't had anything to do with it.

He'd needed Amelia out of town, though. Out of town and away from Anna Corbin.

She was a treasure, his daughter.

He hadn't done well by her, though, he admitted. He'd forced her to drop her final year in college, forced her to relinquish her dream of teaching school and work for him instead.

So he could watch her.

So he could make damned certain she never returned to Crowe Callahan's arms.

He'd had to keep her away from the bastard.

"What should I do now?" She stared back at him intently, sincerity reflecting in her gaze. "It couldn't have been Duclock. Where do we go from here?"

He rubbed his hand along the back of his neck as though he were truly concerned with the subject and he shook his head.

As she laid her head against the back of the chair, her weariness apparent in her expression and the exhausted slump of her body, he decided now was the time to test her loyalty.

"Anna Corbin moved in with the sheriff while you were gone," he told her quietly.

Her eyes opened slowly, derision glittering in them for a moment, before she looked up at the ceiling, once again with a weariness that touched his heart.

"She's determined to get herself killed." She sighed.

"I remember a time when you wanted to be close to Crowe Callahan as well," he stated gently.

"I may not like the method, but I appreciate the effort you made to ensure I took the time to consider the foolishness of that, too," she stated, her gaze thoughtful, regretful. "None of them are worth dying for. And the Slasher's not just killing their lovers now. It's apparently anyone close to them if Katy's death was anything to go by."

"Was Katy close to him?" He hadn't been aware of that.

"Wouldn't she have had to be?" Amelia closed her eyes again, relaxing against her chair as she appeared to be fighting the need for a nap.

Jet lag was always hard on her.

"Archer and I haven't figured out her connection to them yet." He made certain his tone echoed with regret. "That poor child. I've had nightmares over losing you in such a way, Amelia."

She gave a delicate little snort. "I'm not a kid anymore, Dad. And as I said, the means sucked, but I appreciate it more than you know. Even if his lovers weren't being killed off with frightening frequency, he's not exactly the type of man a woman wants to build a future with." She opened her eyes and stared back at him with rueful amusement. "I know you like the Callahans, despite our fights over them when I was younger, but I can see now what I should have seen then."

"And that is?" he asked curiously.

"Crowe Callahan's way too selfish for a woman who wants a family of her own." She smiled softly.

That smile.

It was almost a motherly smile. She'd once sworn to him he would never see grandchildren from her.

"You want a family of your own, now?" he asked, fighting back the hope of a grandchild.

"Yeah, I do." She nodded. "A good husband and a few kids would be nice, Dad. Really nice." She pushed herself slowly to her feet. "I think I'll head home now. Maybe give Anna a call later and see if I can't make her see reason. If I can't, then perhaps it's time to sever that friendship. Losing a friend to the Slasher is more than I want to face."

"I wouldn't go that far, sweetie." He crossed the room, gripped her shoulders, and gave her a gentle kiss on the cheek.

She had stopped stiffening and moving away from him nearly a year before.

"Do you think I should wait?" she asked, clearly torn and asking his opinion. Sincerely wanting his input?

His heart swelled. Could he have been wrong? Could she be worth allowing to live?

"Let's discuss it a bit after you talk to her. Maybe she'll see reason. You always were able to talk to her when no one else could."

Amelia shook her head. "She stopped listening to me when she went to college." She shrugged. "But I'll talk to her. Shall I call you before I meet with her?"

He gave a slow nod. "That would be nice, dearest. You know how I worry."

"And now I understand why." Reaching up, she kissed his cheek before picking up her bags. "I'm going home and going to bed now. Love you, Dad."

"And I love you, baby."

His voice almost thickened.

She was forgiving him.

It had been slow. It hadn't been easy. And the truth was, many things he had done were only to ensure an alibi and lack of suspicion where the Slasher's victims were concerned.

As she left the office, he blinked back his tears.

His precious, sweet little baby.

If only she had been Kimmy's as well.

Anna answered the phone the second the caller ID revealed the name of the caller.

"Amelia Sorenson, it's about time you called me," Anna berated her friend with a laugh. "I've missed the hell out of you."

"As I hear it, you haven't had time to miss anyone." There was a snap to her friend's voice that Anna frowned over. "All shacked up with that sheriff, and playing personal assistant to that cousin of yours."

"Yeah, well, maybe if you had been here we could have discussed it first," Anna snapped back. "Get your ass over here and share a cup of coffee with me. You can yell at me to my face then."

"Would it do any good?" Amelia questioned her, her tone indicating her certainty that it wouldn't.

"You never know." Anna shrugged, a grin touching her lips.

There was nothing the other girl could say to make Anna change her mind, but she was always willing to let Amelia try.

"Hmm, we'll see." Amelia sighed. "You have the coffee on?"

"It will be," Anna promised.

"Is Archer there? Because it would be damned uncomfortable to try to convince you to leave his ass if he were there listening to me," she stated ruefully.

"Archer won't be home until later this evening," Anna promised. "He and his deputy were heading out to one of the farms on the other side of the County. Something about shotgun weddings and the Middle Ages." She laughed.

She knew better.

Archer had left with the deputy to chase down a lead on Elizabeth Haley and her abandoned car. Archer had warned her to keep that information to herself, though, and give the story of the shotgun wedding instead.

The mountains held a diverse set of men and women who didn't always conform to society's rules, and forced weddings after a daughter became pregnant wasn't unheard of. It was actually fairly regular when those young girls forgot birth control.

They didn't happen to just the younger generation, either. Anna knew for a fact such a marriage had taken place several months before between a widow and her former brother-in-law.

"Get that coffee ready," Amelia ordered. "I'll be there by the time the first cup is ready to pour."

"See you then." Anna disconnected the phone before nibbling at her thumbnail and moving to the coffeepot.

She knew Amelia better than she knew anyone, and there had been a tone to her voice that didn't make sense.

The other woman lived in a small house beside her father, several streets north of the city square. Richardson Street was on the more exclusive side of town. There the larger, nicer homes had been built, but that was basically the only difference between it and the rest of Sweetrock.

Most of the blocks were tree-lined with rows of flowers planted here and there. Maintenance was taken care of by those citizens sentenced to community service for whatever legal infraction they had committed.

Anna hadn't imagined she could love living in town as much as she had loved living on her grandfather's ranch, but she was starting to wonder if she didn't enjoy it more.

For a small town, it wasn't boring.

There was always something going on in the city square in the evenings. Alfredo's, the local gas and convenience store, was open all night, and the owner, Bill Alfredo, or the family member working the night shift, rarely shut the grill or pizza oven down.

It was quiet, but it wasn't lonely.

A knock at the back door came just as the coffeemaker beeped its readiness. Crossing the room, Anna opened the door, and the minute Amelia stepped inside she threw her arms around her friend with a happy laugh.

"I have missed you so much." Standing back, she gazed at her friend's exhausted features. "What in hell have you been doing to wear yourself out, Mel?"

"Chasing shadows," Amelia said as she moved to the wide balcony doors that led out to the shaded, hidden patio in the back. "You know, I've never been in Archer's house. I'd heard about the patio, but I've never seen it."

Everyone had heard about his patio. The very fact that it was so completely private made it newsworthy. Everyone wondered what he was doing out there, especially when wood was burning in the small outdoor fireplace.

"Isn't it beautiful?" Anna tilted her head as she watched the dappled sunlight that slipped past the overhead wisteria and ivy that grew across the huge pergola beams. "It's peaceful as hell out there, too. Just listening to the baby birds chirp is enough to put you to sleep. There're several nests in the far side beneath the wisteria and ivy, and they do like to bitch when you're out there."

Amelia turned back to stare around the kitchen as Anna opened the balcony doors.

"I thought we could have our coffee out here." Anna moved to the coffeepot and pulled free one of the trays she'd placed on its side behind it. "Archer and I have our coffee out there before going to work. I love it."

She turned in time to catch the look that crossed Amelia's face.

"Do you disagree with me living with him?" she asked, more curious than upset that her friend disapproved.

"You've lived your life secluded from the world, Anna." Amelia sighed as Anna placed a thermal pot, coffee, cream, and sugar on the tray. "I don't think you should have moved in with anyone if you weren't going to stay with your parents for a while."

Anna tightened her jaw at the slight chastisement in Amelia's tone.

"Yeah, well, I didn't have a lot of choice there." She shrugged. "And I'd prefer not to discuss them, Amelia. They may have been the ones to disown me, but I'll be damned if I'll cry over their decision."

"I don't expect you to cry over it forever," Amelia stated as she followed her to the patio. "But I expected you to be a little regretful."

"Of what?" Anna snapped. "Have you considered the fact that I don't even know who they are anymore? They're the family I visit twice a year, that's it. And it's their fault, not mine."

She wasn't nine any longer. They could have trusted her with the truth. Regardless of what they thought, she wouldn't have betrayed their confidence, even with a friend as close as Amelia.

Setting the tray on a small bistro table in the corner nearest the doors, Anna took her seat on a padded chair and poured them both a cup of the steaming liquid as Amelia took her seat across from her.

"Anna, you don't really feel that way." Amelia watched her with a heavy gaze as Anna spooned creamer and sugar into her cup as she knew her friend liked it.

"Yes, I do, Mel." She breathed out heavily before fixing her own and sipping at it. "I've spent my life begging, crying, threatening—" She shook her head at the memories of the many and varied ways she'd attempted to convince them to let her go home. "I was sick of begging a long time ago."

"Dad said you actually graduated college a year early?" Amelia obviously approved of the coffee, as she held the cup while speaking and sipped from it again.

"Business courses aren't rocket science," she informed her, amused. "What else did I have to do but study? Hell, Amelia, until moving here with Archer, I didn't even remember how to make friends."

And that was the truth. She'd forgotten how to have friends.

"You didn't make friends at college?" Amelia asked, surprised.

Anna shook her head. "I made acquaintances. There's a difference."

And there was. They weren't friends that she would keep up with, visit on vacations, or exchange Christmas cards with.

"But why, Anna?" Amelia shook her head, confused. "I know you had no intentions of living anywhere but your family's ranch, but that has nothing to do with friends. Why not make friends?"

"Because I didn't want to lose touch with someone else I cared about," Anna admitted. "I felt I had lost my family, and in some ways, you changed so much that I had lost you as well. I didn't want to lose anyone else."

Amelia looked away for long moments. "I've been busy," she finally said softly.

"I know that." Anna nodded. "And I was so far away it wasn't as though we could stop for lunch once a month. It wasn't either of our faults, but I just didn't want to make more friends that I might never see again. If you remember, they were trying to ship me off to France, and I didn't know if I was strong enough to stand up to them."

"You sure as hell stood up to them." Amelia breathed

in roughly. "It's just terrifying to me, the cost you could be paying, Anna. Women who associate themselves with Callahans end up dead. And by God, I don't want to have to attend your funeral. It's well known that Archer is their most dedicated friend. As his lover, you'll be seen as associated through Archer. That makes you as much a target as any lover. It's time you leave."

CHAPTER 12

She was tired of being told to leave the one place on earth she wanted to be. She was starting to see exactly how her cousins felt now.

"Their lovers end up dead," she reminded her friend. "I'm not a lover, I'm a cousin and an employee. And Crowe doesn't even acknowledge the fact that I'm a cousin."

"Katy Winslow was not one of their lovers," Amelia argued, leaning forward. Her expression became fierce as the coffee cup clattered to the top of the table. "My God, Anna, women die in this fucking County, and the thought of losing you to that bastard just pisses me the fuck off more than it does that women have died here, period, over this idiocy."

"Katy was connected to them somehow. She had to have been," Anna argued as she placed her cup more carefully on the table.

"Which makes it even worse," Amelia snapped, rubbing her hands over her face wearily. Lowering her arms Amelia gripped the sides of the table with a white-knuckled hold. "Crowe Callahan should have never hired you. Hell, he should have never come back to this County, period. The minute he and his cousins crossed the County line the bloodshed began again. And no, I don't like it one damned bit."

"Then they should have just thrown away everything their parents left them?" Anna frowned back at her, confused. "Amelia, don't you think that's a rather harsh stance to take?"

"It was money. Possessions," Amelia argued. "It wasn't worth the death that's followed them."

"So they should just give up, forget about their homes, their roots, and what's rightfully theirs because someone doesn't want them here and doesn't want them to have what their parents dreamed of giving them?"

She'd never imagined Amelia could be so hard, so judgmental. Sitting back in her chair she stared at the woman she thought she knew.

"I can't believe you feel that way," she said quietly. "I thought you cared for Crowe—"

"When I was a teenager." Amelia's eyes narrowed as anger sparked in the gray depths. "I'm not a teenager."

"And you're not the person you were the last time we visited, either," Anna said carefully, wondering what the hell was going on with her friend. "Or the woman you were when I first met you. That woman would have never believed Crowe and his cousins had no right to their homes."

"Not at the price this County is paying." Amelia slapped her hand on the top of the table, rattling the dishes and shocking Anna with her response. "Go to France, Anna. Go to France, go to California or New York, but get the hell out of Corbin County before you die, too."

Anna rose from her chair slowly. Moving with deliberate control she collected the cups, thermos, sugar, and creamer, and placed them on the tray before carrying them into the kitchen.

Amelia's chair scraped across the stonework of the patio and Anna could feel her following her.

Setting the tray on the counter, she turned to the other woman.

"Anna, listen to me—"

"I want you to leave, Amelia." Anna gripped the counter behind her with desperate fingers, terrified of the anger rising inside her now.

Amelia's eyes narrowed, hiding a response Anna felt she would have preferred to see.

"Anna . . ."

"Leave before I say something I'll regret."

Amelia crossed her arms over her breasts, cocked her hip, and braced one leg to the side. It was her classic confrontation stance.

"I'm not going to lose your friendship because of those damned Callahans," she bit out.

"It's probably already too late to worry about that," Anna assured her, breathing in carefully through her nose, promising herself she wasn't going to lose her temper.

"Because I think they're wrong to come back here? To set up shop and home and pretend as though women aren't dying around them?" Amelia cried out. "God, Anna, do you see how wrong that is?"

"What I see as wrong is the fact that you should decide they should have to give up everything that should have been theirs, every dream they ever had, because some bastard doesn't want them here," Anna all but screamed at her.

There went her temper.

Red blazed through her senses as the building rage began to explode.

"What I see as wrong, Amelia, is the fact that you feel that way, when you above all people know what they've lost. You have no right." She pointed her finger at the other woman furiously. "You have no right, Amelia—"

"It's my friends dying . . ."

"And it's their lovers," Anna yelled. "It's their friends, the women they *would* die for. Do you think leaving would stop it? They left, and that bastard found the lovers they tried to keep hidden. Do you honestly believe anything will stop that son of a bitch, short of fucking killing him, to make him stop torturing those men? And, by God, he sure as hell has no right to force me from Corbin County, or from my goddamned family, and if you can't see that, then no, Amelia, I have no use for you as a friend because you're not the person I thought you were to begin with."

"And what kind of person did you think I was?" A tear fell from Amelia's eye. "The kind of person that would wake up one morning to the news they've found your body, raped and tortured, naked and lifeless, and actually survive it?" Her breathing hitched as more tears fell. "No, Anna, I'm not the person you thought I was, then."

"No, Amelia, I thought you were the type of person that would at least understand why I came home, why I want family that I don't have to beg to be around, and why I want to be with the man I've loved since I was a teenager," she argued fiercely.

"You haven't lived enough to even know what love is."

"Leave, Amelia," Anna yelled. Stalking to the door, she threw it open furiously, not even surprised at the sight of Archer and Crowe as they stared back in surprise from the doorstep. "Get the fuck out, and don't bother worrying. You didn't worry while I was stuck in those damned schools after you left, nor did you bother to fucking come around me unless I defied my family and returned home. And obviously the only reason you did was to convince me to leave, because that was usually the only reason I did go back. So just get the hell out."

Everyone was staring at her as though she had grown two heads and was spitting venom rather than fury.

Turning on her heel she all but ran from the door and raced up the stairs, only barely aware of Oscar slinking from the kitchen and running up with her. He cleared the door into the bedroom only seconds before she gripped it and slammed it closed.

And there, without bothering to run to the bed, she leaned against the wall and slowly slid to the floor, tears finally falling, the sobs finally tearing from her.

The one person she thought would understand was, she was only now realizing, the one who had always convinced her to leave. And she was beginning to wonder, had she been a friend, or merely an instrument her family used to keep her from Corbin County and from her cousin?

And that raised the same question she couldn't stop asking.

Why?

Archer moved slowly into the kitchen, ignoring Amelia for a moment as she turned, obviously crying and attempting to get a hold of herself.

"What the hell happened here?" He turned to her after hearing Crowe come through the door behind him.

Crowe stood to the side of the door, his arms crossed over his chest, his expression dark and foreboding as he glared at the top of Amelia's head.

"Can I borrow your study, Archer?" Crowe asked, never moving his gaze from the young woman.

"Do you intend to get any answers?"

"I do," Crowe said as Amelia turned and moved for the door.

Crowe stopped her. The second he gripped her upper arm she froze, as though something had sucked every iota of energy from her body. "Excuse us, if you will."

He all but dragged Amelia from the kitchen as Archer breathed out roughly, almost regretting the fact that he'd allowed the other man to remove her from his ire.

Anna had been crying. Someone had made his Anna cry, and that just pissed him the fuck off.

Moving to the stairs, he strode up them quickly and within seconds entered the bedroom.

The sight of her against the wall, Oscar cuddled against her side as she covered her face and sobbed, broke his heart.

Hunching down in front of her he grabbed two tissues from the table next to the bed and handed them to her.

Taking them, she held them to her face but the sobs didn't stop.

"Come on, baby," he said softly. "It's just Amelia. You two will make up in a few days and everything will be fine. Right?"

Wasn't that what girlfriends did? They fought, they cried, then they made up.

She shook her head fiercely.

"Come on, it's not like she killed my cat," he tried to joke. "She's your friend."

She shook her head again, though the sobs were easing.

"Anna, talk to me, at least," he urged her. "Tell me what she did. Maybe I can even arrest her for it."

She didn't laugh, and he really needed to see her laugh.

Instead, she blew her nose delicately before lowering the tissues and staring back at him miserably.

"She's like my family," she said tearfully. "She said the Callahans should give up everything they love and have fought for, because of a madman. I should give up everything I love and need, because of some bastard who doesn't want me here," she cried, her voice low now. "But you know, Archer, at least she came here . . ." Her breathing hitched again. "She came. My family couldn't even come to me with the truth. They couldn't trust me. They couldn't love me. They just threw me away to give in to a killer, rather than telling me anything, explaining anything, or even giving me a chance."

The tears were still falling. They were still breaking his heart, and Archer was damned if he knew how to ease the pain he could see shimmering in those pretty green eyes.

It was the pain of betrayal, the pain of desertion and separation, and he had no idea how to fix it.

"You know why . . ." Hell, he had no idea what to say to her. "They love you enough to do without you to keep you safe."

Anger flashed in her eyes again.

Carefully setting Oscar aside, she rose to her feet. Straightening with her, Archer watched as she paced across the room before turning back to him.

"You wanted me before you ever touched me at the weekend social that night, didn't you?" It felt like an accusation.

"You know I did," he said, though he wondered for a second if he should have broken his number one rule where lovers were concerned and lied to her.

"But you wouldn't have done anything about it if I hadn't teased you into touching me that night. I wouldn't be here right now, would I? You wouldn't have tried to contact me or come looking for me, would you, Archer?"

Hell, yes, he should have lied to her.

Rubbing at the back of his neck, he breathed out roughly. "I don't know, Anna," he finally sighed, opting for honesty. "I wanted you, and I wanted you bad. But as long as you weren't here, I could ignore it."

Anna turned away from him.

She could feel the anger burning inside her to such a degree that she felt it would sear her soul to ashes.

Didn't anyone want her?

It didn't make sense.

She wasn't a hateful person, nor was she a complete hag. She didn't think she was someone to be embarrassed over, but maybe she was wrong.

She wanted to scream.

The ache in her stomach was so deep, so spiraling, she could barely stand it. It physically cramped her muscles and had her wanting to reach for her stomach to hold the pain back.

She had to breathe in deep. She had to fight back the same burning anger toward Archer that she'd felt toward Amelia earlier.

She hated losing her temper with Amelia, because as wrong as she had been—and Anna did believe she was wrong—still, Anna knew she had said what she had out of fear and worry.

That didn't mean she deserved an apology, but if

she went off on Archer, then she would definitely be eating crow later, and she so did not like the taste of crow.

She breathed in deep.

"Anna, I've always known you'd come home eventually," he finally said.

But she hadn't been good enough to come looking for.

All those years she'd sat and stared into the darkness, wondering, questioning, trying to make sense of why her own family didn't want her, and she'd never thought to question why Archer hadn't even called to say hello.

"I'm starting to wonder if I shouldn't have just gone to France." She gave a bitter little laugh. "At least someone there wanted me."

It hadn't been her family. It hadn't been those she considered friends.

It had just been a company, but Anna knew the family that owned it and she knew how tight-knit and close that family was. They wouldn't have left her out in the cold after moving there. Hell, all she'd had to do was look out for Jacques' wandering hands and medieval attitude.

Why hadn't she at least tried it? She could have just hit Jacques with a bat or something. He would have kept his hands to himself after that. Right?

Because she wanted to be home.

"Crowe should change his mind about spanking her ass for being such a damned busybody. The little wench doesn't deserve it," Archer growled behind her.

Anna flipped around in shock. "You would have him abuse her? Crowe would actually dare something like that?"

His brow lifted. "Abuse her? I didn't say he should abuse her. I said he should rethink spanking her."

"He wouldn't dare hurt her. And there's no difference between spanking her and abusing her?"

"Of course there is," he assured her mockingly. "One she wouldn't enjoy, one she would definitely enjoy after the initial nervousness."

"You're crazy!" she cried. "No woman enjoys being abused, Archer."

He snorted at that. "Perhaps I'll show you differently one of these days."

"I highly doubt it," she promised him. "I'm moving out of this room. I'll be out of the house come morning. Because I'll be damned if I want to stay someplace else where I wasn't wanted to begin with."

CHAPTER 13

She'd already emptied the dresser of her frilly stuff and thrown her folded jeans to the floor by the chair. She didn't have a lot of clothes with her, just the ones she'd managed to stuff into that bag she stole from her own bedroom and the few things she'd bought from Goodwill.

Son of a bitch, Archer hadn't even been able to convince John Corbin or her parents to pack some of her clothes and bring them to him. And he hadn't been able to make time to take her shopping, either.

He intended to rectify that soon.

Very damned soon.

But first, he had to do something about the pain surging through her, and her belief that she wasn't wanted by anyone in her life that she cared about.

The fact that he was adding to that pain pissed him the fuck off.

Son of a bitch, she had such a tender heart, and such a pure, gentle nature. That tender heart and gentle nature were being tromped on, though. It didn't sit so well with him that he was helping to do it, either.

As bad as he felt about it, he didn't feel bad enough to give in and let her leave him. The minute she was no longer under his protection, then he was terrified she would no longer be safe, either. The bastard was threatening John Corbin nearly nightly, and Archer had received a note or two himself.

He'd ignored them. Just as he ignored the threats Corbin had been given. For whatever reason, they couldn't strike out at Anna yet. But Archer intended to be there when they decided to do it.

He would be there, and he'd kill them.

Staring at her a moment longer, he closed the bedroom door, then propped his hands on his hips and watched as Anna tossed clothes from the closet to the recliner in the corner.

The pretty summer dresses he'd hoped to get to see her in, a few rather short skirts he'd wondered if he could bear to let her out in public in.

Those skirts would have made his dick harder than hell. Just the thought of her wearing those skirts and what it would do for those fine legs made his dick harder than hell.

To get a chance to see her in those skirts, though, he was going to have to keep her safe. And he was going to have to keep her with him.

With him, or with someone he knew who could protect her even better than he and Crowe had arranged to protect her.

The large black suitcase she'd gotten at Goodwill was thrown from the closet next, winging its way several feet past the closet door. That surprised him, considering its size. He wouldn't have expected it to go quite so far.

But enough was enough. She wasn't going anywhere, and he wasn't about to let her fool herself into believing she might actually make it out of the house.

That just didn't seem exactly fair for some reason.

"You're not leaving, Anna. You know damned good and well it's not safe, just as you know the protective measures we have in place aren't going to work near as well if you're living anywhere else. Stop pretending otherwise."

"I wasn't the one pretending!" Outrage and hurt filled her voice, but they also filled her wounded green eyes as she turned back to glare at him with hurt-filled anger.

Son of a bitch, those expressive, sea-green eyes just never failed to make him feel like a bastard or a god among men, whichever mood she happened be in, or however he'd managed to prick her delicate feminine feelings.

Not that he'd ever meant to prick her feelings, but he'd also not known she believed herself to be in love with him.

It had been a crush, he'd always told himself. A schoolgirl's crush, nothing more, and nothing to worry about. She would get over it.

She was moving for the chest now. It was time to put a stop to this crap before she threw out all that silk and lace she called panties and bras.

Striding across the room, he picked up the suitcase, jerked the closet door open, and shoved it back inside amid an outrageous amount of sneakers, sandals, and wicked high heels.

That was the only thing he'd seen her splurge on. That damned yard sale she'd heard of and had to attend the evening before. He swore she'd bought every pair of shoes there that she could wear.

"Twenty damned pairs of shoes might be about eighteen too many, don't you think?" he growled, damned hesitant to broach the war he knew he was getting ready to face.

As John had stated before, she was damned stubborn and too determined whenever she set her mind to something. If she was determined to leave, then the only way to make her stay would be to attempt to make her promise not to leave.

Fat chance, considering the mood she was in now.

Keeping his back to the bed, Archer was determined to keep his gaze away from the very inviting mattress and his thoughts away from what they could be doing there. He didn't need any distractions right now, and letting himself remember the pleasure he could experience with her there would definitely be a distraction.

"It's too damned dangerous for you if I stay," she raged as she jerked the closet door open and pulled the suitcase out again. "And don't worry about my damned shoes. They're about to be the least of your problems."

"They're already the least of my problems," he assured her with a harsh grumble as he grabbed the suitcase out of her hand, shoved it back into the closet, then slammed the door closed.

Turning back to her, Archer placed himself in front of the door before crossing his arms over his chest and glaring down at her.

"Oh, and don't you just look so damned arrogant and commanding," she mocked, but despite the anger, he could see a hint of tears in her eyes.

Damn, he wasn't about to lie to her, period. But right now he almost wished he'd been able to lie to her. To tell her he would have come for her. To tell her he wouldn't have let her stay away much longer. Or would it have been a lie?

"We're going to talk about this, Anna—"

"We're not talking about a damned thing," she informed him furiously. "I don't have to have all my clothes to leave, Archer. I can easily just wear what I have on." She brushed her hand down the front of the T-shirt she'd stolen from him before flipping her fingers toward him contemptuously.

His dick was hardening.

Dammit.

He needed a clear head, not one burning with lust.

"Don't make me tear that shirt off you, Anna," he warned her with the utmost gentleness, determined to remain calm.

"Don't make you tear it off me?" Incredulity filled those wounded green eyes as she stared back at him, as though he were a slug that had crawled out from under a rock.

He felt like a slug, too.

"Who the hell do you think you are to believe you can dictate to me so cavalierly?"

He gave a low snort. "Cavalierly? Honey, don't use that word too often in Sweetrock. Folks might think you're beginning to get a little above your raisin'."

She was going to go ballistic. Anna could feel the rage, pain, and fear growing inside her, and couldn't seem to stem her response to the powerful dominance he was facing her with.

"You can't make me stay here." She was shaking with anger. But at least with the anger she didn't have to face the pain any longer.

"No," he agreed. "But if you make the mistake of stepping out the door I will ask Ivan Resnova to abduct you himself and make damned certain you don't escape until all this is over."

It wasn't a threat. It was a declaration of intent, pure and simple, and Anna recognized it for what it was.

Archer didn't deal in threats. They required effort, he'd once said. No, he simply stated what he would do, then acted accordingly.

In this case, she simply couldn't see it happening, though.

"I highly doubt Mr. Resnova asks how high when you say jump." Her fingers curled into fists as she ached to strike out.

Anywhere.

At anyone.

Oh God, she couldn't bear this.

She had the feeling that if she just disappeared, no one would really miss her.

Sure, her family had tried to protect her over the years. They didn't know her; they had no idea who she was. They wouldn't miss who she was, because they had no idea who she was.

"No, he doesn't ask how high," Archer agreed. "Ivan runs a favor tab, sweetheart. And he believes he owes me for allowing him to continue to butt his nose into my investigations here. Trust me, he would do far more than abduct you if it meant he could continue to do so."

"You honestly believe you can force me into giving in to you, simply because you know some damned Russian hoodlum with more money than good sense?"

"I do." He nodded somberly, sending outrage surging through her. "Leave this house without my express permission, and, before the Slasher has a chance to even consider grabbing you, I'll have Resnova's men come for you. Before you can process the trip, you'll be hidden so deep inside Mother Russia that even Resnova himself couldn't find you without the Slashers' heads on stakes to prove your continued safety. Do we understand each other?"

He wouldn't dare.

Resnova wouldn't dare.

No man had that kind of power to display.

Did they?

"You have no right to do this." She was on the verge of stomping her foot, and that would only piss her off further. "Damn you, Archer, you *can't* do this. It's illegal."

His smile was cold and filled with bitterness. "So are rape and murder, but someone in this County has been getting away with it for more than twelve years. I'll be damned if I'll allow them to add you to their list of victims."

"And to thank you for keeping me alive I'm supposed to just spread my thighs for you and fuck you whenever you please now?" Heat was engulfing her, and it wasn't just from the anger.

His grin was slightly less cool and without the bitterness. "Well, now that you mention it, that would be quite nice of you, Anna," he replied with the utmost seriousness. "It will definitely make the time go by quicker, don't you think?"

Eyes widening, her lips parting in shock, Anna could only stare back at him, certain he wasn't as serious as he sounded.

"I absolutely refuse to deal with you any further," she bit out furiously. Incredulous disbelief filled her. "Go ahead and call your buddy Resnova, Archer, because I'm not staying with you a moment longer."

"Because you believe I had sex with you to draw the Slasher out?" he shot back at her as his eyes narrowed, his entire body tensing. "Anna, you know better than that."

If only that were the reason. She wished she could say

that was the only reason she was pissed. It wasn't. It was the knowledge that, once again, she was pushing herself in somewhere she hadn't been wanted.

Just as she had with her parents.

"Go to hell," she snapped, the ragged, tear-thick sound of her voice another humiliation for her to bear.

She was fighting to keep her eyes dry, to keep from sobbing with the pain and fear she couldn't seem to get a handle on.

"Or is it because I couldn't tell you I was going to come tearing to California or France like some white knight, and declare my undying love?"

Hell, just declaring his undying need would have been nice.

It hurt. It tore a gaping wound into her heart and she had no idea how to repair it.

Anna turned away from him quickly to hide the overwhelming pain from his too-sharp gaze, to keep it to herself before she found herself dying of humili-ation.

She wasn't a child who believed in fairy tales, and she wasn't waiting for Prince Charming to ride in on a white steed. But neither of those were love. And Anna knew she had loved Archer for most of her life. Loved him so much that she had no desire for another man's touch, or another man's kiss.

She'd waited for Archer, and now she wondered if the fairy tale had been believing that Archer was a man who even wanted to be loved.

"Leave me alone." The demand was all she had left. "Just get the hell away from me, Archer."

He could have at least allowed her the chance to run.

Before she could guess his intent, he gripped her arm, swung her around, then pulled her to him.

"The hell I will." One hand buried in her hair, pulling her head back as his head lowered, his nose nearly touching hers, so close she could see the fiery sparks of fury deep in the predatory golden brown gaze now locked with hers. "You gave yourself to me, Anna. There's no turning back. No turning back and no taking it back. Now I'll be damned if I restrain myself from what I know we both want. And I'll be damned if I let you leave."

Anna didn't have a chance to argue. She wasn't even certain she could argue. As Archer's lips pressed against hers heatedly, parting them, his tongue licking inside, Anna fought him and the pleasure. She knew, even as she did so, that she was fighting a losing battle.

Struggling against him, pushing at his shoulders, she struck out at him with her fists, and still her lips parted for him. Her tongue met his, and as he lifted her with his free arm beneath her rear, Anna lifted her knees and gripped his hips tight.

With the hard wedge of his cock centered on her sensitive pussy, Anna couldn't help but move against him. Whimpering with pleasure and rising need she rode the iron-hard erection her body craved, torturing them both with the hunger.

"Not yet," she cried out as he broke the kiss, but then she moved with him eagerly, helping him to dispose of their clothes, stripping, tossing them aside with a hunger that seemed to possess her.

The second they were both naked, his head lowered, lips parting and covering the tight, aching peak of her breast.

"God I love these pretty tits," he groaned, cupping one with each hand, pressing them together, then licking and suckling at each tip until she was certain the pleasure would burn her alive.

He was destroying her with his touch. He always did. There was no way to fight it, no way to resist it.

It was so good. The pleasure-and-pain sensations were impossible to resist. They kept her on such a sharp edge she couldn't fight them.

She didn't want to fight them.

"I won't let you go. Did you really think I would?" he growled.

She needed him far too much to deny him now. She would figure the rest of it out later. Right now, all she wanted was his possession and the release she could only find in his arms.

"Don't make me wait, please, Archer," she cried out, the melting ache in the depths of her vagina demanding the hard thrusts of his cock.

"Don't make you wait?" he growled. "Don't make you wait for what? For me to fuck you until we're both dying of pleasure? For the release you know you'll only find in my arms? Oh, baby, don't worry, I'm all yours now."

He was all hers for this moment. His tomorrows weren't hers, but she was more than willing to give him all her tomorrows. And even amidst the blinding pleasure, she could feel the anger from that knowledge.

"Damn you, Archer, fuck me now. Fuck me like you mean it."

"Oh, baby, I already mean it; every stroke, every cry I pull from your pretty lips, I mean every bit of it."

And just as he had before, he pushed her to her stomach on the bed.

It was almost déjà vu as his hard hands gripped her hips and pulled her to her knees. With one hard knee he pressed her legs further apart before moving in be-

hind her, his harder, stronger body completely dominating hers.

Anna couldn't hold back her muted cry of sensual
surrender as she felt the head of his cock press against
the clenched entrance of her pussy. Her juices spilled
from her inner flesh, slickening it, easing his way before gathering in the swollen folds and torturing the
swollen bud of her clit.

"Archer." Her fingers dug into the blankets beneath
her as his hips pressed and rolled, impaling her flesh.
The rubbing, stroking motion of the head of his cock
stimulated naked, excited nerve endings to a fever
pitch of pleasure as he came over her.

Bracing his weight on one powerful arm, his hand
planted on the mattress next to hers, Anna felt Archer's heated breaths next to her ear.

"Damn, I already love fucking you," he groaned.
"Feeling your tight little pussy all wet and hot, clenched
around my dick, has to be the most exciting pleasure
I've ever known."

His voice was strained, tight, and filled with the
audible proof of that pleasure as he slowly worked
his cock inside her. Moving in and out, burying it to
the hilt before pulling back and surging inside once
again.

Thick and iron-hard, his erection caressed pinpoints so violently sensitive that her orgasm was only
a breath away. She could feel the need for it burning through her, her hunger for it building with every
second.

"Does it feel good, baby?" he groaned at her ear as
his powerful hips began moving stronger, harder. Each
stroke sent a burst of fiery pleasure radiating through
her. She felt locked in a sensual swirl of such brilliant

sensation that nothing mattered but pleasure and the drive to orgasm.

"Tell me you're not leaving," he demanded, his voice hoarse, his own pleasure building.

Anna was so lost in the ecstasy racing through her that she couldn't fight, she couldn't deny him, no matter what he wanted.

"Promise me, Anna."

"Please don't—"

"Promise me." He surged inside her hard, his cock stretching her, burning her with pleasure. "Promise you won't leave, Anna."

"I won't leave," she cried out, knowing even as she said it, she lied. "I won't leave, Archer. Please—"

Pulling back, his hard body tight, powerful as his hands gripped her hips, holding her steady as he let loose the hunger tearing through both of them.

Control was a thing of the past. Anna couldn't help but lose herself in his touch, and if he hadn't lost himself in her touch, then he was doing a damned good impression of it.

With each hard, heavy stroke he pushed her higher, sent the fires burning hotter, harder. Anna cried out his name, begged, fought for release until it took her with a strength and overwhelming rapture she was afraid marked her soul.

Behind her, Archer fucked her through her release, thrusting and surging inside her until at the last second he pulled free of her. The feel of his seed spilling onto her rear, his groan, then the feel of his body coming down beside her as he pulled her against him had her sighing in aching regret.

She had lied to him, and she knew it. Anna had never made a promise that she hadn't kept. She was careful with her promises, stingy with them her grandfather often said. But Archer had used her pleasure against her. He had forced that promise from her, and a forced promise didn't count.

Did it?

CHAPTER 14

She should leave.

And how very ironic that was considering she'd dreamed of sharing Archer's bed and his life for so many years.

Anna told herself countless times over the next five days that leaving was the best thing she could do. While she was at work dealing with Crowe's snide remarks. Each evening when Archer arrived home and watched her with that suddenly cool stare of his.

Each night when they went to bed, silently, and he rolled over and went to sleep, it was the last thing she told herself as she finally drifted off, often hours later.

But each morning she awoke in his arms, never certain how she found herself there. His arms would be wrapped around her, his face buried in her hair, and then he would act as though it had never happened, get up, shower and go to work.

That Friday, as she left the office, then paused at the entrance of the tavern, waiting on Rory, she was still debating what she should do, what she shouldn't do.

He wasn't having her move to the guest room. Each

time she had mentioned it after the first attempt, the look he gave her had her tightening her lips and quickly moving away from him.

She was not going to let it be said she made the first move to fix whatever the hell was going on between them.

"Rory has to work late." It was Archer who stepped from the bar, rather than Rory. "He'll see you in the morning."

Anna was surprised to see Archer; she stared back at him in surprise as he paused in front of her.

"I'm sure I could have walked back alone," she assured him. "You didn't have to take off work."

"I didn't," he growled.

Tucking her hands into the shallow pockets of the gray pencil skirt she wore that day, she considered debating her Archer problem again, now that he was reminding her why she was still debating it.

"How did you manage to get off early, then?" she asked as he shortened his stride to match hers.

"Schedule was made out last month," he answered, his voice short. "I should be off until Monday unless something happens."

"Unless the Slasher comes out again," she guessed.

"Or Caine needs help." He shrugged. "This isn't exactly a nine-to-five job."

Anna nodded. He didn't seem much in the mood to talk, so she wasn't going to push it. It would have been better, though, if the silences between them didn't feel so comfortable, despite the fact that she was mad enough to scream at him.

"How the hell do you walk in those shoes?" he asked as they passed a narrow alley entryway and moved along Main Street, crossing in front of the stone courthouse

as she glanced down at the light pink four-inch heels
that matched the light sleeveless blouse she wore beneath a gray sweater.

"Practice." Glancing up at him again, she nearly
stumbled at the look of pure lust that flashed on his
face. Just as quickly, it was gone. And Anna couldn't
help herself but push. "I started wearing heels when I
was twelve."

Surprise glittered in his eyes for a moment. "Isn't
that kind of young?"

She shrugged.

"Not in California," she assured him, remembering
Jaci Fielding and how she had taught Anna to wear the
shoes. "All the girls wore heels at Tennenbaum's Es-
tablishment of Higher Education." She almost snickered at the name. "It was very exclusive. Every girl
there but me, I believe, had been arrested at least once,
done drugs at least once, and everyone I talked to
claimed to have had sex. At least once."

"At twelve?" He glanced at her in disbelief.

Anna sobered, frowning at the memory of the girls
who were much older than their ages. "They were all
very worldly. I had my first drink there, on my first
night in the dorm. I had my first hit of pot there."

"At twelve?" he repeated, more than shocked now.

"I didn't inhale," she promised with false sincerity.

"Hell, and here I thought I was wild as a kid." He
could only shake his head at her. "How did you handle
it, Anna?" He breathed out roughly.

For a moment, the distance that had grown between
them for the past days had disappeared.

"I cried every night I was there," she sighed, feeling
his hand settle lightly at the small of her back as they
walked. "I would call my parents for weeks on end

and beg them to let me come home. I was always begging to come home and they were always refusing."

"Until you stopped," he guessed, his voice quiet then.

Anna nodded. "Until I stopped. It was my fourteenth birthday. I'd spent every birthday alone since I turned ten. They forgot to call that night. . . ."

"Damn," he muttered. "I never knew Robert to be so fucking cruel."

"Oh, he wasn't cruel, and you know it," she assured him. "Just forgetful sometimes. And I hadn't been home on my birthday since I was nine. It was the first time they forgot."

"But it wasn't the last, was it?"

Crossing Second Street, they passed a café and took the shortcut through a narrow alleyway to Third and Corbin Streets.

"No, it wasn't the last time," she agreed. "A few days before, a few days after. A couple of times, it was like three weeks before my birthday."

His fingers rubbed at the small of her back consolingly.

"I'm sorry."

Anna shook her head, a mirthless grin tilting her lips. "I've been thinking about it a lot the last few days. I told Amelia I didn't make friends, but I did. A few. Not the kind of friends you exchange cards and stuff with, but if I called, I think they would talk to me."

"I have no doubt they would, Anna," he sighed. "But you were meant to have friends. You're too open and generous. I have no doubt you have more friends than you know."

"Well, little Callie Brock next door seems to like me okay," she admitted with a grin. "But I think she just wants an invite to the patio. Everyone is way too curious about that hidden patio, Archer."

She glanced up at him in time to catch his smirk.

"Dad always thought it was funny as hell. The woods border the back of the house, the street on the side of the patio. It kills everyone that they can't see in there."

They paused at the corner across from his home.

It was beautiful. Red brick, two stories, with a four-foot privacy fence around the front yard, an eight-foot fence around the small backyard, and the patio at the back corner on the street side. A heavy rock wall about six feet from the sidewalk was overgrown with ivy and wisteria in bloom. The heavy purple blooms sent a light fragrance through the air of the patio, while trailing clematis, pink and white roses, and lilac bushes and lavender plants sent a sultry scent through the air where they hid the rock wall.

Many of the homes were bordered by stone or tall wood privacy fences in Sweetrock. The people in the small town seemed to love their privacy, even as they loved living within the city limits.

"Ready?" There was a hint of amusement in his tone as he urged her across the street.

Anna stepped from the curb, following his lead as they moved across the all-but-deserted street.

It was still early in the day. Most of the small homes were empty, with only a few older couples sitting on their porches to enjoy the cool, late summer day.

Peace seemed to fill the air until it was suddenly shattered by the scream of tires and the sound of a vehicle gathering speed.

"Fuck!"

Archer's curse split the air before Anna found herself picked from her feet as he raced the last few feet across the street, only inches from a wicked black pickup that had shot from its parked position. And that wasn't bad enough. As it shot past them, the sound of gunfire splitting the once peaceful setting assured Anna the driver wasn't playing around.

Archer dove for the ground, covering her body with his as more shots rang out, the pelting bullets hitting the vehicle he dragged her behind, tearing through her senses as she felt the fiery wash of pain at her thigh.

She'd been hit.

It was a distant realization as she heard Archer shouting something into the radio he kept clipped at his shoulder or at his belt whenever he left the house.

He was shouting orders, giving a plate number, and screaming at someone to get the fuck to the house. Even as he was screaming, the second the truck rounded a curve that would have put them in sight of the shooter again, he was moving.

More gunfire rang out, everything happening so fast, yet in such slow motion that Anna found herself unable to process everything going on.

Lifted against him again, as the pain that tore through her thigh nearly stole her consciousness, she found herself rushed along the side of the house and through the gate of the fence. A second later she was all but tossed into the house as Archer slammed the door behind them.

"Stay put!" he ordered as she collapsed on the kitchen floor. "I have to check the house."

A gun was shoved into her hand and Archer's face suddenly filled her vision. "If anyone comes through that door, you shoot first and I'll ask the questions later. And by God, you shoot to kill."

In the next heartbeat he was racing through the house.

The sound of doors slamming was only a distant awareness of his progress through the house. As she sat on the cool tile of the floor, Oscar slinked from where he hid, moved to her side, and butted his head against her arm for attention.

Glancing down at him, she followed his gaze to the sight of the red stain slowly spreading along the creamy stone floor.

It was her blood.

Her skirt was torn at the side. Shock was obviously keeping her from screaming in agony, she thought.

"All clear!" Archer was yelling as he moved for the kitchen once again.

Anna watched the cat.

Delicately, as though not entirely certain of the slowly, slowly spreading stain, he reached out one huge paw and batted at the thick dampness as Archer suddenly came to a stop, no more than a few feet from her.

He felt poleaxed. Almost unable to function.

"Ambulance," he snapped into the radio at his shoulder. "Now, Caine. Now, goddamm it, get an ambulance here now—Anna—"

She lifted her gaze as he suddenly knelt at her side, pushing the cat away. There was a handful of towels or clothes in his hands.

Where had they come from? she wondered.

Archer could feel the breath suspending in his lungs, the effort to breathe hard as he stared at the blood-soaked material of her skirt.

Ah God, her thigh was so delicate and small, and there was so much blood.

The sound of sirens blaring barely registered in his head.

"I think maybe it just grazed me," she said, slowly feeling the pain as it began to radiate through her leg. "It's going to hurt like a bitch, huh?"

"You're in shock, baby." He was suddenly ripping her skirt up the side and pressing the towels to the outside of her thigh. "You're right, it's just grazed it."

The ragged tear in her flesh had him seeing red. The knowledge of the scar it would leave was like a red flag in an enraged bull's face.

Whatever ammo the bastard had used, had it actually penetrated her flesh, would have shattered bone.

"Archer, we're coming in," Crowe yelled from outside the kitchen. "Don't shoot, man. EMTs are with me."

The kitchen door was pushed opened hurriedly.

Dr. Krista Mayan was suddenly at his side, shooing at him, trying to push him out of the way as Anna's fingers tightened on his wrist to hold him to her.

"I'm right here, baby," he promised, moving behind her instead, holding her to him.

His arms tightened around her as she suddenly whimpered when the doctor began to check the wound.

"I get a doctor instead of an EMT," Anna suddenly quipped, her voice thick with tears and pain as the doctor's competent hands quickly checked the torn flesh. Krista Mayan. She'd forgotten the doctor's mother once worked at the Corbin ranch.

"You got it, girlfriend." Krista flashed her a quick smile. "And a nice comfy ride to the clinic so we can stitch up this bad boy. I'll put a call in to Aspen and have a good friend of mine flown right in. He's a plastic surgeon and treats trauma wounds for a living. We might get lucky and not even have a scar."

"Oh yeah." Her voice was thready and weak. "How did I rate that?"

"Because he really likes me, and I really like you," Krista assured her with a quick smile. "Now I'm going to give you something for the pain here, and it's going to make you a little sleepy."

Archer watched as a needle pierced Anna's arm, and the doctor injected the liquid she'd quickly pulled into the needle.

"It doesn't hurt real bad yet, Krista," Anna assured her.

"It's shock, hon. The shot will help us there, too." The doctor's concerned gray eyes shot to Archer. "Let her go to sleep if she can." She turned to the door. "Get that gurney in here. Let's move it."

Archer moved aside only long enough to allow the EMTs with the doctor to lift Anna to the gurney and strap her in.

"Bullet's in there," Krista said hurriedly. "It's an explosive round, Archer, and it's not gone off. I can see the head of it, but I don't dare touch it. Keep her calm and still. I'm radioing Aspen now."

Behind him, Crowe muttered a curse so vile that even Archer flinched.

"Motherfucker's dead, Archer." Crowe eased to him, danger and death surrounding him like a cloak. "Let me find him, because I'll kill him with my bare hands."

"You'll have to beat me to him, Crowe. Only if you beat me to him."

Waiting took years off his life.

Anna was rushed into surgery the second the ambulance pulled into the emergency entrance, and within thirty minutes the helicopter landing on the roof delivered three surgeons and two trauma-room nurses from Aspen.

Archer paced the hall outside the operating room, terrified he'd hear the explosive retort of that fucking bullet going off at any second.

If it did, she would lose her leg, and only God knew

what other damage it would do. It was lodged in her upper thigh, to the side, in a perfect position to take out her spleen or her abdomen if the second projectile inside it went the wrong way.

Pacing the hall with him were Crowe; Logan and his fiancée, Skye; Rafer and his fiancée, Cami; and surprisingly, Anna's parents and grandparents.

They'd arrived by helicopter themselves, before the doctors had even arrived.

Crowe ignored them. He was good at that.

As he paced away from the doors of the operating room again, the elevator doors slid open at the opposite end of the hall, revealing Wayne Sorenson and his daughter, Amelia.

"Archer." Amelia rushed from the elevator and moved quickly to him. "Have you heard anything?"

Archer shook his head, clasping Wayne's hand as the other man approached him.

"Rumor's running crazy around town," Wayne muttered. "Is it true she has an explosive-burst bullet in her thigh?"

Archer nodded tightly. "She's with three trauma surgeons now who are experienced in removing the ammo. Evidently it's been used several times in Aspen in the past few months. A theft from Peterson Air Force Base last spring."

"Hell." Wayne rubbed at the back of his neck as Amelia covered her trembling lips with one hand.

"I begged her to leave," she said, shaking her head slowly as her father wrapped his arm around her shoulders and pulled her to his side. "She was so angry at me, Archer."

Tears welled in her eyes before she blinked them back quickly.

Archer was damned if he knew what to say.

Thankfully, he was saved from reply as Dr. Mayan moved quickly from the operating room.

Her surgical greens were unstained, other than the line of sweat at the edge of the hair covering, and a smile curved at her Cupid's-bow lips.

Archer turned fully to her. "She's okay?"

Relief was already tearing through him.

"Excellent," the doctor assured him. "The ammo was a real dud, literally. She has some stitches, but the surgeon did an excellent job. She shouldn't have more than a thin scar, which will disappear over time." She squeezed Archer's arm firmly. "Our girl was damned lucky, Archer."

"Our" girl. Mayan hadn't seen Anna but a few times over the years, yet, like everyone else Anna met, the doctor was protective of her.

From the corner of his eye he watched as the Corbins slowly eased back, then turned and left the waiting area entirely. Bastards. He was definitely going to have a talk with Robert.

"When can I see her?" he asked.

Krista frowned, and turned to where the Corbins once stood. "Well, I was going to let the family see her first," she sighed. "But since they've left—" She turned back to him, smiling softly as she patted his arm in understanding. "Come on, then. They should be moving her from recovery now. She's actually been out of surgery for a while now, but I wanted to stay with her until she came out of the anesthesia. She was asking for you before I left the room."

She was asking for him rather than her family?

The knowledge of that had his chest tightening, emotion swirling to the surface that he didn't dare contemplate. Emotions he didn't want to look into or decipher just yet.

"Caine." He turned to the deputy who was entering the waiting room. "I want you at the house. Go over it completely. Someone was at the door to the study. Nash found ammo casings from the shootings; get his report and see what he's found."

"On it, Sheriff," Caine promised. "When you've left the hospital, get hold of me."

Archer nodded and turned to the doctor without daring to pause. He'd seen the message in the deputy's eyes and, whatever the other man had to tell him, he didn't want to say anything in front of witnesses. And Archer didn't want Sorenson or his daughter to suspect if there was information incoming.

Whoever had shot at Anna meant business, and he was damned if he would underestimate them again.

Four hours later

Wayne entered the back door under cover of night, the woods behind the house sheltering his arrival.

"Have you seen anything?" he asked the man who turned from the living room window to watch him solemnly.

"Nothing. If anyone's watching her, then they didn't come out when I fired on her or after I returned."

Wayne nodded slowly. "Excellent. All we have to worry about is Archer and his deputies now. I wondered if Crowe cared enough to place a protective detail on her. It's nice to see he doesn't."

Satisfaction built inside him, as did anticipation. "If she hasn't left within the next week, take her, however you have to. Just make sure you're not caught or identified."

He nodded carefully. Every movement he made was always done carefully, deliberately.

"Your daughter returned, I see," the other man stated. "Why not see if she can get her very good friend to visit? It would ensure taking her without being caught.

"Make damned sure Amelia isn't harmed when you take her."

"She won't be harmed, nor will she be able to identify me," he promised. "If she hasn't made plans to leave, then I'll take her that night."

Wayne was a fool, Amory thought.

He was playing fast and loose with the rules, and actually believed that by making a move on Anna Corbin, he could make it appear as though someone else were trying to kill her.

Someone besides the Slasher.

He wasn't fooling anyone.

It didn't matter when the FBI came in, before or after Anna Corbin died. And it wouldn't matter when the state police took over the investigation. It would still have the same results.

Both their deaths.

Thankfully, he had only a week left in town himself. He'd take Ms. Corbin, and he'd ensure Wayne was revealed in the process.

Revealing himself wouldn't be a problem.

Amory Wyatt didn't really exist anyway.

"Do you think she really loves me as she seems to, Amory?" Wayne asked him then, his voice reflective. "She doesn't seem to hate me, does she?"

His daughter hated him more than anything on the face of this earth. Even as they spoke, she was attempting to find some hint of proof to tie him to the Slasher's reign of blood. Amory could see it in her eyes and her actions each time he saw her slipping into Wayne's office after he left or the house.

Amelia Sorenson was no one's fool. But there was no

proof for her to find in that office, where she was currently going through files and desk drawers. No, the proof was in a very well hidden cabin in the mountains. A location her friend, Anna Corbin, would know soon enough.

"I do," he lied to the other man. "I believe she sees a father whose only goal in life is her protection, and I believe she loves you as any child should."

As any child should love the father who she knows is a monster. An unprincipled, evil creature whose only true hunger is for blood and pain.

Sorenson nodded, a sickening smile of thankfulness about his lips.

No creature such as Sorenson should ever believe himself deserving of love, let alone feel thankful that it might be his.

"She's a good girl," Wayne stated softly. "Perhaps once Anna is gone, one way or the other, I'll reward her for her loyalty."

Amory nodded absently as he turned back to the window to ensure that Crowe Callahan's agents were still well hidden. Too bad they hadn't seen the other man slip into the back of his house.

"She would make you an excellent wife, Amory," Wayne stated then. "We could find my inheritance together. The captain's treasure is just awaiting us, my friend. Enough gold and jewels to finance several generations. Your children's children would be rich."

Amory turned back to him slowly, tilting his head thoughtfully as he watched the other man.

"You'd allow me to court her?" he asked, pretending interest.

"If you want her, then I insist upon it." Wayne nodded. "You'd make a much better son-in-law than any other man I know."

"Thank you." Amory smiled back at him as though pleased. "I'd like that. I'd like that very much."

Fortunately for him, he was already married.

Married, with his own children and wife far away.

Far, far away.

And soon to return to.

Midnight, Archer's study

The meeting had been put off twice.

Entering the study, Archer glanced at the man awaiting him, but he had to admit, the man who had accompanied was unexpected.

"Ryan, what's going on?" he asked, watching Ryan Calvert, the fourth of the Callahan brothers, who had been believed to have died at three months of age from a fever.

He hadn't died. His mother, Eileen Callahan, had sold him to a wealthy couple out of Boston for enough money to save her husband and her ranch.

Now, at forty years of age, the adopted son of a renowned Boston surgeon and his socialite wife, the other man amused himself with the covert lifestyle he'd learned in the CIA.

A covert lifestyle that had been focused on finding the identity of the man, or men, called the Slasher for the past twelve years.

The other man, Deputy John Caine, was another story.

"I asked what the fuck was going on here?" Archer repeated himself, anger brewing in his tone as well as his senses.

"Sorry, Sheriff," John muttered as he turned fully from the map of the Slasher's kills. "We had to be damned sure we could trust you before I revealed who I was and why I was here."

"Who you are?" Archer leaned against the edge of his desk, crossing his arms over his chest and glaring back at the younger man.

"It was my order, Archer," Ryan told him. "When I found John, he was packing for Corbin County. I had his identity changed and used my contacts to build his history. And I ordered that he hold the truth back from you when he would have told you."

"Why?" Archer growled.

"Because you're too close to the man we've been investigating," John answered. "Ryan and I both wanted to be certain, as close as you were to him, that you wouldn't reveal what we told you."

"Who the hell is he?"

Archer could feel the fury really beginning to build in him now.

First he'd get the name, then he'd teach Ryan and John both the error of keeping such vital information away from him.

"You can't go after him, Archer." Ryan rose slowly to his feet.

"Do you want me to kill you instead?" Archer asked carefully.

"I guess you'll have to," John sighed. "You'll give me your word you'll help us continue the investigation without revealing what you know, or we'll walk out of here. And if we do, then we may never find his partner until he actually ends up killing again."

"Then you haven't identified both men?"

All he needed was one of their identities; he could beat the truth about his partner out of him.

"We haven't yet," Ryan agreed, his deep blue eyes

somber. "Come on, Archer. You're an officer of the law. You know how important the proof is. Give me your word. I won't play games, and without it, I'm going to walk out of here in about ten seconds flat."

Archer turned to John.

"I can't, Archer." John obviously read the determination in his eyes. "I'll leave the County first."

Was he willing to let it walk away?

"You have my word," he snarled. "But you'll damned well get out of my way once we find him."

"You'll get there first or stand in line," John bit out furiously then. "Let me tell you why I'm here. I walked into my mother's home four years ago and found her tortured, raped, and murdered. The MO was the same as the Slasher's. Exactly the same. Except I knew the only fucker searching for her and it wasn't a serial killer, and she sure as hell wasn't a Callahan's lover. My sister lay in her bedroom—my fucking teenage sister—all but dead. As far as he knows, she is dead. He's already struck at my family and, by God, I will have my piece of him first."

For the first time since he'd known him, the cool demeanor and cynical mockery were wiped away, replaced by a rage that Archer knew well.

"Who is he? I gave you my promise," he snarled.

"My biological father." John's voice was guttural, burning with such fury that Ryan flinched. "The son of a bitch that fathered me and hunted my mother like a fucking animal in his efforts to find me. Wayne Sorenson."

It was a damned good thing he was sitting.

Archer stared at the deputy in shock.

Not because he'd named Sorenson as a suspect. Archer had a file on him as well. It wasn't knowing the County attorney was a killer, it was knowing John was his biological son.

"He caught up with her in Canada, just after we returned from France with my stepfather and half sister." John's tone was ragged and edged with pain. "She'd changed her name, but somehow he'd managed to find it. My stepfather and I were arranging for a private flight back to France when he found her and my sister. She didn't survive it. My stepfather barely survived it."

"Hell!" Raking his fingers through his hair, Archer turned and moved behind his desk.

Once there, he picked up the side and moved it back to reveal the safe hidden beneath it. Pulling the door back, he quickly keyed in the digital code, opened the steel door, and pulled a file free.

Leaving the safe open he moved to the front of the desk and handed the file to Ryan.

"It details the last twelve years of the investigation," he told the two men as the deputy stood beside the other man, leafing through it. "Everyone he associates with and their backgrounds as well. If I could tie him to just one person, if I could find so much as a hint of suspicion that they could be his partner, then I'd have enough to convince the governor to issue a sealed search warrant."

"You don't have several men in here that we've seen sneaking into his home," Ryan said quietly. "Benson Markle, Tiberius Graeme, and Amory Wyatt. I've run all three of them, and there are gaps in their lives that can't be accounted for. Graeme was actually missing for days after four of the girls were kidnapped twelve years ago. Markle was missing during the last three. Neither Amory nor Graeme even existed before they came here, but I've had several hints from some of my overseas sources that Wyatt may be National Security and could, or could not be, on a case."

"Amory lives several houses down from me," Archer mused. "I've not seen him do more than basically say hello or good-bye to Sorenson. Markle is just a bastard. I've had him under investigation for the past six years for other things, though I've never seen him with Sorenson, or Graeme—" His lips pursed thoughtfully. "It's not Graeme, I'd bet on it."

"Why's that?" Ryan stared back at him intently.

"Graeme's in the Witness Protection Program," he revealed. "What he was, or might be into now, I don't know for sure, but I know the Marshal that oversees his case has had him out of the County giving depositions somewhere each time he's been missing."

Ryan nodded. His hair, a darker blond than Archer's, fell over his brow before he pushed it back.

"That leaves Markle and Wyatt," he stated. "What do you think about those two?"

"It could be either of them," Archer admitted. "Markle is as cold as a blizzard. He puts fucking ice to shame. He attends the socials, but he hides and watches from the grottos rather than joining in. Wyatt's quiet, keeps to himself, and as far as I know he's never had so much as an argument with anyone. But, like you said, before coming here, he didn't exist."

"If you had to pick, which one would you say it is?" Ryan asked.

"If I had to pick, Markle," Archer answered after a moment's thought. "Amory Wyatt's a friend of the Corbin family. He and Anna's father go hunting a lot together, and he's made himself a part of the community. Markle, on the other hand—" Archer shook his head. "I could see him killing without mercy."

"I'm meeting with my nephews in a few days' time," Ryan sighed. "And I'll tell you now what I'll be telling them. Earlier this summer, in my cover as an assassin, I accepted a job in Corbin County. I met with the buyer in a cabin in the mountains. He wanted the Callahans, their lovers, and anyone with so much as a chance of having conceived one of their children, dead."

"Did you ID him?" Archer felt the fingers of one hand curling into a fist.

He nodded. "It was Dave Stone."

"The fucking realtor?" Archer questioned in disbelief. "What the hell does he have to do with this? Besides, he moved just last week. Went to stay with his daughter in California."

Ryan shook his head. "He's being detained in California. The story that he was moving was put in place by the FBI. Evidently he was besotted with Crowe's mother before she married David Callahan. He saw it as some sort of fucking twisted revenge to kill the Callahans when his illegitimate daughter, Jennifer Whitt, was killed by the Slasher."

Archer wiped his hands over his face wearily before facing the two men again. "How do we know he wasn't the partner?"

"Because his whereabouts can be placed at the time of each girl's murder," Ryan informed him. "Once we've identified the Slashers, then we'll have the charges against him made public and have him brought back to Corbin County for trial."

"What proof do you have that Sorenson could be involved in this?" Archer asked him then.

"What proof do *you* have?" Ryan countered.

Archer's lips thinned. "Twelve years ago, my father learned he disappeared for at least twelve hours during the time each girl was missing, except Jaymi Kramer, Cami's sister, but we've always known Thomas Jones went after her on his own. Before the witnesses who saw Wayne leaving town could be deposed, they died suspiciously."

"Keeping a tail on Sorenson is how I've managed to

find each girl that's been killed since." John sighed wearily. "Tracking Sorenson. He's slick though. I've never caught him with the girls or near the areas they were found, but I know he was out when they went missing."

"Katy Winslow?" Archer asked sharply.

"We believe Katy was in the wrong place at the wrong time." Ryan breathed out roughly. "The castings and pictures we took of the tire treads where she was found indicate two vehicles were there with her at the time. She caught them meeting, and they couldn't let her go after that."

"One of the castings is to a very rare tire," John revealed then. "We're having it run now, though nothing's hit yet. We're also checking the area for any property any of the four men might own close enough to use as their kill spot. We're getting closer, Archer, but he's making some damned stupid moves lately. We're worried he's escalating to the point that he could strike against Anna again, and the next time he might actually manage to kill her."

"Why Anna?" Archer snapped then. "What makes her so important that he's kept her out of Corbin County since she was a child?"

Ryan frowned. Holding the file loosely with one hand, he scratched his cheek with the other in confusion.

"This is new information for us," he revealed. "We were going under the assumption she had been targeted because of Crowe."

Quickly, Archer filled the two men in on the story the "Barons" had given him.

As he spoke, and then answered the few questions the two men posed, he admitted to himself there had to be something far deeper going on.

"I'll see what I can find out about her." Ryan spoke as he nodded slowly. "There's something she knows, or possibly something she saw as a child, that threatens him."

"Amelia Sorenson's her best friend," Archer pointed out. "Maybe that's why he put off killing her."

"She wasn't when Anna was younger," Ryan argued. "But you're right about her being a threat if he's kept her away from the County this long."

"And he's breaking pattern," John injected. "Becoming erratic. She's enough of a threat that he can't afford to wait much longer."

"We'll get moving on this," Ryan promised, lifting the file. "Can I keep this?"

Archer shrugged. "I have another hidden in another location. Just in case."

Ryan's lips curved in approval. "I like that about you, Archer. You always have a backup plan."

"A plan isn't going to do me any damn good if he manages to hit Anna again. Nor will it do the two of you any good," Archer warned them both as he uncrossed his arms and straightened from his position against the desk. "Because I'll kill, gentlemen. I promise you that. If she dies, there won't be any stopping me."

"Just make sure you help me keep those damned nephews of mine on a leash after I talk to them," Ryan sighed, heading for the study door. "And if anything happens to your woman, Archer, I can't say I would blame you." He paused at the door before opening it, turning back to Archer as the deputy moved in behind him. "I couldn't blame you at all."

CHAPTER 15

Three days later, Anna lay silently in the bed she still shared with Archer and stared up at the ceiling as dawn began to peek through the narrow openings of the curtains.

It was supposed to be a little cool today. It would be a perfect day to go outside, weed the flower beds Archer seemed to have neglected lately, or perhaps even go back to work.

Brute Force had given her a two-week leave of absence—paid, Mikhail Resnova had assured her—to allow her to heal from the bullet that had been lodged in her thigh.

It had stopped just below the skin. It hadn't touched bone or a vein. And despite the potential explosive power of the ammunition, it hadn't gone off. All it had done was ensure she was laid up for a few days.

No one had *asked* for a two-weeks leave though. A few days would have suited her just fine.

She was ready to go back to work now.

That stupid doctor had demanded weeks though. Two weeks of nothing but rest.

She would go stark raving mad.

Turning her head, she looked at the clock next to the bed on her side before pursing her lips thoughtfully.

"Are you going to work today?" she asked Archer, keeping her voice low in case he was asleep as he lay beside her quietly. "If you are, you better get up or you're going to be late.

"Not today." He surprised her. "I thought we'd take a drive out to Rafer's ranch, where Resnova and his men are overlooking the protection and security of Rafe and Logan's fiancées."

Now didn't that sound ominous?

"Do you think you're going to convince me to stay there?" she asked suspiciously.

Archer turned his head to her at that point, his golden brown eyes narrowed on her as she met his gaze.

"Ivan's come up with some new information." Lifting his upper body, he grabbed the pillow under his head, fluffed it, then pushed it against the headboard before reclining against it. "He called after I came in last night and requested the meeting. I thought you might enjoy visiting with Cami and Skye for a few hours while I'm there. No ulterior motives, no evil designs."

He rubbed at the scattering of curls on his chest as he smothered a yawn and glanced toward the weak sunlight spearing through the edges of the curtains. "Dress warm," he tacked on. "Rafer's ranch isn't much lower than Crowe Mountain, and Crowe's already started getting snow there."

Sitting up, Anna pulled the blankets over her gown-covered breasts as she bent her knees and rested her arms across them.

"Snow already?" She sighed, thinking how much colder the evenings would become.

"A little." Leaning back, eyes closing drowsily, he

acted as though she weren't even there as he asked her, "You want to shower first, or you want me to?"

What had happened to showering together?

"I'll go ahead." She shrugged, moving slowly from the bed as she stifled the bite of painful emotions that tightened her throat.

What had happened?

It was obvious he didn't want her anymore. But Anna knew that without asking. Three days and two nights. He hadn't touched her even once. He hadn't even kissed her.

She hadn't been ready to leave. She hadn't been prepared to lose him this quickly.

But even more, Anna hadn't been ready for the breaking of her heart.

Stifling a groan, Archer watched as Anna limped painfully into the bathroom. Her slender hips moved seductively, if jerkily, beneath the gown, her rounded thighs a shadow of temptation beneath the white spandex and nylon that hugged her upper body, then swept around her thighs and legs in yards upon yards of silky material.

She wasn't wearing panties. As she'd lain sleeping, the blankets thrown from her body, he'd glimpsed the dark shadow of the curls at the very top of the small mound between her thighs.

Teeth clenched, his jaw bunched, Archer reached beneath the blankets and wrapped his fingers around the head of his cock.

He'd been forced to jack off the last two nights. The wound at her outer thigh, though not extremely long or deep, was clearly still painful if the way she walked was an indication.

Tightening his fist around the engorged head of his

dick, it was all he could do to keep from masturbating to hold back the hunger eating him the fuck alive.

God, he wanted her.

Eyes drifting closed, he could see her lying back in his bed, those beautiful pearly thighs wide open, knees bent to allow her heels to dig into the bed and lift to his voracious lips as he ate the satiny, bare folds. Her juices would lie thick and lush and so sweet that the thought of it filled him with a sexual hunger he wondered if he could restrain much longer.

Three days and two nights. Sixty hours of pure, unimagined hell lying next to her, holding her against him because he couldn't sleep without her warmth against his body.

Not that he'd done much sleeping. All he could think about was the taste of her hot little pussy and the tight, clenching hold of it around his shuttling cock.

God, it wasn't as though he hadn't fucked her the night before the attack. And the morning of the attack. If he could have, he would have fucked her pretty, pouting lips the minute he'd closed the door on the world outside the afternoon she'd been shot.

Now she was hurt, in pain, and all he could think about was paddling her pretty rounded ass, then fucking it with a need that threatened to overtake him.

Almost uncontrollably his fisted fingers stroked down the thick, hard shaft as it flexed with furious hunger at the thought of fucking her so intimately. Of having that tighter than tight little entrance furl open around his penetrating cock. He ached to clench his fingers in the rounded globes of her ass, to part the curves and watch his possession of her.

He'd watch the impalement, he decided. He'd spread the cheeks of her ass apart and watch as his heavily lubricated dick worked its way inside her.

Once buried to his balls inside her anus, there would be no stopping him. Her sensual submission would be like an aphrodisiac, powering his arousal.

"Archer, have you——"

His eyes jerked open, his head turning to stare at her in frustrated shock as she stood, still and silent, in the bathroom doorway.

The accusation in her gaze was almost more than he could stand.

"I'm sorry." She backed up, reentered the bathroom, her face pale, her green eyes moist with tears. "I'm really sorry."

The door slammed closed, then locked behind her a second later. And there Archer laid, his dick still clenched between his fingers, the sheet covering him now slick and wet with his seed where he'd spilled his release the second he saw her.

So much for self-control.

One look at her—— It had taken just the sight of her in that sexy gown to steal his will and send his release spurting onto the sheets.

And if the look on her face was any indication, she felt nothing less than betrayed.

"Fuck!" Rising from the bed, Archer flipped the blankets from his body, rose from the bed, and stalked from the bedroom to the guest room shower.

He wasn't going to survive this.

It had been only three days since he'd had her. Three miserably, painfully aroused days, and he didn't know how much more he could stand.

And he had a feeling one more night of it might make him insane.

He didn't have to actually fuck her, he thought to himself. He could bring her to her release with his lips and tongue——

The doctor had made the "no exertion" thing clear. Hell, if he got her off, those sweet little thighs were going to grip his head, tighten, and the stitches the plastic surgeon had placed so carefully could stretch or tear, leaving a scar she might eventually hate him for.

He knew women in some things. A scar could completely change her éntire perception of herself. Hell, she might never wear a bikini again. And he knew for damned sure just how good she looked in a bikini.

Stepping beneath the icy spray of the shower, he wondered if a man could actually die from arousal.

The ranch the Callahans had set up as a base of operations, and for Ivan Resnova to oversee the safety and security of Rafer and Logan Callahan's fiancées, was the same ranch the Callahan cousins had been raised on after their parents' deaths.

Previously, the Triple R, or Ramsey Ranch, had belonged to Clyde Ramsey, Rafer's great-uncle on his mother's side. Had it not been for Clyde, Anna knew, the three boys would have ended up in foster homes, and only God knew what would have happened to them.

Even so, their lives had been hard enough as Clyde fought to deflect the often cruel barbs that had come not just from kids their own age, but also adults. Add that to the twenty-year court battle to keep the inheritances their mothers had left them, and it had made some years pure hell for the cousins.

Despite the Barons' attempts, or that shadowed *he* who had attempted to destroy them for most of their lives, and the cruelties of the fine, upstanding, God-fearing citizens of Corbin County, the Callahan cousins had still managed to turn out pretty decent.

They were hard, though Rafer and Logan had softened considerably since falling in love and becoming engaged. Crowe was still considered hard core, cynical and too rough around the edges. He sometimes still gave the impression that he was just looking for a fight, a means to expend the violence that three decades had built inside him.

He was a man ready to explode, and Anna had heard that comment from more than one person in the County. Most people were wary around him, and had been for some time.

As Archer turned his big black four-by-four pickup onto the ranch road, Anna narrowed her eyes and gazed at the wide valley and rising mountains. She had to admit, if what she had heard before returning to Corbin County was true, the Ramsey and former Callahan Ranch would be perfect for the rumored plans they had for it.

Gossip was running rampant on her grandfather's ranch that the Callahans were combining the Ramsey Ranch property with the property their Callahan grandparents had owned, and were turning it into a year-round spa and resort that would also cater to scheduled wilderness-survival parties.

The cousins were partners in two related businesses that were migrating to Sweetrock, then also setting up year-round offices at the resort they were planning.

Off Road Excursions, a camping and mountain adventure store, had just filed a legal agreement with the Callahans at the courthouse last month, giving the business limited use of both properties for a period of three years, which many said substantiated the rumor.

There was also talk that Brute Force, the security company Anna had been hired to work at in Sweetrock, had signed an agreement—though this one private— for use of the land for small, private survival-training parties, but also for the guerilla warfare–type games designed to train security agents in the best possible protection of their clients.

The cousins would be crazy not to do so and take advantage of the rising tourism traffic into Colorado, but especially into Aspen and Sweetrock itself.

The mountains were a magnet for adventurers and families alike. Camping, fishing, hunting, skiing, and exclusive mountain vacation cabins were all rumored to be part of the business the Callahans were setting up.

"Is it true Crowe and his cousins are really going to set up the resort everyone's talking about?" She turned to Archer, asking the question as curiosity ate at her.

She'd been dying to ask Crowe, but hadn't yet found the best opportunity to approach him with the question.

Archer glanced at her in surprise. Not that she blamed him.

"You haven't said two words to me since walking in on me earlier, and this is what you ask when you finally decide to talk?" he asked, a hint of rueful amusement playing at his lips.

Shrugging, Anna turned back to stare straight ahead. "I was just curious."

"Why haven't you asked Crowe?"

"Because he's an asshole when he thinks I'm being nosy about his life," she countered, glancing over at him once again. "And he tells me to mind my own business."

Which drove her crazy.

Archer's lips quirked at the admission.

"He has a thing about privacy," he agreed.

"So are you going to answer me?" She turned and glared at him, silently demanding the answer.

Archer rubbed his nose thoughtfully. "If the Callahans were considering such a move, I bet they would have taken on silent partners," he mused. "And if they had, there would be a silencing clause until they had everything ready to roll. Don't you think?"

"Do they?" She frowned.

"Who the hell knows?" He shrugged. "I'm just saying, that's probably why no one knows for sure."

Anna's lips twitched.

Archer could be devious; she'd known that for years. It had taken her just a moment to figure out what he was saying.

"I'm sure he would. So the very fact that no one can say for certain would basically indicate it's pretty much a given," she stated.

"That's what I would assume, myself." He nodded.

Anna stared around at the passing vista.

"They'll make a fortune," she breathed out. "The Callahans, as well as anyone lucky enough to be invited into the venture."

"This is true." The smile that shaped Archer's lips was one of pure satisfaction. "This is true."

The former Ramsey Ranch was incredibly beautiful, but Anna knew the Callahan property and the bordering Crowe Mountain were so breathtaking that for decades JR and Eileen Callahan had had to fend off buyers and resort investors desperate to utilize the property.

The very things that the founding "Barons" considered too rough and unfitting to use for ranching, made the land excellent for tourism and the horse ranch it had originally been designated for by the founding Callahan.

The hunting itself was phenomenal. Where the Rafferty, Roberts, and Corbin Ranches were mostly valley and bottomlands, the Callahan Ranch was mostly rolling hills and mountain vistas, clear streams, white-water rapids, and hidden caverns and caves where wildlife made dens and homes.

There was one small mountain lake, and another much larger one, in one of the few wide valleys the Callahan property possessed.

She was guessing Archer was one of those lucky investors.

He and the Callahans had been friends since they were boys. No matter the obstacles Archer's father had placed between the friendships, they had not just maintained but thrived.

As the house came into view, Anna narrowed her eyes on it, remembering what it had looked like the only time she had accompanied her father when he'd had a meeting with Clyde Ramsey years before.

There had been a lot of security upgrades since she'd last seen it, though, according to gossip, most of those changes had occurred only in the past six to eight weeks.

High fences surrounded the back, with a thin sight-barrier netting stretching around and over it to allow Cami and Skye the opportunity to enjoy a newly installed pool without having to worry about the sniper who had shot and killed one of the security guards hired to protect Cami several months ago.

The fact that the security guard had taken a payoff to kill Cami himself wasn't the point, Rafer had raged. The point was, there was a sniper out there with a bead on his fiancée.

Armed security guards now prowled not just the main ranch yard, but the mountain overlooking the ranch house, where they had turned away several hunters. Several of those security guards held the leashes of some vicious-looking trained German shepherds, as well.

"This place is starting to resemble an armed camp," she sighed. "Skye must hate it."

Archer glanced at her somberly. "Most of the protective additions were her idea."

That surprised her. Skye had never cared much for armed camps, armed guards, or security strongholds. But then, love changed a person. She had not just her safety and security to think of, but also her lover's, and their unborn child's.

"They may have been her idea, but I know Skye, and I know she's hating not just the necessity of it, but also the fact that this is how she's being forced to live."

"But she's alive." Archer sighed. "The fact that you survived that shooting is more a testament to your own reflexes than the shooter's lack of skill or my ability to protect you. You could have died, Anna, or lost your leg and been paralyzed from the waist down because of that fucking bullet and the bastard who's targeted you."

Once again, why her?

What made her so important to a killer?

Pulling the vehicle into the graveled parking area, Archer parked and jumped out with a muttered "Stay put."

Stay put?

She watched as he strode to her side of the truck, opened the passenger door for her, and helped her out. He'd insisted on helping her into the truck earlier, though she had been certain she could have managed with the running board on the side of the vehicle.

Swinging around, she gripped his shoulders as he clasped her hips and swung her easily to the ground.

"I could have managed," she assured him, not certain how to take the gesture.

"I'm sure you could have." Setting his hand at the

small of her back, he placed himself carefully behind her as they made their way to the front porch.

The front door opened as they reach the last wide step.

"Oh my God, Anna." Skye was out the door, her long red-gold hair flying around her, her eyes filled with tears and regret as she wrapped her arms around Anna for a fierce hug.

Instinctively, Anna held on to the other woman, suddenly remembering how Skye had always been into those hugs the year they had attended private school together.

Skye had been the big sister Anna had always dreamed of having. The fact that, more than a month before, Skye had also faced the killer determined to destroy the Callahans wasn't lost on Anna. It was the reason her friend was here, on Rafer's ranch, rather than in town.

Thank God she was here, Anna thought silently. Otherwise, Skye would have gotten involved in Anna's problems and likely have been hurt or killed. Instead, she was safe and sound, her fiancé, Logan, watching over her and their unborn child.

"It's so good to see you." Skye drew back, a tear tracking down her cheek as she stared back at Anna.

Oh God, how she had missed Skye over the years. Missed her caring and warmth, her friendship. They had reconnected over the years at odd times, and Anna had been overjoyed when she'd learned Skye was living in Sweetrock.

Until she'd learned who Skye was living beside.

Until she'd learned who Skye was sleeping with.

Until she'd learned Skye was placing herself in just as much danger as Cami Flannigan had.

As the six victims of the Sweetrock Slasher had twelve years before, and the four who had died in the past six months.

She had placed herself in the path of a madman.

Just as Anna had managed to place herself there.

CHAPTER 16

Skye was outraged.

She was insanely furious.

Helping Anna into the house, she clasped the other girl's shoulders and stared into her pain-shadowed eyes. What she saw in Anna's face was more than physical pain. The soul-deep hurt reflected there made her want to smash faces. Old, stubborn, arrogant faces such as John Corbin's, and younger, stupid faces such as his son Robert's.

"What have they done to you, Anna?" She sighed as she lifted her fingers and touched Anna's pale face.

"Completely trashed my life?" Anna suggested with a rueful smile. "It's good to see you again, Skye. I've been so worried about you since the attack. Are you sure you're okay?"

An assailant had managed to catch Crowe off guard and render him unconscious just before Logan and Skye arrived at his mountain home. The second half of the team known as the Stalker had been intent on killing her, and would have had it not been for that lone bitch wolf Crowe had raised from a cub. She'd crashed through the window, and they had thought, actually hoped, she had managed to kill the assailant. Instead, he had disappeared, his identity once again uncertain.

"I'm fine," Skye finally assured Anna, though she wanted to wail at that painful limp and the knowledge of the wound her friend had sustained. With it, that glimmer of hurt and betrayal in Anna's eyes broke her heart.

Skye hadn't seen Anna as often as she had wanted to over the years, but each time she had, the other girl's eyes had held just innocence and hope, despite the constant rejections of her family.

That innocence and hope were slowly dimming.

Anna was more reserved than she had been as a teenager, but she was still the Anna that Skye remembered, even several weeks before when they had met for lunch. This woman facing her now was little more than a lost, lonely version of the friend Skye cared so deeply for.

The most painful part was the fact that Anna probably thought she was hiding the lost loneliness inside her.

"See, we told you she was doing fine." Jack Thompson and his wife, Jeanne, moved to them from across the room. "She's so damned cute those bullets just couldn't bear to be the ones to hurt her, is what it was.

Jack swept Anna up in a tight hug before smacking a kiss on her cheek and winking at her outrageously. Skye watched Archer subtly tighten.

How interesting, she thought. Archer knew well that Jack was about as happily married as a person could be—to his delicate little wife, Jeanne. The male animal subconsciously claiming Anna was a different story though. Until she was fully his, Archer didn't want another man anywhere close to her.

God, it was so much fun watching these intensely hard, totally male creatures as they fought and failed to remain distant and hard in the face of love.

"Jack, you're outrageous." His wife, Jeanne, laughed as he released Anna.

"Eh, you're just jealous 'cause you want a hug too," Jack accused her playfully.

"From her and Cami," Jeanne declared as she glanced at Cami, who was currently being hugged by her fiancé, Rafer.

"Cami's busy," Rafer drawled.

"You can get a room later, you wicked man." Jeanne laughed as she released Skye and stepped over to the couple. "For now, she owes me a hug."

The next few minutes were taken up with greetings until the tall, black-haired, savagely handsome Ivan Resnova entered the room by the glass patio doors that led to the pool.

Behind him, a young woman, perhaps sixteen or seventeen years old, glared at his back while an older woman walking next to her glanced at the teenager with a firm look.

"Ivan, stop torturing Amara and introduce her to Anna. I know she hasn't had a chance to meet her yet." Skye introduced them, "Anna, meet our wicked Russian busybody, Ivan's sister, Sophia. And his daughter, whom he currently believes he can still control." She snickered at Ivan. "Amara."

"Sophia, Amara." Anna shook each of their hands, impressed with their confident grips. "It's good to meet you."

"It's good to finally meet the terror of the Corbin family," Amara quipped, laughing. "Crowe makes you sound like a cross between an ogre and a troll."

Anna turned to Crowe and lifted her brows mockingly. "I thought you already announced both of those titles were yours?"

Everyone laughed but Crowe, who glared back at Anna instead.

Anna gave a mental shrug. She was damned if she was going to kiss his ass to make him like her.

"And here I thought Daddy had possession of those titles," Amara drawled, with only a subtle hint of her father's Russian accent.

As she came closer, Anna amended her first guess of sixteen or seventeen. Amara Resnova was, at the very least, twenty-one, and she'd seen enough life to know, all the way to her soul, that it didn't welcome one with open arms.

With long, silky black hair and dark, intense blue eyes in a lightly tanned aristocratic complexion, the younger girl's facial features assured she would look far younger than her age no matter how old she was. Amara was dressed in a thin peach-colored chiffon skirt that fell just barely below her thighs and a matching sleeveless blouse that showed a hint of midriff when she turned.

Her feet were pushed into tan leather thong sandals revealing delicate, peach-colored toenails that matched her painted fingernails. A gold chain circled her neck and held a small, poignant gold representation of the crucifix.

She was a very-well-put-together young woman, Anna thought, wishing she was that well dressed and sophisticated herself.

The sound of the front door opening had everyone turning to the newcomer. The man resembled Ivan so closely that Anna wondered if he had a twin.

"And this is Gregor." He frowned intently as though

some description eluded him. "He is the brother of my father."

"Ivan, your uncle. He's your uncle." Crowe rolled his eyes.

"This is what I keep telling you, Crowe. Do you forget?" Ivan asked, deadpan but for the wicked glint of laughter in his eyes.

"He got you again, Crowe," Sophia laughed before turning back to Anna. "Crowe seems to keep forgetting Ivan has an excellent command of the American vocabulary."

"I only forget because he continually insists on using that damned peasant accent," Crowe grunted. "If he wants to play dumb, then he shouldn't get upset when others treat him as though he were dumb."

Dressed in a long, ankle-length white cotton skirt and matching sleeveless blouse, her feet pushed into sandals similar to Amara's, Sophia looked cool and playfully flirtatious as she shot Archer a teasing grin.

"Crowe also forgets that Resnovas remember well their roots. We weren't always suspected international-crime figures." Gregor moved into the room with a predatory stroll. "It's not that hard to remember how to speak as a peasant, especially when you remember well what it's like to be that peasant."

He came to Crowe's back and clapped him on the shoulder as he grinned at Anna. "Hello, Ms. Corbin. I've heard quite a bit about you."

"Don't pretend much of it was good if it came from Crowe," Anna stated.

"All good, and most of it actually did come from your cousin," he assured her as he shook her hand with a broad, calloused hand.

Anna crossed her arms over her breasts and shot Crowe a chiding look as Gregor released her.

"He is a very bad boy," Sophia sighed, though she slid Crowe a teasing, sideways look. "They are all bad boys though, do you not agree?" The look she shot Anna invited feminine secrets and an air of conspiracy against the males surrounding them.

"Just as the good sheriff is," Gregor stated, his accent sensual and thick with Russian influence. "I see he has managed to capture one of the most beautiful of the women it's been my pleasure to meet since I arrived."

"Watch it, Romeo," Crowe drawled mockingly. "Archer might seem like a man who will tolerate your flirting with his woman, but trust me, he has ways of getting even."

Archer shot Crowe a surprised look, as though he had no idea what he was talking about.

Of course he didn't, Anna thought mutinously. A man was only jealous or possessive when he acknowledged he might not willingly allow a woman to leave his life.

Archer didn't even appear to desire her anymore, let alone care if another man flirted with her.

"Gregor is my head of security, and currently training several of Brute Force's agents in the job," Ivan stated. "Archer was kind enough to provide a reference to Gregor's naturalization application."

"No matter the crimes he's suspected of," Crowe muttered, then grinned at the glares Ivan and Antoli shot him.

"We ignore him when he turns into a brat," Sophia assured Anna with a grin that revealed her pleasure in his smart-assed comments.

"Which means they ignore him often." Archer chuckled as Crowe leveled a mock warning look in his direction.

"One of these days we might be tempted to teach him the error of his disrespect." Gregor's comment was more a warning.

"Ah, such children," Sophia chided them before turning back to Anna. "Now I must see to the snacks my nephew has requested for this evening. Excuse me, if you please."

Giving Anna another quick hug, Sophia turned and swept from the living room to the open kitchen, from which the most delightful scents were coming.

"Rumor's rampant you brought the Resnovas here," Anna stated, more than a little impressed. "Where the hell did you meet them?"

"I was one of the agents with the FBI, assigned to protect Amara from the DC Vigilante just before I took my leave of absence from the bureau." Skye linked her arm with Anna's, then Jeanne's, as Cami moved behind them and led them to the patio doors on the other side of the room.

"She knows every damned FBI agent who's walked through the front door," Cami quipped. "And there've been a lot of those."

"She knew the CIA agent who slipped onto the property last week to talk to Ivan too," Cami pointed out.

Cami wrinkled her nose at the accusation. "A female CIA agent who flipped him on his ass the second she saw him."

Amara rolled her eyes at Cami. "She was just flirting with Dad. She has an odd way of showing her affection."

The younger girl moved past them as she headed for an outdoor television on the other side of the patio, beneath a shaded pergola next to the newly installed pool.

"God, I love that pool," Cami sighed as she stared at the glistening water.

"What an odd admission, considering you called the crew responsible for installing it assholes and backwoods yokels with more inbred genetics than common sense," Skye pointed out with a laugh.

"Well, he implied Rafe didn't have the money to have it installed, then once he found out about Off Road Excursions and Brute Force Security Training he had the nerve to imply Rafe, Logan, and Crowe didn't have enough business sense to make them profitable, and perhaps he should check with the Corbins for permission to build the damned thing," Cami sniffed. "A good businessman doesn't give a damn as long as he gets paid.

Anna took a seat beneath the umbrellaed patio table a few feet from the door as Cami and Skye chose their own seats, while still bantering back and forth.

Listening to their laughter, Anna stared around the well-fenced backyard wishing she had the ability and the comfort to laugh and tease with the others.

Once, years ago, Anna had had that ability to tease and play. Then Skye had graduated and Anna's parents had moved her again, requiring yet another school transfer. After that move, trying to fit in once again, then another move, Anna had finally just given up. Skye hadn't been there to ease her into the transition, and no one else had seen the stomach-knotting nerves and dark loneliness Anna had dealt with.

"Anna, are you okay?" Skye reached forward, her hand covering Anna's knee as she stared at her in concern.

Cami was watching as well, her gaze concerned, her expression encouraging.

"I'm fine, Skye, Cami. I promise." They were making her extremely uncomfortable now as she reached up and scratched at her collarbone.

A move Skye watched worriedly. Anna was uncomfortable; she knew all the signs of it and regretted it.

"Considering you were disowned, abducted, and you're now being stalked and shot at, I think you're doing amazingly well," Cami stated.

Anna shrugged. "The two of you have faced the Slasher as well."

"We weren't disowned and left all but alone with no one to turn to," Cami pointed out. "My father never cared much for me anyway, and I knew it, but I had my aunt and uncle, friends, and Rafer. It has to be harder the way you've been kept from the County. It must seem as though you have no connections here at all."

Anna just gave an uncomfortable shrug.

"Anna, talk to us," Cami urged her then, sympathy marking her expression as her eyes filled with a rare empathy. "Skye and I have learned that talking about it goes a long way to easing the nightmares."

Anna's gaze jerked between them in surprise.

"Yeah, the nightmares are brutal," Skye sighed. "But, Anna, your eyes are breaking my heart. I swear, the pain and fear are so clear in them that it makes me want to kill the Corbins as painfully as possible."

Anna quickly averted her gaze. She'd forgotten about that. Skye had always told her that her innermost emotions reflected as clear as day in her eyes.

There was no way to hide it, she thought in resignation. Once she would have just hidden in her room, weeping until she couldn't cry any longer. When she was finished crying, her natural optimism would return.

She wasn't a child anymore though, and sitting and crying took precious time that she could be using in her attempt to enjoy life and to carve a future for herself in Corbin County.

"Have you even tried to call your parents—"

"Skye, please," Anna protested, wanting nothing more than to just hide again. They had to stop this. They had stop poking and prodding at the pain radiating with each question. "I don't want to offend you, but I really can't talk about this."

Not without getting out of here and crying like the child she used to be.

The understanding in Cami's and Skye's eyes was comforting, but she couldn't handle it right now. The pain was too close to the surface and too hard to deal with.

She could ignore it, if she didn't have to talk about it. But if she had to talk about it, and be honest, then she actually had been able to deal with her family. They were doing what they felt they had to. She didn't agree with them. She couldn't understand how they had imagined that was the best route to take, and she missed them so bad sometimes it ached.

But she knew there was hope they loved her.

No, if there was pain in her eyes, then Archer had helped put it there.

"Anna," Skye drew her attention. "Promise me, if you need someone to talk to, day or night, you'll call one of us."

Anna nodded swiftly. *Anything,* she thought, *to divert their attention elsewhere.* "I promise. Both of you, I promise."

Skye wasn't happy, and the look she shot Cami was doubtful. Anna wasn't the teenager she had been when they had first met.

Disillusionment and a lifetime of loneliness and empty promises had led to all the emotional misery that lay trapped inside her now.

Skye just prayed that Archer, with his disbelief

of being "in love" and his determination to remain commitment-free, didn't permanently break the heart that had already been broken far too many times.

"Tell me, Sheriff Tobias, have you yet found someone, anyone, that I can punish for the hell those three young women are being put through?" Ivan asked as he turned back to them after watching Jeanne step onto the patio to join the other women.

She'd become a steady visitor to the house, bringing information, gossip, and often helping Sophia, as she had just finished doing; his sister had arranged cheese, meats, and crackers for a snack while the Callahans and their friends were there.

"Stand in line," Archer sighed as he tossed back the remainder of the whisky he'd been sipping. "I'd beat you there."

"And her parents' disavowal had nothing to do with her pain? Nor her grandparents'?" Ivan asked with icy calm as Antoli joined them from his normal position close to the front door. "Do not deny what I have already learned myself, my friend."

Archer slid the bottom of his glass back and forth in front of him, refusing to answer the other man just yet.

"They've kept her away from Corbin County since she was nine," Jack said as Archer lifted his gaze and looked out to the patio, at the woman who made his chest both tighten and melt whenever he saw her smile. "Her parents changed her schools almost yearly. They moved around as though money didn't matter, and old man Corbin financed every move. For a few years my cousin was employed by his accounting firm. The things he heard and saw where the Corbins' determination to keep her out of Corbin County were concerned, were outrageous."

"Such an accounting firm should not exist," Ivan murmured.

Jack's look was cynical. "Come on, Ivan. I like you, man, I do, but we both know ole Mother Russia ain't much better."

Ivan's lips quirked. "Perhaps not. But my sense of outrage over that young woman's pain and the danger she faces has nothing to do with such things. I want to know why— Why have they kept her from the bosom of her family? Why was she made to be alone, forced to be isolated, by parents who should have wished only to have her with them and to see to her happiness, who should have only wished to love her."

"These are questions that I would wish to have the answers to as well," Gregor growled, his dark expression somehow more dangerous for the lack of fury in his cool eyes. "And these questions, my friends, are perhaps yet another piece to your puzzle where the Corbins and the Callahans are concerned."

"How so?" It was Crowe who beat Archer to the question.

Gregor shook his head, frowning. "They have kept her out of this County, and I can think of only one reason to do so."

"To keep her away from her cousin," Archer murmured, feeling the tension that was beginning to settle in the pit of his stomach.

"There is no other explanation." Gregor shrugged, his dark gaze assessing now. "The five of you have not been born and bred to suspicion, paranoia, and the daily threat of your lives and those of your loved ones being in peril. You have not yet learned—no matter how you think you have, not to the bone—that in all things, the more they are made to appear they do not connect, the more they connect. And that girl—" He nodded to Anna. "Many people, for many years, have worked hard to prove she is not connected."

Breathing in hard, Archer looked to the Callahans, his jaw clenching. "There's more," he stated, glancing back at the patio, seeing the incredible distance between Anna and the other women, despite the fact that they were sitting close together.

"More? In what way?" Crowe asked, the low tone of his voice a heavy warning.

"There's more going on," Archer growled. "The killings have been going on far longer than we guessed and have had more to do with your lives than we ever imagined."

"And you know this how?" Logan leaned forward, his gaze suddenly intent.

"Because your uncle, Ryan, and my deputy, John Caine, arrived at the house last night, well after two in the morning, with an incredible story."

Gregor's expression was hard, pure stone as Crowe's amber-brown eyes suddenly seemed to burn with fury.

"And?" Rafer injected impatiently. "This ain't a reality show, goddamn it, and I don't need to be dangled on some fucking string."

"Has Ryan been in contact?" Archer asked.

"He was," Crowe growled. "And he told us about the contract he accepted this summer to kill all of us. I can't believe Dave Stone was so fucking crazy and we never knew."

Archer shook his head slowly. "They're watching three men as suspects to the identity of the Slasher team."

"Who?" Crowe asked, his tone guttural as he demanded the identities of the three men.

"We have to wait for more proof, Crowe," Archer warned. "We have just enough right now to make a hell of a mistake and end up killing an innocent man."

"Come on, Archer. I'm not a fucking kid. None of us are," Logan snapped. "Who are they?"

Archer revealed the names and detailed the majority of the meeting he'd had the night before with Ryan and John Caine.

He didn't mention Wayne Sorenson. He couldn't, not yet. Not until he had a chance to check a few things out himself, because right now there was just enough proof to get him killed.

Rafer, Logan, and Crowe slowly straightened. At the same moment, Archer glimpsed both Cami and Skye as their heads suddenly turned, their gazes intent, their body language concerned as they looked for their fiancés.

There was instinct, and then there was just plain weird, because at the same time Anna had turned, as though searching him out as well. There was no way she could have turned in response to the other two, because he was damned if the three women hadn't turned at the exact same moment.

Just as they were rising to their feet, then turning to look at each other in confusion for a single heartbeat. Then they were moving faster.

It would have been damned amusing if Archer hadn't seen it for himself. That instinct. That bond and connection confused the fuck out of him, and he couldn't understand how Anna had felt what Rafer's and Logan's lovers had felt.

"Caine believes the killer is his natural father, but his mother never revealed the identity of his natural father, right?" Crowe mused quietly as Cami, Skye, Anna, and Jeanne made their way back into the house. "What would be the point of killing her?"

"Unless she knew something, had some way of identifying the Slasher. She'd been out of the country for nearly thirty years. If she returned and reconnected with anyone who knew and heard about the Slasher, she might have been able to reveal their identities, or even give pertinent information on JR and Eileen Callahan's murders," Archer stated softly, his gaze on Anna, that tension in his stomach tightening further. "And perhaps that's even why it's so important to keep the Callahans out of Corbin County, and the Callahan property away from its rightful owners."

"Perhaps," Ivan mused, "what I have learned can add another piece of the puzzle."

Ivan waited until Cami, Skye, Anna, and Jeanne had joined them before he recounted John and Robert Corbin's visit to Archer's study.

Archer watched Anna as the Russian quietly explained the visit and their suspicion that, if not the Corbins, then the Slasher and his partner, were desperate to hide something.

"Perhaps they are also desperate to find something," Ivan stated as he finished. "We Russians, we understand family, and we understand tracking and tracing family in ways Americans have forgotten. You make a hobby of tracing your ancestors. To a Russian, it is not a hobby; it is a part of who and what we are. It is a part of our honor and has much too high a potential to be a part of our disgrace as well. So we must know."

"I'm getting really impatient, Ivan," Crowe warned him.

Gregor snorted. "Remember, Ivan," he mused, "what impatience gained you?"

"Don't make him smack the back of your head, Crowe," Ivan suggested. "We may never finish this part of the tale if you do."

Crowe slid Antoli a smug, mocking look, but he said nothing more.

"As I was saying," Ivan continued. "Russians know how to find ancestors. Knowing this, I placed several families of the Resnova clan, particularly talented in collecting family rumors and following them where they may go, onto this particular problem. Some worked on the Internet and followed what was found there, contacted others in the appropriate cities and so forth. I have at last collected quite a history on the Barons of Corbin County, and the Callahans as well, as to what may have fueled the killings of the past forty years that seem to have no explanation."

"When you've finished bragging on your fine Russian talents, you could get on with the story." Crowe sighed.

Ivan chuckled, then began. "Nine generations ago, the founding fathers of Corbin County pooled their money, filed a land grant, and bribed certain officials to ensure their land was secured against all other claims that might come in. Then Patrick O'Hara Callahan, Douglas McQuire Roberts, Dennis O'Halloran Rafferty, and Augustus O'Ryan Corbin made the journey to the land of green pastures and wild mountain passes in Colorado. They had been here once before, plotted the land they fell in love with, and rushed to Washington to ensure their claim before a retired ship captain—some said pirate—and his son, could make their claim. The pirate, known as the Raider, and his son, known only as Blood, were only days late in attempting to claim the land when word reached them that the lush valley they had been building their cabin within was no longer theirs. They confronted the four men, and in a shoot-out with Patrick Callahan and Augustus Corbin, Raider and Blood took a bullet in the heart apiece. There were rumors though, and many believed them, that the two men, each captain of his own pirate ship—Raider for

nearly three decades and Blood for more than two—
had brought their chests of gold, jewels, and priceless
plunder with them to the valley they called Raider's
Valley. There, it was said, the pirates had found a cav-
ern so well hidden, so perfect to preserve their treasures, that they had no fear of it being stolen. They
were a paranoid lot though. The men who had come
with them came on the promise of rich land to raise
cattle, horses, and crops, and that the numerous chests
of treasure would be divided once the pirate son's wife
and small son arrived. They had worked hard ensuring
the two captains had everything they needed. When
Blood's wife and son arrived, though, the pirates were
dead and no one knew where the treasure was hidden.

"Now the wife, strangely enough, had never known
her husband's true surname. He gave her the name
Clavern, promising that she would know everything
once he had built their home and sent for her.

"When the wife and child showed up at the Callahan
Ranch, she begged for mercy, claiming to have no funds
and no way of returning to her brother's house in New
York. So Patrick Callahan, being the kind soul he was,
allowed her to stay in the cabin built for her until she
could reach her brother and have funds wired to her.

"Not long afterward, the Indians who hunted those
mountains came to the Callahans with tales of a
madwoman and a child with dead eyes whom they
called 'Devil.'

"A few months later, Patrick and his friends found
this madwoman in the back of a cave, her fists bloody
from pounding on the hard stone walls, her eyes
glowing with madness as her son looked on with no
emotion, no sense of a soul in his gaze.

"It was said the wife had driven herself mad searching for the treasure, and the son whispered a curse

on the Callahans and the Corbins each night as he watched his mother claw her hands bloody searching for the doorway to the treasure.

"Nothing was ever found, and the rumors of treasure faded into the past, but the pirate's bloodline did not. With each generation the tale is retold, the eldest son is taught the stories and told from the cradle that it's his fate to find this vast wealth. At least every other generation, whichever son decides to take on the task of vengeance changes his last name, moves, sometimes fakes his death, so it was rather hard to find a few of them." His lips quirked in amusement and pride.

Crowe rolled his eyes as he crossed his arms over his chest and leaned back against the counter.

"Now, shall we fast-forward to a mere three generations ago? Corinne and Cable Ritchie, living in San Bernardino, California, received word that their eldest brother had changed his and his son's names, and had arrived in Sweetrock to begin the quest to search for the treasure—a treasure said to be hidden in Raider's Valley, a vast sweetgrass valley belonging to JR and Eileen Callahan. And that he had a plan to restore to the family all that had been stolen from them." He glanced at each man and woman now listening intently to his tale. "I have the letters arriving by courier tomorrow, actually," he promised them, eager to see such madness and attempt to make sense of it. "Corinne Ritchie's brother said he and his son had created bonds with one of the four families, known then as the Barons, though he did not say which. But his first order of business was to poison JR Callahan, kill him, then marry his wife before their sons could return home from the war. That is, if they returned. Many of America's sons were dying in Vietnam, and he was certain luck would be on his side. Eileen had just given birth to an infant boy, a child he was certain would be easy to kill without suspicion. But then there was word Eileen's son died of some fever, and within weeks JR was out of the hospital and well on his road to recovery. JR was also aware he had been poisoned. He managed, Ritchie wrote to his brother and sister later, to throw suspicion on the other three families he was now plotting against.

"By now, Joseph was getting on in age, and growing ill himself, and this was when his son decided he would take this quest and complete it. He had fallen in love with the daughter of one of the landowners, and an employee heard father and son raging violently over the son's decision to halt some quest and to live a life of idyllic, blissful love by his bride's side.

"The young woman was headstrong, determined though. He wrote to his sister that he didn't believe the daughter of this family would marry his son, as the son believed she would.

"That was the final letter they had from him. There was no word what he and his son had changed their names to, and no way of finding out when this occurred. I would guess they began this quest of vengeance somewhere around the nineteen thirties, give or take a good five to ten years. The daughter Joseph's son was wooing would have been one of your mothers." Ivan shrugged. "What I do have are records, news clippings, and a Mulrooney family history that would make your hair turn gray." He cast an amused glance at his uncle, who deliberately ignored it. "Suffice to say, you're looking at nearly two hundred years of deliberate deaths and attempts to either frame or murder the Callahans, and to find a way to acquire Raider's Valley."

"Wasn't it around forty years ago that JR and Eileen Callahan lost control of their truck and went over that cliff?" Archer mused.

"Close enough." Crowe's tone was so hard that his cousins looked at him warily.

"The 'Barons' said the event someone was attempting to frame them for happened around forty years ago," Archer told them. "Joseph Ritchie wrote that he and his son were attempting to frame others for this attempted poisoning of one of the parties as well?"

"And JR Callahan's illness was proven to be a poisoning," Ivan agreed.

"You know," Anna spoke then. "When I was little, before I went away to school, there was this guy that came to Grandfather. I was staying the weekend while my parents were away. I forget who he said he was; I wasn't paying a lot of attention," she admitted. "But I do remember he said he was researching an old pirate rumor written in a captain's journal centuries before, that two bloodthirsty pirates had settled in Sweetrock or nearby. He'd identified some valley on Callahan property as the area they had first settled. Grandfather gave him permission to search the valley, and they sat and discussed where that treasure could have been hidden. He was supposed to return a week or so later, but he never came back. That was probably fourteen, fifteen years ago."

"His name was Greg Cabot," Ivan revealed with an approving nod in her direction. "And for the record, Gregory was a college professor actually researching Raider and Blood, a father-and-son pirating team who were said to have stolen as booty the actual crown worn by the king of Spain during the English and Spanish War. The treasures they looted, not just from other ships but also from private homes along several different coasts, would be considered priceless now."

"Hell." Rafer rubbed at the back of his neck in shock. "There's no way something like that is on our property. We were all over that place as kids, and later as teenagers."

"And there are two hundred years of death and blood-shed that prove otherwise," Ivan pointed out. "There's also a rumor that this family line has a sickness. A sickness that requires blood to ease the madness. They're serial killers, my friends. They often work with some-one else, someone they can control or feel they can control. They're always in some way close to their vic-tims, and are rarely suspected of being the monsters they are until they're caught. They've changed their names so many damned times I doubt many of them even remember their original surname."

"And that surname is?" Logan demanded.

"Mulrooney," Ivan stated, his accent giving a lush, broad flavor to the name as he said it with an air of expectation.

When no one seemed surprised, or seemed to have heard of the name, his face fell with disappointment. "Ah well." He shrugged. "I had hoped someone had heard it before." A grin curled his lips. "I believe, though, with my excellent help, we shall indeed solve this mys-tery, save the damsels in distress, and I shall once again watch them ride away with their white knights on their white steeds."

"Always a best man and never a groom, Ivan?" Jack laughed.

"Ah yes, the trials and tribulations of a man such as I," Ivan bemoaned as he laid his hand against the white silk shirt covering his heart. "So many women, so much heartache to mend, and so very little time."

"Even less time, Dad, if you keep pissing me off. Even less time," Amara warned him as she strolled past him, then headed upstairs.

Ivan watched her with a mock glare.

"She threatens to dare to be a prosecutor," he muttered, and though his expression was fiercely mutinous, his tone was filled with pride.

Chuckles sounded around the group as it slowly broke up. Jack and Jeanne announced they had to be going and minutes later, Archer and Anna made their good-byes as well.

As Ivan and Gregor watched the sheriff's truck disappear down the lane, Antoli sighed heavily. "She has heard the name," he murmured to his nephew.

Ivan nodded. "Is there some way we can perhaps aid this memory in returning?"

His uncle had solved harder problems in the past. And it wouldn't be the first time Gregor, Sophia, and Ivan had adopted a family or an individual with none other to stand for them, and fixed whatever tormented their lives.

Sometimes the world was a cruel and dark place, filled with shadows and monsters, if one had no one to look to for laughter or love.

Gregor narrowed his eyes and gazed into the mountains thoughtfully before he shoved his hands into the pockets of his slacks and gave a slight nod. "I will work on this," he promised Ivan. "Give me a bit of time. I work on this."

And if it could be done, then Gregor could damned sure do it.

CHAPTER 17

Archer's arrogance was driving her crazy.

Four days later, four days of miserable, solitary sleeping arrangements and boredom the likes of which Anna had never experienced before.

She couldn't leave the house without enough body-guards to make her crazy. Ivan Resnova had actually listened to Archer when he requested six men to guard her. And they listened when he said she wasn't to leave the house except to go onto the patio.

And that left only one option. If he was going to be all possessive and male, then the least he could do was give her something to make the confinement seem not so intolerable.

And if he couldn't stomach going to bed with her and actually touching her, then she would take the Resnovas and the Callahans up on their offer to move to the ranch. Because she couldn't stand living with him without touching him.

Putting the finishing touches on the dinner prep, she heard the front door open and close, announcing he'd arrived home for the evening.

Moving into the foyer, Anna leaned against the

walnut sideboard positioned halfway to the door, propped one hand on a hip, and watched him coolly.

"I cooked tonight. I hope you're hungry."

"I could eat," he stated, his tone cool.

"Then go ahead and shower." Straightening, she let her gaze narrow on his face. "Is everything okay?"

He shook his head slowly. "Everything's fine, Anna. I'll shower."

Moving past her, he headed up the stairs to take his shower.

Limping back to the kitchen, Anna moved to the cabinet, took two more pain pills, then returned to fixing dinner.

Restraining herself from turning and sticking her tongue out in the direction he had taken upstairs, Anna instead took a slow, deep breath.

Moving to the other side of the counter, she checked the text she'd sent to Amelia earlier, her lips pursing at the lack of an answer.

She knew Amelia was pissed, but she hadn't expected her friend to take it to such an extreme as to ignore her calls and texts.

She pulled marinated steaks from the fridge, and the lettuce she'd broken up earlier. The vegetables she'd cut up went into the lettuce; potatoes were in the oven. Once dinner was done she would find out exactly why Archer felt the need to sleep in the guest room and what the hell made him think he could ignore her so easily.

Skye had laughed at her when she called earlier, asking her friend's advice on the best way to handle the situation. She had asked why Anna was bothering to fix Archer's dinner. She should be pissed instead, Skye had drawled. Give him hell. Don't let him get away with it.

She wasn't going to allow him to get away with it any longer, that was for damned sure.

He stepped out to the patio and Anna glanced at him from her position by the grill as she laid the steaks on the rack.

His dark blond hair looked darker wet, his jaw harder and freshly shaved, without the short shadow of a beard and mustache. There was no missing the uncompromising set of his chin or the rough-hewn lines and angles of his face.

Inherent male stubbornness, determination, dominance, and arrogant pride were now fully revealed. The challenge in the natural set of his jaw was enough to set a woman's nerves on edge.

Or ensure a woman set her own challenge.

There was no mistaking the fact that he was pissed as well, but that was okay. Because, Anna decided, she might be more pissed.

To reinforce the fact that she was not making the first move, Anna gave him a long, hard look, then pretended he wasn't even there and went about finishing the meal.

Archer recognized the challenge snapping in her gaze, as well as feeling it tug at the dominance and possessiveness already rising inside him.

She hadn't even realized he was home early. Early, because Sophia Resnova had called and informed him that Skye was under the impression Anna would be moving to the ranch, if not tonight, then tomorrow. And as Anna had called earlier to ask for Skye, she was giving it great credence.

Like hell she was. He dared her to even mention such a thing to him. Of course, that would be hard for her to do considering she hadn't spoken to him since he stepped out to the patio. He was damned tired of it, too.

Narrowing his gaze on her as she set the meal of steak, potatoes, and salad on the small table, he waited.

Anna took her seat, and still she didn't speak. She lifted her fork and knife, and pretended he wasn't even there.

As a matter of fact, as his own ire grew, she finished the meal and never once spoke to him.

"If you're that pissed, then why bother fixing my dinner?" he asked, jaw flexing as she moved to rise from her chair and stack the dishes.

Anna paused, her nostrils flaring as only her gaze lifted.

"You provide a roof over my head and keep me safe. I appreciate it."

She appreciated it?

He provided a roof over her head and she fucking appreciated it?

"You fixed my dinner because you appreciate being able to live here?" he asked carefully. "Fuck you, Anna. I don't want or need your damned gratitude. That's not why I do it, I do it because—"

Because—the thought of anything happening to her had the power to make him enraged. Because he had to hold her. Because she fucking belonged to him.

And he knew he couldn't tell her that.

"That's what I'm supposed to do."

Fuck. That sure as hell wasn't the right thing to say.

"Because it's what you're supposed to do?" Fury lit in her gaze. "How dare you look me in the eye and say something so damned asinine? Are you actually trying to tell me you're protecting me because it's your fucking job?"

Archer almost winced. Hell, he hadn't wanted it to come out that way. That wasn't actually why he did it.

"That wasn't exactly what I said."

"That's exactly what you said. You said you were doing it because you were supposed to. Because it's your job. Well, I'm not your fucking job, Archer." She smacked the plate she was holding to the table.

Archer stood up slowly, leaning forward, his hands bracing on the table as he came nearly nose to nose to her. "No, what you are is driving me damned fucking crazy."

"Then why do you even bother having me here? Why not just go ahead and ship me off to the ranch with Skye and Cami?"

"Because it pleases me at the moment to have you here," he snarled back at her, feeling his body heating, the need to grab her, to kiss her—

Hell, if he didn't fuck her pretty soon then he was going to have a stroke from the blood pounding directly to his dick.

"Well, I'm so glad that much pleases you at the moment, because I'll be damned if I'm in the least bit pleased, Archer Tobias," Anna snarled back at him. "And since you evidently appreciate dinner, you can take care of the damned dirty dishes."

She turned to leave.

"Oh, I don't think so, sweet pea."

Moving into her path before she could rush from the kitchen, Archer blocked her way. Grabbing her hips, holding her to him, he glared down her as her slender hands pressed against his chest.

"Get out of my way," she demanded, her voice rough. "Now."

"Like hell."

He wasn't stupid. Her nipples were as hard as his dick was. Her eyes might be spitting fiery anger, but the hunger, the need was just as hot.

Despite the anger sizzling through her, Anna could feel arousal beginning to melt inside her womb. There was something about the dark, brooding dominance in his expression and burning in his eyes that almost mesmerized her.

His hands clenched at her hips. "I'm damned tired of trying to stay the hell away from you to keep your stitches from stretching or your exertions from scarring your thigh. So if you're going to have problems wearing those pretty bikinis if you have a scar, then you better get the hell away from me before I strip your ass down and fuck you until you're screaming with pleasure."

Her eyes narrowed.

"You haven't touched me because you were afraid I would scar my leg from that wound?" she questioned him furiously.

"I don't give a damn," he growled. "I said, if it will affect your opinion of yourself or your ability to wear a bikini, then now is the time to say something."

"My opinion of myself? You think a scar would change my opinion of myself? Do you really think I'm that damned shallow, Archer?"

Her arms went akimbo, her fingers spreading over her hips as one cocked, delicate foot pointed toward him like an exclamation of anger. Archer watched as her lips pursed, her skin flushed, and both anger and burning arousal heated in her gaze.

"No, I don't think you're shallow, and neither do I believe the scar should bother you, before you get that one in your head. I just didn't want to take the chance that it would. The doctor was very specific, Anna. No exertion or there will be a scar."

"What exertion?" Her arms lifted in exasperation before spreading across her hips once again. "Sex?"

"Sex," he snapped back, suddenly uncomfortable with that description of being with her. "That wound is at the outside of your thigh. During sex your thigh muscles flex and tighten often, Anna. It could tear the stitches or stretch the newly bound skin."

"Or maybe you just prefer not to have sex with me any longer." The sudden uncertain, bleak pain that filled her eyes sliced at his chest.

"Where the hell did you come up with that?" Incredulity snapped through his senses as he stared back at her in disbelief.

"Only a man who no longer wants a woman could come up with something so asinine," she retorted as moisture shimmered in her gaze. "Because it's not possible to use your thighs more having sex than you do sitting down, standing up, or walking all damned day long," she cried out. "Go to hell, Archer, because I know how to pack too, and how to get my own ride out to the ranch with Cami and Skye."

And that was exactly what she would do.

"Like bloody fucking hell," he snarled. "I won't let you deliberately misunderstand this, Anna, just because I've done something you didn't agree with."

"Oh, is that how you see it?" she snapped, giving him a hard push with her hands flat against his chest. "And exactly why should I stay with a man who arbitrarily believes it's just fine to make such decisions for me? To force me to do without my pleasure, without one of the few things that son of a bitch, the Slasher, hadn't been able to take from me. You took it without so much as discussing it with me. I'll be damned if I need someone who believes they can simply take over my life and control me without so much a by-your-leave."

Archer almost paused, because she was right. He should have discussed it with her; he should have given her the choice rather than believing it was his place to protect every aspect of her life.

And where he had that idea, he didn't have a clue.

He wasn't about to admit that to her though. Instead, Archer shook his head, smiling slowly as he backed her against the kitchen counter.

"That excuse isn't going to fly," he warned her.

"I don't have to have an excuse," she informed him, sensuality suddenly gleaming in her expression, flushing her face. "I'm right and you know it! You held back my pleasure and my right to an orgasm because you have a damned He-Man complex."

A slender, delicate finger dug into his chest with each of the last few words of that declaration. But it was the word "orgasm" that tightened his stomach and his balls simultaneously.

Archer glared down at her, his hands tightening at her hips. "Do you really think you're going to get away from me so easily?"

"Pretty much," she assured him, her brows arching, her chin tilting defiantly. "What are you going to do, Archer? Arrest me?"

The thought of handcuffing her to his bed held definite appeal.

His cock jerked at the thought, hardening impossibly more.

"Oh sweetheart, you have no idea of the appeal of handcuffing you to my bed."

"You wouldn't dare." But excitement was slowly gathering, burning in her eyes. The challenge burning there was definitely a dare as well. Feminine, rife with arousal and challenging him to control it.

She was right; he had no right to make decisions where her protection was concerned without discussing it with her first. It was a mistake he would not consider making again.

That didn't mean he was going to let her get away with this little display of hers.

Hell no.

He'd spent far too many years watching out for her, maneuvering to get her home for vacations because he knew that was what she wanted, what she needed.

"I would dare many things, Anna, to ensure your safety."

"To ensure you kept your playthings about is more like it," she protested, albeit weakly as his head lowered, his teeth nibbling at the sensitive lobe of her ear.

"Make me *your* toy then," he told her. "Come on, Anna. Show me how you play." He nipped the side of her neck, licked the little wound. "You can even show me how you get serious."

A shiver raced up her spine and heat sparked, hot and tempting, spearing straight to her womb as her pussy began to ache, to clench in hungry need.

"I've been dying to see you in these pretty little skirts," he breathed out roughly, his hands sliding from her hips to her thighs, bunching the soft material in his hands, pulling it up far enough so his hands could cup the curves of her ass, left bare by the silk of her thong panties.

Slick and hot, her juices gushed from her vagina, the feel of them sliding over the sensitive inner flesh dragging a low moan from her.

Archer's lips covered hers, his tongue licking over the seam of them. Pleasure washed over her, through her, as his lips sipped at hers, his tongue licked and stroked, penetrating her lips with a slow, sensual glide.

She could be pissed again tomorrow, Anna decided. Tonight she wanted him, ached for him. She'd ached for him for over a week, needed his touch.

Tonight she wanted to fill the loneliness with his touch, the hurt and betrayal with pleasure.

Parting her lips, Anna's tongue peeked out as his licked over the lower curve of her lips. Her hands, first pressed against his shirt and then moved to the buttons holding the material together.

Clumsy, fumbling, Anna struggled with the too tiny discs until, finally, the last one came free, revealing the hard contours of his chest and the light mat of dark blond curls that tempted her fingers.

Pushing back from him, she stared up at him, and Archer had no idea what was causing his chest to tighten. His body hardened with such feeling that making sense of it was impossible.

"Archer," she whispered, her hands tightening on the material of his shirt, trying to still the trembling he'd glimpsed.

There was a need in her eyes, a hunger he couldn't decipher.

Her lips trembled before she stilled them, but she couldn't erase the unconscious plea in her gaze, which she had no idea she was showing him.

"Whatever you want, Anna," he said, his lips brushing against hers. He watched her pupils flare, watching the lust, seeing some deeper, darker emotion he couldn't allow himself to acknowledge in the dark sea-green of her eyes.

Clenching his fingers in the curve of her ass, feeling

the muscles clench beneath his hold, had him fighting
the need to take her as fast, as hard as possible.

But it wouldn't be enough, Archer knew. It wouldn't
be enough for him, because he could sense what she
was silently aching for, feel it in the tightening of his
chest, though he was unaware of exactly what it was.

"Tell me, Anna," he said. "Tell me what you want,
baby. Don't you know I'd give you anything you asked
for? If I have it, it's yours."

If he could give it to her without asking, then he
would. If he could read the desire raging in her eyes,
then he would do whatever he had to, to ensure she
had it.

She licked her lips, the sight of her little pink tongue
tasting them tightening his balls. Her breathing accelerated, her breasts rising and falling beneath the light,
silky material of her white sleeveless blouse.

Her gaze turned somber then, a flash of uncertainty
sparking deep in the pretty green orbs.

Archer lowered his lips to her ear again, caressing
the curve of the delicate shell as he spoke.

"Whatever you want, baby. Don't you know, in this,
I would give you whatever you want, Anna, however
you want it."

She arched against him, her head tilting to the side
to give him greater access to the flesh beneath her ear
as he continued kissing the soft curve.

"Please, Archer." She shook her head, and he could
see the uncertainty, the hesitancy raging inside her.

"Don't you trust me, Anna?" he asked, kissing the
corner of her lips. "Do you believe there's any pleasure
you want that could possibly turn me off?"

Her lips trembled.

There were no tears in her eyes, and the need was
only growing, burning hotter inside her.

"Archer." The uncertainty filled her voice.

Lifting his hand, his fingers touched her cheek, his thumb brushing against her lips. "Yes, baby?"

"I want the fairy tale." Hoarse, nervous, the plea caused him to slowly still as he held her against him. "Just tonight, Archer. Just this once, let me know what the fairy tale feels like."

The fairy tale.

Archer's eyes closed.

Burying his face against the curve of her neck, a grimace tightened his expression as he fought to hide it from her.

Just for tonight, his Anna wanted to be loved. She wanted to know what it felt like to be loved, to have someone be "in love" with her.

He didn't believe in being "in love"; Archer knew what the illusion of it could do to a man though. How it could destroy his life, rip his guts out day by day.

But women—

Love could strip the life from a woman's soul and leave her drifting, her heart and her soul torn from her body as she existed, nothing more.

He didn't want that for Anna.

But didn't she deserve just one dream in her life? Didn't she deserve just a little illusion to make up for everything that had been taken from her?

But how could he give her that dream?

He was a man who didn't believe—

She stiffened beneath him.

"Just for tonight," he whispered, feeling something slowly loosen so deep inside his soul that he had no idea what it was. "Just for tonight, let me love you, Anna."

CHAPTER 18

There was a hunger in Archer's kiss that Anna hadn't felt before, a need she hadn't known could exist, except in her.

When his lips covered hers, gently—oh God, so gently—his lips moved over hers, rubbing against them, stroking, warming them as sensation mixed with emotion to flare in heated pulses rushing through her.

Wrapping her arms around his neck, Anna parted her lips further as she eagerly accepted the deeper intensity that filled the kiss.

This was what she had needed.

This was what she had ached for.

As Archer's lips devoured hers, his tongue pushing and teasing hers, the hard curve of his knee tucked high between her thighs. The heated warmth against the sensitive flesh of her silk-covered pussy pulled a moan from her lips. It was so good. It was the most incredible kiss she had experienced. Even in her deepest fantasies she hadn't known a kiss that fired her blood, her heart and soul, as well as her pleasure, at once.

The slow arch and lift of her hips rubbed the aching

flesh against his knee, blindly following the sensations suddenly tearing through her.

Burying her fingers in his hair, Anna licked at his lips as he had hers. As she moved into his kiss, a muted cry of pleasure was lost beneath the harsh male groan that rumbled in his chest. The combined sounds of pleasure moving through her senses, multiplying the intensity of her pleasure.

Tightening her thighs on his knee, Anna slid her fingers from his nape, along his neck, then to his chest. Lowering her other hand, instinct and need guiding her actions, Anna was pushing at the material of his shirt, needing to feel his flesh against her own.

As the soft cotton slid over his powerful shoulders, catching on his hard biceps, Archer suddenly lifted himself from her, jerking the shirt off and letting it fall, forgotten, to the floor.

Lowering himself to her again, the sight of the short skirt pushed above the silk of her panties as she rode the hard curve of his knee drew a harsh groan from his throat.

God, what she did to him.

How the hell had he forced himself to wait to have her like this? To touch her, to taste her?

The pleasure was a high he was quickly becoming addicted to.

Fuck, she was killing him.

Lowering his hands to her thighs, Archer pushed the skirt back further. His jaw clenched at the sight of her silk-covered pussy rubbing against his knee, the moist heat dampening her panties.

Holding back a desperate groan, Archer lifted his hands to the buttons of her thin blouse, hurriedly releasing them as her lashes lifted.

Her hands flattened against his stomach, smoothing up over his chest, spreading a heated wave of pleasure over his flesh as the silk of her hands caressed him.

"Anna," he groaned, as her hands moved to the belt of his jeans.

How the hell was he going to maintain his control when her hunger was like a flame licking over his flesh?

Lifting her, he quickly pushed her blouse from her shoulders, forcing himself to patience as it fell from her arms.

Her fingers loosened his belt, pushed it aside, then tugged at the snap of his jeans.

"I want to touch you." The husky need in her voice had his thighs tightening further as she struggled with the zipper of his jeans until it, too, parted beneath her trembling fingers.

Archer breathed in roughly as she parted the jeans, gripped the thick length of his cock, then eased it from the fabric.

The broad head flared, thick and smooth, the flesh dark with the need to fuck her, as Archer eased her back on the couch. Pushing his fingers beneath the skirt he gripped the side of her panties and tore the silk from her hips.

He would buy her more later.

Anna shuddered, exquisite pleasure rushing through her in a wave of fierce, heated sensation.

"Oh God," she breathed out, the sound ragged and rough as Archer moved lower, spreading her thighs apart as he came down between them.

His fingers brushed against the top of her mound.

Damn, he loved her pussy.

Soft curls covered the mound above her clit. Below them was sweet, silken pink flesh saturated and glistening with slick, hot, feminine honey.

Archer licked his lips, took his finger, and eased it up the narrow slit, feeling the slickness of her wet heat as more flowed from her hot little pussy.

"So pretty," he murmured, circling the hard, swollen bud of her clit.

He felt mesmerized, fucking drunk on the temptation of that wet heat lying slick and glistening on her swollen folds.

Easing her thighs further apart, Archer felt her heels digging into the couch as her hips arched again, the soft curves of her delicate little pussy parting again, flashing the pretty, soft pink flesh at the entrance of her vagina.

"Archer, I don't know——" A whimpering moan fell from her lips. "I don't know——what you do to me."

The sound of her arousal, the need in her voice, had his muscles tightening, the temptation of her tearing at his control.

"I'm loving you, Anna," he promised her, his hand flattening against her belly to hold her in place. "I'm loving you, baby."

And God, how he wished love, the love she ached so desperately for, actually existed. He would give it to her. He would fill her life with it. He would give her so much damned love she would never remember what it felt like not to have love.

For now, all he could do was give her the illusion, but that illusion——

It rose inside him, overtook him, and for a while, for just a little while, Archer let himself believe it could exist.

Lowering his head, Archer slid the tip of his tongue through the narrow slit of her swollen folds. The silken flesh parted, the sweet honey of her juices clinging to his tongue as he licked and stroked the sensitive flesh.

Sliding his hands beneath her hips as she lifted to him, Archer worked his tongue from her clit to the clenched, heated opening of her pussy, feeling the snug, tight opening flex against his tongue, trying to draw it inside the heated depths.

Staring up at her as she pushed her fingers through his hair, Archer licked his lips again, held her gaze, then swiped his tongue quickly through the swollen slit as her cry of pleasure echoed around them. The sweet spice of her feminine heat exploded against his senses, the sweet, heated taste of her drawing him back for more.

Anna felt her breath catch, then rush through her lungs as his tongue slid through the swollen, sensitive folds of her pussy.

Her clit throbbed in impending release, sending a rush of brutal need to tighten her nipples as her clit throbbed with a deep, pulsing demand.

As his gaze held hers, his tongue working through her pussy, licking, stroking, Anna was certain she couldn't bear the pleasure.

"Ah, Anna, I swear the taste of your pussy makes me drunk. All I thought about today was tasting you." His tongue licked along her slit again. "Sucking your pretty clit." A sucking kiss was delivered to the little bud. "And stroking my tongue as deep inside you as it'll go."

His tongue pierced the entrance, pushing inside, stroking along nerve endings that flared in heated response. As his head came back, his fingers found the entrance instead, pushing inside her again. the tight depths requiring several stretching thrusts before they lodged fully inside her.

"Archer, oh God, it's so good," she moaned, her hips pressing his fingers deeper, riding them with tight, desperate movements. Forcing her pussy against the impalement as pleasure rushed through her senses.

His lips covered the hard bud of her clit, surrounding it with the wet heat of his mouth. Anna whimpered with the sensations as he began suckling it, slow and easy. His mouth and tongue worked the little bud, the fingers buried inside her fucking her with deep, rhythmic motions.

"Oh God, Archer, yes" she moaned, the pleasure tightening through her pussy, her clit, building in her womb as she cupped her breasts. Her thumbs and forefingers caught the little buds, working them firmly and sending sharp peaks of pleasure slashing along an erogenous path to her clit.

Archer's lips tightened on her clit, his tongue flickering against it now. The thrust and rub of his fingers inside her, the heavy male growls of pleasure vibrating against the tender bud, overwhelmed her.

Sensation exploded through her in sharp, body-jerking bursts as she came around his fingers a breath before her clit exploded against his tongue.

As her vagina clenched and rippled in waves of fiery sensation, her clitoris exploded, shards of sharpened ecstasy racing through her as she screamed his name. Pressed tight against his thrusting fingers and suckling lips, his tongue keeping the fiery storm of rapture racing through her clit, Anna could do nothing but arch, her hands clenching in his hair, her hips lifting to him as the obliteration of her senses continued.

Perspiration coated her flesh as a cry of completion became a wail of continued ecstasy. Shuddering, her body jerking against him with each violent pulse of rapture, Anna was certain she would die in his arms before it would end. But as she collapsed against the couch, her breathing harsh as Archer's fingers slowly slid from her inner flesh, she admitted she might live.

She might.

Forcing her eyes open, she watched as Archer sat at the side of the couch, jerking his boots off before standing and quickly shedding his jeans.

Anna forced herself to sit up, sliding around until she faced him her gaze locked on the flared, heavily throbbing crest of his cock.

She licked her lips, seeing the bead of pre-come that glistened at the tip.

"If you wrap that pretty mouth around my dick, I won't stop until I'm pumping my come down your throat," he warned her as he watched the intent fill her gaze.

The explicitness of the warning shouldn't have sent her juices spilling again, and her clit immediately throbbing in interest.

But it did. And, she realized, it had curiosity filling her just as quickly as the lust.

She'd never had that, and she realized she wanted it. She wanted to experience everything with Archer. When this was over and he walked away, she wanted to know every act with him.

She wanted to know what it meant to belong to him.

"But I want to wrap my lips around your dick," she said softly, watching his expression as it tightened and brutal lust filled his face.

Leaning forward, his hard body pressed her into the back of the couch as his hand braced against the top of the cushions. Archer gripped the base of his cock, the flared crest pressing against her lips.

"Ah baby," he groaned as her head tilted back, the angle of the penetration allowing her gaze to connect with his.

"Fuck, I love your mouth." Burying the fingers of one hand in her hair, a heavy grimace tightened his face. "Sweet, hot, sucking mouth . . . That's it, baby, suck my dick. Let me fuck those pretty lips."

Fingers clenched tighter in her hair, his hips moved, thrusted the head of his cock into her mouth. With each thrust her tongue licked and stroked with heavy demand, pushing Archer closer to the brink of release.

Sliding her hands up his thighs, Anna found the tight, heated sac beneath his cock as a heavy groan filled the air. Stroking the taut flesh, feeling his cock head throb against her tongue, Anna tightened her lips around him. One hand stroked the hard shaft, the other cupped and caressed his balls as her need for him overwhelmed her.

Watching the flared crest of his cock as he thrust it slow and easy inside her mouth, Archer groaned desperately at the draw of her mouth against the sensitive head.

Controlling the thrust of his hips, he felt the depth of his penetration into her exquisite heat was killing him. The need to fuck her hard and deep had his balls throbbing, the blood pounding hard and heated through the engorged length of his dick.

God, he loved the feel of her mouth.

"So sweet." Watching his cock stretch her lips, redden them, was so damned arousing he couldn't believe it.

He'd never had lust grab him by the balls in the ways it did with Anna. There was no maintaining his control and no way in hell to hold back with her. She did things to him he couldn't explain and couldn't make sense of.

As her tongue licked and rubbed beneath the flared crest, her mouth enveloping it with innocent heat, her expression cleared of the somber pain that had filled it. Her eyes were no longer dark with the misery trapped inside her, or the fears haunting her.

And she was stripping him to the very core of who and what he was, Archer realized.

He'd never known pleasure like this. He'd never known the pleasure could burn through the depths of her body as it did with her.

Fiery heat surrounded the head of his dick, her mouth drawing at it. Pleasure stroked straight to his balls as the need to come began to overwhelm everything else.

Staring into her eyes, lost in the dark depths of the emotions swirling in her gaze, the intensity of those emotions pulling him under, pulling him in—

Archer meant to pull free of her. The intent had been to fuck her pretty mouth only to the point of coming. He'd had no true intention of giving her his release in such a way.

As her mouth tightened, her tongue pressing and rubbing against the ultrasensitive nerve endings, her fingers lightly rubbed against his balls. Archer stared into her eyes and saw emotions he couldn't define. Yet he could feel them resonating inside him until his control shattered and his release erupted from his cock.

There was no warning.

One second he was ready to pull back, the next second his come was spurting from the head of his cock and filling her tight, sucking mouth in rapid pulses of semen that jetted from the tip.

Anna's eyes widened, then darkened. Tightening her mouth on the pulsing head, her fingers stroked the throbbing shaft as low pleasure-filled moans vibrated around the thick head.

Pleasure was almost agony. It was like having a part

of his soul stripped from him to meet with the fire and brilliant emotions in her heavy-lidded gaze.

When it returned, slamming back into him as the last thick pulse of his release spurted into her mouth, Archer knew he wasn't the same.

Just as he knew he needed more of her.

The release that tore from him wasn't enough.

He needed more of her, more of a pleasure so addicting that he wondered if he could ever let her go.

Staring up at Archer as he pulled free of her gripping mouth, Anna couldn't help but lick her lips with sensual satisfaction.

"Oh baby, we're not done yet." He surprised her with the harsh growl of his voice.

A gasp escaped her lips as Archer jerked a pillow from the couch and tossed it to the floor in front of him. Then, bending to it, he gripped her knees and parted them before pulling her hips to the edge.

"Oh yes," the whispered need passed her lips as she spread her thighs, her knees lifting to grip his lean flanks.

Quickly rolling the condom he'd pulled from the back pocket of his jeans onto his erection, Archer then bent to her.

"Did you think I'd leave you unsatisfied?" he asked, gripping the thick stalk of his cock as he eased the engorged head through the swollen, juice-laden folds of her pussy.

"I would—" A moan parted her lips as the thick crest pressed into the now oversensitive entrance. "—would have understood."

"Watch." The hoarsely voiced order had her gaze following his.

Reclined back as she was, her thighs spread wide,

Anna could see the hard flesh of his cock parting her intimate lips. The swollen curves hugged the wide crest, her juices clinging to it as he began pressing inside.

The slow, controlled stretch of her delicate inner muscles had pleasure rising rapidly as the fiery pleasure-pain began streaking across her nerve endings.

"Archer." The intensity of the pleasure beginning to overtake her. "It's so good, Archer."

Angling her hips to him, her fingers gripping his arms, Anna watched as, with a final hard thrust, he buried to the hilt inside her.

The heavy pulse of his cock had her knees tightening on his hips as the imperative need to orgasm came racing through her again.

Lifting her gaze to his, Anna felt her chest tighten, almost felt the tears that would have filled her eyes.

The look on his face—

Her breath hitched, a whimpering moan filling the air around them as he began to move. His hips thrusting, dragging his cock nearly free before pushing inside her. He worked the heavy flesh to the hilt, pulled back, then thrust hard and heavy inside her again.

The stroke and caress of his heavily veined shaft and his thick, blunt head built inside Anna.

Pleasure rose in intensity as overexcited nerve endings began to burn, to flare. Thrusting harder, faster, he locked his gaze on hers, his expression so tender so—what?

What was it?

What emotion was whipping between them?

The intensity of it, like the ecstatic pleasure, only strengthened, increased.

"Archer, please!" The need, the overwhelming sensations were pulsing, expanding inside her.

When he was groaning, perspiration running in rivulets down his chest, along the side of his face, his golden-brown eyes seemed more brilliant, more predatory—

"Anna. Sweetheart." His groan was hoarse, his body tightening as he lifted one hand from her hips to cup her cheek. "Sweet Anna—"

Archer's teeth clenched as Anna cried out, her pussy tightening around his cock as it shuttled back and forth, harder, faster.

Flames erupted inside her.

Electric, pulsing, ecstasy exploded like fireworks inside the clenched, pleasure-tortured depths of her vagina.

"Fuck! Baby!" His hand tightened at her cheek, some battle raging in his expression as she felt his release suddenly tear through his corded body.

"Ah fuck!" His face tightened, his gaze turning savage. "Anna. Ah God. Mine!" His hips slammed forward as she felt his cock flex, pulse.

The muscles of her pussy rippled and tightened around him.

"Mine! Damn you, you're mine!"

His lips covered hers.

Possessive, demanding. The kiss marked her soul and stilled the words being torn from his lips.

Caught in the cataclysm swirling through both of them, Anna swore she felt a part of herself merge with him. Felt a part of him merge with her.

And for one precious moment out of time, Anna knew what it meant to belong—

CHAPTER 19

The alarm that began blaring through the house brought
Archer instantly out of bed and reaching for his pants.
Jerking them on, he grabbed his weapon from beside
the bed and turned to Anna as she quickly dressed.

"Archer, what the fuck?" Rory yelled outside the
bedroom.

Archer jerked the bedroom door open. "Stay with
her and get two men in here. Send the others next door
to the Brocks."

Archer was running through the house as he shouted
out the order.

Archer had tied the Brocks' alarm into his after an
attempted break-in the year before. The parents worked
midnight shifts at the Emergency Care Clinic, leaving
their teenage daughter, Callie Brock, alone in the house.

"Jerking his cell phone from his jeans as he ran
down the stairs, he quickly hit the speed-dial number
for his deputy.

"Caine," the deputy answered.

"Get your ass to the Brocks." Disconnecting,
Archer was out the back door of his house and racing

across the short distance to the side door of the Brocks' house.

He could hear Callie even as he shoved the key into the lock and twisted it to unlock the door.

Pushing into the house he was aware of two of Brute Force's agents coming in behind, one of them the single female on their protective payroll.

Callie was screaming upstairs.

The sound of her cries had a growl of fury tearing from his throat. He'd spent enough time in the military overseas to suspect what had happened from the sound of those hoarse, terrified screams.

"Cover me," Archer ordered, though he was certain no one was in the house any longer.

"Callie. Callie, it's Archer," he yelled as he tore up the stairs.

Following her screams he burst through the bedroom door, instantly finding the teenager where she was huddled, a sheet drawn around her naked body, the cell phone she'd used to activate the alarm clenched in her fingers.

Shoulder-length blonde hair was tangled and tear damp as she stopped screaming only to collapse in tears. Callie laid her head against her up-raised knees, sobs tearing from her chest as Marta moved quickly around him and bent to her knees in front of her.

"Callie, sweetheart." The agent's calm voice and compassionate tone made the young girl's head lift as her breath hitched violently and her sobs became harder.

"Callie, how badly are you hurt?" Marta asked softly as Archer and the other agent moved quickly to the open doorway. "I need you to tell me how badly you're hurt."

Archer glimpsed Callie shaking her head quickly, though the sobs became louder for just a moment before she seemed to control them once again.

"I was able—able to turn—the alarm on." Jerky and tear-roughened, her voice had fury stabbing at his senses. "He was in dark clothes—" she sobbed raggedly. "And a mask." She was rocking herself as Marta moved cautiously to rub her arm. "He said, said I was a means to an end," she cried. "I was just bait—like a worm on a hook—" she sobbed. "He said don't forget, you're just a worm on a hook."

Just a tool.

Archer's head lifted and turned, suspicion suddenly exploding through his mind.

Jerking his cell phone from his pants he hit Rory's name in his contact list and listened to the phone ring—and ring

His heart stopped in his chest as Caine raced to the top of the stairs and Archer turned to him slowly.

Just a tool—a means to an end.

"Caine, with me." Archer didn't hesitate.

Leaving Callie with Marta and the other agent he was down the stairs and out of the house in a matter of seconds.

He'd closed the side door to the house and it would have locked automatically.

But it wasn't closed. It was open.

"Anna." Archer yelled her name, knowing, he knew— "Anna."

"Rory's not answering his phone," the deputy yelled.

Archer all but tripped over Rory's fallen body in the foyer.

He went to his knees, staring at the back of the younger man's head and the amount of blood that stained his black hair, white shirt, and the honey-colored wood of the floor.

"Calling the EMTs." Caine's voice was distant, barely heard.

There was a buzzing in Archer's ears, in his senses. As he checked Rory's pulse, there wasn't even enough emotion left inside him to feel relief that Rory was alive.

He rose to his feet, knowing—

Ah God, he knew.

Moving up the stairs, he turned and walked into the bedroom.

Oscar was lying on the floor, dazed, obviously hurt.

Kneeling, Archer checked him out. There were no broken bones, but blood smeared his head from a cut, and more blood smeared his face.

Pulling the cat's mouth open, Archer saw threads, blood, and possible flesh between the cat's teeth.

"Archer?" Nash and Caine entered the bedroom slowly.

Handing the cat to the surprised CSI he said, "There're flesh and fabric fibers in his teeth. We have the Slasher's DNA, thanks to Oscar."

He could hear the dull lifelessness in his voice.

"We found tire imprints in the woods behind the house. One of Ivan's men is casting and photographing them."

"They have her." Archer stared around the bedroom.

Her gown was tossed to the floor; she'd been dressing when he tore off to check on Callie.

The clothes she had worn that day were still on the chair, but he'd seen her jerking jeans on as he left the bedroom.

"I left her alone," he said, his chest tightening to

the point that he wondered if his entire body would explode.

"Rory was here, Archer," his deputy argued. "And he's a damned good agent. Whoever took him out caught him unaware."

"Or it was someone he suspected he could trust," Nash interjected.

"I left her alone," he repeated. "I should have taken her with me."

"The two agents outside saw the truck leaving the woods and rushed to attempt to get a tag number. There were no tags, but they've seen the truck before." The agent he'd left with Marta was suddenly at the door.

"It was the same truck the shooter was driving," Archer stated.

He felt—fuck, he felt broken inside.

"It was," the agent agreed.

"The tires from that truck were unique, Archer," Nash said then. "I've been running them. They're not even sold in Colorado. They're extremely expensive and custom made—"

Archer turned back to him and saw the cat missing. "Why aren't you digging that meat out of Oscar's teeth? That's fucking human flesh. It's an ID."

"And Gregor Resnova just carried him straight out of here with a message that's he's called someone else in straight from New York. He took the cat to the labs."

Archer turned to Caine. "Get to the labs."

"He had half a dozen of Ivan's agents with him," the deputy reported. "They're covered, Archer."

Archer turned back to the other agent. "Callie?"

"Her parents are on their way. She wasn't raped, she was used."

"She was bait," he said softly. *Like a worm on a hook. Don't forget, you're just a worm on a hook.*

It was a message.

The abductor was Sorenson's partner. It wasn't Sorenson, but the County attorney would be waiting wherever he took her.

"Archer?" John questioned, watching him closely.

He turned to the other agent. "Get to Wayne Sorenson's house, see if he's there. If he is, I want him here, and I don't care how you get him here. If he's not, see if you can find any hint of a cabin, or a residence near a lake, or fishing hole. A vacation home, anything. It would be close to Corbin County, if not in Corbin County."

The agent turned and rushed from the room.

God, he left her alone.

"Ryan's on his way," John assured him.

Archer nodded.

Flipping his phone open, he hit another contact.

"Jordan Malone," a dark voice answered.

"Rory's been hurt, bad," he told the former Navy SEAL. "They took my woman, Jordan," he said, his voice tight. "The Slasher has her, and I have no idea where he took her or how long I have."

There was a moment's silence on the line.

"Rory called in last week about the case," Jordan told him then. "Noah Blake and Micah Sloane are currently in Corbin County, and have been for several days. As soon as they know something, they'll contact you. I'll be there within hours."

The line disconnected.

Archer inhaled slowly, aware of John Caine watching him, his gaze narrowed.

"There are two shadows in town. Stay out of their way and pass the word along," he warned the deputy.

"And we know them from the other fucking shadows in this goddamned place, how?" John cursed. "There are so many fucking players here I'm about to get whiplash."

"You can get whiplash on your own time," Archer informed him. "Callie's attacker left us a message. She was a worm on a hook. Think John. She's bait. A means to an end. A worm on a hook."

"They have a hold on her somehow, or have her in a position she can't escape from," John answered instantly. "Bait—it's more literal. They're holding her next to a place where you could fish."

"Jaymi Kramer was killed next to the lake outside of town," Archer remembered. "Thomas Jones was screaming for help when Crowe caught up with him that night. Crowe said once he had the impression Thomas thought his partner was nearby, in the area, and expected him to help. Maybe he knew his partner was close. Maybe he was taking Jaymi to his partner when he decided to stop and rape her first instead."

He and his father had gone through every rental cabin in the area that summer—

He flipped his phone open again and hit another number.

"Tell me what you need," Ivan answered.

"Private cabins around Broken Bow Lake," Archer told him. "I'm looking for any way the Mulrooneys, Wayne Sorenson, or the suspects Ryan named might be connected to those cabins. I'm on my way up there now."

"Got it. Give me five minutes."

He prayed Anna had five minutes.

Running from the house, he ignored John as he attempted to call him back, ignored the security agent who yelled something about the Callahans.

He didn't have time to worry about the Callahans.

Anna—

He'd left her and Rory alone. He should have taken her with him. He should have never left her alone, not after he'd loved her, not after the mark he'd seen on her back and the realization of exactly why the Slasher wanted her out of Corbin County.

He'd given the bastard the perfect opportunity to take her when he raced to the Brock home. And he should have known.

He should have known he was being played the second that alarm had pierced the house.

Reversing his truck from the driveway, he threw it into drive and tore off along the back roads out of town toward Broken Bow Lake.

Sorenson had to have a private cabin there. That was why Thomas Jones had taken Jaymi to the lake to kill her. It was the reason why he and his father hadn't been able to find any evidence in the rental cabins there.

There had been no evidence in them, because those girls had been raped and murdered in one of the private homes instead.

And tonight he'd know exactly which one.

"She's beautiful, isn't she?" Insidious and filled with malicious amusement, the vile compliment had terror threatening Anna's composure. "Did you inject her?"

"Just as you ordered," Amory lied through his teeth. Sort of. The injection had stilled the majority of the terror; it kept her from giving in to the horror and agonizing fear.

She could think though. She could think, and she could move, and she hadn't been tied down. She wasn't restrained in any way by anything but the warning Amory had given her earlier.

"Be still and be quiet, and you'll live. If he tries to rape you, then you can fight. He won't expect you to fight. Go for the eyes first, hurt him, then run. The front door will be open. But only if he tries to rape you, Anna. Do as I'm telling you and you'll live."

She definitely intended to live.

And she intended to kill Wayne Sorenson herself.

Oh, she might be blindfolded, but she knew his voice, just as she had known Amory's. All she had to do was stay calm, she told herself. Calm and in control.

What she feared, though, was that calm and control might not do her a hell of a lot of good in this situation. Restraining herself could be the least of her worries, and God knew screams, tears, and pleas weren't going to help her in the least.

The Slasher had no mercy, and hearing the voice, putting together the things she knew about her best friend's father, Anna knew he would be particularly merciless with her. He would have never allowed Amory to take her otherwise.

Amelia couldn't know about this, could she?

Or was that why she had been so furious when Anna had refused to leave Corbin County?

"Do you think she knows who she is?" Wayne asked Amory then. "That mark on her back is like a red flag. She's sleeping with Archer, and there's no doubt he'd know that mark."

Her birthmark? What did that have to do with anything? It was just a birthmark.

"I doubt it," Amory answered. "If Archer knew what it was, then he's evidently kept it to himself."

What did it mean?

Lying still and quiet, lethargy still gripping her and holding back the fear, Anna wondered what the hell could be so important about the birthmark.

"She looks so much like her mother," Wayne sighed then. "It's really too bad she wouldn't stay away, isn't it? It might have saved her this fate."

This fate. Rape, torture, murder.

Somehow, the Slasher had chosen her, and she couldn't figure out why.

She hadn't fucked a Callahan.

Hell, she didn't want to fuck a Callahan.

The fact that she had no interest in her cousin, or his cousins, ensured that what Amory and Wayne were doing just wasn't fair.

Every victim the Slasher had taken had at least given one of the far too handsome Callahan cousins a blow job. She had never considered it—not to the Callahans or any other man until Archer.

For some reason, a Callahan cousin had never been her preferred sexual turn-on. Nope, that distinction went to one of their best friends. The man she loved.

Where was Archer?

Was Callie okay?

"Is she still asleep?" Wayne asked, his voice filled with anticipation.

"Completely," Amory promised the other man. "But I'm still uncertain why we've taken her, and why we took her in this way. If you rape and kill her, Wayne, you'll only bring the state police and the FBI down on the County. Fun and games will definitely be over then."

"It would have been much better if my warnings had been heeded by her grandfather. I can't risk Crowe learning her true identity." *What the fuck?*

Her true identity? She was Anna Corbin. She knew who she was, and her family knew who she was. Who the hell did Wayne Sorenson think she was?

"But can we risk the state police and the FBI here?" Amory asked again.

"Such a pretty, perfect little body." Regret filled the voice. "You're right of course. I've already thought of all of this. We can't risk killing her, and we can't risk allowing her to stay here. If we're very, very lucky, when she awakens she'll be frightened enough to leave Corbin County."

"The abduction was only a ruse then?" Amory asked. "And if she doesn't leave as you anticipate she will?"

"Then the next time we take her, we'll enjoy her to the full extent of our abilities," Wayne murmured. "She has no idea who we are, nor does the sheriff, evidently, or Crowe Callahan would have already gone insane I believe. Learning the baby sister you believed was dead is actually alive, and that the family that disowned you raised her, knowing full well who she is, would make you crazy. He'll kill the entire fucking family, except Anna, if he ever learns it."

"Wouldn't that achieve your aims?" Amory asked then.

Wayne was silent for long moments. "You would think so, wouldn't you?" he said softly. "But each time I consider it, all I can see is Kim's face. All I can see are her tears, and all I hear are her pleas. No, Amory, that wouldn't achieve my aims. Sarah Ann Corbin can't die before she turns twenty-five."

She was a Callahan?

She was Crowe's sister, Sarah Ann. And her family knew it?

Thank God Amory had given her whatever he'd given her. Otherwise, she would be screaming in rage right now.

This was why her family had never allowed her to be home for more than a week at a time.

She'd been eight the first time she'd asked about Crowe. She'd questioned her grandfather and Wayne

Sorenson about her cousin Crowe, and why he couldn't be a part of the family.

Six months later she had been shipped off to her first private school.

Because she was Crowe's sister, and Wayne Sorenson couldn't risk anyone other than the Corbins knowing that.

Anna knew some of the details of Kimberly Corbin's will, and the estate she left to her son. Crowe wasn't the only child mentioned in those papers. David and Kimberly Callahan's daughter had been mentioned as well. Sarah Ann Callahan would receive the entirety of the estate if Crowe ever left the County. If he died, all the property would be put up at auction, just as it would be if Sarah Ann died at any time after she turned twenty-five years old.

She would be twenty-five soon.

"Keep her another twenty-four hours." The order was delivered crisply, the voice above her no longer crooning or filled with amusement——and it was now so very familiar. "I've made my point with her disappearance. Once the drugs wear off, remove the restraints and leave. When she awakens, she'll find her way out of here and back to the bosom of her family." Sarcasm filled the cruel voice.

"That's a long time to keep the drugs in her." There was no emotion in Amory's voice. No approval or disapproval. He was simply relaying information as though whether she lived or died really didn't matter to him.

"Ease her back slowly then. Just be certain to be gone before she awakens."

"She may remember who I am." Once again, the tone was completely devoid of caring. "If she recognized my voice when I took her, then it'll all be over with."

Of course she would remember who he was. The question was, why had he ensured she would know who he was, that she would remember each second of this little meeting?

She would have him crucified. He might have saved her, but he'd done nothing to save the other girls who had been murdered this year.

"I doubt she will remember, but if she does, you and I were at my house putting together that budget for the Community Center. That's all you have to say."

"You're not sacrificing me, then?" Amory seemed surprised. "I was afraid you would, to save yourself. And I couldn't have blamed you."

Oh, he was good, Anna thought in surprise. Real good. He even sounded convincing.

"Of course I'm not sacrificing you, my friend. Who would aid me in my little hobby if I did so?" The familiar voice was gentle, and so convincing. "Everyone at the Community Center knows we were supposed to get together to go over that budget. I wouldn't sacrifice you, Amory. We cover each other's backs and we live to enjoy our next little play date."

"Hmm." The noncommittal little hum sent a chill racing up her spine.

"You worry too much," Amory was told with a vein of amusement. "And you're far too suspicious."

"Well, you have managed to kill your two previous partners," Amory pointed out. "That would make a man suspicious."

"Not so. Not so," the voice objected. "The Callahans killed both of them. They were stupid, and refused to heed my directions. Everyone wants to lead and none want to follow. Keep following my advice where the Callahans are concerned, and you won't have to

worry about them. Nor will you have to worry about
getting caught."

Smug satisfaction filled Wayne's voice.

"I believe I've shown great aptitude in following
your directions," Amory assured him.

"Yes, my friend, you have." His partner's tone was
one of triumph and satisfaction. "And for that reason,
I'm looking forward to an excellent partnership. Just
remember, whatever she may remember when you
grabbed her, we can easily explain away. If she remem-
bers any of it."

Oh, she was going to remember. She promised them
both she would.

"Have you found Ellen Mason yet?" the familiar
voice asked, his tone changing to one of impatience.

"That can't be her real name," Amory answered.
"The apartment was clean. I mean real clean. No fin-
gerprints, no DNA of any sort. It was completely ster-
ilized."

"Interesting," the partner murmured. "Were you able
to find anything about her when you questioned her co-
workers? Social security number? Driver's license
number? Anyone who knew anything about her?"

"She was being paid under the table and she didn't
make friends."

Ellen Mason. She was the third lover Logan had
contacted after Marietta Tyme had been found several
months before. Logan had had three lovers that he'd
attempted to keep hidden. None of them had lived in
Corbin County, and he hadn't seen any of them more
than once. Still, two had died.

"I want her found."

"Why? We didn't try to grab her, so there's no chance
of her identifying us. Why is she so important?"

"Because she's obviously not who she says she is,

and she's hiding. That makes her dangerous. Trust me. If Logan managed to knock another bitch up besides that O'Brien whore, then it would be Ellen Mason. I know exactly how those whores work. I want the Callahan line to cease and desist. Do you understand me?"

"What about the assassin you hired?" The faintest hint of amusement filled Amory's voice then. "Have you managed to contact him?

"You didn't answer me." Dangerously dark, Wayne's voice lowered warningly. "Did you understand me?"

"I understand completely." There was no emotion, no fear, nothing in Amory's voice to indicate what he actually felt. "I always understand the orders you give implicitly."

He didn't understand shit and he didn't care. For whatever reason, he was part of this team, and all he cared about was getting out of it whatever it was he was after.

"Call me when you leave then," the partner ordered.

It was only seconds later that the door closed, and no more than a breath later that she heard the sound of footsteps nearing her.

Amory.

Why was he coming over to her? He was just fine on the other side of the room as far as she was concerned.

"He's an interesting man, isn't he?" Amory commented.

Anna forced her eyes open and felt a tear that slipped free. And here she'd thought she'd done a better job at holding back her emotions.

"Why are you helping me?" She needed to know. What made a monster suddenly pretend to have an iota of mercy?

He sighed heavily. "The major reason is the fact

that you remind me so much of my own daughter. You would like her, Anna. She's outspoken and full of spirit, just as you are. And, like you, she has a heart and a soul. Not all of us have such things, you know."

"And," he continued, "sometimes such addictions such as mine are simply a part of who and what you are." He shrugged, glancing up at her once again with a somber look. "But even such addictions can be handled. Managed, to a point." His gaze was still cold, but the expression on his face seemed a little less merciless now. "But only if you adhere to your own rules. Mr. Sorenson has broken far too many of those."

"Such bloodletting should have limits. I don't care much for what he would do to a young woman he knows as well as he knows you. One of such innocence and integrity." He stopped.

Anna heard the sound that had him pausing, had his expression tightening again into one of icy, murderous intent. A slight, distinct click, almost that of a lock easing open.

"They're early," he murmured, moving away from her, his expression suddenly imperative as he bent and jerked open a trapdoor in the floor before turning back to her. "Tell them I helped you, Anna. If it hadn't been for me, you'd be dead. You'd just be another loose end for him to tie up if I hadn't found the clause that stated you had to be twenty-five for your death to benefit him. Remember that. Remember, I repaid your father's kindnesses and more."

CHAPTER 20

It happened so quickly.

Amory threw himself into the opening the trapdoor made in the floor.

Weak, struggling, Anna threw herself to the floor.

Glass shattered as a harsh, acrid scent began to roll through the room in heavy columns of lung-searing smoke. Raised voices, shouted commands, and blinding lights lit up the smoke-filled interior of the cabin as darkened shadows rushed through the door.

Smoke attacked her lungs, tightened them, and made it harder to breath.

As close to the floor as she could get, Anna fought to breathe and to control the instinct to cough against the harsh smoke filling the room.

"Archer," she cried out. "Archer, where are you?"

She knew he was there. She had known he would come for her. The sound of sirens began to fill the night, along with the harsh male voices raised from the darkness outside. Anna could hear orders being shouted from outside the cabin.

Shards of splinters rained through the room as the

back wall and door seemed to explode into tiny fragments. Chaos exploded around her.

The prick of a splinter being forced into her arm, then her hip, had her crying out, her head jerking to the side. Geez, she was getting tired of losing her own blood. She liked keeping it inside her body, if that was okay?

The stitches in her thigh had torn as Amory dragged her from Archer's house through the night. There went Archer's hope that it wouldn't scar.

"Dammit, Archer, make it stop," she cried out as she heard another of the smoke canisters explode in the house. "I can't see." Her voice was so weak, ineffective as she fought against the smoke that made breathing difficult.

The sense of powerlessness that tore through her as she tried to crawl for the door was the most horrifying thing she had ever known. Surely she hadn't escaped death by the Slasher's hand only to die at the hands of her rescuers?

That would just suck. Panic welled inside her. Her heart began to pound harder, a cold chill racing over her body as the shadows began to converge on her. A shirt was quickly whipped over her head, filtering some of the smoke and easing the searing burn in her lungs.

The instinct to cough was finally mastered, though it wasn't easy.

Powerful arms pushed beneath her knees and shoulders, pulling her against a hard, muscular chest where she was held securely.

"Where is he?" One voice yelled over the din. "There's too much damned smoke here, Archer! I can't see him!" Crowe called out.

The Callahans were with Archer and what sounded like an army.

"We have movement in the trees, Archer. He's on the run! Night vision shows a vehicle moving fast." Another harsh, male voice rang through the area as fresh night air filtered through the shirt covering her face. "Fuck me! Hell no, that bastard's not getting away!"

Amory was on the run, but he wouldn't get far if the Callahans had anything to do with it.

"Make sure no one else is in that building," Archer ordered, his voice furious. "Then start gathering evidence. I want those fuckers to fry when we find them."

Archer was snarling, his voice furious as he shouted out orders while he held her against his chest, carrying her away from the hell other young women hadn't survived.

"Sheriff, we have two sets of tracks here! They were both here," Deputy Caine called out.

"I want photos and cement castings, Caine. Make sure everything matches up with what we already have," Archer called out as Anna felt herself being lowered on something much softer than the floor of that cabin.

He had come for her.

No more than two or three hours could have passed. Dawn was only just beginning to lighten the night sky.

Her throat was tight with tears, with the knowledge that she could have died. That she could have lost any chance to tell him how she felt.

God, she should have told him before now. It didn't matter that he might never love her. That he might not want to love her. She loved him.

A sob escaped her lips as he removed his shirt from her head, his hands cupping her face as those wonderful golden brown eyes stared down at her.

"It's okay, sweetheart." His voice was softer now,

gentleness replacing fury, though she could still feel that rage pulsing just beneath the surface. "It's okay, I have you. I have you, baby."

"Don't let me go," she whispered, her arms tightening around his neck as she fought to hold onto him. "Please, Archer, don't let me go."

"Never, Anna," he swore, holding her closer, the heat of his body sinking into her skin, into the chill that had been wrapping around her soul. "I'll never let you go, Anna."

"Don't leave me." She tried to make her fingers fist in the material of his shirt, but without much success. "Don't leave me, Archer."

"I'm not going anywhere, darlin'," he promised. "And neither are you. Never again, Anna. I won't let this happen ever again."

She was so tired.

"Amory drugged me," she told him. "I'm still so weak, but I have to tell you—Amory and Wayne——"

"I know, Anna," he breathed out roughly. "We know who it was, and officers are waiting for both of them at their homes. We'll get them, I promise."

"I have to tell you so much." And she was so tired.

"You can tell me when you're ready, baby." One large, broad hand caressed up and down her back, and she could swear it felt as though Archer was trembling.

"Make sure I wake up." She couldn't hold her eyes open much longer. "Swear it, Archer. Make sure I wake up."

"I swear it, Anna," he swore, his large hand cupping the side of her face gently as he pulled back to look at her once again. "I promise, I'll make sure you wake up."

It was all she had to hold on to. That promise, the assurance from the man she loved—

Because she couldn't stay awake any longer.

Her lashes drifted closed one last time, the sedative pulling her under, but relief eased her into peace.

She was safe.

Archer had come for her. He would have been there if Wayne Sorenson had actually decided to rape and torture her. He would have saved her, and he would have protected her.

Archer rubbed his hand wearily over his face, the sense of relief that assailed him almost weakening his knees.

God help him, he'd thought he'd lose his mind when he realized she had been taken.

For the first time since he'd realized the mistake he had made in leaving her behind, he could finally breathe comfortably again.

That tight knot of pain was slowly easing away, but it was being replaced by a core-deep fury and a need to kill that hardened inside him to the point that he wondered if he'd ever be the same again.

No, he would never be the same again. He'd almost lost the most important thing in the world to him. No man came back from that without changing.

"We're ready to transport, Sheriff," the young medic Sanja Fallon informed him somberly. "You'll be able to find her at the Emergency Care Clinic, and Doctor Mayan told me to assure you she was in charge."

Archer had to force himself to lay her on the gurney, then to step back from it and not jump inside the ambulance as they lifted her inside and secured the small bed.

She was asleep now, but all he could remember were those frightened green eyes as she stared up at him.

Locked inside her gaze, Archer had felt things he'd sworn all his life didn't exist.

Tipping his hat back on his head, Archer propped his hands on his hips as he turned and stared around the secluded area silently.

Two County deputies and three deputized Callahans were searching the area, along with the sheriff and two deputies from a neighboring county.

No doubt the FBI would be showing up soon.

Archer had received a searing objection regarding the Callahans' participation from the director of the Aspen FBI office, though it had been on voice mail.

That was one phone call Archer had known better than to answer.

"Not much has been left, Sheriff." Deputy Caine moved toward him, his expression tight and dark with anger as his turquoise gaze narrowed against the bright lights of the vehicles pointed toward the cabin.

"Did you get those tracks?" Snapping his hat from his head, Archer wiped the perspiration from his brow with the sleeve of his shirt.

"Casting and photo." The deputy nodded. "Those boys must not have known about the rain that hit up here the other night. The ground directly beneath the trees where the other vehicle parked was still soft. Only those areas that the sun could actually hit were completely dry. I still have to run the tests, but I'm ninety percent certain the tracks under the tree will match Sorenson's. The others definitely match the truck parked behind your house.

Yeah, a lot of folks, even the old-timers, sometimes forget that just because the weather's nice in Sweetrock doesn't mean the mountains are going to be hospitable.

The valley that housed Sweetrock was far enough below the mountains that it was often weeks to a month later before they saw the snow that fell ass deep this far up.

It was already cold here.

A chilly breeze ruffled the trees and slid through the threads of the shirt he wore.

"I'm finished here, Sheriff. There's simply nothing left to gather." Nash moved across the small clearing, his strides long, powerful.

"Caine, start rounding everyone up," Archer sighed as he turned and headed for the Yukon the investigator was loading. "Let's get back to town."

"I have an APB out on Wyatt and Sorenson," the deputy informed him, following Archer to the investigator's County vehicle. "Sheriff Dillen from Montrose sent his deputies to the bastards' houses."

"That's where I'm heading as well." Nash turned from storing his supplies and the sealed tote of evidence in the back of the vehicle.

"I'm heading to the clinic." Archer jerked open the door to his vehicle as he turned to the deputy. "Have the Callahans wait for me at the ranch. I'll bring Anna there."

She wouldn't like it. Hell, she would hate it. But maybe once she learned he was taking Rafe and Resnova up on the offer to stay as well, then she would be okay with it.

He couldn't risk this again, ever.

Starting the SUV, he threw it into drive and tore out of the area, racing for the clinic and for Anna.

He didn't bother to call the Corbins. They would find out soon enough, if they hadn't already begun getting calls. He knew how gossip worked in this town.

If they didn't know yet, he'd tell them later, after Anna was safe, after he could stand to breathe without the remembered fear rushing through him.

Just as soon as he had a chance to tell her he loved her.

CHAPTER 21

She was fine.

She was so fine that by the time Archer arrived at the clinic, Anna was waiting behind the nurses' station rather than in the waiting room, obviously amusing herself on the computer.

"I see you're ready to go," he stated as he leaned against the nurses' station she was sitting behind, her gaze locked on the computer screen.

"Archer." Her head jerked up, the dark pain in her eyes not exactly something he was expecting.

"Are you okay, Anna?" He started to move behind the counter.

Anna quickly rose to her feet and tugged at the T-shirt she wore.

"I'm ready to go home," she told him as she quickly moved around to meet him. "Let's go."

She didn't pause and she didn't wait for him.

As she swept past him and headed for the main entrance, her limp more pronounced now, indicating that the healing wound at the side of her thigh was bothering her, Anna still made quick progress to the Emergency entrance.

"This isn't a race, Anna," he reminded her as he caught up with her.

"Good thing," she rounded mockingly. "I'd so lose. I couldn't even run fast enough to escape Amory last night."

"Well, we couldn't run fast enough to catch him either," Archer relayed quietly. "Him or Sorenson."

She came to a slow stop. "Did you find Amelia?" she asked, fear apparent in her voice.

"She was unconscious in the bedroom she used as a child," he told her. "Drugged. Evidently, he'd had her there for several days after he caught her poking around in his basement. From what she told Logan and Nash, she's suspected for some time that he was connected somehow to the Callahans. Something he let slip the year he jerked her from college. She's been trying to prove it ever since."

"That was why she wanted me to leave," Anna guessed as he hit the auto open feature for the doors.

"That's why." Archer nodded, leading her through the exit. "She's been playing a very deadly game, Anna, and judging by the letter Sorenson left on my truck while I was in his house, it's just gotten deadlier for her."

Head down, her hands shoved into the pockets of her jeans, Anna hunched her shoulders almost defensively.

"He's evil," she whispered.

"Well, that's a good word for him," Archer agreed.

Hitting the remote door release, Archer followed her to his SUV, opened the passenger side door, then gently lifted her to the seat.

Helping her swing her legs around and latch her seat belt, Archer waited for Anna to say more. When she didn't, he closed her door and loped around the vehicle before stepping into the driver's side.

Damn, they had to talk. He had to explain her birthmark to her, make the most sense out of what little he
knew and still didn't fully understand.

"You said you want to go home—"

"Your home," she finished for him, uncertainty
flashing in her gaze.

Archer nodded, started the vehicle, then slid it into
drive and pulled out of the parking spot.

"Was Wayne just crazy?" she asked him.

"Not from what I've seen, Amelia." He glanced
over at her quickly. "Driven. Arrogant and bloodthirsty, but I don't think he's crazy at all. Just certain
he could have his hobby, keep it a secret, and acquire
the Callahans' land in the process."

"No one can acquire the Callahans' land," she
stated. "He should have read the fine print."

She had read the fine print, but even more, she understood it. Wayne Sorenson hadn't taken the time to
really believe her grandfather and the other Barons
would so blatantly fuck the terms with all the clauses
that had been added. It was written to be misleading,
and it had been just that.

"Why can't anyone acquire the Callahans' land?"
he asked as he pulled into the driveway of his home
and turned to look at her. "The Barons tried for years."

"The terms of the estate," she said as she stared
down at her hands. "John Corbin and Wayne Sorenson
both knew there was no way to acquire that land until
I turn twenty-five."

She could almost feel Archer tense, confusion raking the air around him.

"What do you have to do with the estate, Anna?" he
asked. "Only Crowe Callahan stood to inherit that
portion of the estate."

She shook her head slowly. "So did his sister."

Anna lifted her gaze and stared up at him, expecting to see shock or surprise. Confusion perhaps. What she saw instead was bleak suspicion.

"You know who I am, don't you, Archer?" Had he always known?

"I remembered where I saw the birthmark last night," he finally answered, his voice soft, filled with regret. "Sorenson told you, didn't he?"

Anna could only shake her head as she took a ragged breath and reach for the door latch.

Once again, Archer beat her in exiting the truck. He was around it and standing at the open door to help her out before she could navigate getting out herself.

She turned to face him as he closed the kitchen door behind them, then turned to face her. "Anna?" he questioned her, reminding her of the conversation.

She didn't need a reminder.

"He told Amory," she admitted. "He had no intentions of doing anything but frightening me out of town last night. He just wanted me to leave. He needs me alive until I turn twenty-five. The judge ruled, based on my grandfather's suggestion, of course, that the portion Sarah Ann Callahan would have inherited be held in trust until the end of the year that she would have turned twenty-five. Sarah Ann Callahan would have turned twenty-five three weeks before Anna Callahan. I turn twenty-five at the end of August."

A tear fell down her cheek as all the years of loneliness and unanswered questions began to come together in her head.

It had taken a while for her senses to clear of the sedative Amory had given her. With the slow dissipation of the drug, Anna found herself putting so many things together.

"I'm sorry, sweetheart," Archer said.

A second later Anna found herself in his arms, her ear against his chest, the feel and the sound of his heart a comforting beat beneath her head.

"That's why they kept me away from the Callahan cousins," she said. "Away from Crowe and Corbin County. That birthmark."

Shaking her head, she moved away from Archer, turned and faced him again as fists clenched at her side. "Do you know how many times I've heard about the Callahan mark since I moved into Sweetrock? Or how the Callahans were marked so there was no way one of them could hide?" A sharp pain-filled laugh left her lips. "And I was so stupid, because I didn't even think to question the unusual mark I carried myself."

The birthmark resembled a broken arrow with the point pointing toward the middle of her back.

"I hate them," she suddenly screamed, anger pouring through her, from her now. "I hate them. I hate their lies and deceit, and I hate all the years we had to suffer and all the evil that thought it could destroy us. I hate it!"

She was sobbing. Her heart was breaking in her chest as she felt the strength that had kept her upright suddenly leaving her knees. She was sinking and the only thing that kept her from falling to the floor was Archer.

"I have you, baby," Archer said as he caught her and pulled her against him again. "I have you, Anna, and I won't let you go. I swear I won't let you go."

Her hands fisted in his shirt as she held on to him, her tears dampening the fabric.

"It's okay, baby. It's okay, my heart." His words shocked her, stealing her breath for one long, impossibly unreal moment before she forced herself not to question it, not to hope for more.

"You—" She shook her head. "You knew I was a Callahan?"

His hand reached up and cupped her cheek, a thumb brushing a tear from beneath an eye. "I saw the birthmark, really saw it, last night. I hadn't paid enough attention and I'm sorry for that, sweetheart. I should have known, but to be honest, I've only seen it once, and it was a lot of years ago."

"I'm scared, Archer." A bitter, broken sob escaped her lips.

Thankfully, she was able to hold the rest of them back. She didn't want to cry now, not now. First she wanted to figure out how to handle it all.

"Even knowing what we're going to face when all this blows up," she said, "will you still want Sarah Ann Callahan?"

Would he ever be able to love her?

As the question left her lips, she saw Archer's gaze lift to a point behind her as he suddenly stiffened, his golden brown eyes narrowing.

Anna jerked around in his arms, staring at the three men standing in the kitchen doorway at the foyer, staring back at her with anger so deep and black that for a moment, one helpless moment, she felt consumed by it.

Then Crowe blinked. He blinked and swallowed tightly, glancing away for a second as his cousins stared back at her in shock.

"He couldn't help but love you," Crowe said, turning back to her, his tone as bleak as his expression. "Just as I couldn't help but love you, even when I believed you were my cousin and no better than any other Corbin you lived with."

His voice was so hoarse, so ragged, Anna flinched.

"You didn't know?" she'd wondered, feared he had and hadn't wanted her.

"If I had known, you would have never been left alone all those years," he swore, his wolf eyes burning with inner fury and pain. "God help me, I would have given it all up. I would have given those bastards whatever they wanted, Anna, to know you were alive and to protect you from the isolation you suffered. If I had known—" As though he couldn't bear his thoughts or the sight of her any longer, Crowe turned and stalked away.

Seconds later, the slam of the front door caused her to flinch violently and a sob to escape her lips as she faced her cousins.

They were her cousins too, not just Crowe's. They were her family.

Logan and Rafer stared back at her as though she were an apparition, a ghost so insubstantial they couldn't be certain she was actually standing there.

"John Caine told us to be here." Logan cleared his throat as he glanced at Archer, shifting his stance and running his fingers through his hair with a rough movement. "We weren't eavesdropping. When you came in, we came looking for you." He shrugged uncomfortably.

"It's okay, Logan," Archer breathed out roughly.

Logan's lips tightened before, with a jerky movement, he was suddenly stalking across the room.

Anna didn't know what she expected, but she hadn't expected Logan to pull her away from Archer and into an almost desperate hug. "Welcome back, cuz," he murmured at her ear. "It's damned good to see you."

As he stepped back, Rafer was there as well to pull her into his embrace.

"Crowe will come back, you'll see," he told her. "When he was a kid, he would hide and cry for his little lost sister just as much as he hid and cried for his parents. He'll be back."

She nodded as he released her.

"Archer." Rafer extended his hand. "I hope we're welcoming you into the family, man, because you break her heart, and Crowe just might kill you. I know for a fact we will." He grinned.

"I wouldn't expect anything less," Archer promised as he accepted the handshake.

He turned back to Anna then. "Crowe will be back when he can think again. I promise."

Anna nodded, then watched as the two men left the kitchen through the foyer. Seconds later, the front door closed firmly.

She turned back to Archer slowly. "You were going to tell them, weren't you?" she asked.

"Only after I told you," he promised, his rough features tightening into a grimace. "It's been kept from the four of you too long now. You deserved to know."

Reaching up, she laid her hand against his hard jaw as he stared down at her, all the emotions, the gentleness and the love she had dreamed of seeing clearly reflected in his eyes.

"I thought I'd lost you." He lifted a hand and covered hers, holding it against his face. "When I realized Callie had been attacked to draw me away from you, I felt everything in my world turn dark, Anna. I've loved you all along and I wasn't even smart enough to realize it."

"Of course you realized it," she told him with a teary smile. "You haven't let me go even once since you came after me, Archer. You knew, you were just too stubborn to admit it."

He nodded slowly. "Okay, we can work with that

explanation," he promised, a smile tugging at his lips. "We can work with that."

His lips touched hers. "I can work with anything but losing you."

What had started as a soothing kiss became something more, something far deeper than Archer had expected.

His lips brushed hers, parted them, let the taste of her draw him in, and the sudden feeling of a connection, a bonding he hadn't known how to describe before, tightened around them again.

It had always been there, he realized. Since the first moment his lips touched hers, it had been there.

Her breathing accelerated, her cheeks flushing a delicate pink as her pert little tongue swiped nervously over her lips, brushing against his and sending a surge of lust to explode in his senses.

She had come to him, had given every part of herself, even believing he didn't believe in love. He could see it in her eyes every time he had touched her; he had seen the hunger and need for his love, the need to love him fully, openly.

There was no way he could turn from the aching feminine need that matched the hardcore vein of emotion throbbing inside him.

Archer brushed his lips against hers.

Holding her gaze with his, he watched as the agony slowly eased from her eyes, the inner pain and conflict being replaced with a slow, easy quest for pleasure.

That was what he wanted. He wanted that dark pain eradicated, and if this was the only way to do it, then who was he to deny her? After all, there was nothing he ached for more than her heart, her touch, her kiss.

His cock throbbed with aching insistence beneath his jeans as he eased the kiss into a deeper caress. Brushing against her lips again, again using his own lips to slowly part hers, he watched the pleasure build in her gaze.

Archer took her kiss slow and easy.

Leaning into her, his head tilted as she lifted hers up to him, giving him unlimited access, giving him everything he could have ever wanted in life.

His kiss was hot and tempting. The need beginning to flame through her body, arrowing between her thighs and striking at her clitoris and vagina, rose with the knowledge that she didn't just love, she was loved in return.

Each time his lips sipped at hers, his tongue licked at hers, sensation swirled at the sensitive, nerve-laden flesh between her thighs as though ghostly kisses were being laid at her pussy as well.

Tightening her thighs, a little whimper escaped her and slipped into the air around them. Beneath her fingers the hard muscles of his shoulders bunched, flexed as though the battle to hold his hunger back was as much physical as mental and emotional.

Anna, innocent though she might be, had been kissed before Archer. She hadn't just accepted that she belonged to Archer. She had often at least attempted to find pleasure, to find happiness without him.

It just hadn't existed without him, that was all.

Pressing her lips further apart, Archer's tongue licked against hers, teasing her to play.

She wasn't completely certain how to play yet, but following his lead, she licked back at him, retreating quickly, only to lick at his lips as he eased back, to shift her head just enough to evade a full possession of his lips before nipping at his lower lip when he returned.

At that little nip Archer's arms tightened around her. Pulling her closer to the hard strength of his chest while his lips covered hers, taking them, possessing them with his lips and tongue as a moan escaped her throat.

Pinpoints of sensation began to prickle through her body, charging her nerve endings with hot, dancing jolts of pleasure.

Hunger raged through the kiss now. Pleasure licked over her senses, charging her nerve endings and awakening parts of her body she'd never imagined could be so sensitive.

Such as the skin at her side where her shirt and the band of her jeans separated: calloused fingertips stroked and smoothed the sensitive flesh. Pleasure washed over her in waves, the need for more growing with ever increasing demand.

More of his kisses and more of his touch. She wanted his body fully against her. Turning in the chair to press into him, she gasped as he gripped her, his head pulling back to growl, "Straddle me."

A second later Anna found her legs embracing his thighs as she straddled his hard body, the wedge of his cock pressing into the mound of her pussy through the layers of denim.

His lips immediately returned to hers, growing excitingly rougher and more demanding. His tongue was less playful and more intent. His hands became questing and entirely serious in their explorations as one palm pushed beneath the hem of her shirt to find the swollen curve of her breast.

The heat of his palm seared her flesh through the lace of her bra, creating an exciting friction as his thumb found the swollen tip of her nipple and rubbed it slowly.

Arching into the touch, her hands buried in his hair, Anna heard her own whimper of pleasure and could barely believe she would ever make such a pleading sound.

"Please." She might as well actually beg.

As he pulled back, his lips moving over her jaw to the side of her neck, finding the ultra-sensitive nerve endings there as he licked and kissed a meandering path to the lobe of her ear.

"Archer, it's so good," she moaned, the sensual lethargy that overtook her more intoxicating than the liquor she had consumed earlier.

His hands tightened on her sides, holding her still as his hips arched to grind his cock harder into the vee of her thighs.

Exquisite pain raced through her pussy. Her clit throbbed with an ache she had no idea how to ease. Riding the hard length of his erection with their jeans separating them was an exquisite agony she wondered if she could bear for much longer.

His hands moved from her waist once again, pushing her shirt up, cupping her breasts as his thumbs raked over the lace covering them.

Shards of sensation tore from those swollen tips to the engorged bud of her clit. Her womb clenched, her juices spilled to her panties as she forced her lashes open, staring into the drowsy, lust-filled expression on Archer's face.

As their gazes locked, she moved her hands from his hair, watching as surprise flickered in his gaze when she reached behind her back and released the catch of her bra.

Immediately his hands pushed beneath the loosened cups, his thumbs and forefingers gripping her nipples and tugging at them with an erotic pleasure-pain that had her pussy melting in wicked hunger.

Arms lifting, she pulled the shirt as well as the bra from her body and tossed them to the floor.

"Oh God—Archer."

Every muscle in her body clenched and threatened to explode in rapture as a hot, hungry mouth surrounded the painfully tight tip of a nipple and sucked it inside.

His cheeks hollowed as he drew on the swollen bud, his gaze still holding hers, locked with it, the too-responsive tips of her breasts gloried in every touch.

The one buried in Archer's mouth was in such agonizing pleasure she was certain she couldn't bear it much longer. Her pussy spilled its sensual wetness, her vagina clenching at the emptiness there, aching to be filled.

"Take it off." Tugging at his shirt as she made the demand and ground herself against his cock, she swore she was close, so close to the rapture of release that she could almost touch it, almost allow her body to slide into it. If only she knew how.

"Unbutton it," he ordered, his lips and sucking mouth moving from one nipple to the next.

Sucking the matching, pebble-hard tip into his mouth, one hand captured hers and pulled it to the buttons of his shirt.

Anna moaned, knowing she would never manage to control her fingers enough to get his shirt unbuttoned.

She didn't even try.

As his teeth surrounded her nipple and nipped, Anna gripped the edges of his shirt and pulled.

Buttons popped and flew across the room. The ping of the little discs hitting the floor was forgotten as he released her nipple from his teeth and immediately surrounded the nipple again, suckling at it strongly.

Devouring it. Eating at the tip as though nothing mattered but ensuring he sated the hunger for the taste of her breasts.

"Oh yes," she panted, the painful pleasure that attacked her nipple streaking to her pussy. "Archer, please. Oh please, yes."

Her hips shifted, ground, rode the ridge of his cock as she searched hungrily for release.

It had to be there, just over the edge—

Perspiration began to gather on her flesh, her cries becoming more ragged as her head tipped back on her shoulders. His hands at her back, he pulled her closer.

His tongue lashed at her nipple, his teeth rasped it. His thumb and forefinger gripped its twin, rolled it, tugged at it, sending increased fingers of lightning-fast sensation to crash into her womb and surround her clit.

Thighs tense, Archer dropped his hands to her hips, guiding the desperate movement of her pussy against the thick erection beneath his jeans. The clothing that separated them was a painful friction and agonizing pleasure.

Heat and nearing ecstasy began to gather into increasingly tight swirls of growing sensation. Anna could barely breathe as so many, too many sensations began to fill her at once.

The suckling of her increasingly sensitive nipples, one, then the other, then back again. The lash of his tongue against the tortured peaks, the thumb and forefinger of one hand returning to the other nipple to torture it with those growing circles of blistering heat and nearing release.

Her womb spasmed, her pussy clenched. Her clit tightened further, throbbing, expanding, sensation surging, striking against it with each lash of sensation as he pressed silk and denim against the steadily sensitized bundle of nerves.

She was tortured, her body strung tight as she fought for the center of sensation, searching desperately for the edge where she dropped off into sheer sensation and ecstasy.

It was close—

It was so close—

Muted mewls of desperation sounded around her. She knew they were hers, knew she would wince at the begging, pleading sound of them later.

Then one hard male hand grabbed the side of her ass, as Archer's hips moved faster against her, dry fucking her with heavy strokes until those gathering, tightening swirls of ecstatic sensation seemed to rupture inside her.

Her body imploded with a pleasure so violent it seemed to shred through her.

Her clitoris expanded, then exploded like a sun going supernova, tore through her, and flung her into a climax that rocked her body and almost, just almost, touched that center of her being she had placed in lockdown deep inside her soul.

Her nails dug into Archer's shoulder as his lips released her nipple and buried in her neck. He tensed beneath her, a muted male groan rumbling against the curve of her neck and shoulder.

Holding her close, his body so tight, so hard it was like iron against her, Archer kept her poised within the exploding heart of the ecstasy surrounding her.

One arm was clamped behind her back, the other clenched in the curve of her rear as her sensitized nipples raked against his chest with each breath she took.

The sensual rapture held her, suspended in its grip

as the world stopped around her. The swirling sensations began to slow, to ease. The violence of her release echoing weaker, then weaker still until she was left trembling against him, little shudders of her climax echoing through her until she was left slumped against him, wasted—

The pleasure, the exacting explosion of release, still left her strangely aching for more.

Beneath her, Archer's cock was still iron-hard, throbbing. He'd eased the painful, aching need torturing her, but he hadn't—

"I'm sorry," she said, as his hand stroked down her back.

"For what?" His head lifted, his lips pressing against her temple.

"You didn't—" She stopped, heat flushing her face as she felt and heard the chuckle that vibrated in his chest.

"Well, yeah, babe, I did," he admitted, abashed as she lifted her head to stare up at him.

She swallowed tightly. "You did?"

His grin was one of male bemusement. "Hell if I can explain it. Haven't done that since I was a damned teenager."

"Oh." She blinked back at him.

"Yeah. Oh," he teased her.

Anna wished she could smile so easily, wished she could find the laughter inside her that she used to find so easily whenever Archer was around.

"Come on, pretty girl. We've both had a hell of a night and day. I think it's time we went to bed." Gripping her hips, he lifted her from him, steadying her until he rose to his feet as well.

Taking her hand, he led her through the house to the staircase and upstairs.

As they stepped into the bedroom, she suddenly broke away and rushed across the room.

"Oscar." Going to her knees beside the cat bed, she stroked the suddenly pitiful-acting feline with gentle strokes.

Oscar stared up at her as though he'd had bones broken from the attack the night before. And if Archer didn't know better, he would have sworn the cat actually gave a little moan rather than a purr.

"Poor baby," she said, avoiding the shaved area of his head where his cut had been checked at the vet. "Poor Oscar." She turned to Archer then. "He bit Amory, you know. Right on the inside of the thigh. It was all he could do to make Oscar stop attacking him."

She continued to rub the cat's fur, and he ate it up like cream, the little bastard.

"Oscar did good," Archer agreed as he moved to her, gripped her arms, and lifted her to him. "Now forget the cat for a minute and come to bed with me, Anna. Let hold you, baby. Just for a little while before we have to fight the world again, let me hold you."

He wanted to hold her, and Anna admitted she needed to be held by him, comforted by him.

As he said, before they had to fight the world once again.

CHAPTER 22

Elizabeth Haley was laid out and waiting. Strapped to the metal table, gagged, the drugs having worn off, and he couldn't kill her.

He'd known before having Anna Corbin—or rather Sarah Ann Callahan—abducted that he couldn't kill her. Knowing that, the moment Amory had located Elizabeth Haley, the woman whose name had been Ellen Mason, he'd had the other man abduct her and bring her to the small cabin in Aspen that he kept for just such occasions.

Unfortunately, so very unfortunately, there was another young woman there as well. One he hadn't ever imagined having to kill, not really. But betrayal was betrayal, and he couldn't allow it to go unpunished.

There were few things so frustrating, he thought as he paced the floor in front of the large monitor, as knowing the daughter a man trusted and loved could betray them to the point that his sweet, precious Amelia had attempted to destroy him.

Why had she done this?

Because he'd forced her away from Crowe Callahan's arms?

Or had she somehow learned the truth about her mother?

There was always that chance. She could have found the basement room where her mother had been buried, the gravestone marking her grave and listing her crimes.

And all the inconsequential thoughts or questions in Corbin County weren't going to change the decision he had to make where she was concerned. Nor would it change the fate of the young woman he viewed now.

Staring at the screen, watching as Elizabeth struggled against the straps, he could feel his cock hardening, anticipation rising despite the circumstances, and resentment building.

How dare those fucking Callahans interfere in his fun? Every time he turned around in Corbin County now, they were locating yet another of his little hidden playhouses.

Not that they could possibly know who he was, but they were finding and destroying the secluded line cabins he and Amory often used for their fun and games.

It wasn't as though there were many ways to find recompense for everything he and his ancestors had been cheated of.

This one pleasure was all that was to be had for so many decades of searching.

Naked, young, and so very beautiful.

Finding Elizabeth hadn't been easy.

Hell, it had been damned hard because Crowe was real damned careful. Finding his lovers was an almost impossible task. Catching up with Elizabeth had been even harder, and he couldn't figure out why.

It was almost as though she had been aware danger stalked her and refused to back off. Hell, she had nearly managed to escape again. If he hadn't gone looking for her himself while Amory ensured Anna was released, then she would have escaped again.

"Are we sending her back?" Amory asked, his tone lazy and unconcerned as he tipped back in his chair and watched the monitor.

Amory didn't seem in the least concerned with the fact that they couldn't kill this girl either. At least, not at the moment.

Wayne had been set to enter her room and begin the fun himself when Amory had arrived with the news that word was sweeping Corbin County that Anna Corbin was actually Sarah Ann Callahan and Amory had been identified as her abductor.

"Do we have a choice?" he growled, knowing they didn't. "If we don't and she doesn't show up, then the governor will have the excuse he's looking for to take over that investigation."

He couldn't allow that to happen. "Carter Ferguson has a hard-on for us like it ain't nobody's business," he continued. "The last thing we need is the FBI and the state police on our asses. Dammit, Elizabeth Haley isn't even a resident of Corbin County. No one should have even known about her."

"True," Amory agreed. "But it's not every day two teams of U.S. Marshals are beating the damned bushes searching for one of our playthings either."

"Ferguson is fueling this," he snarled. "He just won't let it go."

"Yeah, that's what happens when you rape and murder a man's daughter. They just get all out of sorts and want to kill ya."

Sliding a sideways look Amory's way, Wayne thinned his lips in irritation. Amory was so damned critical of the past, and he was getting sick of it.

"And just how would you have handled it, Amory?" he asked snidely. Damn, he was getting real sick of Amory's assured attitude that he could have handled everything so much better than his previous partners.

Amory pursed his lips thoughtfully for several seconds before grinning back at him. There was no doubt the other man had been waiting for this question for months now. If he had thought of it, he would have never given the younger killer a chance to answer it.

"First off." Amory lowered his chair and stared back at him with a smug look. "I wouldn't have touched a representative's daughter. Never ever choose a high-profile victim."

"She slept with Logan Callahan." What the hell did Amory think the point was here?

"She was a badge," Amory drawled with a mocking smile.

"What the fuck do you mean?"

"She was an FBI agent, a badge," Amory repeated. "That made her a challenge to you, and we both know it. Add to the fact she was a representative's daughter and she was more or less deliberately goading you." Amory shrugged. "If I had been working with you at the time, we wouldn't have touched her with a ten-foot pole."

Since when did Amory think he would have had that much control? The past days since they had taken Anna, Amory had acted differently. More confident, perhaps? As though he were certain he suddenly knew more, had more experience than his trainer had.

"She was the perfect target," Wayne all but snarled, hating the fact that Amory was making him feel stupid.

"The point is, she was a friend of the Callahans, not a lover," Amory stated. "Your partner did not do his research well."

And Amy Ferguson had been such a joy to kill.

Particularly sweet, and such a fighter.

"So she hadn't slept with him?" he mused.

"Does that make a difference?" Amory asked.

He had to grin. "No, not particularly."

He would do it again.

There was a flash of something dark and disapproving in Amory's eyes for a second. *How amusing, a killer with a conscience.*

"We're still left with another problem," Amory pointed out, flicking his fingers to the monitor as he leaned back in his chair, one leg crossed over the opposite knee as he cradled a cup of coffee in his other hand. "Ms. Haley is very high profile. I don't know who she is yet, but she's obviously in the Witness Protection Program. Two teams of marshals are already searching for her and they won't stop. She could be the end of us if we keep her."

"So we don't get to play for a while?" Wayne asked in disappointment.

"Not for a while," Amory answered as he forced himself to contain his fury.

This attitude was pissing him off.

"I think I'll see about finding someone far enough away that they won't be connected to the Callahans." Wayne grinned. "Even though they are connected."

He wasn't pissed any longer.

"You think that's possible?" Amory asked.

Wayne's grin widened. "They were away for twelve years, my friend, I'm certain they had many bed buddies in that time. We just have to find them then we can continue having our little snacks."

Amory watched the other man, restraining a sigh of regret. At this rate, he would end up having to kill the bastard himself.

"I look forward to it," Amory agreed, though. "Does this mean we let Ms. Haley go?"

Wayne rose slowly to his feet and glanced at the monitor. "Get her out of here. Thank God you had the foresight to sedate her well before bringing her in. I'll head back to Corbin County and see what the hell is going on there."

"I'll take care of it." Amory nodded as he rose to his feet and headed for the door.

Halfway there, he paused and turned back with a frown. "What about Amelia? Ms. Corbin has called her cell phone and texted several times. The sheriff will begin asking questions soon. Once he does, her disappearance will be tied to the Slasher."

His jaw clenched. "It would have been so much easier to get rid of her. She might not have found anything, but it doesn't change the fact that I caught her searching the basement. She's suspicious of something."

"Whatever you want to do." Amory's shoulders lifted negligently. "Perhaps the governor will overlook her disappearance."

"Bastard," Wayne growled, his fingers curling into fists. "I should have killed him rather than his daughter."

"What is it they say about hindsight being twenty-twenty?" Amory asked, mocking.

Wayne clenched his teeth furiously. "Let her go," he snapped. "We've kept her well drugged while I've been in her room, correct?"

Amory shrugged. "You injected her before taking her blindfold off," he reminded Wayne.

"Let her go," he sighed, then smiled slowly with relish before rubbing his hands together gleefully. "Dump her on Crowe Mountain. That clearing before reaching the cabin. Let's see if she's learned how to keep her legs closed where he's concerned. If she can, then maybe we'll let her live."

Amory's grin was amused. He obviously approved. "I'll take care of it."

As the other man left the room, Wayne turned back to the monitor to watch Elizabeth in disappointment. He had so been looking forward to her.

As for Amelia, he had no desire for her himself, but she was a danger to the future. Not that she was aware of his identity, because she wasn't. What she was was a danger to the plans he envisioned for Anna if she suspected something or, God forbid, managed to actually find something that he might have missed in his efforts to cover his own ass.

She was definitely suspicious, though what she was suspicious of he wasn't certain. What he did know was that his daughter was damned intelligent and damned devious. Considering who her mother was, he should have guessed that last part. He had time though.

With the governor's threat now hanging over all their heads, he had at least six weeks to figure out what to do. At the most, he and Amory would just have to separate for a while. Or as he had told Amory, there were twelve years the cousins had been out of Corbin County. They could continue their hobby elsewhere.

He wasn't willing to lose Amory though. The other man was the perfect partner, despite his sometimes superior attitude. And perfect partners were so very hard to find.

Amory stepped into the room Amelia had been placed in, amazed Wayne was unaware of the APB out for both of them.

He hadn't wired this room, but that didn't mean his partner hadn't placed, at the least, a listening device inside it.

He'd learned over the years to be paranoid and very careful. Not that he didn't still make mistakes, because he did. His present partner was proof of that. He'd made a hell of a mistake there, and he had less than six hours to fix it.

It was nearly time to go home, thank God.

All his preparations had been made.

The private plane was in place, thanks to his eldest son.

His alternate identity had a vehicle waiting close by.

Within a matter of hours, he would shed Amory Wyatt and become Steven Glasglow until he managed to get out of Corbin County and arrive safely in Aspen.

The plane was waiting at the airport.

The private plane his son had purchased the year before under the umbrella of the family business. Who would ever suspect a well-respected businessman from England to have managed to alter not just his face, but his whole persona for over a year as he worked himself into the Slasher's little game?

By the time he left, he would have fulfilled his blood lust for a while, and on leaving he would ensure his partner was ruined and no longer a threat. After all, learning the Callahans were innocent of the crimes laid at their feet had pretty much ruined this game anyway.

The rules had been a lie to begin with, because their basis didn't exist. Because of this, his partner would have to pay.

Amelia, though, had done nothing to deserve her punishment, just as Anna Corbin had not. Yet both of them had paid. Both of them would still pay yet further.

And that was truly a shame. They had already paid a lifetime for crimes they had not committed. For men they had not been with.

The men too had been innocent.

What a disappointment to learn the family of Callahans had always been innocent. For generations his family had been led to believe the Callahans had begun the bloodshed all those generations before. That they had deceived his ancestor. That the Callahans worked with his ancestor and Jonathon Mulrooney in their quest for blood, only to have betrayed Jonathon and his partner, Devon Castle—not that that had been his real name—and caused them to be hanged while escaping unscathed himself.

To learn that early Callahans had nothing to do with the betrayal of Devon Castle changed the rules. They could only shed the blood of the enemy, and the Callahans had done nothing to the family of Devon Castle to be considered the enemy.

No, family had always been most important, and they had tried to teach that to the Mulrooneys at one time.

They had never learned their lessons.

Releasing the straps that held Amelia to the bed, Amory mentally shook his head. No, the Mulrooneys had never learned, but they would now.

Wrapping Amelia's slight body in a blanket, Amory carried her from the room without ever speaking to her. Just in case his partner was listening. Just in case he had become suspicious. And that was always possible.

Carrying Amelia's body outside the remote cabin to the SUV he'd acquired, Amory slid her into the back, grinning at the tension in her body. The mild dosage of the drug was even less than Anna had been given.

He had readjusted the active drug in the mix himself. What Amelia had been given had only made her mildly disoriented and completely capable of maintaining her control. It kept her from appearing conscious, while all along she had been. Just as Elizabeth Haley had been fully conscious. Fully aware of Wayne Sorenson's identity.

Sliding into the driver's seat of the SUV, Amory chuckled.

His partner had no idea who Elizabeth Haley was, but Amory knew full well. He had run the search on her through his partner's home computer. He'd even gone so far as to attempt to hack the U.S. Marshals' network, which had immediately resulted in more than the two teams Amory had told Wayne about being sent to the area. They were awaiting Wayne.

Within the next couple of hours, there would be two young women found. Amelia Sorenson and Elizabeth Haley would be found in Crowe Callahan's mountain cabin, and what an incredible story they would have to tell. A story that would destroy his partner's life, and for a while at least, would allow the Callahans to live in peace.

CHAPTER 23

The Corbins had had over two decades to explain their actions, and to explain the truth to her, Anna thought the next day as she dressed.

Buttoning the silk white-and-maroon-striped sleeveless blouse, she straightened the hem over the creamy calf-length full skirt she'd purchased from the Goodwill store after first moving in with Archer.

He liked the skirts. She liked the way his gaze darkened, then flared with hunger whenever she wore them.

The skirts or dresses made her feel more confident. Three-inch or higher heels gave her an illusion of height while the skirts or dresses made her feel more feminine, yet stronger.

One of her professors had always claimed that a woman held her greatest power when she looked her most feminine. That soft, flowing dresses gave a woman an illusion of hope and forgiveness. Straight skirts and stiffly starched blouses beneath blazers gave a woman the appearance of superiority and power while casual day dresses gave the appearance of maternity, of mother's love and cookies and brownies baking in a kitchen filled with love.

Today, her skirt was soft and flowing, her blouse silky and warm, her heels at three inches, adding height but giving the aura of hope and forgiveness.

When she walked into her grandfather's home, she wanted them to think she was weak, that she was all love and forgiveness and please-allow-me-to-come-home.

She would never return to the ranch and Anna knew it.

She would never see her family in the same light, because she had changed since leaving. She hadn't just changed in becoming Archer's lover, or in knowing she loved him versus just believing she loved him. She had changed in the fact that since she had left, she'd learned everything she knew about herself was a lie.

She'd changed because she wasn't the child she had been when she had announced she wasn't returning to a college she had already graduated from. She wasn't that naive, uncompromising young woman she had been when she had started walking down a mountain road, all but daring a killer to take notice of her.

She didn't need her family to be her life any longer. She needed her family to be honest with her. She needed them to look her in the eye and answer the questions she had and be willing to find common ground with her once it was over.

"Anna?" Archer stepped into the bathroom as she completed her makeup and came to a hard stop.

The woman who faced him was unlike any side of Anna he had seen since she had come to live with him.

Her long hair was piled to the back of her head in a

loose pile of silken warmth, then secured with a tortoise-shell clip.

Dark ringlets fell around her face here and there and haphazardly down her neck and back.

She looked like a college student dressed for a day of shopping or lying around the house reading.

Or his lover arming herself for a meeting that meant so much to her.

"What do you think?" She breathed in deeply as she turned to him, laying the slim tube of satiny lipstick to the side as she faced him.

Her makeup was so subtle, so well applied that it took a minute to realize she was actually wearing anything other than the slight shininess of the lipstick.

"You look like a very beautiful, lovely, innocent young woman who loves her friends and her job, but more importantly, she loves her family," he put his thoughts and the appearance she projected into words. "You just want answers, Anna. It's time they give them to you."

She nodded slowly before brushing her hands down the material covering her hips and breathing in once again.

"Have you heard from Crowe?" She didn't look at him as she voiced the question. Instead, she looked at the candy-pink shade of polish on her toenails and the effect of the strappy sandals on her feet.

"Nothing yet," he admitted. "Rafer called earlier to check on you though. He, Logan, Skye, and Cami will be here tonight. Hopefully Crowe will be here as well."

"Amelia?" Her voice lowered.

They hadn't found Amelia in her home. No sooner than she had left the hospital, she had disappeared.

"We'll find her, Anna," he promised, though he was

afraid once they did, what they found would break Anna's heart.

Amelia was Wayne's daughter. She could have been aware of what he was doing and currently aiding his escape. Or she could have become a victim instead.

"We'll find her," she nodded, but he could see the fear in her eyes.

"Are you sure you want to see your family today, Anna?" he asked her then. "There have been a lot of changes in your life and a lot to get a handle on."

She nodded her head. "I'm ready to go."

Anna gave herself one last glance in the mirror before stepping from the bedroom and picking up the tan leather purse she'd left at the bottom of the bed.

Archer remained behind her as she left the house, then as he always did, he moved to the passenger side of the SUV, opened her door, and helped her inside.

The drive from Sweetrock to the Corbins' ranching operation was the longest ride she believed she had ever made in her life.

They didn't even attempt to make small talk, the questions and lack of answers stood between them like a chasm. Anna prayed that once those explanations were made that she would find some measure of peace with her family.

Archer glanced at her as they drove closer to the ranch.

Realizing what he felt for her had been the hardest battle he believed he had ever fought. Letting go of those lifelong obstacles to giving his heart hadn't been easy. But, God, the thought that he'd lost her, that he'd been too late to save her, had nearly destroyed him.

"You okay?" Reaching out, Archer covered her hand where it lay in her lap and entwined his fingers with hers.

"I'm fine," she promised.

He could hear the edge of nerves in her voice now. She was a little angry, and perhaps even a little frightened.

"I talked to Rory's uncle, Jordan, today," he informed her as he made the turn to the Corbin property, his gaze going over the vast pasture that stretched out before them and the cattle dotting the landscape. "Rory woke up once early this morning before lapsing into what the doctor called a healing sleep. Amory hit him hard."

Anna nodded. "With a baseball bat. I tried to warn him, but it was too late. Amory acted like he was hitting a baseball for a damned home run, the way he drew it back."

She had been stepping outside the bedroom. She'd seen Amory first, drawing that bat back, then Rory had come around the corner, his expression hard and cold. He'd known someone was in the house, but he'd seen her and hadn't expected anyone to be around the corner. And she hadn't been able to react in time.

"It wasn't your fault, sweetheart." He tightened his hold on her hand as his thumb caressed her knuckles gently.

"It was my fault," she denied. "It really was, Archer, because I refused to leave, even knowing the danger I could be drawing to myself and those trying to protect me. I should have made other choices."

What other choices could she have made other than leaving the County as Wayne Sorenson had attempted to ensure she did?

"Anna, you have the right to be safe," he retorted

with that arrogant determination that turned her on even when it shouldn't.

"Not according to my family," she said roughly. "They showed I only had the right to be sent away, to be kept alone." A bitter laugh passed her lips. "I guess I had to be isolated for everyone else's protection."

And that was exactly how it felt.

"Why haven't they found Wayne yet?" Anna asked as they drew closer to the main ranch house, the nerves in her voice clearer now.

Archer inhaled slowly. "I don't know. He didn't have plans to leave town though, that much I know."

"How do you know?" Her fingers tightened on his as the truck rounded a curve and the two-story ranch house came into view.

"He had scheduled several meetings today and to-morrow, one of which was with his stockbroker who had flown in from New York and arrived at the hotel this morning. He was cashing in some of his stocks and having them routed to an account in the Caymans to cover an account he had routed from Aspen."

"He was getting ready to do something then," she mused. "Any idea what?"

"You turn twenty-five soon." He shrugged. "He was allowing you to live for that reason alone, according to him. Whatever his plans were, he knew he would need cash."

At one time, the Barons, including the Callahans, had discussed merging their properties and turning them into a vacation resort along the lines of the Cal-lahans' plans. It was the Callahan Ranch that was pivotal in that plan, though.

Archer's father had mentioned it to him when he was a teenager, how they had all discussed the plans with Randal and made him the offer to enter the partnership so they could show one non-landowner in the deal. That would have given them an edge at the time with several organizations who gave favoritism to tourism businesses with partners who owned no land, nor held large amounts of money.

Then JR Callahan had become ill, his wife's family had threatened to disown her if she didn't stop working herself to the bone to save a ranch that was going broke, and her infant had, everyone believed at the time, died.

Those plans had just drifted away. Then just when it looked as though everything would come together again, JR and Eileen had died in that blizzard, going over the same cliff their sons and daughters-in-laws had gone over years later.

The coincidence, as his father had stated more than once over the years, was too much to believe. Too many deaths, especially those attributed to the Slasher, were tied together, and it had haunted him.

Just as it had haunted Archer.

Now that the threads were finally coming together, it was beginning to make sense, and realizing exactly how far back the bitter hatred and greed had gone shocked him.

Nine generations were far too many for such secrets to have been buried, and for one family to torture and torment four others without being identified. Ivan had finally tied Wayne Sorenson as a direct descendant to Clavern Mulrooney, the pirate father known only as the Raider.

But he'd also identified another family, one far more secretive than even the Mulrooneys, and much, much smarter at hiding.

With Clavern Mulrooney and his son Blood, the

pirate's first mate and boyhood friend, Edward Bosworth the third, the son of a titled family and closely related to the English throne.

He'd been a serial killer. He and Clavern had preyed upon not just the settlements of Colorado Springs and Aspen, but also the Native American tribes in the area.

All women. All whose reputations were those of witches, prostitutes, adulteresses; all women who, at the time, had broken some of society's most sacred taboos.

The Bosworth name had not shown up again. The tie to the throne had never been given a surname that had been proven, and the first mate's family had drifted into the shadows of time.

Archer dragged himself from the past as the main yard came into view.

Situated at the end of the small valley with the mountain rising around it on three sides, several barns and pristine outbuildings scattered in the general area, the ranch had the appearance, almost, of a small town.

Glancing over at her, Archer caught her expression before she turned her head to stare over at the waterfall that fell from a steep cliff behind the house. It cascaded gently to the fast-running stream that ran through the valley.

Corbin County was one of the wildest and most beautiful areas in the state, he often swore. Hell, the world as far as he was concerned. And the four ranches that had once dominated it held the majority of that beauty.

Pulling into the graveled drive in front of the ranch house, Archer gave her hand a gentle squeeze.

"I should have known before it ever came to this." Her voice suddenly filled with dread as she stared at the house. "If they had wanted to explain anything,

Archer, they would have come to the house yesterday. They would have sought me out."

"This is your call, Anna," he stated, the gentleness in his voice tightening her chest further as she fought against the fears rising inside her. "We can leave."

She was a grown woman, yet she felt nine again, realizing her family really wasn't going to let her come home.

"He told you that night at the house that once you learned the identity of the Slasher, then they would tell you everything," she said, lifting her gaze to him as she fought against the fear that they would throw her out before she had the chance to ask the first question.

"You won't know until you try, Anna." Lifting his hand, he ran the backs of his fingers over her cheek, warming her chilled flesh. "We can turn around and leave now, or we can go to that door and demand the answers you deserve. The worst they can do is not answer the door."

She nodded slowly. He was right. That was the worst they could do, and Crowe had faced so much worse over the years.

She had been the treasured, coddled princess until she refused to obey the demands a madman had forced them to make. She deserved to know why they hadn't trusted her with the truth, and with the knowledge of who she was. "Thank you, Archer." She blinked back her tears.

"Anytime, sweet pea," he promised, his voice stroking her senses with the tenderness his eyes reflected. "Anytime."

And nothing more.

Dropping his hand, he exited the vehicle before moving to the passenger side and helping her out as

Anna fought to restrain the disappointment tearing through her.

After his desperation and determination to hold her to him since Amory had taken her, Anna was certain he would eventually tell her he loved her. That he surely would have done it by now.

"You do know I'm capable of getting out on my own," she reminded him.

"My momma was alive long enough to teach me *some* manners." He snorted as he closed her door, twined his fingers with hers once again, and led her to the house.

Anna could feel her heart racing as she stepped up to the porch, remembering those years as a child when she had played on the rough, natural stone, the evenings she had sat in the large swing with her father as he sang to her.

Straightening her shoulders, Anna stepped across the porch, lifted her hand, and pressed the doorbell twice.

She didn't have to wait long, but she was rather surprised when her grandfather answered the door rather than the butler who had been with their family for years. "What's going on, Archer?" As her grandfather's gaze flickered to her, she saw the soul-deep pain that filled them and felt her throat tightening in agony

"Damn, Grandfather, you can't even acknowledge my presence?" Aching, so hungry for this man's notice that she was ready to beg for it, Anna used mockery to shield it.

Acknowledging that hunger was one thing, showing it was another.

Her grandfather's jaw clenched as a spasm of such

agony crossed his face that Anna couldn't hold back a slight sob.

"John, we've identified your problem," Archer told him quietly. "But Anna's known what's going on since the night you were in my study with your friends. She heard it all as she stood outside the door."

Her grandfather gripped the door frame quickly, paling as his gaze shot to hers.

"Tell me, Grandfather," she said painfully. "Would my mother understand what you've done to her daughter?"

"What?" He swallowed tightly, shaking his head as he turned back to Archer and Anna felt her heart breaking, for her as well as this man who had helped raise her for so many years. "What happened?"

"You haven't heard about Anna's abduction by the Slasher last night?" Archer asked then.

If John could have paled further, then he would have. For a second he seemed to sway on his feet, his fists clenching spasmodically at his sides as he seemed to fight to get control of himself.

His gaze turned to Anna.

"I didn't know," he wheezed. "Oh God, Anna, I didn't know." Then fear seemed to flash in his eyes as he turned back to Archer again. "You know the identity of the Slasher then?"

Archer breathed in roughly. "It was Wayne Sorenson, John," he told him quietly. "He was your blackmailer as well as Amory's partner."

"No." Her grandfather gave his head a quick shake. "He's Robert's best friend." He turned to Anna. "Amelia's father. He helped—" He broke off quickly, as though what he had been about to say was something she couldn't hear.

Oh God, what secrets was her family hiding? What had happened that could be worse than what she already knew?"

"Helped with what, Grandfather?" she asked. "What did he help do? Hide the proof that my parents were murdered? Or hide the proof that the daughter David and Kimberly Callahan had had three weeks before their death hadn't died with them after all?"

CHAPTER 24

John gave his head a hard shake, as though unable to believe the words had come from her lips.

Her grandfather's gaze was tortured as it met hers, years of pain, fear, and decisions that broke all their hearts filling his eyes.

"You better come in." Her grandfather stood back then, his hand shaking as he shoved it into the pocket of his slacks and hung onto the door with the other. "We were all on the back patio."

"No one told you Anna had been abducted last night?" Archer questioned him again as they followed him through the house.

"No one," he answered, his voice hollow. "But then, we were out of the house most of the night and into this morning. Some of the fences went down near the interstate, and we had cattle trying to play speed bumps for the cars. It was a hell of a mess. We were all out until dawn."

That explained why they hadn't at least called to see if she was okay, Anna tried to tell herself.

Stepping onto the patio, she stood still, silent as her parents and gran'ma stood from their seats around the ceramic top table and stared back at her, their eyes holding an edge of desperation.

Archer's hand settled at the small of her back, his fingers subtly caressing as she drew in a long, slow breath. "Last night, Amory Wyatt and Wayne Sorenson had me abducted from Archer's house," she stated.

"Oh God. No," her mother said, her hands covering her face as Anna found herself battling her tears once again.

"I listened as someone other than those I loved told me how another couple gave birth to me. Wayne was quite triumphant that he had ensured I was no part of my family, not part of any family really, since I was nine, and that by abducting me he would ensure I would leave and be out of the county when I turned twenty-five." A tear slipped down her face. "Why didn't you just tell me?" Her gaze centered on her mother. "I haven't always been a child, but I've always begged to come home, to be a part of this family. Why couldn't you just tell me the truth and at least allow me the knowledge that you loved me? That you weren't ashamed of me or just indifferent? Why?"

"Anna." Her mother came to her feet, her face lined with sorrow and with guilt. "There's so much you don't understand, so much that would be impossible to explain."

Her father rose from his chair more slowly, his expression heavy.

Everyone now seemed frozen, as though they didn't know what to say, or what to do.

Archer stepped closer to her.

"My deputies have found irrefutable proof that Wayne's has been blackmailing the Corbin, Rafferty, and Ramsey families for the murders of JR and Eileen Callahan, also their sons and daughters-in-law's, Benjamin and Ann Callahan, Samuel and Mina Callahan, and David and Kimberly Callahan, that he committed."

Everyone seemed to be waiting.

"There was also proof of Clyde Ramsey's murder and a cowboy, Dale Layden. It seemed Clyde and my father were working together for a number of years to find proof that Wayne had committed the murders. Dale was JR and Eileen Callahan's workhand just before they were killed. He saw Wayne loading their bodies into JR's ranch truck and driving off with them just before the blizzard. He followed on horseback and witnessed him sending the truck over that cliff. Unfortunately, Wayne saw him as well. Knowing Wayne's father was a judge in the County, rather than telling anyone what he saw, Dale ran. Clyde tracked him down but somehow Wayne learned of the meeting and followed him. After Clyde left, Wayne killed him. He then came out to the Ramsey Ranch and killed Clyde out in the field before rigging the tractor accident."

"My God." Her grandfather sat down in the large easy chair that had always been his favorite, his hands shaking. "But why?" He stared back at Archer, his gaze beseeching.

Taking a seat as well and watching as Robert and Lisa Corbin, the couple Anna believed were her parents for so long, take their seats, Archer began.

He had explained this part to her as they dressed, and she still had problems believing the story.

"Do you recognize the surname Mulrooney?" Archer asked.

Her grandfather frowned. "There was a story of a Mulrooney claiming the land when our ancestors bought it from the state," John said, confused.

"Same family." Archer nodded. "Wayne's a direct descendant. He needed control of the Callahan property to find and claim the treasure those early Mulrooneys were rumored to have hidden on Callahan lands. He abducted Anna to force her to leave out of fear until he could make use of her when she turned twenty-five and could take possession of her part of the estate."

"There's no treasure. It's a rumor, nothing more." Her grandfather stared back at her, his eyes filled with a desperate pain. "It was just a rumor, Anna. There's nothing anyone could gain from all this."

"It's a rumor the Mulrooney family has always believed." Archer sighed. "We found generations of journals in Wayne's home, detailing the search for that treasure and early efforts to drive the Callahans out of the area and make the other Barons pay for their supposed parts in the loss of the treasure. Investigators are still going through the journals but it appears there are generations of them."

The family sat still and silent. Her mother's head was lowered, her hands covering her face, refusing to look at her.

Then the woman Anna had always called Mother lifted her face and Anna's breath caught at the pain and tears that filled it.

"The night your mother died, my newborn daughter died," she told her tearfully. "Your grandfather flew out to California." Her breathing hitched with a ragged sob. "He flew out, gathered us all together, and told us what happened, and how he had to protect Kimberly's child. He looked at me." She laid her hand on her heart, her lips trembling. "Lisa," he said. "That sweet baby girl we've all waited for you to have is gone." She sobbed. "But her death could save Sarah Ann's life. You could save her, he said."

She could barely talk now the pain was so thick, the memories so ragged.

"I had you with me," her grandfather stated as Anna held onto Archer's hand like a lifeline, her tears falling along with her mother's——no, the woman she had called mother. "I begged her," he admitted. "Me and your gran'momma, we begged. Within hours we flew home. When we landed, Lisa carried you and I slipped her beautiful baby girl to the M.E.'s office where the coroner and Archer's father were waiting on me. We buried Lisa and Robert's daughter with David and Kimberly. Their wills demanded they be buried together, and it was a damned good thing, because if Wayne was the Slasher all these years, then he was the one who demanded that David not be buried with the wife that loved him so much." He shook his head and focused on her once again. "They loved each other desperately, Anna, but they loved you and Crowe just as much. So much, they did everything in their power to protect the two of you and themselves. And she would have been very, very proud of both of you."

Anna stared at the couple who had been her parents for nearly all her life, aching so deep with such furious pain that she couldn't force herself to say anything. She couldn't rid herself of the aching hurt or the sense of desertion that had followed her for so long.

Her father——no, not her father.

No, no matter why, no matter the hurt——

"Da," she whispered.

His face twisted with pain as her momma gripped his hand tighter.

"Why couldn't you just trust me?" she asked the question that had been tearing her apart and laying waste to everything she believed in. "Why, Momma? Da? Why couldn't you just tell me instead of allowing me to feel as though you had deserted me? As though I meant nothing to you, or to my family?"

It was Archer who kept her grounded. Keeping her hand in his, his warmth close to her, letting her handle her tears, her anger, and her pain without assuring her everything was going to be fine.

Because it wouldn't be fine for a long time.

Her mother wiped desperately at her tears while her father inhaled sharply and blinked back the moisture in his eyes furiously.

"We were so scared, Anna," her momma rasped, her tear-roughened voice strained. "We never knew when he would call or what he would demand. All we knew was that we were losing you more and more every year. And more and more every year my soul was dying." She sobbed. "I had lost one child already, I couldn't bear to lose another."

"You are our daughter," her da stated hoarsely. "No matter what you feel, or what you will feel later, you are and always will be our daughter, Anna. I loved my sister. She was the baby of the family, treasured and cherished. And you were her child. But you're our daughter."

Her grandfather pulled his handkerchief free and wiped his face with trembling hands. "The day we buried your parents, you were quiet. The perfect baby," he said. "For a while. When you heard Crowe scream at me when he learned he wasn't coming back to the ranch with us, you woke instantly."

Anna's heart shattered at the knowledge that Crowe had suffered far more than she had.

"You screamed for hours," her grandfather said. "You were sobbing for him, I knew. I was sure you couldn't cry anymore, that your tears had to empty themselves, but even after we returned to the ranch, you still screamed. And that day I would have given my life, Anna, my life, if I could have had both of my grandchildren here.

If I could have helped Crowe with his grief, if I could have sheltered him. I would have given everything, all the bastard would have had to do was tell me what he wanted."

As Anna's lips parted, a sudden pounding on the back gate had her swinging around and watching in shock as it was suddenly pushed inward and fury itself stepped onto the patio.

Crowe stood like a dark visage of death, his amber-brown eyes filled with murderous fury as they swept the room and found her.

The look didn't change, but the tension, the killing rage that tightened his body eased somewhat.

"Crowe?" Archer questioned the entrance as they all came instantly to their feet.

Crowe's gaze sliced to John Corbin. "Well, if it isn't the martyr of Corbin County," he sneered. "Tell me, old man, have you sacrificed yourself for anyone else this year? Hell, I hope not. Your brand of help sucks."

Surprisingly enough it was his grandmother who reacted.

"James Crowe Callahan, your mother raised you better than that, and I know she did," Genoa rasped, her voice weak, and for the first time Anna noticed the tear tracks that glistened on her lined face.

Crowe's jaw tensed until Anna thought it would crack.

For a moment, she actually thought he would ignore her.

"Look at you," Genoa said. "As proud and stubborn as your daddy, but with your momma's eyes and with her way of staring at a person like you could run through them."

"Don't do this." His voice wasn't as cruel, but neither was it respectful. "You haven't been a grandmother since I was ten, and I don't need one now."

"I've always been your grandmother," she told him. "And you need one now, Crowe, far more than ever. Let's hope you don't wait too late to ask your own questions."

"I don't have any questions," he told her, the anger throbbing in his voice. "I don't have any questions, requests, or time to play these games." He turned to Archer. "We found Amelia Sorenson and a young woman, Elizabeth Haley, bound and suffering dehydration and exposure on the front porch of my cabin." His voice was so harsh, so filled with fury it was animalistic.

"Amelia?" Lisa whispered in a tone filled with the same shock Anna could feel tearing through her. "Why?"

"According to Amory Wyatt," Crowe sneered, "because Wayne wasn't playing by the rules." He turned to Archer. "Amelia is prepared to testify it was her father, Archer. She's—" He shook his head wearily before rubbing the back of his neck. "She's with Doc Mabry and his wife. Cayna's keeping an eye on her."

Leaning against Archer, his arm wrapped tightly around her, Anna could only stare back at Crowe, barely able to comprehend everything.

Amelia had disappeared from the hospital in the early hours of the morning.

"I was heading here when Amory called me," he continued, and the look he gave her parents and grandparents was savage.

"Don't leave without me," she told Archer softly, drawing his gaze as the emotional upheaval tore her apart inside.

"Never," he promised. "Let me see what's going on, and I'll be right back."

"Rafe and Logan are outside," Crowe all but snarled. "Along with those damned Resnova misfits that won't stay the hell out of my business."

Bending his head, Archer kissed her cheek gently. "Give me ten minutes."

Anna nodded, watching as he strode from the patio with Crowe following close behind.

Anna turned back to her family, her gaze settling on the two who had nurtured and raised her.

"You're my parents," she told them, clasping her hands in front of her, her fingers twisting and twining together as she watched her momma and da warily. "If you don't want to be my parents, then I can't force you, just as I can't force them." She glanced back at her grandparents. "But I love you," she said, the tears falling again as she faced life without the man and woman she'd always called Momma and Da. "Crowe will always be my brother and I hope some way, one of these days, we can find that relationship as it should have been, and I'll wish I had known the man and woman that gave me life. But you gave me manners, honesty, security as best you could, and I always thought, until I was forced from my home, you taught me to love." Her voice broke as she lifted her hands, covering her face for a moment, hoping to stem the tears. "But you also taught me to fight for what I want. And I want to be in Corbin County. I want to be a part of my brother's and cousins' lives, and yours."

But nothing could stem the pain resonating inside her. Just as nothing could change the love she felt for this family. Faults and all, and in spite of the past that had nearly destroyed them all.

Her father's arms went around her.

She knew the feel of them.

Other than for the first three weeks of her life, this man's arms had held her, this woman's had comforted her, and the grandparents she so loved had done their best to spoil her.

And her momma was there. Pulling Anna to her, Lisa Corbin tucked the only daughter she had ever truly known against her heart, and they sobbed together as her gran'pop and gran'momma came to her, their hugs, their whispers of love perhaps not healing, but easing her heart.

They had lost time, years spent in fear and fighting to protect the child who stole their hearts with her broken sobs at such a young age.

They were praying the tears were over.

"My baby girl." Her momma said as Anna stepped back. "No matter the name you carry, you'll always be our baby girl."

CHAPTER 25

She felt broken when they returned to Archer's house that evening.

Amory Wyatt and Wayne Sorenson had disappeared entirely.

Thankfully, Rory Malone was coming out of the hospital in a day or so with a clean bill of health.

"Hey, babe." Archer entered the kitchen after his shower, moving to her to place a gentle kiss at her nape. "I ordered dinner in. It should be here soon."

Anna stared back at him, her heart aching at the warmth in his gaze.

She knew just this: the warmth and sexual need would never be enough. She needed his love. She deserved his love.

"Thank you," she said. "I'd forgotten about dinner."

The doorbell sounded at that moment, an announcement that the food had arrived.

Archer winked back at her with wicked, lustful intent. "You can show me how appreciative you are after dinner."

And she would, because she needed him. Because

his touch, his warmth would haunt her once this was over.

Archer returned to the patio with the food long minutes later. Stopping in the kitchen, he'd transferred the still hot fries and sandwiches to plates, collected the salt, pepper, ketchup, mayo, and hot sauce.

Stepping back to the patio area for a second, Archer was taken aback by the sight of Anna and the romantic glow the fire cast around her.

Dressed in the ankle-length, full gypsy-type cotton skirt and pale peach camisole top that revealed soft shoulders gleaming with a silken sheen. The tops of her firm, rounded breasts with a hint of a lacy bra pulled at his gaze and had his mouth watering to taste her nipples.

Long dark hair hung loose around her face, heavy curls falling over one shoulder to curl over the lush curve of her breast.

Lower, beneath the thin material of her blouse and the lace of her bra, her nipples pressed pebble hard, and waiting for the heat of his mouth.

Every inch of the tempting, curved body hardened his dick and made him ache for her touch.

She was sinking inside him, he admitted silently. Never had he brought a lover to his home or dealt well with the thought of having some female imprinting her presence inside his house. But this woman, this lover—he simply couldn't imagine his home without her.

As they ate their food, conversation stilled, and the sounds of the waterfall in the far corner and the flames licking at the wood opposite turned the patio into an intimate, warm cocoon.

Intimacy couldn't dispel the concern that Wayne

and Amory couldn't be found though, because of the
threat they represented to Anna and to Cami, Skye,
and now Amelia as well.

"You look worried," she stated as they finished the
last of the food and the beer.

Archer watched her face, watched the light of the
fire flicker over the pretty features, the somber cast of
her eyes. She'd smiled at him earlier, and he swore his
heart was going to beat right out of his chest with excitement.

A woman shouldn't be able to do that to a man, he
told himself. It was damned dangerous. It started him
thinking that maybe the fairy tale could be more than
just an illusion.

"We have to figure out where Wayne and Amory
are hiding," he breathed out roughly. "Neither Amelia
nor Elizabeth knew where they were holding them,
but they're certain the drive there was more than an
hour, but no more than two."

Anna turned her eyes from Archer's and stared into
the fire instead. The flames were lower now, the wood
more than half consumed as they sat before it and ate.

"They can't hide forever," she stated as she rubbed
her arms, knowing that as long as Wayne and Amory
were free, they were dangerous.

"Do you know how it tortures me? I'm terrified I'll
blink, and he'll snatch you again." he told her as he
moved his chair closer to hers, then pulled her into his
arms. "Knowing he's still out there, knowing he won't
stop until he's dead."

And he wouldn't. Anna remembered the pure evil
in his voice, as well as the need he'd felt to hurt her.

Leaning against his chest, feeling his heartbeat beneath her ear, she couldn't stop the chill that raced up
her spine at the memory of it.

Tilting her head back, she stared up at him, catching his gaze as he stared down at her and seeing the determination inside him.

"If anyone can stop them, you will, Archer." She knew that to the bottom of her soul. "You're not the kind of man who will give up just because others think you should. You'll catch them, and when you do, Amory and Wayne both will regret each drop of blood they shed."

As she stared up at him, his head lowered, his lips brushing against hers.

She was sinking inside him, and he had no idea how to make it stop, how to make her stop. The problem was, he didn't want it to stop. And that scared the shit out of him.

"I wish we had happened another way." The regret in her voice had him tightening his arms around her. "I used to imagine I could slip out to one of the socials. That you would see me. Your eyes would touch mine and in your eyes I'd see how much you wanted me." Tears might not be falling, but he swore he could feel them falling in her soul. "You'd walk across the dance square, all tall and handsome, and you'd take me in your arms. We'd dance until you danced me right into one of those little grottos, and there you'd kiss me. You'd tell me how you'd waited for me and were never going to let me go." Her head fell back against his shoulder, the long strands of her hair feathering out over his arm. "And now there's just not even a chance."

Because now it had already happened. They had come together in a way that was certain to tear them apart.

He hadn't invited her to move in with him after they became lovers. He had been forced to bring her to his home because she had no other place to go.

Archer turned her in his arms, one hand sliding into the back of her hair, clenching in the strands and sending pleasure racing through her nerve endings.

Lifting her gaze to his, she could see the hunger burning in his eyes, lust and something more. Something she wished was love.

Then his lips were covering hers, easing over them, his tongue licking over the fullness of her lower lip before pressing inside and finding hers.

Anna moaned at the rich seductiveness of the kiss. The feel of his lips caressing hers, taking sipping kisses and burning her with the hunger in his touch, tore a whimpering cry from her.

He couldn't know how deeply her heart beat for him. How deep the hope that she could fill his heart went. And how wide was the certainty that when this was over, she would be without him.

Wrapping her arms around his neck and lifting to her toes, Anna parted her lips for him, taking his kiss with a need she didn't bother to control.

Her hold tightened.

Sliding her fingers into his hair, Anna moaned with rising pleasure, lifting against him, feeling the thick ridge of his cock, iron hard, iron hot, pressing against her stomach as his tongue thrust inside her mouth and rubbed against her own.

Before she could stop him, he was drawing back, releasing her, then pulling her to the fire.

On the other side of the patio a wide lounge chair had been pushed against the house. Archer jerked the thick, heavy pad from it and tossed it to the patio in front of the fireplace.

A second later, he'd shed the sweatpants he wore before gripping the scarf she used as a sash around the elastic band of her skirt.

Staring into her eyes, he untied it, loosening the ends before gripping the elastic band and pushing it over her hips and down her legs to pool at her feet.

With a flick of his fingers between her breasts, her bra was loosened, the straps pushed over her shoulders and smoothed down her arms until he could toss it away as well.

"Sweet God, have mercy on me," he breathed as he cupped her firm, sensitive breasts, his eyes caressing her nipples. "I love your breasts, Anna. And your sweet, berry ripe nipples. Do you know I dream of sucking those pretty little nipples?"

Bending to her, his lips surrounded one hard tip and sucked it into the heat of his mouth.

Staring down at him, her fingers feathering through the dark blond of his hair, Anna fought to control her accelerated breathing, to find enough strength in her legs to remain in place.

"What if someone sees us?"

"No one can see," he promised, brushing his lips against her nipples before easing her to the wide, firm cushion he'd tossed in front of the fire. "You might want to watch those little cries when you come though. You never know if the neighbors are listening."

Lying before him, wearing only the pale peach panties riding low on her hips, Anna bit at her lower lip, wondering how in the hell she was going to manage that.

Lowering himself beside her, his lips came down on hers again, stroking against them, licking over them as Anna fought to hold back a needy moan.

"Shhh," he murmured as his head lifted, his eyes glittering a rich golden brown as rising hunger reflected in the depths.

Calloused fingertips stroked her thigh as his lips moved across her jaw, down her neck.

Anna turned her face to him as his kisses fell to the upper rise of her breasts, her lips finding the hard flesh of his neck.

As he drew the sensitive tip into his mouth, Anna had to clench her teeth to hold back her cry.

Warmed by the fire and by Archer's hard body, Anna lifted to the heat of his mouth. With her hands buried in his hair, her lips and tongue caressing his neck as he tormented her nipples with searing pleasure, Anna felt the world around them receding. Pressing the hard curve of his knee against the mound of her cunt, Anna could feel the flames rising higher, pleasure sinking deeper inside her.

Sucking first one hard nipple, then the other into his mouth, Archer groaned against the hard tip, his tongue stroking, rasping against it until she cried out his name. Throttling the sound, desperate to keep the unknown neighbors from hearing her, she pressed the back of her hand to her lips and prayed that would work.

Then those diabolically clever, wicked lips began moving down her body. His tongue peeked out to play, to lick and draw heated patterns of erotic pleasure against her stomach before trailing lower, lower.

When his lips came to the elastic edge of her panties, his fingers moved from her thigh, gripped the band, and eased them slowly over her thighs.

Drawing back, he pulled the silk past her knees, down her legs, then dropped them to the side of the makeshift bed.

Her breathing ragged, pleasure whipping through her, Anna stared up at Archer as he pushed slowly between her thighs, his hands gripping her knees as she lifted them, planting her feet next to the pad on each side to lift closer to him.

Spreading her legs apart, Archer stared down at the dew-slick, juice-laden folds of her bare pussy. The swollen bud of her clit peeked out beneath the small, short tuft of curls while her juices saturated the flesh below it.

She had the prettiest pussy, he thought, licking his lips in anticipation. The need to taste the sweet, wet heat spilling from her was a hunger nearly impossible to control. It was all peaches-and-cream perfection outside the tight, slick embrace of her hot little vagina.

Fucking her was euphoric.

It was better than any drug any dumb son of a bitch could imagine.

Moving his lips to hers once again, Archer took her kiss amid her small, muted little moans. He couldn't help but groan at the pleasure.

She did something to him. Something far deeper even than the sight of his hat on the coat hook. Coming home to Anna, touching her, tasting her, was like *really* coming home.

With his lips settling against hers, pressing closer, his tongue tasting her, Archer let his senses become fully immersed in her. Stroking his tongue against hers, tasting a hint of the wine and chocolate she'd had for dessert, he let his hand caress her side before moving in to cup her breast.

The firm, swollen flesh fit his palm perfectly. The pebble hardness of her nipple beneath his thumb, the responsive arch of her body to his caress, held no deception or hint of ulterior motives.

She was completely lost in the pleasure. So lost in the sensations whipping through her body that she dragged him deeper into his own pleasure as well.

Sensation rose like a blazing sun burning in the pit of her belly and sending heat radiating through her pussy.

Anna arched into his touch, whimpered with the lash of pleasure and the rising clash of sensations that were impossible to keep up with.

It seemed every cell of her body ached for his caress. She craved his kiss. Her nipples throbbed, swollen tight, ultra-sensitive nerve endings eager for even the slightest touch to send burning arcs of sensation striking at her clitoris, at the clenched muscles of her vagina.

Flattening his palm at her knee, Archer stroked slowly up the inside of her thigh, parting her legs further. Bending one knee, her foot pressing into the thick pad beneath them, Anna lifted herself closer to his touch.

Her hips lifted in anticipation as his palm stroked like a tease, a taunt of what was to come. Flat, short nails scraped against the sensitive flesh of her thigh but refused to come closer to the aching center of her body.

The rasp of his nails had sensation prickling beneath her skin, racing along nerve endings to strike at her clit as she jerked closer to his touch.

"You're teasing me," she panted, her neck arching as his kisses returned to it.

"I'm enjoying you," he growled. "God, I don't think I can get enough of you."

She didn't want him to get enough of her. She never wanted him to stop aching for her because she was afraid she would never stop aching for him.

"I need more, Archer." She didn't think she could be held on this edge, as violently sharp as it was, much longer.

"How much more, baby?" His lips moved from her neck to her nipples.

Suckling a tight peak into his mouth, his teeth rasped it, drawing a short, sharp cry from her lips. Gripping it between his teeth, his tongue rubbed against it until it felt as though her orgasm was only a heartbeat away.

The tender tips were so sensitive now, so incredibly hard that the pleasure bordered ecstasy and the pain bordered agony until they merged to create a clash of such intensity she didn't know if she could bear it.

She felt suspended, poised on an edge of ecstasy so sharp it was all she could do to breathe.

"Archer, fuck me," she moaned, her back arching as his lips moved lower. "Please, you're killing me."

Sliding his fingers to the wet folds of her pussy, he parted the intimate lips slowly. There, with only the tips of his fingers, he rubbed against the clenched entrance to the sensitive inner flesh.

Arching closer, a strangled moan falling from her lips, Anna tried to force his fingers inside her, to find the release that tortured her.

"Archer, it's so close," she gasped, her nails biting into his shoulders. "So close. Please. Please let me come."

Her nails raked across his shoulders as he moved closer. The wide, engorged head of his cock slid through the heavy, slick moisture. Parting the hot, wet folds he angled his hips to press the wide head against the weeping entrance to her pussy.

"Oh yes," she moaned, the pinch of the incredibly tight fit beginning to bloom at the narrow slit as he began to push against it.

Heated, stretching, the impalement was pleasure and pain. The pinching heat speared through her as Archer worked his cock inside her.

The hardened flesh parted the sensitive muscles with short, strong thrusts of his hips. Working the

wide, hot crest inside her, inch by slow inch, he pushed
the pleasure higher, pushed her closer to an edge she'd
never suspected could exist.

"Archer." Her low, desperate moan filled the air as
ecstasy began to fill her. "Oh God, it's so good. It feels
so good."

It was better than good. It was a rising wave of sensation swirling through her with burning sensation
and rising rapture.

Deep, sharp, the aching need for release rushed
through each erogenous zone and stroked over each
nerve ending as his cock shuttled inside her, pushing
into the clenched, snug tissue milking his engorged
erection.

Each thrust stroked against painfully sensitive
nerve endings. It rasped over them, igniting flames of
such fiery intensity that Anna felt as though she were
melting around him.

Each fierce penetration, each hard thrust rasped over
areas so sensitive, nerve endings so burningly alive
that each stroke sent ecstasy slamming through her.

Her body tightened, every muscle straining, aching,
as she reached for release.

"Look at me, Anna." The harsh male groan had her
lashes lifting, her gaze meeting the fierce glow of lust
in his eyes.

One hand gripped her thigh as his hips thrust and
rolled, stroking inside her harder, faster.

"Let me see you, baby," he demanded. "Let me watch
you come, Anna."

Anna felt the last restraint holding her to earth shat-
ter. With her gaze locked to his, his hands gripped her
wrists, pulling them from his shoulders and lacing his
fingers with hers as he pressed them to the pad above
her head.

Entwined with hers, his fingers tightened, holding her to earth as his hips moved harder, faster, thrusting desperately inside her. Anna felt the cataclysm erupt within. Exploding, blazing, shattering through her system with a rapture that stole her breath and sent her flying through ecstasy.

Archer's lips came over hers as his release rushed through him as well. His tongue tangled with hers, his cock burying deep as she felt his release spurting inside her, filling her with the hard, heated jets.

Crying out into his kiss, her fingers tightening with his, Anna shuddered, her body trembling, jerking against his. With each spasm of her pussy around his cock, each heavy, milking clench of her inner muscles, a surge of rapture raced through her again. Again.

Archer lost himself in the release he shared with Anna. The power of his orgasm rushing through him, through her, over them, was a pleasure he knew he had never experienced before. It was a pleasure he knew he would never have with any woman but Anna.

He had fallen into the trap he had sworn he'd never allow himself to fall into. That trap where pleasure and emotion combined to lock a man's soul to a woman's and leave him lost at the thought of ever being without her.

He'd fallen through the rabbit hole and he was very, very afraid he was in danger of the illusion taking control of him.

Archer was beginning to believe he might have found the fairy tale.

CHAPTER 26

It was time to pack for good.

Anna realized that this time she had accepted the fact that she wouldn't be coming back, because this time she remembered to pack her toiletries from the bathroom.

Packing her toiletries, Anna was zipping the bag when the bedroom door opened.

"Anna, I thought we were out of the grilling steaks? I know I laid out the last two the other night—"

Anna lifted her head and watched as Archer came to a full, hard stop.

His gaze went to the luggage.

Straightening, she stared back at him, her heart breaking as she watched his fierce, predatory gaze flicker between her and the bags several times before he reached back and slammed the door closed.

She flinched, her heart jumping and racing furiously in her chest.

She had never seen such a look on his face before now. She had never seen that look on *anyone's* face before now.

"What are you doing?" There wasn't so much as a hint of emotion on his face, but his eyes . . . there was so much rage in his eyes that Anna couldn't have kept up if she'd had an emotional dictionary.

"We know who's behind it now," she stated calmly. "I know what both Wayne Sorenson and Amory Wyatt look like. They can't catch me unaware again."

"And just where do you think you're going to go?" He advanced into the bedroom by only a few feet before coming to a stop.

"For the next few nights I'll stay at the hotel in town," she answered with a shrug, wishing she could take her eyes off him. Wishing she could take her heart back from him. "Momma wanted me to come back to the ranch, but . . ." She shrugged. She couldn't. Not yet.

"I'll be fine, Archer," she promised, turning away from him and pretending to make certain she hadn't forgotten anything. "You're not responsible for me any longer."

"Is that what you think?"

The slow, furious drawl of the question should have warned her. She should have known the second that tone snapped across her senses to beware.

She was a second too late in turning, not that she could have avoided him, no matter how fast she moved.

One hand gripped her arm, the other went around her back as he pulled her the rest of the way around.

Locked to the length of his hard, aroused body—he hadn't been aroused before—there was no pushing away from him.

"Why are you doing this?" She pushed against his chest, despite the fact that she knew there was no breaking free.

"You think I'm going to just let you walk out?"

"Why not?" Glaring back at him, fighting to keep from melting against him, Anna pushed her fists against his chest as she tried to angle her hips away from the length of his erection.

"Why should I?" he questioned her instead, his lips lowering to part, his strong teeth nipping at the lobe of her ear.

She shouldn't respond so easily to him.

Biting her lip, Anna had to fight to keep from tilting her head to the side and giving him full access to her neck as she felt the whisper of a kiss against the sensitive flesh.

"You should—" Lashes fluttering as sensual weakness flooded her body, she had to fight to remember why. "You should, Archer, because I'm weak." Bitterness returned with a rush, but it didn't dissipate the need for his touch.

Stilling against her, his lips against her neck, one hand pressed against the small of her back, the other a scant breath beneath her breasts.

"Anna," he protested softly. "Why do you think you have to leave?"

Pressing her forehead against his chest, Anna felt tears filling her eyes again.

"Why leave me, Anna?" he asked.

"Why doesn't matter, Archer." Her voice sounded as hoarse, as aching as her soul did.

How was she supposed to fight this need for him? The hunger that raged through her and had no intentions of abating?

"Why always matters, Anna." Lifting his head, Archer stared down at her, his gaze still raging but his expression not hard or unemotional any longer.

Savage, fierce.

Possessive.

The dark emotions brewing in his gaze were reflected on his face as hands tightened at her hips.

Shaking her head, she fought the need to respond to that look, to give into the demands, the dominating strength of his body and the hunger that only burned hotter in his gaze.

"I'm weak, Archer," she reminded him bitterly. "Too weak to be able to give you what you need."

"Like hell." Stark, echoing with denial and rich with possessive intent, Archer lifted her, turning and pressing her against the bedroom wall. "The last thing you are is weak."

A shift of his hips and, before Anna could stop him, he had her thighs spread, her knees gripping his hips. The full length of his cock notched between her thighs, pressing hard and hot into the mound of her pussy through the cotton panties she wore.

The full skirt she wore fell back, pooling between their bodies as he held her with one hand and dragged the hem of her sleeveless blouse from the band of her skirt.

Before Anna could do more than attempt to lower her arms, Archer gripped them in one hand, dragged the shirt up and over her breasts, her head, jerking it over her arms.

A second later her wrists were free and the shirt was gone, leaving her breasts covered by nothing more than her flesh-colored bra.

That did nothing to hide the hardness of her nipples though. They pressed against the lace of her bra as the swollen flesh of her breasts rose over the half cups.

"Why are you doing this?" Anna slapped at his hands as he released the catch between her breasts and quickly got rid of the bra.

"You're not leaving me," he growled, his hands cupping her breasts, his fingers finding the hard tips of her nipples and applying just enough pressure that she stopped fighting and stilled with a sharp moan of surprised pleasure.

"And you can't make me stay," she cried out. "I won't stay, Archer, and you can't keep me in a damned bed twenty-four hours a day."

"The hell I can't."

His lips covered her, his tongue pressing against the lush curves of hers, pressing, easing past them until he owned the kiss he had taken. With his lips and tongue, the heat of the hunger that swirled between them, he stole her objection and her will to object.

She could have him, this one last time.

Her arms went around his neck, fingers spearing into his hair.

She could love him this one last time.

A moan pushed past their kiss as his hands stroked and massaged her breasts, his thumb and forefingers pressing and rolling the tender tips of her nipples until flames were shooting in a path straight to the swollen, heated bud of her clitoris.

As his lips left hers to blaze a path of pleasure down her neck to the sensitive curves of her breasts, heat trailed in their wake.

Her nipples throbbed. His lips moved closer, the threat of their firm pressure, the fiery dampness of his mouth and the wicked strokes of his tongue had them pulsing, throbbing in anticipation.

When it came, a whimpering cry filled the air.

Anna tightened her fingers in his hair, her head falling back against the wall as his lips began to draw at the tight, over-sensitive peak he held captive.

Teeth rasping, his tongue flickered against her nipple as his cheeks hollowed, sucking with firm, even draws of his mouth as his eyes glittered between the thick cover of lashes.

How wicked he looked. How completely sexual and dominant.

One hand slid to her thigh, lifting her skirt further, and she knew what was coming.

Anticipation slid over her flesh in the wake of his touch, her pussy throbbing, clenching in need as she felt his fingers tighten at the side of her panties.

At this rate, she was going to have to buy new panties.

Before she could process the move, he released her breast from the heat of his mouth and turned. With a gasp, Anna found herself sprawled on her back, his hands gripping her panties and pulling them down her legs. The skirt came next, the elastic waistband making it even easier to dispose of.

Before he returned to her, his pants were shed, the heavy length of his cock spearing out from his body, flushed and dark with lust, the tip beading with pre-come as he came over her.

Quickly, the condom he pulled from the bedside table was torn open and rolled over his cock before he flipped her over on the bed and once again came between her thighs.

"What are you doing?" she gasped, trying to pull herself from the bed but only making it as far as rising to her knees.

"Perfect." Hard hands gripped her hips as the head of his erection pressed into the slick curves of her cunt.

Her juices pulsed from her body, spilling their slick heat against the tip of his cock as he began pressing inside.

Anna moaned.

Pleasure began whipping through her body at the first press of his cock against the entrance, stretching the tight opening and pressing slowly inside.

The pinching pleasure-pain of the first few inches of his cock working inside her had the blood searing her veins, pounding harsh and overly fast through her body.

A deep, desperate moan welled in her throat, the need to bed him was nearly overwhelming.

As the width of his cock pressed deeper, her hips jerked against him, lightning strokes of pure sensation whipping through her body as her pussy began contracting around his erection.

Breathing in hard, the hunger burning higher by the second, whimpering moans coming from her throat. The fingers of one hand clenched in the blankets beneath her as she reached back with the other and gripped his hard thigh desperately.

Lust wracked her body. Ravenous, burning, it stormed through her senses and shredded her control.

"Anna." Dark, deepening with need, his voice only stoked the flames higher. "Ah, baby. I love your pussy wrapping around my cock like that. Clenching and hot, sucking me in like your sweet, hot little mouth."

Anna tossed her head, pressing her hips back, taking no more than an additional inch before the hard hands at her hips stilled the backward thrusts.

"Not yet," he growled. "I want to feel it slow and easy. Feel every little sucking motion of your pussy as it draws me inside."

Hunger pounded through her with thundering force. It rocked her body, burned her with the need for more.

Anna could feel her body trembling, fought to control it and lost the battle.

Pulling back from the advance inside her hungry

pussy, he paused, only the head of his cock parting her entrance. The fierce throb echoed through her flesh, pounded at her clit, and clenched her inner muscles tight.

Then he moved, plunging forcefully into the tight channel as Anna screamed her pleasure. Bucking against the impalement, desperate for more as he lodged to the hilt inside her, she could only wait, quivering in his arms.

She felt poised on an edge of insanity. The need for him twisted inside her, spiraling through her body with a force that left her begging for more.

Moving behind her once again, Archer began working the broad length of his cock inside her, pushing into the clenched depths of her cunt as the slickness of her juices spilled along his rigid flesh.

He was moving too slowly. She needed—she ached for the heavy hard strokes filling her, shafting inside her with destructive pleasure.

Hard fingers tightened on her hips as he began moving, slowly at first, working his cock inside her with steadily increasing thrusts that rasped and raked along delicate, naked nerve endings. Tunneling inside her over and over again, stretching the intimate depths with each tight clenching of her vagina until pleasure and pain began to merge and become a sensation so heated and powerful Anna was pleading for release.

She could feel it building, burning in the swollen bud of her clit, clenching around the burrowing length of his cock and triggering tiny, fiery explosive sensations that became stronger, deeper—

"Oh God, Archer—" Shock, deepening rapture, and a sudden flaming expansion of the sensations rocking her began to surge across her nerve endings.

Archer came over her. One arm slid around beneath

her, his hand tucking between her thighs as his hips moved faster, harder.

Fucking inside her to the hilt before pulling back, then thrusting hard and deep again. Capturing her clit between two hard fingers and tightening them on the tender bud as he fucked her with deep, desperate lunges of his hips, was that one sensation too much.

Anna exploded.

Screaming out his name, her back arching, her head tipping back, she began to shake, to shudder from the deep, breathtaking surges of ecstasy that attacked her.

Clamping down on his cock, her inner muscles began to clench and milk the shuttling flesh as her clit pulsed with fiery sensation and her body came apart in his arms.

His groan echoed in her ears, vibrating with the same desperate pleasure as she felt him thrust in hard, then again, before his body tightened, slamming against hers and trembling as she felt his cock expand and begin throbbing in release.

Deep, desperate surges of sensation rocked her body until Anna collapsed, feeling Archer follow her, his thighs holding hers braced apart, his fingers still snug around her clit.

Anna shuddered again, her fingers tightening, twisting in the blankets beneath her, little cries erupting from her lips as the powerful quaking sensations erupted again, leaving her shuddering against him until they eased.

Exhausted, sexually replete, Anna lay beneath his body, refusing to open her eyes, to accept that this changed anything.

Easing from her, the feel of his still semi-hard flesh pulling free of her body dragged a weary moan from her and an exhausted little shiver of delight. She loved his body more than he could know.

She loved him more than he could know.

"My sweet Anna."

Archer's hand curved over her cheek as her head lifted, bringing her lips to his. He kissed her, caressing her lips with his, sipping from them. The gentle caress pulled all the emotions she had fought to push back, suddenly surging forward until Anna caught her breath and felt her eyes filling with tears again.

"Stop." Pulling from him, she shook her head, gaining only a few inches between them. "Please, Archer, I need to sit up."

He let her go slowly, watching as the slender, delicate line of her back tensed with what he was certain would become a confrontation.

Hell, he didn't have the will to deny her any longer, and Archer knew it.

The long, softened strands of her hair caressed her back, tempting his fingers. Archer stilled the need to touch her, rolling to his back instead and pulling the condom from his still-hard dick before rising to his feet and pacing to the bathroom.

Disposing of the latex, he washed, then returned to the bed, carrying a warm, wet cloth and towel.

Before she could do much to protest, he pushed her back on the bed, spread her legs, and began cleaning her gently. Glancing up at her, he saw the confusion in her face and the wariness in her eyes.

Drying the soft flesh, Archer tossed the washcloth and towel aside, then sat on the bed next to her as she eased up.

"Anna, let me say this first." Laying his fingers against her lips for a second, he waited until she nodded. "When you came to stay here I really didn't care how long you stayed. To be honest, I never considered the day when you would leave. Let alone the day when I would push you into staying."

Tears glittered in her eyes. "I don't need lies, Archer," she said.

"Damn good," he growled. "Because I'm not lying to you. So would you shut the fuck up for two minutes and let me finish this?"

Her lips pressed together tightly.

"If you leave me, Anna, if you walk out of that door, then, I'll say you're weak as hell." Her head jerked back, her gaze widening with indignation.

Archer pressed his fingers to her lips again and kept them there.

"I'll say it," he repeated. "But I'll know better. Just as I've always known you are one of the strongest women I know. But you're also one of the gentlest, and one of the most loving. And if I have to watch you walk out my door, my heart's going to break."

He lowered his fingers, but she didn't say anything. She just stared at him somberly; her green eyes, though, they were filling with hope.

Her eyes began to fill with tears again.

Anna tensed, her eyes widening, her breathing becoming ragged as Archer lifted her hand and placed it against his chest, leaning closer to her. "Feel my heart, baby? It's racing. I'm terrified of what I feel for you. It fucking gives me nightmares, because all I can do is see my father's face the day he realized he couldn't save my mother. The second he accepted the fact that cancer couldn't be fought with his strength, his diligence, or his training, and that he was losing her."

A single tear slipped down her cheek as he turned her more fully to him. "Since the day you turned eigh-

teen, every time I've seen you, I've ached for you. I
dreamed of you. I fantasized about you. And each time
I tried to reach out for you, that was what I saw. Because, Anna." He cupped her face in his hand, staring
into her eyes, begging her to believe him. "I love you.
I've loved you since you were eighteen. I've hungered
for you. I've lain in my bed and stared at the ceiling and
swore I didn't love you. That it wouldn't kill me if you
were suddenly gone. Until the night Amory took you
and I had to face the fact that I could have already lost
you."

"No. Stop." She shook her head, her voice ragged
now and filled with disbelief.

"Don't you dare call me a liar again." Gripping her
shoulders, he held her in place, refusing to allow her to
jump from the bed and desert him. "Don't you dare
walk out on me, Anna. Because I swear, if you do, if
you leave me and walk away from me, I couldn't blame
you, but God as my witness, I would grieve every
fucking day of my life."

She jumped from the bed, moving away from him
to grab a long shirt from the nearby chair and slip it
on. "You believe love is a fairy tale."

Archer narrowed his eyes on the white fabric.

So that was where his favorite shirt had gotten off to.

Wrapping it around her, she held it closed in desperate hands and stared at him as though somehow, some
way, some divine intervention would allow her to see
inside his soul.

Archer reached down and pulled his pants on. This
was evidently a discussion that required clothes.

"Are you going to deny it?" she demanded fiercely.
"Pretend you didn't say it?"

"Only if you'll let me," he retorted as he turned

back to her, his hands going to his hips in irritation. "Hell yes, I'm going to deny it. It didn't happen, Anna. That was a very, very bad dream you had, baby." He gentled his voice and moved to her, gripping her shoulders and staring down at her in sympathy. "Come back to bed, and I'll make all the bad dreams go away for you."

She blinked up at him. "You so are not serious." She couldn't believe he would joke about something so serious.

The hell he wasn't, Archer thought.

"It must have been something you ate," he mused with all seriousness. "You know, I heard if you eat mustard before going to sleep, it will give you nightmares. What did you eat?"

Her eyes narrowed. "This is not a joke."

"Hell no, it's not," he agreed as though it was the height of seriousness and wondered if she would actually let him get away with it. "I take your nightmares very seriously, Anna."

Was that a twitch he saw at the corner of her lips? A hint of a need to smile?

"Don't play games with me, Archer." Desperate, uncertain hope began filling her eyes. "If you care anything at all about me, please don't play games with me."

Lowering his head, his gaze holding hers, he touched her lips with his. "I love you, Anna. You gave me a gift no one can ever take from me but you. A gift that will only be a part of me as long as you are with me. The truth, baby."

Her lips parted as the question rose in her eyes.

"Shh," he shushed her, kissed her lips with the utmost care before pulling back and explaining.

"You showed me that fairy tales do exist, and the

illusion was my fear of having you taken from me. A fear so fucking deep and strong that I almost pushed you away so I wouldn't ever have to face you walking away from me."

Her gaze searched his for long, long moments.

"I can't even swear you won't ever have that nightmare again," he sighed regretfully. "Because I'm just a real dumb man, darlin'. One that's spent a lot of years loving a woman so damned pretty, so damned smart, and sweet and gentle, that sometimes it just messes with his mind and makes him forget all those lessons she taught him over the years."

"And what lessons were those?" she asked, her voice husky with those unshed tears.

"Acceptance. Gentleness, and most of all, Anna, love. You taught me to love. And if you love me at all, then you won't leave me. You won't be able to leave me. Because God knows, I can't let you walk out that door."

Her lips were trembling.

Tears spilled from her eyes now, but it wasn't pain that filled the emerald orbs. For the first time in all the years he had known her, Archer watched her eyes fill with joy.

"You really love me?" Her voice quivered, a hint of a sob in her voice as she reached up, her fingers shaking as she touched his face.

"Anna, baby, I don't just love you," he swore. "I'd die for you. I'd kill for you. You own my heart, and you're my soul. If I lose you, then I've lost everything important in my life."

And only then, only in that second did Archer realize he'd shed his own tear or two.

All for Anna.

For the heart he was terrified he'd broken, for the

gentle spirit and loving heart he hadn't known he would die for, until he had almost destroyed it.

"Archer—"

He saw it then. Slowly at first, almost hesitant. So hesitant, that at first he was terrified it would happen.

Then it bloomed.

The sweetest smile on the face of the earth. That soft, gentle smile only his Anna had, because only his Anna could infuse it with all the love she felt for him.

"I love you," she said, and with the smile came her tears.

Tears born of happiness, joy, and love rather than the dark fears and betrayals that had marked her life for so many years. A smile so bright, so filled with every part of Anna's heart that Archer swore it made his knees weak.

"Oh God, Archer. I love you so much."

She was in his arms, her arms wrapped around his neck, her lips pressed to his, but before he could hold them, her lips were touching the dampness of the tears he'd shed, his eyes, then his lips once again.

Pulling back, staring up at him, that smile still in place, filling her eyes, her beautiful face and he could see, filling her heart.

"I've loved you since the first moment I saw you." God, her voice. It was like the soft warmth of summer and the golden rays of the sun.

It just made him warm inside.

"Just always love me." He would have gone to his knees to beg if that was what he needed to do. "Just that, Anna."

"I'll always love you," she swore.

EPILOGUE

Wayne stared at the small town from his vantage point above it.

How peaceful it looked.

How calm.

He wasn't finished here yet. The Barons owed him, and by God he would have his due one way or the other. He would have it. And every fucking Callahan living would pay for all he'd lost.

Especially Crowe Callahan.

Crowe and the traitorous slut no doubt sleeping in his bed. Wayne breathed out heavily. His own traitorous daughter . . .

Midnight Sins

Cami lost her sister in the brutal murders that rocked her hometown so many years ago. Some still believe that Rafe Callahan, along with his friends Logan and Crowe, were involved. But how could Rafe—who haunted her girlish dreams, then her adult fantasies—be a killer?

Deadly Sins

A newcomer in town, Skye O'Brien is a mystery to Logan Callahan. Like him, she is a night owl. Like him, she is fighting her own demons. Like him, she hides a secret in her eyes—a fire that consumes him with every glance. Could she be the one to heal him?

Secret Sins

Sheriff Archer Tobias has watched the Callahan family struggle to find peace and acceptance in the community—despite the murders that continue to haunt them. But he is torn between duty and desire when Anna Corbin becomes the next target.

Ultimate Sins

Mia, left an orphan after her father's death, was raised amid the lies and suspicions against Crowe Callahan. But nothing could halt the fascination she feels for him, or the hunger that has risen inside her.

St. Martin's Paperbacks St. Martin's Griffin

Wild Card

Navy SEAL Nathan Malone's wife, Bella,
was told he was never coming home.
But if he can get back to his wife, can
he keep the secret of who he really
is . . . even as desire threatens to consume
them? And as danger threatens to tear
Bella from Nathan's arms once more?

Black Jack

The Secret Service can't control him.
The British government can't silence him.
But renegade agent Travis Caine is one
loose cannon you don't want to mess
with, and his new assignment is to die for.

Maverick

The only way for the Elite Ops agent to
uncover an assassin—and banish the
ghosts of his own dark past—is to use
Risa as bait. But nothing has prepared him
for her disarming blend of innocence and
sensuality, or for his overwhelming need
to protect her.

Renegade

Elite Ops agent Nikolai Steele, code name
Renegade, is asked to pay an old comrade
a favor. This friend swears he's no killer
even though he's been mistaken as one
by Mikayla. Nik goes to set her straight,
but the moment he lays eyes her, he
knows he's in too deep.

Heat Seeker

John Vincent has every reason to want
to remain as dead as the obituary had
proclaimed him to be. He'd left nothing
behind except for one woman, and one
night of unforgettable passion. Now both
will return to haunt him.

Live Wire

Captain Jordan Malone has been a
silent warrior and guardian for years,
leading his loyal team of Elite Ops
agents to fight terror at all costs.
But Tehya Talamosi, a woman with
killer secrets and body to die for, will
bring Jordan to his knees as they both
take on the most deadly mission

🐾 ST. MARTIN'S PRESS

CPSIA information can be obtained
at www.ICGtesting.com
Printed in the USA
LVHW111737230621
690957LV00005B/913